FIRE

CAROLINE ALLEN

FIRE

a novel

Book Three
of the Elemental Journey Series

Caroline Allen

Copyright ©Caroline Allen 2018

Published by Art of Storytelling
PO Box 2598
Estacada, Oregon 97023
www.artofstorytellingonline.com

Publisher's Note
This is a work of fiction. Names, characters, places, and incidents either are the product of the author's imagination or are used fictitiously, and any resemblance to actual persons, living or dead, business establishments, events, or locales is entirely coincidental.

PRINT ISBN: **978-0-9975824-4-4**
E-BOOK ISBN:**978-0-9975824-5-1**

The scanning, uploading and distribution of this book via the Internet or via any other means without the permission of the author is illegal and punishable by law. Please purchase only authorized electronic editions, and do not participate in or encourage electronic piracy of copyrighted materials. Your support of the author's rights is appreciated.

Illustration by Greg Simanson
Cover Design by Greg Simanson
Edited by Caroline Clouse

ACKNOWLEDGMENTS

The first person who read this book besides me was my editor and friend, Caroline Clouse. It is rare to find someone you can trust so implicitly with your deepest creativity. What I love about Caroline, and what I'm profoundly grateful for, is how we connect, how we're almost telepathic in our mutual understanding of what makes a profound story. Her advice consistently breaks open the writing to higher levels. Thank you, Caroline. You're a light in a very dark world.

I did not want anyone but designer Greg Simanson to do the illustration and design of the cover. Greg designed the covers of EARTH and AIR, the first two novels in this series, and each time, he connects deeply with the subject, listens carefully to my needs, and comes up with something that is both exactly what I want, and a complete joyful surprise. It has been said that Greg takes book covers and "sprinkles them with fairy dust". Thank you so very much, Greg.

My novels are its readers. Without readers, I have no voice. A big thank you to Kenya Moore for her marketing prowess on all three of my books.

To my nephew Alejandro Josue Boza, thank you so much, dear

godson, for helping me with some of the Spanish translation in this novel.

To Stephen Munger, you opened my eyes to the world. How can I ever repay you? You just being you changed my life.

To all the therapists and healers I have had along the way on this difficult but soulful and edifying journey, there aren't words to convey how your commitment to healing saved my life, and continues to save the lives of so many others. What a noble profession! You do the real work in the world, nurturing the souls of so many hurt people in this broken world, and I have so much love and gratitude in my heart.

I always like to thank the clients I work with as a book coach. During my hours helping you with memoir, novels and self-help books, I continue to learn and grow as a writer. Your courage and commitment inspires me, and I'm grateful for the trust you give me in allowing me so deeply into your creative process.

Spirit guides showed up for FIRE, as they did for EARTH and AIR, and guided the writing. I have such a gratitude for my ancestors, and all of the guides that honored me with their presence, and guided my hands. I certainly did not write this alone.

And, finally, a well of gratitude to all my readers, and to all readers of all books. I'm so grateful for the written word, and for others who love books as I much as I do.

*This book is dedicated to all people,
past and present, who have been struck by lightning
and tempered by fire.*

"The way of love is not
a subtle argument.

The door there
is devastation.

Birds make great sky-circles
of their freedom.
How do they learn it?

They fall, and falling,
they're given wings."

— **Rumi**

THE PHILIPPINES

1

The man clung to the briefcase handle as he fell. Why would he not let go? His business shirt blazed, the flames a blue-freeze on hot white. Others flew, behind and below. Clothes and hair ablaze, fiery meteors. A woman's arm was twisted backward, a broken wing. A child—its face a white shadow of cheek and forehead. I refused to remember the child.

When they hit the ground, which they would, nothing would ever be the same again. Nothing would ever be the same again, when they hit the ground. Which they would. Something would rise from the ashes, when they hit the ground. What would emerge would be dark, and what would emerge would be light.

To know this, I would have to watch them hit the ground. And I would not watch them hit the ground. I would not.

I awoke floating on my back in an orange life preserver on the ocean in the middle of the night. Above a meteor shower. One scenario was a memory, a vision, another the reality. People falling from the sky, on fire, was a memory. The other, watching a meteor shower on my back in the bay on the Pacific Ocean, that was reality. Reality and illusion—sometimes one wasn't more real than the other. Sometimes the veil between today and memory, between the water lapping through sodden wrinkled fingers and a broken rail bridge in another country and another time, between a meteor shower and children on fire flailing through sky, was cut from the thinnest, most diaphanous cloth. Sometimes the veil was missing altogether.

Finn floated on his back next to me, intent upon the shooting stars overhead. We were in the Philippines visiting an island whose name meant Enchanted. Our jackets were like glowing phosphorescence in the black ocean, orange against the purple mirror of the water, the only two spots of color in an infinite universe. My body shook with tiny explosions from the memories, the vision, the meteor shower had triggered. I could deny much, but my body always told the truth. Water was perfect. My body had no heft, little weight. My flesh was not of dry land. I could live my whole life like this, floating in a black sea, cushioned.

Tokyo. The earthquake. The broken rail bridge. They burned up, or jumped to their deaths. I knew Finn was tortured by the memory, too. I'd heard him cry out in his sleep. I'd reach for him and hold him to keep him from falling.

I did not know the people I saw fall from the burning train, but I had my own personal haunting, Usui. His death in my arms below the rail bridge, with people plunging to the earth all around us. A single death is a tragedy—a million a statistic. Usui was my tragedy.

Earlier that evening, a boat boy had motored Finn and me out to a floating bar in Miracle Bay. We'd gotten drunk on gin and tonics as the sun set in rainbow stripes. When night fell, the tide pulsed in and the shore receded. The boat boy came to ferry the drunks back but Finn and I wanted to stay. It grew late, and the child with the boat was supposed to return but didn't. At two or three in the morning, the bartender took our drinks and put in their place two tangerine life preservers. We put them on and howled as we threw ourselves into the black ocean.

Even in rural Missouri, I had never experienced a sky like this, a meteor shower that dribbled and sparked, dotted reflections in sky and sea. The stars were quilted fire, dripping molten ash. Streaks of fervor. Delicate explosions. I felt the fat drippings upon my heart, a gasp, a sputter, a singe.

I turned from my back to my belly, turned away from the memories, started paddling toward the white glow of the sandy shore.

"Queenie, love, how can you miss this?" Finn said, his soft voice echoing into the blue-black sputtering night. "Queenie. Come on." I heard him splash and paddle behind me. "God damn it. Stay close…for fuck sake." Still I swam, a ginger dot in a vast black world beneath a sky raining with fire.

2

Our home on this island called Enchanted was a rutting place for chickens. A two-story makeshift hut with a pitted yard where roosters mounted hens. Clucked, and mounted and tucked and fucked. We'd rented a falling-down plywood A-frame, one table, four chairs, a bed, mosquito netting, an indoor hammock. The more expensive cottages for the tourists had ocean views and exotic landscaping—flowering vines, spiked blossoms, fat leaves, plants I could not name. We could only afford a scrubby yard full of horny fowl.

We were on the first leg of a one-year journey through Southeast Asia on our way to set up home together in London. I was not in a good place. The dark moods took hold of my leg and wouldn't let go. Savage animals, yanking me backward. It didn't matter how sunny it was, or how beautiful the island. I called them walking depressions, like walking pneumonia, a low-grade sickness that colored everything I saw. Usui used to call them "black dog," and now Finn was calling them that, too.

Finn would say, "I see the black dog is back." Or "Can we subdue the black dog for a few hours?" Or "When you sit and smoke and ruminate on everything wrong with your life or the world, you're just feeding the black dog. You know that, don't you, Queenie? Queenie?"

You could blame the Tokyo earthquake, the death of so many. You could say I worked too relentlessly hard as a journalist in Japan post-quake, that I was tired, that I was exhausted beyond all reason. You could go further back than that, and blame the initial move to Tokyo from rural Missouri years ago. Moving from the grit and grime of the earth to the steel and smog of one of the most congested cities in the world—it was the loss of culture, a loss of identity, as if a rug had been pulled from beneath me. Who was I? What did my life mean with no cultural references? And now, we were spending a year with only backpacks for a home, with no house to call our own, and no country. Sometimes I felt like I was floating with only a frayed rope to tether me to the planet. Not only was I free from parental expectations, I was devoid of any of society's rules. I could cobble together a self from the cultural cast-offs of different countries, adopt a custom here, a religious ritual there, but were these really "me"? Living in Japan changed my life. I had no regrets. Travel through Asia would transform me further, I had no doubts. It was exhilarating, mind blowing, epic. It also drew up anxiety, though, and a fear that were difficult to fathom, confusing to mold into an understanding. If truth be told, it all went further back than that. I was not in a good place before moving to Tokyo. You could say I had lost the real me years earlier, as a little girl. You could argue I'd been upset all my life, that the black dog had been my companion since infancy.

On rickety rocking chairs on the crooked porch of the house on Enchanted, we sat smoking cigarettes, drinking Coca-Cola and watching the chickens fuck. It was hot. Sweltering. Sticky. The sky relentlessly cloudless, the beaches burning to the soles. I lit one cigarette off another.

The rooster snagged the hen. He climbed onto her and kneaded her back, scraping her feathers apart with his claws. "He's raping her," I said. The hen pierced the yard with her scream.

"Rape most fowl," Finn said, without looking up from the guidebook.

Agitated, I lit another Mighty off my butt. It tasted like mold. Asian cigarettes were cheap. "At least someone is getting some." Finn ignored me.

Unlike the birds, we were not fucking, not touching. We were whirring in our separate universes, devoid of our bodies, separate from flesh, floating in the mad corridors of the mind. There was a scream between my thighs that he would not go near, a scream I was scared would build to a roar. Every night I roiled and boiled and slithered beside him, sweat dripping between breasts, but he would not have me. I was skinny. I had boobs. Men checked me out. For the first few years of our relationship, all Finn and I did was fuck. Four times a day.

"Why do we not have sex anymore? Finn? I'm in my 20s. You're in your 30s. This is crazy…"

Tears ran down his face. Finn was a crier. A beautiful sunset made him weepy. Jazz made him blubber. In movies, he'd openly weep.

I'd asked him many times before if it was my moods, and he'd never answered. I was tired of taking the blame on myself.

"What?" I sighed. "What?" He shook his head. I gave him a hard look. Sometimes I worried the black dog took over my face. Sometimes I thought that when Finn looked at me he saw a snarl, and sharp, bared teeth.

It took him a while to get out the words. "Pearl," he said. This wasn't good. He never called me by my name anymore, even during our most intense arguments. "Queenie," he said, and wiped his nose. "I don't…" Again the tears. "I don't think I love you anymore." He said it so softly, I wasn't sure I heard him correctly. I curled forward over my knees. How did a person respond to that? I held my ankles. I'd heard this enough as a child, Father's whispered hate: *Nobody gives a shit about you, kid.* When you are suckled on such madness, you do not act appropriately when someone un-loves you. You had no compass for authentic reaction. The message landed in a space that was like a whiteout with no walls and no floor, a place of perpetual falling. I held my ankles and rocked.

Still the tears in his eyes. I didn't understand. Was I supposed to feel sorry for how badly it hurt him not to love me anymore? I tried to breathe. He sighed, picked up his backpack, went down the steps to the sand.

"I'm going to find Henri." Henri was a local musician who lived on the other side of the island, a long-haired European hippie who'd married a local woman. Finn and Henri had jammed together at one of the beach cafes. Neither of us had yet been to the dark side of the island, though, and that was where Henri lived.

Enchanted was an island divided. Five miles in circumference, angled like a butterfly, the west held calm seas, the east pounding waves. One side dark, the other light. Bipolar. Clear skies here, threatening clouds there. One coastline powder sand, the other sea detritus littered like dead bodies. Seafood restaurants for tourists with seating on the beach to the west, ramshackle battened-down cottages for the locals to the east.

I went down the steps and pressed my body against Finn's. My hipbone cleaved to his thigh. He was so tall, thin legs, a lean torso. He seemed to be floating, white hair on top, white sand below, the thin vocabulary of his body. I could feel last night's meteor shower in him, the stardust and the fire. Some would say he was too skinny, in that heroin-chic British way, but I loved his knuckled body. With my hips I was trying to say *but I do love you, Finn.* If I just loved more, I would receive the love that was withheld me. Right? I'd figured that out as a child. Hold on. Don't let go. Like a dog. Even if they kick you. I had nowhere else to go, then or now. I reached into his hair, gritty with salt, and bent his head toward mine.

"Queenie," he said, trying to pull away. "Pearl…" I pulled him hard to me, tasted the sweat and salt on his wide lips. "Bloody hell, stop." I didn't. He yanked away. We stared at each other. "I'm *going*."

He headed into the coconut grove, his tall frame curved forward as he walked, the lean question mark of him. I watched him go. *I have nowhere else to go,* my soul screamed at his receding form. In the yard, the rooster mounted a second screeching hen.

CHAPTER 2 ½

When I lifted a soggy arm from the sea, something was wrong with it. It was not my arm. I studied it with rising anxiety. It was a child's arm, thin, brown, with small, nail-bitten fingers. On the flesh, sun blisters so hard and deep they might never heal. When I licked my lips, they were swollen and cracked. I was so thirsty, so desperately thirsty.

I tried to make some sense of it. I had come to the tourist side of the island, to swim and float and not to think. When I'd arrived, Western tourists swam farther down the beach, and a row of shack restaurants blared pop music. Now, when I looked around, I was surrounded by nothing but sea.

Thoughts that were not mine became my thoughts. I was the child again, with the brown arm. I had been in the sea a long time. More than two days.

It is the oarsman's eyes that haunt me, the whites of them blood red. I was sleeping the sleep of the overworked on the deck of the boat, a group of us boys worn thin by too little food and too much labor. How many months had we been out to sea? How had he tricked my grandfather, and the others' mothers, into letting us go? Time made no difference in our bowed-down exhaustion.

While I slept, the oarsman tied me and tipped me over the edge of the boat. When the water woke me, I tried to scream. He had tied my mouth and my hands, gagged and hobbled me.

I caught a watery glimpse of Santiago, my friend. He was lying on his side, his arms tucked between bent knees, eyes wide with terror. He dared not scream or move, dared not let the oarsman know he was awake, or he would be next. Santiago and I had talked about escaping, but he was always too afraid. "I do not have your courage, Enrique," he would say, but I knew he was scared that I would fail, and I would take him down with me. I was proving that to him now, thrashing in the dark ocean, hands and feet bound.

Squirming to keep my head above water, I caught the burning eyes of the oarsman. He smiled, showing black and broken teeth. He wanted me to watch as he turned the boat, watch as he rowed away. He was leaving me to die. I had underestimated how much he wanted me dead. I was the only one who spoke up against him, against this life of slavery he had tricked us all into. I knew he hated me, but I could not remain always awake and watchful.

Sinking deep now in the black water, I fumbled hysterically with the bindings. Close to passing out, I tore flesh as I wrenched a hand free, ripped off the ropes at my feet, clawed my way to the surface.

The boat was gone. It was just me and the darkness. Two days went by, and now, here I am floating, thinking of the oarsman's eyes. I am strong, and I can tread water. I was born and raised in water. The sun has already had its way with me, burned holes into my flesh, cracked and bled my lips.

I will survive. I will show you, oarsman. "A sleeping shrimp is carried away by the current," Grandfather Juaco used to say. Grandfather, I will not sleep. I will not be carried away. Oarsman, the sea is my home. I have lived and breathed it since birth. I will show you. I will survive. I will walk on dry land again. You will not win!

I fumble into the pocket of what is left of my trousers. It is still there. The thin wooden man that Grandfather whittled for me—a talisman for safety. I gave Santiago one, and I imagined he too was taking his out, holding it and thinking of me. "Santiago," I say out loud, but my voice, like my lips, is cracked. I clutch the wooden man in my palm until it presses a symbol into the flesh. I put it to my lips to pray, and to remember my grandfather, the one person who has loved me the most.

3

F inn's side of the bed was empty. I'd come back to the house after the vision to sleep. The visions always left me utterly spent. I had them once to twice a week, and often had no idea what they meant, or who they were about.

Mostly, I didn't try anymore to figure the visions out. I just waited for them to pass, slept off the time afterward like sleeping off a hangover. Often the images, the sounds, the smells lingered as if the event had really happened.

Sometimes a memory would thrust me into the same visionary state, like remembering the falling bodies. Sometimes, out of nowhere, I would be transported back in time, forward in time, into someone else's body. They started when I was 13, though from what my mother said, they could have started much earlier, but I couldn't remember.

People would talk about their vivid dreams or wild imaginations, and I could not impress upon them how this was different. This was something from the annals of Catholic mystics and Sufi poets.

From the outside, I was told it looked like an epileptic fit. From the inside, I would be taken over by images and messages that seemed to have some meaning I often could not understand. People would visit me, or scenes would unfold, more real than dreams and imagination, more real often than real life. Each time, I felt something was wanted from me that I could not quite ascertain.

There were visions of people I knew who'd once been alive, and visions I knew of people who were now spirits. Often I did not recognize those who came to me. But that was not true. I knew them in my bones. I knew them like they were some home I used to have. They were people and events from the past, or from the present or from the future, but really that did not matter, because in whatever realm this was, time did not exist in linear fashion. The boy drowning out in the dark ocean existed now.

Unsettled souls, were they also seeking home? One thing I was beginning to understand, the dead, the spirits that came to me, seemed to know only marginally more than we did in this reality. They were learning, too. It was our job as humans to help the spirit world learn. And vice versa. It wasn't about praying to them, it was about saving them.

Mostly, the humans I'd met in my life had responded to me and my visions with fear, hatred and violence. It wasn't good for a girl's self-esteem when people you met wanted you dead because you were different. When a father wanted his daughter dead, she grew up with dreams of death. She fumbled along with a desire to be anything but herself. She also wanted herself dead.

Others showed up though, too. Good people in this normal reality. Or people who had moments of good. That was all one could hope for in today's world anyway. Embers of acceptance. Flickers of compassion. Flashes of empathy. Moments that came and went. Rare candles lit in dark windows. Most of the world couldn't sustain the love. Love had been lost such a long time ago.

Sister Alice, Usui, Jason, Yuriko, others. It was my life, though, and I had to live it. I had to brave the storms and let myself be struck by lightning, again and again. Friends and lovers were embers and flickers that kept the flame alive.

Still, if you grew close to me, I could not hide the visions from you. If you fell in love with me, my haunting became yours.

In the ocean today, it was lucky that I hadn't drowned. When I came to, I was in the shallows, a family with children watching me curiously nearby. I had no idea how long I'd been floating there, lost in that other world.

Finn's absence scared me. I got up, went to the porch and stood staring for a long while into the coconut grove, willing him to magically appear. Warm wind batted at my hair, and the ocean pulsed in a far-off drumbeat. Tree trunks threw purple stripes onto the white sand beneath a half-full moon. An animal howled and a night bird cawed.

I walked down the steps, made my way into the trees. I was in a singlet and shorts with no shoes. I had no flashlight, no idea if it was safe, if locals mugged tourists or tourists raped each other.

Palm fronds waved a shadow dance on white sand, the way the wind blew through them in unfamiliar melody, the sound like thin slices of waxed paper. The sea breeze from the darker side of the island smelled hard and of death. This wasn't a simple story about a girl losing a boy. That would be too easy a tale. It was about losing home. It was about being homeless, a wanderer in a makeshift world. It was about a girl who had left a rural farm and escaped to a foreign land looking for somewhere she fit. It was about having nowhere else to go. It was about love, but it was also about fear. For some reason, I thought about Santiago then, the boy in my vision, still on the boat. I realized then he reminded me of Finn.

The winds gusted and blew the tops of the trees sideways, and at the same time blew my hair sideways. We were one, these tall palms and I. The night full of whisperings, unknowns, titillations of fear.

The sand made it difficult to walk. My calves ached. The pitch of the screaming trees grew higher as I neared the west side. A storm was brewing.

Who was that dancing in the shadows of the palm fronds on the white sand? Usui? I was dreaming. Usui was dead. He was one of the few people who made me feel I fit. I belonged. As I grew closer, the shadow Usui danced up the white trunk of the palm tree and was gone.

After his death in Tokyo, Usui had not gone away. I saw him regularly, heard him call my name with his Japanese inflection, "Purr. Purr." I loved him, but every day, I willed him to leave me alone. Just leave me. Alone. It was enough to contend with the black dog.

I tried to hide the visions from Finn. He hated them. Lately, when I came out of one, he pretended he did not see it, and I pretended I did not have it. Who could blame him for hating them. I hated them too.

I would find Finn, and I would bring him home. I would hide the visions, and I would make him love me again, and we would spend this year traveling with our backpacks across Asia and get married in London, and live happily ever after.

As I came out of the trees onto the dark beach, wind gusts carried me backward. The ocean roiled, moonlight performing a jarring rumba on the spray. The sky was engorged and furious. Debris and the wind made it almost impossible to walk. The tide was out, a moonscape of sea wreckage, twisted driftwood, slimy kelp, shattered shells, blackened bamboo fronds. Lightning clarified in sudden shock. Riled-up clouds marched across the blackened sky.

"Finn?" I yelled, my voice ricocheting back into my face.

I felt the lightning in my shoulders, the wind in my gut. A fat dollop of rain smacked my forehead. The storm was me and I was the storm. It was the first time I wasn't scared in a long time. It was the first time I'd felt at home in a long time. This was what calmed me? This fury? I wished Usui was alive so I could talk to him about this. How in the middle of the night, in a place I didn't know, during a sea storm, I suddenly felt at home.

I heard Finn's flute, a wisp of a fluttering note.

"Finn?" My voice melded with the storm howl. My clothes were soaked, hair slapping against cheek.

A row of huts sat back from the beach at the edge of the tree line. I heard another riff of music, a guitar. I labored against the wind to follow the sounds. At the thatched huts, all were dark except one. Through slats of a makeshift shutter, I saw Finn inside on a small stool, playing his flute. I went around and knocked. Anxiety in the gut. I knocked again.

A tiny Filipino woman opened the door, nodded, smiled. "Finn?" I said once and then twice. She let me in. I dripped pools of water onto the dirt floor. Finn looked up, eyes unfocused. He was on something.

Henri was in tie-dyed pants, sitting cross-legged on the floor, strumming a guitar. Two half-caste kids ran around in tattered shorts. I did not like Henri. Finn often said I was too critical, that I judged too harshly. He was right, at least about Henri. I judged harshly men who were lazy, men who used women.

Another man lay on his back in the middle of the room, eyes closed. The woman, who I assumed was Henri's wife, went behind a curtain and emerged with beers that she handed to the men, and a Coca-Cola for me. Henri patted her ass as she passed.

An odd aroma, a sour smoke. Henri handed me a pipe, but I refused. I went to Finn, whispered, "We should go." His eyes were fogged, backward looking. He was on something. Fin was often on something.

He put his flute down. Henri kept playing, a disjointed piece that sounded like chimes hit by a psychotic wind. Finn cupped my face. His eyes were scorched. He kissed me hard on the mouth.

"Sorry for what I said," he slurred. "I'm just all messed up." He tried to scale me with his cold fire stare, but his gaze was too inward and I would not play. He sat back down and picked up his flute.

He had a way of saying hello. Whenever he was playing music and I entered the room, he would change the tune. He would play for me a song of my soul. It was our special thing. He did this now, staring at me with ignited eyes.

I found space along one wall to squat. I listened to his dark and fretful melody, a lonely rendition of me, a grief full of the love that went with not-loving. The woman went back and forth to serve the men durian and sugar apples. When she held the plate up to me, I waved her away. I wanted to grab her and whisk her away from this life, to save her from the likes of Henri, but instead I squatted and sipped my Coca-Cola.

Outside, the wind threw debris. An object hit the house, and I felt the shock of it in my shoulders.

4

I **was roaming** Enchanted seeking ideas for travel articles. I'd arranged to be a travel writer for the year I was in Southeast Asia with my former employer, the Kaze newspaper in Tokyo. I wanted to call the column "A Broad Abroad," but the other editors wouldn't let me. I'd promised the Kaze one article per month.

Everywhere the Filipinos waited on white people like me; they hauled, cleaned, swept, cooked, and served. They fished, haggled, gutted, gleaned and grew. They served. They smiled. They nodded and bent. They shuffled. It reminded me of Missouri, the relentless work, but back home we were just barely serving ourselves. I had not expected this, the Filipinos lives so centered around serving the tourists. It shocked me. I wanted to write about it, but knew it wasn't what a travel article should be.

As I meandered, I knew I didn't want to fit here. I didn't want to write an article about scuba diving, or luxury cottages. It wasn't the kind of story I wanted to tell. I didn't want to fit here as a white woman from the States, writing about a tourist haven for more white people. It sickened me. Again, I felt the exhausting pang of not fitting. I didn't fit here, with the tourists, or with the locals. I'd spent my life thinking I belonged on some island of misfit toys that I couldn't seem to find. I'd spent my life, and was spending this year, looking for some semblance of home.

"Where, truly, is home?" Usui had asked me that once. He'd been a Jesuit, and he'd made himself homeless in Tokyo to "find himself." He'd gone from clean-cut and clean-smelling to dread-locked and ripe, and I loved him for it. He couldn't find home in the dark and twisted normal world. He wanted to find it in some deeper way, on his cardboard beneath the rail bridge at the edge of the park, surrounded by origami cranes.

I'd felt more at home sitting with Usui on his cardboard than I had anywhere else in Tokyo. Before that, when was the last time I truly felt at home? The woods in Missouri, when I was little, when I thought I was no different than a tree or a ladybug or a weed.

Home had become even more complicated since then. Home was no longer the Missouri I grew up in. It was no longer Tokyo, where I'd lived for four years. Home was now a backpack. Home was a boyfriend who just said he no longer loved me.

You didn't know how much you depended on your family, your town, your home country, for what to think and how to act, until it was no more. How much you relied on roots and patterns, until it was ripped away. I'd left rural Missouri and moved to Tokyo, fitting there by not fitting, like so many other non-Asian expats. Now I'd left Tokyo to roam Southeast Asia. Home was a game of musical chairs. What was home when walls, furniture and neighborhoods changed year after year? Where was home when you had no country? Who was home when you left family and friends, again and again?

It wasn't just terrifying to have torn away the shroud of expectations. It was also exhilarating—to have no one to answer to, to float high with greater perspective, to reinvent yourself, to be someone else, *anyone* else. How did you go back to anything "normal" after such freedom, after such wanton disregard for the norm? I often felt I was scooting out onto a branch, farther and farther, to the very tip, where the limb was weak, and might bend and break. I often dreamt of myself falling. I wasn't sure what scared me more, the fear of homelessness or wild joy of utter release.

I was walking down the beach, near the cafes. Olivia Newton-John was singing "Let's Get Physical." It was a white-hot cloudless day, sharp and burning. A boy was at one of the tables, talking to a couple about a cockfight: "Good action. You come. Place bets. Big winner."

He was the boat boy who had motored Finn and me out to the floating bar. He was talking to a white hippie and his blonde girlfriend in a bikini. "Dude, I'm vegan," the guy said, flipping his blonde dreads, hair beads jangling. "I don't want to see sentient beings bloody each other for man's enjoyment." He crossed long, tanned legs. "Come back when you've got something more earth-friendly."

The boy turned to the leggy blonde. "You?" He rubbed index finger and thumb. "Much money..." The girl tinkled with laughter, her glowing teeth and freckled nose an American chewing gum commercial. The child blushed. She leaned over and tousled his hair. "You are *so* adorable." His face turned cherry red.

The roar of an engine blew in suddenly from the bay, and we all turned to look. A group of European jet-setters, polished men with tight bodies in Speedos, and their brunette girlfriends in bikinis buzzed the shore in a speed boat. I'd seen them already whipping around the island, heads thrown back laughing. In the evenings, in sparkly clothes, good-looking and moneyed, they'd sit with umbrella drinks at one of the fancier ocean-side bars.

"Cockfight?" I stopped the boy as he walked away. "I'd like to go to a cockfight." He was about ten, had thin legs, red shorts with a red racing stripe. He smelled briny and brackish.

"How much you bet?" His brown eyes were too old.

"I just want to observe it." He looked at me confused. "I just want to see. Just go and see."

"We take a boat. You have to bet. Pay for boat."

He wore a beige dress shirt that once was white. His feet were bare. The sun reflected daggers and forced us to squint.

"Can you translate?" I'd studied Spanish in high school and understood some, but it wouldn't get me very far.

He held his fingers up and counted. "Bet, boat, translate." He rubbed his index finger and thumb. "Much money."

"Deal," I said. I was supposed to haggle. I hated haggling. It felt wrong. These people had so little. Still, when I didn't bargain, they came at me like I was a rabbit and they were hawks.

I reached down and took his small hand, his touch suddenly flashing me back to the boy left to drown in the sea. "Pearl," I said.

"Raul." His palm was sandpaper. In his speckled eyes, a recognition. It was unsettling. It was as if I knew him, as if I'd known him all my life.

Longer.

"One, Dallas. Two, Starsky and Hutch. Three, Wonder Woman." Raul counted on his fingers. "American TV. American English. Good. You pay ten dollars for translate." The Filipinos seemed to prefer to deal in dollars over pesos.

Raul worked the rusty outboard motor with one hand and bailed a leak near his feet with the other. Three planks served as seats. A fat German sat at the stern, stomach rolling over bikini trunks. He didn't appear to speak English and seemed annoyed every time he looked at me.

"Seven," I countered.

"Eight dollars. Eight." Raul lifted his chin, his unkempt brown hair framed by indigo sky and emerald sea, the motor sputtering the stench of burning gasoline and oil.

"Okay, eight," I said.

There were no life jackets. Without a life jacket, I couldn't swim. My mother had insisted on swimming lessons at the public pool, and I'd splashed around in rivers my entire childhood, and still I could not seem to remain afloat.

"Okay eight for translate. How much bet?" he asked. "Village champion El Loco will fight upstart newcomer El Jefe," he said in perfect English.

"I'll put twenty on El Loco," I said. His eyes lit up. Twenty dollars was a lot of money. "I'll pay another five for the boat."

"Ten for boat."

"Six."

"Eight."

I reached over and grabbed the small plastic bucket from his hand. "Six. I'm paying you six for this boat ride since someone's got to do the bailing or we aren't going to get there." I filled the bucket with water from the bottom of the boat and threw it overboard.

Hands passed over my ass. Men whistled. Fingers brushed my breasts. It wasn't personal. They would've acted this way with any single foreign woman daring to put themselves in their midst. The German man was not with us. I didn't know where he'd gone. A group of about forty men stood on the scrappy shore, next to a ring of chicken wire. Two men handled the roosters inside the ring.

I twisted to try to avoid the hands. The boy saw, felt how agitated I was becoming. He stopped and turned us around so that we were facing the group.

"This stupid American has bet twenty on El Loco," he shouted in Spanish. The men laughed. "She is friends with my mother, so we must be nice. Yes? She is a periodista (journalist)." He explained that I was a crazy *gringa*, who had a fascination with cock fights. Everyone laughed. A man slapped me on the back. Others nodded. The tension broke. I reached down, took Raul's hand, and squeezed it. *"Gracias,"* I whispered.

The surprise was the glistening beauty of the roosters. I raised my 35-mm camera and snapped. Plumage of obsidian, crimson, canary. Festooned. Regal. Nothing like the grubby rooster raping the hens in our yard on Enchanted. Snap. The one sporting indigo feathers on wing and ankles was El Loco, Raul told me. The hackles of the other was intense red of burning embers. El Jefe. Snap.

I saw the German on the other side of the fence, his face red like a heart attack. In the ring, El Jefe's owner held him tight around the wings and jabbed his face into El Loco's. Neck feathers ballooned, orange and fiery. A screeching, a clawing. El Jefe's owner put the rooster down and grabbed his tail feathers. El Loco's owner did the same. Held back, the birds tried to yank themselves forward and claw out the eyes of the other. Snap. Snap. Snap.

A man in a dirty baseball cap yelled, "En sus marcas, listos, fuera! (Ready, set, go!)" The owners released their roosters. The birds went into a frenzy, attacking, blades slicing. Blood spattered through the fence, whipping Raul, me and another man in the face like a slap. We reeled back. The crowd laughed. I guess I hadn't expected the violence. I guess I hadn't expected the blood.

Finn often said to me: "You can take the girl out of Missouri, but you can't take Missouri out of the girl." This was the rough brutality of my homeland. My childhood had been a feral mix of filth and the guts of hunted animals, of raised livestock. I had with my own hands killed hundreds of chickens in my short life. I had been born in blood and mud.

When I was a little girl, I was in charge of collecting the eggs. Redneck Rooster would chase me. Wings flapping chaos, he'd climb my calf, my thigh, my back, sinking spurs into clothes, into flesh. He'd hang onto my back. I could barely see to find the gate, unhook the wire and plunge out of the pen. He'd draw blood.

Why couldn't I be more like the European jet-setters? Why couldn't I write a travel article about a speed boat or a fancy villa? Or luxury vacations? Why was I here in the dirt with these bloody chickens? Why did all of these fucking and fighting fowl seem to be more home to me than a drink with a fancy umbrella?

Pecking, slashing, pummeling, El Jefe and El Loco squealed amidst the wild grunts of men. The onlookers' rabid faces. Snap. Bloody roosters with incandescent feathers. Snap. Crazy paint against a filthy background. Snap.

A final slash, and El Jefe fell, guts spilling and mixing with dirt. People cried, and jumped. Raul grabbed my shoulders. Everything seemed to go silent, the sounds of the crying cock and the guttural shouts of the men fading into a low hum. Raul turned to me in slow motion, jumping like the little boy he was, mouthing: *You are winner. You are winner,* but his voice was lost in muffled silence. The crowd held up wads of pesos and dollars and waved them, faces contorted, teeth bared.

I won.

CHAPTER 4 ½

The crowd parts. *He sits in a circle of light, his back to me. He wears an old black coat, even in the heat. All around him the men dance in shadow, waving grimy money.*

I come up behind him. How could I not have recognized him sooner? Usui. Dear Usui. My friend. My tragedy.

He still has the dreadlocks, his black hair matted into ringlets. The arms of the coat are too short, and lanky wrists protrude. He is bent over doing something. I move in closer to look. Long, elegant fingers fold origami cranes. Musky incense clings to him. I ache with how much I miss him.

"Usui, what are you doing here?"

He looks up and back at me. "Like you, I am here. This is where I am."

A wad of bills is wedged beneath his bare foot. He is using money to fold the cranes, Japanese yen, American dollars, Filipino pesos. He finishes the bird in his hand, the body green, the beak purple. He has used a thousand-yen bill. He places it in the dirt, then chooses a five-dollar bill from the middle of the stack. He folds it into a square, and tears off the excess, the sound of the tearing money like a sacrilege.

"Why do the others not see you?"

"Why do you see me, Purr?"

"That is a question I've never had an answer for Usui. That is a question I have always wanted an answer for."

He finishes the five-dollar crane, green and white patterns, and holds it up for me to see. I've long wished American money was as colorful as the bills in other countries. I reach down to cradle the thing in my palm, but Usui shakes his head. He has such a glint in his eyes, more happy, more mischievous than when he was alive.

He pulls a book of matches from the pocket of his wool coat. He holds the crane by its tale, bends one match with one hand to the strip, clicks his fingers and lights it. He puts the flame to the beak. When the fire reaches his fingertips, he lets it go. The burning bird flies up and disappears in a sudden burst.

"What are you doing?"

Usui laughs. He takes up the yen crane, lights the match, burns it in the same way.

"Usui?"

"Purr, perhaps I am helping you to find home."

The men in the shadows dance.

5

"**H**ace mucho calor! (It's too hot!)" Raul yelled. My cheek was in the dirt. Men's faces peered down. "Too hot. Some air." Raul swung his arms. "Get out of the way."

He tipped a water bottle to my lips. I sipped. Water dripped into the dirt so that my cheek was now in mud. Raul pulled on one arm, trying to help me stand, but I couldn't quite manage it. He and some other guy grabbed me by my arm pits, dragged me into the shade, and leaned me against the trunk of a lone tree.

"Missus Pearl. Too hot for foreigners." Raul fanned me with both of his hands. I tried to get up. He pushed me back. "Take it easy, man." He handed me my camera, a small dent to the lens where I'd dropped it.

The referee came up and handed Raul a stack of crumpled pesos. "You a winner! You won!" He put the money to my face. Some of the bills were covered in blood. I half expected them to turn into birds and burst into flames.

I tried to sit up, but the dizziness swirled the scene. Raul looked me in the eyes. His brown eyes had flecks of red like tiny flames. "So tired," he said. "So tired, my friend. There must be rest for you." I felt it again, that somehow Raul and I knew each other, that we went back years, and lifetimes.

The German walked up, frowning.

"How ya doin'?" I said up to him and smiled. He spoke to Raul in Spanish. He wanted to get out of there and get back to Enchanted.

"I just need a moment. Tell him that, Raul."

Raul grabbed one of the dirty bills the referee had brought, took the German over to where some men were drinking, and bought him a beer. I blinked in the fiery heat, took a swig from the water bottle. The smell of my childhood wafted around me, wood fire, damp blood, wet feathers and chicken shit. I turned to see a camp fire several feet away, a banged-up pot sitting on rocks on top of the flames. A man was dunking the now dead El Jefe upside down by his ankles. He squatted and started plucking.

Raul came back, saw me staring at the man, leaned to me and said, "Here is a man to interview. I ask."

"No..." I couldn't fathom doing the journalism article now.

He went over and spoke to the man in Spanish. The man nodded. He came back. "Okay, you ask me questions. I translate."

I shook my head.

He grabbed my arm and pulled me to my feet. "We are hurry. The German lost much money. Not happy. You ask. I'll ask. He answer. I'll answer. Quick."

I walked unsteadily over, Raul under one arm like a crutch. The old man offered me a bloody stump. I took a reporter's note-book out of my fanny pack, and a pen. I could barely sit up.

How often do they hold the fights? Why? Who trains the roosters? How?

I asked what had happened to El Loco, and the man pointed behind us. A man was sitting behind a tree with the wounded rooster, sewing him up with a needle and thread. I picked up my camera and took a shot of him sewing up the wound. What will happen to this one he's plucking, to El Loco? The man held it up, I snapped a photo. The man rubbed his belly, said something in Spanish I couldn't quite understand. Raul translated: "For the loser, the boiling pot." I had my title for the article.

"Okay, we go now," Raul said, looking over to where the German stood staring daggers.

"Okay," I said. I lurched toward the boat.

"You are losing your money." I'd crammed the dirty bills into my fanny pack. Raul picked up wadded pesos and handed them to me. After I got into the boat, I took out all the money and counted it, almost one hundred dollars. The German turned his back with a huff at the sight of the money. Raul stood up to his knees in the ocean, holding the side of the boat, and looked at the bills in my hand with reverence.

The man said something gruffly in German. Raul hauled the boat out from the shore, jumped in, started the engine, and bailed as we made the 30-minute ride back to the island. I hunched forward, tired, so very tired.

On the shore now, just wanting to get home, to rest, to sleep, I paid Raul for the boat ride and the translation. I'd already paid him for the bet. As I was counting, I saw Usui burning the bills, and shoved the rest of the bloody pesos into the little boy's hands. I didn't want the money.

"No. No, gracias," he said, pushing the money back. "It is God's will."

"How much is a new boat?" I asked. He shook his head. I was too tired to argue. "How much?" I shoved the cash back. "Get a new boat."

He stared at the crumpled stack of bills.

"How about this. You be my translator and my transportation for all the articles I'm going to do. But you gotta get a new boat. And life preservers, please." He looked at me confused. I made motions with my hands as if I was lifting a life jacket over my head and tying it. He nodded.

After a vision, I was hypersensitive. I could see the essence of a person for hours. It was not good to be that clear in this crazy world. Seeing the soul of a person with that clarity in such a toxic world could make a person crazy. I looked at Raul and felt again the other boy who was left by the oarsman, floating in the sea. "Raul. Do you know about a boy who fell off a boat and who was floating at sea for a while?"

"In America?"

"No, a Filipino boy. Around here. He would've been a little older than you. He would've been on a boat with an oarsman."

"What is oarsman?" he asked. I explained as best I could. "You mean like old time? Like long time ago?"

"I don't know."

He looked confused. "Maybe. Maybe I know." He squinted his eyes in memory. "I ask *mi madre*."

"No," I said. "It's okay. Don't worry about it." I was sure the vision was real. About a real person. But I didn't want to get Raul's mother involved. I didn't want to spread the craziness.

Raul put the money up to his nose and sniffed it. He danced a waltz, holding the money out as if it were his partner. He sang to the money, "Let's get physical. Physical. I want to get physical." His sharp shadow, the white-hot sand, the slow ritual of his bony legs and arms, the way light swirled around him as he danced.

6

His penis was long like his legs, wet blond hair between his thighs and more framing his long face. He had a way of holding his naked body, without shame. He'd just taken a shower.

All night I'd been on the toilet. Or on my knees with my head in the toilet. The water Raul had given me… I knew not to drink the water, but this had been in a water bottle. It didn't matter. Sometimes the locals filled bottles with tainted local water.

The noise from my festering stomach was audible in the large ramshackle room. Finn laughed and sat on the bed.

"You smell like soap," I said. "I smell like vomit and poop."

My stomach rumbled. He reached his hand to move a sweat-soaked strand of hair off my cheek. I flinched. Besides the visions, another thing I tried to hide from Finn was the fact that I flinched every time a man's hand moved toward my face.

"You know, when you're feeling poorly, you're actually normal, more like an actual person," he said.

"What does that mean?"

"When you're unwell, your energy decreases to a place where one mortal man can handle it."

"I never thought of you as…" I moaned and held my stomach, "mortal."

He kissed my sweaty forehead, got off the bed, walked around the room and didn't rush to put anything on. It appeared we'd both decided to ignore his comment about his not loving me. Or his later apology. This was fine by me.

"Listen, we have that windsurfing lesson," Finn said, running his long fingers through his wet hair. "I'll forgo it if you so desire, but they won't refund us the money."

I stared at his penis, the tops of his thighs. His hair was white all over his body. Even deathly ill, I was turned on. Even when he didn't love me anymore, I wanted to fuck him silly.

"You don't want to spend the day here?" I flung my arm out across the sheets that smelled like vomit. "With me? In this glorious sweet-smelling bed?"

In the middle of the night, Finn had moved to the hammock. I didn't blame him. He stared at me with an intense focus. He had these blue crystal eyes, cracked like ice, that would pierce right into your soul.

"Oh please, go," I said. It came out sarcastically, but I didn't mean it that way. What could he do? Watch me vomit? Watch me sit seething on the toilet? He'd already gone out and gotten me fresh fruit, bottles of water and juices, and some Coca-Cola. I wouldn't be eating anything anytime soon. There was a little pharmacy on the island, but I was wary of pharmaceuticals, especially the unmarked, unlabeled, unbottled pills available in Southeast Asia. He knew not to ask if I wanted him to go get some medicine. I'd always had a monstrous reaction to pharmaceuticals, my body swelling up, hives so bad I worried I'd go into anaphylactic shock. Some people were highly sensitive. I was apparently too sensitive for this mortal world.

"Seriously," I said, grunting. "Go. Go, before I have my way…" I rolled off the bed, and ran bent over toward the toilet. "With you."

The bodies started to fall again, burning behind my eyes. I begged them to stop. Usui floated in and out of the room, and once, he blew into me, entered into my body. I could see out of his eyes. I could understand more. I didn't want that knowledge, and I begged him to leave, to just please leave me alone.

Throughout my life, the people who had loved me told me that these visions must mean something. That they had a purpose, and I just needed to figure out that purpose. There were those who did not love me, who feared me, who thought of the visions as evil or crazy. They had had me committed.

These people who loved me, who thought the visions had merit, did not know what it was like to be raped by such thoughts, with no control of the feelings and images that haunted you. What they called a gift, they did so out of ignorance. It was a curse, a darkness that needed to be boxed up and shoved into a pit. I had spent my entire life trying to out-run this "gift." I wanted to live in *this* world, not *that* world. That world had no rules and made no sense and drained me to the bone. No matter how many times I tried to lock it away, the monster broke its bonds again and again.

Friends told me to turn to these apparitions and own them, question them, find out what they meant or what they wanted of me. The very thought terrified me. If I gave them free reign, wouldn't there be nothing left of me to survive in this real world? If I turned to the visions, and accepted them, wouldn't that just make me crazy? I was trying to walk the middle road, just stay on a strip of earth that was called reality.

The way the visions terrified Finn—there was a reason for it that was deeper than what I knew of him. There was some past they triggered. How we thought we'd left our childhoods behind but we grew up and met those childhoods everywhere. We thought we'd left home, but home kept showing up in the people we met, in the people we fell in love with.

To appease Finn, I went to a doctor in Tokyo a couple of

months before we left. The doctor gave me drugs. They made me a zombie, with muddy thoughts and turbid passion. I'd stopped taking them. Finn didn't know. Or maybe he did, and we were both pretending.

I t was night, a lifetime in my feverish mind, when the door opened and Finn came home. The sheets were soaked with illness. I rolled painfully off the bed, intent upon finding a new set of sheets and changing them.

He stood before me as I bent hunched over, opening the one large cupboard in the room. I looked up at him. He was a bruised mess. The left side of his face was swollen, and blacks and purples ran up his long white legs.

"My god, what happened?"

He looked about to cry. He told me the story. He took the windsurfing lesson and then went off to try the board by himself. Right away, he was knocked off by the boom. Bruised and winded, he wrested himself back onto the board. By the time he gained control, the shore was lost from sight. He went adrift. Hours went by. He was in such pain. More hours. The wind died down. The adrenaline wore off and his body screamed. He was terrified he would be lost at sea.

"When would you have even noticed I was missing?" he asked. I remembered the little brown boy left at sea in my vision and shuddered. My stomach roiled. I ran to the toilet and vomited.

When I came back in, Finn had found sheets and was gritting his teeth as he changed the bed. As we lay down, he moved this way and that, trying to find a position that didn't hurt. He tried to put an arm around me, but any touch was unfathomable. I tried to put my arm around him, but he gasped from the bruising. We lay side by side, not touching, each in our own painful worlds.

Finn's bruised profile, the angularity of his face. This was not just about me being sick and not being there for him. It had deeper roots. Someone somewhere hadn't noticed Finn was missing, and it was a wound that festered. Someone somewhere had not been there for Finn, and let him float away, untethered, and he ached from the neglect. We'd been dating for years, but still Finn had not told me all of his childhood story. I only knew that an uncle had raised him. That he'd left home young, and traveled Europe, then moved to Japan.

I looked at his profile, his long nose and sharp chin and thought that right now someone needed to go get the poor guy an ice pack. I was so sick, I wouldn't have made it past the fucking roosters.

I sighed. What did you do when both people needed saving? Who would save whom?

Finn opened his eyes and turned his face to mine. He smelled like salt, and that flavor of musk that was so very Finn, that smell that turned me on every time. He smiled and gasped from the pain of stretching his bruised mouth. My stomach made a loud growling sound and I grunted.

He started laughing, and moaning from the pain of laughing. Laughing and groaning. Laughing and gritting. He held his belly and opened his wide mouth with his crooked teeth and let out a guffaw. And groaned.

"What's so funny?" I asked. One of his eyes was swelling shut. He moaned and put his palm to his bruised cheek and laughed harder. It was contagious. I started giggling, and groaning from how the giggling was upsetting my stomach. Soon we were both hysterical, rolling around the bed in pain and mirth. The energy roiled my belly so hard, and I had to run to the toilet, the sound of diarrhea filling the cavernous room.

From the bedroom, Finn roared.

7

A teenage **Filipino** boy sat in the stern of the small wooden boat that was lodged in the sand. He placed his finger to the side of his pursed lips and cocked his head. In a high-pitched voice, he said in English, "My name is Lisa. I am American. I'm so pretty."

A boy next to him on a plank seat slapped the boat's side with his palm and said, "Hurry. I am British. Hurry. Fast. Quick. Now." A handful of other kids laughed and ran circles in the sand and surf.

Raul squatted with a bucket of red paint by the bow. His new boat was bigger than the old one, with an extra plank and a shiny new outboard motor. I looked inside, but didn't see any life preservers.

"Now, I can have five tourists. Good money," Raul said, squinting up to me, a slash of red paint on his cheek.

"You need to get the life preservers, Raul," I said.

"Yes, woman who is not my mother." He looked me up and down. "You look too skinny. What happened? You look like us, not like American." One of the kids, overhearing, stood and puffed out his cheeks and put his arms out to represent a fat body, and tipped the boat back and forth. "I am fat American," he said. "I am rocking boat."

"I've been sick," I told him. "And I have a job for you." After four days of vomiting, I was finally able to sit up in bed. I'd written the cock fight story. It was not an easy article to write. I didn't want to talk about roosters slashing each other. And the Usui vision would not fit in a travel article. Finn was getting exasperated as I whined about the story. "Queenie," he said, "are you vegetarian?"

"You know I'm not."

"You eat chicken, right?"

"You know I do."

"Somebody has to kill the chicken you eat."

"Look, city boy," I said. "I grew up butchering animals. I know how to kill a chicken. The problem isn't killing a chicken."

He shook his head. "Why even choose a cockfight story? Who writes a travel article about chickens killing each other?"

It was a good question.

Afterward, I just shut down and whipped out the article. I could do that. Shut down and pretend, even be normal. The shutting down took its toll, though, so I couldn't maintain it for long.

The one thing I'd always liked about journalism was how the story wasn't about the writer, how anything could be happening to the reporter, but the reader would never know it. The whole process had absolutely nothing whatsoever to do with how the reporter was feeling. You could be suffering panic attacks while you were writing the piece and no one would know. You could be secretly dying inside. No one would care.

I'd gone around the island and couldn't find a manila envelope. I'd written the article on fragile local paper, and had a canister of film. The best I could do was wrap the paper around the film canister and tie it with string. I was woefully behind deadline. I handed Raul the small package.

"Can you take this to the mainland, find an envelope to put it in, put this address on it, and make sure it gets mailed?" I'd already asked around about the island's mail service, and was told it wasn't reliable. A boat ferried the mail to the mainland once a week, sometimes it got there and sometimes not. The mail boat operator was known to pocket the money for postage and dump the letters into the bay.

"Ten dollars," he said.

"Four! Ten is too much."

"Eight."

"I just bought you a new boat."

"Eight."

"Five."

"Seven."

I shook my head, handed him an extra $7.

He put down the brush, took the money, the pages and canisters, and smeared red paint on the article.

I squatted to look at his handy-work. He was painting letters on the side of the boat in surprisingly attractive script: "El Je.."

He smiled and said, "Honor to the old rooster!"

"Not the winner, El Loco?"

"I cannot call boat crazy."

He stood up and reached into his pocket. "*Tengo un regalo para ti*," he said. (I have a gift for you.) He pulled out two small carved figurines. They were replicas of the ones owned by the boy left to drift in the ocean, the boy in my vision. I held them in my palm. They were both men in hats, each one no more than three inches long, arms, head and legs narrow and streamlined like a small totem pole, nicks in the wood as if they were carved with a primitive instrument. They were browned, and old.

"*Mi gran gran gran abuelo...*" (My great, great, great grandfather...) I looked at him in shock. "Do not worry," Raul said in English. "This *abuelo*, he carved many, many such small men, maybe hundreds. Maybe thousands." When I still stared at them, speechless, he took them from my hand, unzipped my fanny pack, and put them inside.

"The little man is for protection. Keep safe. He will make you safe."

8

Usui was bothering me. He kept showing up. More than normal—beneath the tree where the fucking chickens met, in the corner of the porch when Finn wasn't there, floating beside me in the sea. I liked to float, it was the only thing that calmed the small explosions in my body. One night, when Finn left to seek out music, I was on the porch smoking, and saw Usui floating at the edge of the coconut forest. I stormed to him and demanded he leave.

Why do you think I come to you?

To scare me. To freak me out. To piss me off. To make it impossible for me to live.

You will not listen. I come for you to hear. We all come for you to hear. Very few have such a gift as yours and you throw it away as if it is trash.

La la la la la. I put my hands over my ears.

There isn't much time, Purr.

Go bother someone else! I shoved at him, pushing at air.

Worlds exist beyond this one. You know. We want you to remember who you are. This world. That world. You separate them. No separation. It is one.

You're driving me mad! I yelled out loud.

Yes, madness. Madness. That is why there is so little time. Do you think you are the only one we visit?

Where are these others? Where?

You will meet them someday.

Oh joy. What fun that'll be.

We are the doorway to the "home" you seek, Purr.

You mean the insane asylum.

The real world, it is insane. The world you live every day, that is the insanity. We are asking you to wake up.

La. La. La. La. La.

Purr...

La. La. La. La!

The plan was to stay on Enchanted for three months, to decompress from Tokyo. Raul became our guide, boating us around. Finn liked him as much as I did; there was an instant bond there as if they, too, had known each other before. I'd given Finn one of the little wooden men. He'd teared up at the sight of it and now carried it everywhere.

We became quite a sight around the island, with the jet-setters whipping by us in their power boat, Finn and me and rib-skinny Raul in a skiff named after a rooster who lost. Raul still didn't have life jackets.

Finn was determined to teach me to snorkel. We had to start in the shallows, with just the mask and the snorkel. He showed me how to put my face in the water and breathe through the tube. He was so patient. *He loves me. He loves me not. He loves me.* It took so many tries. He knew I could not swim, swore to me snorkeling wasn't swimming, since I didn't need to keep my head afloat and the flippers would turn me into a fish. We stood in the water at the shore. From a beach cafe, David Bowie sang "Let's Dance." It was the '90s, but the island seemed to be stuck in the '80s.

I could see my feet in the clear shimmering water. I'd grown up on muddy rivers and was used to seeing nothing below the surface. The Missouri, the Mississippi, the Current, lakes and ponds, murky affairs, dark reflections on the surface and grimy glimpses below. Here, I could count my toes. It freaked me out. Being able to see color, texture and form below the surface scared me more than muddy blind faith.

When I finally succeeded in floating on my belly and breathing through the tube, I barreled upward with eyes wide as saucers beneath the mask. Finn, standing crooked in the lapping sea, belly-laughed. He laughed and laughed.

Learning to use the flippers was rapid. It reminded me of running. The feel of the thigh muscles, the pacing, the forward propulsion.

Raul boated us out to a reef. It was the kind of washed-out day where sea and sky became one, where the horizon line was just the faintest whisper, the thinnest veil between air and ocean. Cliffs rose out of the water, slick-stoned and spotted with trees. Here I would not be able to touch the bottom. As we jumped in, I clung to the side of the boat. I thought of the boy, Enrique, floating in the ocean, and how terrified all my life I had been of drowning. My body clenched like a cramp.

"You sure you're ready for this, Queenie?" Finn asked. His hair was matted to one side of his head, and his blue cracked eyes matched the landscape. "You were quite keen at the shore."

How many times had I been this frightened? So many. The first time I walked into my university classroom with students from all over the world, me with my redneck accent and thrift store clothes. The first jump as a skydiver, when I froze, clung to the strut and almost died. When I'd left the Midwest and arrived in Tokyo, where I knew no one, and the taxi driver took more than half my money.

I had an alter ego, a "me," that had never left Missouri. When I was scared, I would conjure her. She was the me that I never wanted to be. She had big hips, permed hair, five kids, and a husband she didn't like. She was stuck in that dark place of my childhood. She sat in the boat watching me. She was always my motivation to take risks.

I let go. Before I could get the mask on, I sunk below the surface and took in a mouth of salt water. I spat, sputtered, flailed and got the mask on. Finn treaded water nearby. And then I was seaborne. Like a fish. Nothing could stop me. Finn had a hard time keeping up. We first checked out a reef near the surface by the cliff, but soon we were diving down, swimming into caves cut into the rock of the cliff face.

Symbiotic structures, fantastical frameworks, sharp plates and piercing tentacles, snails and starfish and schools of darting fish. It was as if I was plunged into another world, as if I was looking at pictures of the universe sent back from some far-off space ship. The colors—meringues and polar whites that flamed blue, sunset speckles, and a crimson that glowed like embers. The next hour proved to be one of the most profound experiences I've ever had of beauty. A vibrant, iridescent world lived just below the surface of normal.

Asteroid starfish, clown fish, angel fish, stone fish, lion fish, scorpion fish, ring-eyed and pixie hawk fish. I'd grown up catching fish in the Missouri rivers, gutting and scaling them, but they were gray and ugly and had names like catfish and carp and trout. We got back into the boat only because we had to. The sun was setting. We watched the stippled variegated sky, and I marveled at a world so full of grace.

"What I like about you, Queenie, is that you are up for any adventure." I looked up at him, this glowing man. He'd said that to me before. *He loves me. He loves me. He loves me.*

W e went out daily for the next few weeks. Our skin turned brown, and our faces cleared of the dark confusion of that other world, that normal world. I hadn't realized how coiled up I'd been, how much Tokyo had corkscrewed itself into my flesh. I felt free, and I knew Finn felt free. We didn't talk, just swam, and experienced. And lived.

On one of the days, when we got to Raul's boat, someone was sitting on one of the planks. I gave Raul a look. I'd paid for the boat so we could have Raul's private services. I'd made that clear to him. He rubbed his index finger and thumb together and shrugged.

A British accent, a lanky man in khakis with wire glasses, eyes that looked down into some deeper place. We introduced ourselves. His name was Ian and he was an environmentalist from the UK studying coral reefs. He was with a group of environmentalists, but he'd seen us come in the day before with our snorkeling gear, and wanted to come with us instead.

As we made our way, Ian spoke of stressed reefs, and tourist development. There was some energy that I could not quite understand. Subtle swing of blue, melting and washing. I felt myself today as the ocean, felt my body leaning toward Ian as he spoke. I kept my eyes on the water as he told us about the 5,000-, 10,000-year-old reefs, the hard exoskeletons of invertebrates piling one on top of the other, growing one tiny exoskeleton at a time, the multifaceted marine life, striped, spotted, iridescent, who ate, sheltered and bred amongst it all. His job was to record the damage, the voracious needs of tourists, the over-fishing, blast fishing, cyanide fishing, the dumping of sewage, the poisoning of the body of the waterways.

The way he spoke about stressed reefs, I could feel the anxiety in him, as if Ian were the reefs, and when they suffered, he suffered, sore toe, aching knee. The damaged coral lodged in my body as I listened, broken coral in the shoulder, silt in the lungs. I couldn't look Ian in the eyes, kept my head bent. He smelled of caramel with a faint hint of cigar smoke.

I knew I wanted to write an article on this man and his tales of battered coral reefs. The story of the battered environmentalist who felt himself no different than coral he studied.

Raul stopped in the small semi-circle bay of an uninhabited island, an oval less than a half-mile in circumference, most of the island a towering dolomite cliff with a narrow strip of pure white sand at the base. We dove in. Finn said something about exploring nearby caves and took off by himself.

I could fall into nature like falling in love. It'd started as early as I can remember. A tear of dew reflecting blades of grass, a strand of river water turning white as it tumbled over rocks, mottled bark against palm. Give me natural wonders, and I would fall headlong into them as if I were falling in love. Rain forest, mountain path, slimy cave— any wonder would do. This had already happened with the reefs, a falling into. Love.

Ian seemed magnetized to me. He entered my orbit, swimming next to me and behind me, letting me lead, as the hues like liquid dye bled out and enveloped us. I could look at him now, through the protective obscuring goggles. Here there was no damage. Here there was purity.

A luminous red starfish. I could not believe the colors here, other-worldly tints and hues. I could not believe this whole other world existed below the surface the entire time. Such beauty that was there all along, that I could not see.

I looked up at Ian. His eyes reflected the pulsing starfish. *He is my people. He feels the world in the flesh the way I do.* The realization stunned me. I'd never met anyone like me before, where the earth was their very flesh.

We are showing you something here, Purr-chan. Usui's voice. You are not alone. There are many like you. Many are hurting like the earth. We are showing you that below the pain are prisms. We are showing you something. Pay attention.

R aul handed me matches and asked me to build a fire, while he gutted the fish he'd caught while we were snorkeling. We were on a strip of beach at the base of one of the large rock formations, a jutting piece of earth that couldn't even be called an island, perhaps an eighth of a mile in circumference. Finn was ignoring us. He had his flute, and roamed to the other end of the beach to play it. Wisps of sounds made it back to us.

I was good at fires, having built them almost every day in the winter as a kid. Ian and I gathered dried-out driftwood and twigs. I dug a shallow hole in the sand, made the twigs into a teepee, lit the fire, and fed in twigs.

"A woman of many talents," Ian said, and I smiled, but couldn't look up. The colors of the reefs were still too evident behind my eyes.

I impaled the gutted fish Raul handed me, put them on sticks and balanced them over the flames. Squatting in our bathing suits, the sun high and blazing with heat, the white, flaky, smoky taste of the fish, around us, placid ocean. It was the first time I'd felt truly happy in a long time. Finn was eating rice and fish with his hands. He wasn't saying much. I knew he felt this energy between Ian and me. I hooked my arm around Finn's neck, and planted a kiss on his forehead.

"Not around the children," he whispered against my hair, his lips leaving a greasy fish streak across my right cheek.

I was not conventionally attractive. I had the body, large round breasts, a small waist, muscular thighs. But my hair was dark and ratty, and my face too serious, frown lines, circles beneath the eyes. Many men spoke of how often I frowned. *You'd be pretty if you just smiled.*

We helped Raul clean up. Finn took off to walk the circumference of the island and take pictures. Ian sat with a notebook in the small strip of shade made by the cliff. I went over and joined him.

We'd already decided I would interview him for an article, on another day, not today. Today wasn't for work. I squatted beside him while he took notes and looked out to sea. We didn't speak.

When I was little I could see so far. I'd stand on a hill and look across a field, with those Missouri wide-open skies overhead, and my vision would go farther, to land beyond, spreading out like a wind-blown sheet on a clothes line, and farther still, rivers snaking the landscape, and deeper, the roots of the trees tangling and talking. As I squatted on the beach, this happened again, my sight flew out beyond the horizon, to the dotted islands and inlets, and farther still, flying across the massive roiling ocean.

A movement, and I turned my head. Ian was watching me, and before I could stop myself, I looked into his eyes, and saw myself there. My pure self. The coral rainbow of my soul, the wide sight, the depths of my despair, the dark art of me.

He put his hand to my cheek, a long, fingered touch. I was terrified. Of the touch of him that went so beyond normal. You could think the gesture was romantic, but it was greater than that. Finn came around the corner. Ian dropped his hand. I put my fingers in its place, touching where he had touched.

"Queenie, come see this," Finn called. I went to where he was taking pictures of reflections in shallow waters. *I love Finn. I love him not. I love him.*

I an spoke in low tones, his voice like a musical note or the slick hum of a motor, putting me under hypnosis. We were at an outdoor cafe, sitting in chairs in the sand, the sea behind him, watering down the edges of him. I was interviewing him for the article, taking pictures of him. I wore large black sunglasses that covered my face and darkened my vision, so that if he tried to look me in the eyes I would be prepared.

He murmured his grief for the culture of the coral reef, the chronic stressor of development, how more people meant over-fishing, with some fishermen now resorting to explosives. How coastal cities were developed to accommodate tourists, and how they built on top of the reefs, or they dug up the reefs to build channels, or how so much more sewage was being dumped, and more algae grew and took over the coral.

"In five years, if you return here, you will not recognize Enchanted," he said. His team had a professional underwater photographer who took pictures every year. Already, year after year, you could see the destruction, the dimming of the vibrancy.

"It's as if man just cannot take the true beauty of this planet," Ian said. "As if it pains us to see what we are missing."

His eyes stirred sediment in the depths. I wished he also had worn sunglasses to hide his eyes. After that touch on the beach the day before, I spent all night tossing and turning for the light he invoked in me and the darkness it drew. I had Raul's figurine out of my pocket and was worrying it between thumb and forefinger. I did this twenty times a day. Sometimes I picked the flesh around my thumbs until they bled and sometimes I massaged a little wooden man.

Ian watched my hands. I hurried to put the thing away, but he took my wrist. He took the figurine and extracted an eyepiece magnifying glass from his bag.

"Where did you get this?"

"Raul," I said.

"There's something so very familiar about it." He turned it over, checked the weight of it in his palm. "Would Raul sell me one, do you think?"

I nodded and looked at the little man, the folk-art roughness of the carving, the hat, the chipped nose, the enlarged bare feet. It was familiar to me too, as familiar as Ian.

"He's for protection," I said.

Ian put the object on the table, his elbows on his knees, his face close to the figurine. He nodded. "Yes, that is what is needed. Protection. Of this," he waved his hand across the bay, "and of this." He pointed his long fingers to his chest. "I know you see it, too. Feel it."

I thought at first he meant his feelings for me, but I knew quickly that he meant more than that. His way of seeing, and my way of seeing, wasn't just about another person. It was too big for that.

"Every abuse to the ecoculture is an abuse to the soul," he said.

I'd never heard anyone use such words, the vocabulary of my flesh.

I took him to the water line and took his picture, the sea behind him, the blue of his shirt melding into the ocean, but it was his eyes that told the story.

CHAPTER 8 ½

*"**Enrique. Me llamo Enrique.** Enrique. Enrique. Enrique." My lips and tongue are swollen. I cannot speak. So unfair, to be surrounded by water, but not to be able to drink. A cruel joke.*

It's been too many sun cycles. I will not make it. The oarsman has won. No one can win if the sea goddess refuses you. I have kept afloat for three nights. I cannot fight anymore. It is time. It makes my heart heavy. Grandfather's carving in my palm, I am clenching it for safety, but really I do not even have the strength for it.

The salt eats at my sores. I let my face fall into the sea. It will be difficult to die, but I will try not to fight it. I have no more to give to the work of remaining afloat, to staying alive.

Only a few will miss me. Only a few love me. I am surprised by the love I feel as I sink. I am below the water now, sinking, sinking. Then it becomes impossible not to breathe, and I open my mouth and lungs, and water rushes in.

It is true what they say about drowning, it is serene. But at first, it is not. At first, it is frantic and desperate. It is full of guilt and shame. As I thrash, I feel I have squandered the life I was given. I have squandered a great fortune.

As I die, I think of silly things. I left a ball of rope unattended when I left home and went with the oarsman, rope that I was supposed to untangle and store. How could I have left such a simple task undone? I never cleared that field, visited that cove, spent more time with those people I loved.

After the tearing and burning in the chest, after the desperation and the flailing, after the darkness closes in from all sides, then the calm comes. Serenity. A deep love for this floating place. Water like a womb, a poetry of dancing limbs and floating hair, sunshine glimpsing down from the surface. I die and all I can think of are the people I love.

A final deep sigh, and my soul flies free. We are all so scared of death, so grief-stricken by it, but it is just... normal. To me, the surprise is how boring death was. Mundane.

I can see the body floating there, my old body, Enrique's body, the poetry of the floating death. Upward my soul ascends until I reach the surface, then I fly along the top of the sea, like Jesus walking on water, just like Jesus.

I travel to the oarsman first. He is at a diving site with the other boys. As he has been doing for years, he is sending them down into the ocean to find and bring up trinkets, sunken treasures from another ship that has gone down. The oarsman is a treasure hunter who uses local boys to dive for baubles. He is screaming at a boy, and I see that it is my friend, Santiago. Santiago turns his face skyward as I fly, as if he knows I am there. "I am here, my friend. I am here." He grows petrified. I can feel it in the clenching of his body. I want to help and am only hurting. I start to float away. The oarsman is shaking Santiago, pulling his arm. He gets angry for the slightest reason, this oarsman.

I scream as loud as I can, as I leave, "Te amo, Santiago. Te amo." (I love you.) Now, without a body, there is nothing more I can give. I am only love now.

Santiago bursts into tears. The oarsman slaps him. Crying is not allowed. I am doing more harm than good, and so my spirit flies away.

I now go to my home, and see you there, below me, Grandfather. You are a very old man. You sit on a stump, working a knife. On the ground in front of you are a hundred little wooden men. You are careful to whittle the debris to one side, to create a pile of splinters separate from the pile of wooden men. As I hover, I read your thoughts—the little men are for me, to keep me safe. You have been working on them obsessively day and night for three days. You know somewhere deep inside that I am not safe.

You look up from your meticulous task. You sense me there. You throw your head back. It is raining and the drops prick your face and fog your eyes.

"It is just a dream, Grandfather. It is all a dream," I say, my voice like a breeze traveling through palm fronds.

"All a dream," you say out loud, as your knife drops from your hand and clatters to the earth.

9

It was a hard fall from a vision back to normal reality. It was a crashing down from this spirit place of no body to the heavier compacted energy of the physical.

I fell backward when I came out of the vision. We were on Raul's boat, my butt in the bottom of the boat. My back was against Raul's legs. I blinked and tried to remember. It was the middle of the night, overhead a torrent of stars. Raul was boating Finn and me eight hours through the middle of the night to a place called The Nest. Ian had wanted to come on this sojourn, much further out into the wild than any snorkeling trip we'd yet taken, but his team needed him.

"A sleeping shrimp is carried away by the current," Raul whispered in my ear. I looked backward. His face flashed green with the phosphorescence, a crown of stars circling. Our souls knew each other. Not just this lifetime, but before and always. "It is just a dream," he said. "It is all just a dream." I stared at him wide-eyed. The veil between realities was still slipping, and I needed it to be solidly in one place or the other, this reality or that, or I might lose my mind.

"Queenie?" Finn called from his plank near the bow. I strained to look at him. "What's wrong?" He leaned toward me.

"She fall asleep and fall down," Raul said. Yes, this time we could pretend it was sleep.

"I'm okay." I put my hand on the bottom of the boat and tried to lift myself back onto the bench. Finn reached a long arm out and took my hand and pulled. Raul pushed.

As I sat, exhaustion nagging, Finn kept turning to stare back at me. "I'm fine," I said. He narrowed his eyes. "I'm fine."

I looked back at Raul and felt such grief. His face was Grandfather's face. I looked up at Finn's concerned stare, and felt the grief there too. In his face, Santiago's. We seemed to be actors in some play that spanned lifetimes. Actors who were thrust together in different bodies, and differing scenarios. My chest ached from it. Was I Pearl? Was I Enrique? Who was I? My body ached with the deepest loss.

The bowl of stars reflected in the water and it was as if we were suspended in the dark universe. Phosphorescence shot green lightning from the tips of the oars. We floated, no up, no down, no ground, no sky, just a bubble of black and light. I put my hand in the sea, the silken liquid turning my flesh to water.

Raul knew these darkened waters, the wiry boy in torn shorts. I thought about his mother, letting him boat tourists overnight. I thought about my own bicycle trip across Missouri when I was a kid, how some people couldn't believe a child would do that, would go on such an adventure. But there were some places in the world where children still had great adventures, where children still faced real danger, looked it in the face, and learned how to live with it.

Dawn broke to giants rising from the ocean. Broad-shouldered dolomite monsters, hunchbacked gargoyles of the sea. We were surrounded by cliffs rising up from the ocean. Seagulls in echo against sheer cliff walls. Raul told us the town lay just twenty more minutes away, but Finn had him boat to a strip of beach at the bottom of one of the outcroppings.

Finn didn't speak, just grabbed his snorkel and flippers and walked into the sea. I had to run to catch up. Here it was even more spectacular than Enchanted. I became the fish, swam with them in and out of the coral, and my body echoed the color of them, with the nighttime journey a brightly lit universe anchored in my being. I thought of the oarsman beating the boys for treasures, and of these fish and coral treasures we were so willing as humans to destroy. I so wished Ian could've been here to see this. Another layer of my anxiety washed away. For the first time in months or years or maybe decades, I was good again.

Tokyo had been a study of nature's trimming, an overlaying with concrete. Why was Missouri so hard-bitten and angry? Before I was twelve, I remembered such oneness with the earth. Where did Father's rage come from? It wasn't just him, everyone seemed so angry all the time. Father had a connection with the earth. His soul was dirt and river. I suspected it was his connection to the earth, my connection to the earth. Such oneness was not allowed. It was beaten out of you. Until you learned to beat it out of yourself.

Finn didn't want to go find the town. He wanted to stay on this strip of beach. There was something released in him here, too. We ate the fish Raul caught over an open fire. We slept on the beach under a blanket of stars. Finn and I on our backs in the sand, holding simple hands. *He loves me. He loves me. He loves me.*

Raul curled up nearby. I looked into the black spaces between the stars, and wondered how people stood living in houses, if they were really happy. Because here, I was happy in a way that I hadn't felt since I was on my back in the grass behind the farmhouse when I was little.

Two nights later, we took the night-ocean trip back to

Enchanted. No visions to throw me off the plank this time; I was at peace, at peace for the first time in such a very long time. Usui had said that I was already on the path, that I just had to pay attention. The island had touched me deeply with its simplicity, with the beauty of the coral hidden beneath watery depths. It wasn't something other-worldly. It was this world, and it was as real as dry land, and it was here all the time.

We pulled into Enchanted Bay at dawn, and as we came to the beach, a group of people were lined up to take the small ferry boat back to the mainland. The last person in line was Ian. He had his luggage with him. He was leaving.

I leaned to Raul. "I need one of the carvings. I'll give you good money. How long would it take you to run get one for me?"

He reached into his pocket, and handed me his.

"No that's yours."

"I have many," he said.

"No," I gave it back to him. The line was moving fast, and Ian was almost to the boat.

Raul reached into his pocket and pulled out another one. "Mi madre asked me to carry two for double protection for this trip. See? Take one. Take it."

"Are you sure?"

He rubbed index finger and thumb together. *For a price.* I laughed, grabbed the figurine and jumped out of the boat. I was full of the swirling colors of the depths of the sea as I ran the beach to Ian. I was in my swimming suit, holding the figurine, my hair wild, bare feet slapping wet sand.

When I reached Ian, he moved so that he was shielding me. I didn't understand what he was doing, and looked behind him and saw that men eating breakfast at the cafes were staring at me. Finn was in the distance watching too.

I leaned over to catch my breath, and held the figurine out to Ian. He stared at me with that wide-open look. I stood and stared back. I felt my love of the coral and the fish leave me and enter him. I saw him. Like he'd seen me earlier, I saw him, the torn-up coral of his soul, his despair and his love. I was still holding out the humble wooden man. The driver of the boat was taking Ian's luggage and putting it into the skiff. I lifted Ian's hand, placed the figurine there, and closed his fingers.

"For your protection," I said, holding my fingers on the hand that held the tiny man. I would've embraced him, but stood and didn't move.

Then he was on the boat, sitting in the stern, looking back at me, becoming smaller and smaller until he was the size of the wooden man I held deep in my own pocket.

NEPAL

Snow seared the flesh in pinpoints of fire. Beneath my boots, the crunch of brittle ice. A middle-aged woman on crutches labored five step forwards, five steps back along the narrow stone road. The crutches clicked, clacked on frozen earth. Click. Clack. Click. Click. Clack.

We were the only two people on the narrow old road. Our breath made clouds in the frigid night air. I wore a sweater, coat, socks and boots bought at a second-hand shop in Kathmandu. The warp and weave was the color of the locals, wild wool on hands and head. She wore a red wool stocking cap pulled low over heavy brows. Her crutches kept catching on patches of ice between the stones and slipping. Her legs were swollen beneath short leggings. Pus dripped from open sores. Five forward, five back. Five forward, five back. Click click. Clack. Click.

She mumbled, garbled words. I moved in closer to hear. Sweat and urine bled out of her like shame.

Finn waited for me behind an ancient door with rivets just twenty feet away, but I couldn't seem to stop watching her. She must've been here when we arrived, but with the small plane ride through the peaks, the ancient village of wooden structures built into the side of the mountain, the thin mountain air, and the view of the Himalayas in the distance, there was too much to notice at first for me to really see her. Over the next thirty minutes, my fingertips grew numb even in the woolen gloves, my toes ached. Some ancient custom—her as penitent, me as witness.

Travel was a perpetual leaving, and a sudden arriving. Short-lived bonds, shifting tableaus, snapshots with no through line to connect the plot. Bursts of love, sudden goodbyes. People you should've never met. People you were meant to know. People you would never see again.

I'd left Raul on the beach at the mainland. I'd taken him in a fierce hug, but he'd pulled away and run to his boat.

I was becoming a master at leaving, a virtuoso at goodbyes. It was beginning to worry me. Mother, Bonnie, Jason, Yuriko, Usui, Raul. It wasn't just about the people; I'd left the earth too many times to count. That filthy patch of poor Missouri dirt, the mud of my soul. The distancing concrete of Tokyo, the fiery singe of the Philippines. I could feel the limb I was climbing out onto beginning to bend, I could hear the branch moan.

The door was heavy, and with my frozen fingers, they were difficult to open. You could call the place a restaurant, but that would conjure an image that would not fit. A big dark room lit by tiny halos of candlelight, the ceiling two floors high, two big tables, in the corner an open fire where Nepalese women stirred, boiled, chopped and fried. The only windows were two narrow slits two floors up, near the ceiling. Earlier, when the sun was setting, a beam of light flew in through one of the windows like some message from God.

Finn and three German trekkers sat at one of the tables. They were stoned out of their minds, listing sideways, eyes narrowed to slits.

"This is some bloody good shit, Queenie." Finn handed me the spliff. "Nepalese kids sell hash for fifty pence for a chunk the size of a golf ball." He held his fingers three inches apart. The Germans nodded and laughed and listed. I took a hit and wished I hadn't. I didn't need drugs. My mind was already tripping. The weed seemed to amplify the sound of the penitent woman just outside the door, the clack of her crutches like an irregular heartbeat, or the beeping of a hospital monitor, echoing around the cavernous room.

I was still on Enchanted, my blood pulsing with the sound of ocean waves. I was still with Raul, in his one pair of shorts. It was difficult for my soul to make this transition to a place of ice. My body was here, but my heart still sang the song of the coral. This was travel, your spirit running to catch up with your body.

Finn began to play his flute, a stoned and rambling improvisation. One of the Nepalese women placed tin dishes of food on the pock-marked table, fried rice, unleavened bread, dahl, veggies in sauces, lamb in yogurt sauce. The men ate voraciously. I sipped my beer and watched the women serving us.

They wore green wool robes over pantaloons, handmade sheep-wool shoes, red-patterned scarves wrapped around their brow. The woman in charge looked about thirty, her face brown and lined by the mountain sun. Two girls were helping her, in their teens, dragging in water in buckets, using the same buckets to drag out dirty dishes. One of the girls went out again, and came back in with a basket of dung and wood, and bent to feed the fire. The other girl took up a handmade broom and started sweeping. Meanwhile, the woman chopped, mixed, simmered, boiled, moving from the pot dangling over the open fire to a work table behind her, her movements subtle and utilitarian, her face blank and her eyes downcast. The fire glowed her up like poetry, like something ancient. I brought up my camera to take her picture and tried to catch her eye but she pretended not to notice. I took the picture but felt guilty, sure I wasn't the first tourist who had stuck a camera in her face.

The laboring reminded me of Missouri. You wanted food, you went out and hunted it, or you went to the fields where you kept your livestock and you killed it. You skinned and gutted. You wanted vegetables, you went out and picked them from the earth. You earned your dinner.

Finn's flute playing was entering my flesh and lodging there, and not in a good way.

"Kitchen bitches" is what my half-sister Meghan called us. Runaway, prostitute, now missing in action, Meghan. *Where are you now, my sister?* I hated that the girls were doing this endless, mindless work. I hated it in Missouri. I hated it in Japan. I hated it in the Philippines. I hated it. Women thrust into the role of this kind of caregiving boiled my blood. That everyone everywhere seemed to accept it as the norm made me verge on crazy.

Growing up, Father threatened overt violence if we refused to comply. Deeply disturbed, heartbroken Father. Enraged, fisted, abusive Father. *You're dead but you're here, aren't you, Father?* Violence gave way to just the threat, a sudden standing up from his chair at the dinner table, a look from his mad-cracked eyes. It was enough to keep us chained to garden, stove and cutting board. The more compliant we were, the more compliments we received. Compliance was the only way to wrench any love out of that dark-hearted man.

What I was learning during my time in Asia, was that the archetype of Father existed everywhere. He was in Japan. He was in the Philippines. And he was here.

Thinking about it brought on the black dog. The dark force wept around me like a ghost. When the black heart descended like heavy smoke, it could fog me for days or weeks, sometimes months. The darkness settled in my shoulders, and I felt my face grimace up.

Finn, laughing with the Germans, turned, and even as stoned as he was, saw it and handed me the joint. "Doing alright there, Queenie?" he asked. I tried to smile, but it came out a smirk. I took a small hit and handed it back.

"Let it go," he said, leaning sideways and looking up into my face. His eyes were unfocused. I took the spliff and took a deeper hit. Finn always said it was all baggage and you could just drop it and move on. We'd done that with our summer clothes before we left, given shorts and singlets and flip-flops to Raul, and whatever he didn't want, we walked around Enchanted and gave to the locals. We'd filled the packs back up in Kathmandu and when this trip was over, we'd dump it all again.

I was supposed to drop the baggage. But how? How would I let it go? Like the man falling from the burning overhead train in Tokyo, my hand firmly attached to my briefcase full of woe. Were there instructions? Where would I put the darkness? Did I place it at the feet of the Nepalese woman bent over the boiling pot? Was I meant to give it to the penitent? Should I walk deep into the mountains and place it there?

Something hot pricked my face. I swiped at it and tried to fall back into sleep, but there it was again, hot liquid spat upon cheek, chin, eyelid. I sat up. Finn was asleep in a single bed against the wall. I was in my own bed. Snow hawked in from outside through cracks in the walls. A snowstorm had kicked up and the snow was coming in sideways. It burned my flesh like hot ash.

We'd rented a small room in an old building with no heat and gaps between the wooden slats. We were both in bed fully clothed and in coats, hats, gloves and socks. I could see my breath. There was a window, nothing more than a hole in the plywood, covered by a tarp. I heard the penitent's click and clack, got out of bed, untacked the tarp. She was still there, fumbling down the street. *I am her and she is me. We are the same.*

---

inn was holding me. I was in his arms, my face was against his chest. We were outside. It was frigidly cold. My feet hurt. I looked down and my toes were blue. *Where are my shoes?*

It was just before sunrise; the black world dawned gray. The owner of the house where we were staying stood at the doorway with a look of concern as we passed.

Finn said, "Thanks for waking me. Sorry. Really." He carried me up the stairs, placed me on the bed. *Is it a dream? A vision?*

He took a plastic water bottle from the floor, grabbed a T-shirt from his pack, poured water onto it. The clacking of the penitent's crutches like a ticking time bomb outside the window. The tarp was flapping and the wind and snow flung into the room like confetti.

Finn put the wet T-shirt onto my feet, and it was as if he'd lit a fire against my skin. I cried out. He sighed heavily, put the shirt again on the soles of my feet. His breath came out like smoke. "This is not good. You can't go on like this, Queenie."

When he tossed the T-shirt on the floor, it was dark red. I did not understand. We had a small medicine kit in each of our packs, and he pulled out mine and applied antiseptic cream.

I could feel his fingers and the cream on my toes, and the ball and heel of both feet. The pain was excruciating. My feet were on fire.

"What happened?"

Finn shook his head. His sigh was like something final. *He loves me? He loves me not?* He climbed into his bed and curled beneath his sleeping bag.

"Finn?"

CHAPTER 10 ½

Somehow you became stuck *on your way to the temple. Is that right? Is that what happened? You came all the way from India, this is the story I tell myself, I do this— create stories for people that become even more real than the truth. I don't know the truth, so I create a myth.*

You came all the way from India, five hundred miles on crutches, begging for food along the way, sleeping on the side of the road, behind trees, even once in a cave. You gave up your husband and children. You had to do a penance. For what crime? You wanted to be closer to whatever god it is that you praise. You were desperate to feel something.

Did you start out lame? Or did that happen on the way? How much worse has the trekking here made your legs?

For years, the gods have been punishing you and your family, a string of bad luck. You've come to seek absolution. No, it is worse than that isn't it? Someone raped you, or they raped your daughters, and you cannot bear it, you cannot hold that kind of pain.

You are searching for the sacred, seeking some relief from this thing they call real life. I honor you for this. I know the others might look at you and think you are crazy or worthless, but I hold you in the highest honor. I know that desire. For relief, for something beyond this mess. Oh,

I do. Crawling on my hands and knees until they're bloody for some blessing, some ease from this anguish.

I have such a great desire to help you. I want to be with you, walking beside you, five forward and five back, five forward and five back.

I am trying to talk to you. Why will you not acknowledge me? Do you see this road? I am gesturing and not using words to get you to follow me. Come this way. I will show you the road to the temple, so you can find your way, and you do not have to be stuck in this perpetual coming and going. Follow me to the end of the village. Another rocky road veers to the right up there. Can you see it? I want to point you in the right direction.

Why will you not follow me? Why do you act as if I am not here? Shall I walk with you for a while?

Why am I barefoot? Where are my socks? Five forward, five back, the stones are so cold, so jagged. Like you I start to hobble, I can no longer walk upright. Five forward, five back, five forward. I cannot seem to stop. I can see there is some comfort in it. Like knitting or solitaire or saying the rosary.

Let me join you in your purposelessness. I shall commit to this task that goes nowhere, five forward, five back. It is a rebellion. I begin to laugh. Will you not laugh with me?

My face and head grow heavy. I look at you through dark eyes, as the two of us pace side-by-side. I understand now, Penitent. I get it. The mind is clear. There are no thoughts. That is it, right? No thoughts. No feelings. No awareness. This is your religion. Right? Right?

The truck clanked hard from left to right and I banged my head on the metal passenger door. We were on a mountain road—the drop-off to our left so sheer and plummeting that Finn and I kept gasping.

To the right of our truck, a stream of people covered in dust from the road walked like ghosts, in foggy robes, saris, head scarves, hiking gear. They labored with sticks, staffs, and metal poles. The dust turned them the color of stone.

This was the Mustang trek to the Bullhead Temple at Muktinath. The temple was a place of cleansing waters, but what really interested me was the attached monastery with a perpetual burning flame, the Goddess of Fire.

"Pilgrims," the driver explained, "most from India. Only March to October does the weather permit it." I knew from the guide book that Muktinath was a great spiritual sabbatical for both Hindus and Buddhists.

We passed a man with his arm lifted above his head, the appendage withered, emaciated, disabled.

"He is holding it for penance. I know of him. Every year he

passes through the village. He is Saddhu, gave up wife and children in India. For Shiva. Gave up all the luxuries, and raised his arm up to remember suffering. He has been holding it this way for years."

In Tokyo, Usui had made himself homeless for the same reason, forsaking what he saw as soul-crushing "normality." I thought of the woman on crutches. Was I doing penance? Were we all?

Our tires kicked up more dust as we passed, and the people became even more ghostly. The sight of them was ancient, the beat of it somewhere in the depths. With so little sleep, and with the ogres the middle-aged penitent had evoked, I should've been paying attention to what was being drawn up from the core.

We made it to the temple entrance, and Finn and I joined the dusty crowd up a long steep pathway. Prayer flags hung on long strings, from roof to ground, flapping in icy mountain wind. Shuffling feet, dust in the back of the throat, the terrain rocky and hard, feeling high from the thin mountain air.

I'd had to spend two weeks convalescing after the incident with the penitent. My feet. Finn was annoyed and disturbed and stayed away. I spent most of the time reading a book on Buddha's Eightfold Path.

"There is a difference between what *is* and what one desires *to be*." I lay in bed, propped against the cracked plank wall, huddled in coat, hat and gloves, with only my wrapped feet sticking out at the end of the metal bed frame.

The sentence was pissing me off. So, I accept all the rampant sexism and poverty? Murder? Wars? Climate change? Not expect anything more from this sorry-ass place that we humans were horribly messing up?

Finn opened the plywood door. He carried a tray of food,

walked over and put it on my lap without looking me in the eye. He smelled of wood smoke and snow. He'd lost more weight, and his jeans hung low on his hips. I wanted to say: *I know you're upset with me, for hurting my feet and messing up our plans. For losing my marbles, and scaring the piss out of you. For being crazy, when all you want is someone normal. For making it so very hard to love me.* But I said nothing.

Finn turned and left without a word. I wished he'd yell at me, tell me to keep my shit together, anything but the silent treatment.

"Happiness or sorrow—whatever befalls you—walk on, untouched, unattached." I wanted to throw the book across the room. How? How is it possible to be untouched? Absurd. Undoable. I flipped through the tattered paperback.

"Three things cannot be long hidden: the sun, the moon, and the truth." That was better. I could live with that. Anything to do with the elements always calmed me, the consistency and simplicity of them.

This wasn't the first time I'd looked into Buddhism. I'd devoured Finn's collection of Buddhist books in Tokyo, taken meditation classes, discussed Buddhism with expats, with Usui.

Oh how I used to believe in "God." Oh how I used to sing high and mighty to the rafters, as a girl at Holy Cross, shins against the kneeler, light streaming through stained glass. I had a passion for it then, for the world and for what was beyond this world. I could feel the love then. I believed in my cells that life was something good and epic and big.

When I was little.

I grew up. The world took its best shot. And won. How did you believe in anything when everything was just so wrong? How could anyone possibly go through this world "untouched"?

Could a spirit be broken? Was wholeness there beneath the rage? People could be broken. I'd seen that. I knew that. When I was five, my father would hide in the dark corners of the hallway, sneak up, bend down and whisper hate in my ear—*stupid, ugly, fat. No one will ever love you.* He did it so many times I lost count. I grew up with this monster over my shoulder. The monster entered my head, and lodged there.

I'd told my friend Jason about it, later, when I was nine or ten. He'd laughed. "Come on, what father would ever do that?" He with no father, he with no understanding of how a father could be. I'd tried to tell Mother. She'd looked at me aghast. "Pearl, you and your stories." And then later, "Don't you dare talk about my husband like that."

Mother, who walked behind Father, cleaning up his messes, serving him, always serving. The nuns who walked behind the priests, always secondary, always serving, always cleaning. And "God" himself a man.

Buddhism too was about the men. That's why I'd stopped pursuing it in Tokyo. Still, I didn't think God was a woman, because I knew the sacred was also a tree, and a river and a fish. I knew that before I could walk.

"There is a difference between what *is* and what one desires *to be*." The book kept opening to that quote.

What *was:* so many versions of "father." At home, in the church, in God. What I desired *to be:* loved. Just that. Loved. How did one walk on untouched? How? How do I accept what was? The words were like gristle and bone and wouldn't give beneath my teeth. The dark ghost came back, settled on my shoulders like a putrid shawl.

"Menstruating women do not enter," the sign at the temple gate read. On the other side of the gate were dozens of people who'd come to cleanse themselves in sacred waters. Westerners and locals, nuns and monks in saffron robes. In the center, a white-washed pagoda. All around sharp-edged frozen landscape, mountain peaks in the distance.

I'd seen these menstruating signs at Hindu temples in Kathmandu. The guidebook explained that women on their period were unclean and unfit to enter sacred spaces. The sign invoked a fury that shook my entire body.

It wasn't just my father's words: *Nobody gives a shit about you.* Nor Finn's: *I don't think I love you anymore.* It was never *just* personal. The personal had to come from somewhere, some larger paradigm. People weren't that original. The hate started in a way that was bigger, or deeper, or collective before it reached you on a personal level. I knew that even when I was a kid, that Father's rage was not just his own, that my pain was not just my own.

In some traditional places in Nepal, menstruating women were not even allowed to touch things, lest they make them dirty —water and food and such. I'd read a personal account from a Nepalese woman who'd left the country and moved to the West, about how much she thought of her body as unclean.

I wished I was on the rag. I had visions of reaching between my legs, taking out my tampon and flinging it at one of the saffron-robed monks with prayer beads.

Finn put his hands on my shoulders. He did this sometimes to calm me. We'd been here before. We'd talked about how these were ancient cultures and we had to respect where they were. That it wasn't anyone's place to oppress them with Western ideas. I didn't disagree with him. I respected these holy men. I honored their commitment.

Rage, though, had a mind of its own. The fury stirred like the dust on the mountain road. The anger had its own soul that required a reckoning. The rage had a past, a present, its own collective consciousness. Even as I pretended to calm down, even as I entered the gate with Finn, I shook with a pulsing desire to bloody the monks with the drippings from between my thighs.

Along the courtyard walls, sacred water poured from the mouths of 108 metal heads of bulls. Each was a statuette of horns and ears and snout affixed to the wall, and looked like the stuffed deer heads hanging in my childhood home.

People took their shoes off and doused themselves in the water. I put my hand beneath one of the spigots. The water was icy, frigid. While Finn took off his boots and socks, I left him and roamed.

You could feel the vibe of the place. There was something here, some confluence of energies, some force. I believed places had a force, to heal or transform. I had come from such an earth place.

In me, the place seemed to draw even further up the panting rage I'd had at the gate. I did circuits around the temple to walk it off. My feet ached, but I couldn't stop and I couldn't calm down.

In the center of the courtyard stood a pagoda temple. I peeked inside the whitewashed building at a golden life-sized statue of Vishnu, then paced around the base, once, twice, three times, four. I felt like the penitent. One, two, three, four, five. Again. Again. On my ninth circuit, I had to get out.

I couldn't find Finn to tell him I was leaving. At the gate, I quelled my temptation to rip down the menstruation sign and stumbled down the pathway. Signs led me down a side path. People were entering a small wooden door and I blindly followed them.

In the center of a main room, a fire burned. This, then, was the Goddess of Fire. Painted bricks and a base of stones protected a thin flame, with miniature bowls of herbs on the floor around the flame. I'd expected a raging inferno, not this flickering fire. Still, it was magnetizing. I stared into the hot-blue center. Soon the people around me became opaque like spirits, and it became a finger beckoning me.

Suddenly I could barely stand, I stumbled outside and leaned against the monastery wall. Why did things have to affect me so deeply? I leaned against the wall and tried to catch my breath. I couldn't put into words what had happened in the flames, preverbal, or post-verbal or proverbial. Meaning before language.

Next to me was a window that opened into a small room. The sun created a beam that landed on a single male monk, sitting in profile, in meditation. I could feel the pure spirit of the monk, and it was as if that piety shot into me. It was as if this holiness met with my rage and the two went into battle. *This man refused entry to my menstruating body into the sacred. What did his "purity" have to do with me?*

The battle raged until I grew sick to my stomach, a force of diarrhea that sent me scrambling over a low stone wall, squatting from view, dropping my trousers and letting out a stream of shit. I rolled back over the wall and went to look at the monk again. He was sitting in the lotus position in an orange wool robe, palms up on knees, first finger and thumb joined in a circle. Again the purity. Again the battle in the gut.

A Buddhist nun opened the door. In her hands was a tray, a single cup, a teapot. She bowed, bent to her knees, and placed the tea tray on the floor at the doorway, stood, bowed again and left. *Women are your servants. Women are your bitches.* My stomach clenched. *How can you expect me to have any kind of faith in any religion like this?*

The monk turned. He looked me in the eye. He said but did not say, *Dear one, Buddha cannot help how people choose to praise.*

I stumbled backward, threw myself over the low stone wall, tripped and fumbled over sharp jutting stones until I found a path that led away from the temple. I stumbled as fast as I could, wanting to put as much distance between myself and that cursed temple. I had to control whatever it was that was happening to me, this epic fight in the soul. My feet hurt. Inside the boots, I was sure they were bleeding.

I stumbled on sharp rocks, fell, pulled myself up again, stumbled again, kept weaving down the path like a drunken person. It had worried my mother when I was a girl in Missouri how deeply things wedged into my heart. *You ain't going to be able to live no normal life if you keep feeling things so hard,* she'd say. Believe me, if I knew any other way to be, Mother, I'd be it.

After maybe two miles, I flopped onto a rock. My feet throbbed with pain. The sun pierced my forehead, the rugged unrelenting peak in the distance. Air so thin.

The buzzing started at the base of my skull. *No. No. No. Please!* I put my head between my legs: *Someone, help me. Please!*

CHAPTER 11 ½

Nine women pulsate across the sky, their bodies amorphous puffs of smoke, disintegrating and forming, falling apart and reforming. Ladies of the Light. They are familiar. I know them. I cannot name them.

They fly naked, primitive, tribal. Carnal. The light of them a scouring like too much sun on alabaster skin. The flesh of them a throbbing, a gestating.

One of the women shows her teeth in primordial ferocity.

"Rage" she spits. "Rage is your fire. We have been told the fire within us is wrong. For so long, and in so many ways, we grew to believe it. How can fire be wrong? It simply is."

The nine fly down and weave through me, enter my flesh, my mind, my soul. I understand then that this rage is part of some kind of journey, a coming of age, unlike any that I could have possibly known if I'd stayed in the American Midwest.

I miss my sisters. My heart breaks open for the women I have loved, the women who like me are so broken. I miss my mother, Meghan, Bonnie, Choko. I miss Yuriko, the closest I'd come to finding a strong woman, with her mixed-race confusion, her voracious sexual appetite, her easels and paints. I can almost smell the turpentine grit of her. I miss being around women.

A profound protection emanates from the Ladies of the Light, these are my protectors on this open-souled journey, a path that will immolate me if I let it. They are a sacred circle of something feminine, and bigger than any of us. "You are one of us. You are one of us. You are one of us." Whisperings of their souls to mine.

The one whose eyes burn with fury says, "The men are not stupid. They know our power. In their groins. They put upon us so much weight as to break us. Because they are broken. They know we can heal them. The pain is too great to let us near. They wish to break the healer. To prove that healing is not possible. There is nothing worse than hope. Nothing more terrifying than love."

The weaving women are breaking me apart, turning the rigid into the fluid, muscle into liquid, until I too become amorphous, and I too seem to form, disintegrate and then reform.

"We know you despise religion. Yes, it wishes to control, but there is spirit behind religion. Even if you eschew, ignore, or pretend, the spirit is there. People misunderstand. They praise incorrectly—this does nothing to decrease true spirit."

She loves my rage. She wants me to be infuriated with everyone who tells me who I should be, how to act, the roles they expect of me.

"Who am I then?" I cried. "Who am I without culture or expectations, without constructs or context? Without form?"

She swoops into my face, hair dissipating like wood smoke, face fat with fury. "You are raaaaaaaaaaaage. You are fiiiiiirrrrrrrrre."

"How will I survive it?" I cry.

"Who said you will survive it?" she hisses.

She joins the others, and the nine dance into the clouds, their bodies like great art, a Sistine Chapel of torsos, breasts, pudenda and thighs painted into the clouds swirling around the rugged and snowy tip of Annapurna.

And then a cloud moves in and obscures them, and they are gone.

The **guidebook said** anyone of average fitness could handle this. Perhaps we were not of average fitness. Bending, gasping, stumbling, puffing. Trudging, coughing, spitting. Wheezing.

We were hiking the Annapurna range, from the village of Jomsom at the Tibetan border down to the base. We'd given ourselves a week. Each day, the plan was to hike six hours to the next village, where locals gave trekkers room and board.

Things were not going to plan.

We'd hiked one mile in two hours. The village we'd just left was still in sight behind us. Our packs felt like double the weight at 9,000 feet. The air was so thin we could barely breathe. One step, stop, bend over, gasp. Two steps, stop, hold side, breathe in great gasps. It was like slogging through treacle. The earth beneath our boots was cold and hard-fisted, rocky, unrelenting.

Around us, a desolate gray landscape, everything but the sky devoid of color, stones and dirt and the path and the sheer rock wall to our left, all different shades of beige. The sun threw such sharp shadows, they appeared to be objects. I'd step over them, walk around them. Our shadows, too, were sharp and real, like dark dogs on our heels.

Two boys carrying baskets of toilet paper ran past us the other way up the path toward the village. They were barefoot. We tried to engage them, but they flew past. I threw up my hands in surrender, flopped on a big flat rock and lit a Mighty.

The cigarette along with the thin air made me high-altitude stoned. I took another drag and leaned back, blew out the smoke, and then gasped for breath. The sky was brilliant, the light dazzling, dizzying.

"I'm sure these fags are helping," Finn said, lighting one himself. Below us was a massive boulder-strewn, dry riverbed, the Kali Gandaki River. The gorge, said to be the deepest in the world, separated two major peaks, Dhaulagiri to the west, and Annapurna, which we were hiking. Dhaulagiri loomed like a white-capped monster on the other side of the riverbed. Around us, the path did not appear steep, but who knew what steep meant at nine thousand feet. This was a place of skewed perceptions, what you thought was up, was down, shadows were as real as the people they echoed, and not being able to breathe made you feel light, giddy and other-worldly.

Over the past few days, we'd both been drinking too much, smoking too many cigarettes, and getting stoned out of our minds on hash. Often I sat alone in the room while Finn wandered. He'd come back in the evening and we'd both be smashed. I marveled at our chutzpah at taking on such a hike without any physical training at all, or worse, anti-training.

Finn bent in half at the waist so the pack would rest horizontally on his back, to take weight off his shoulders. It was easier to keep the pack on than haul it off and on again. Bent sideways, he lit a Mighty and blew smoke toward the ground.

After the visitation from the women of the light, I was left with a vision of women all over the world. In my mind was now a map of women, and how hard we all found it to "choose to praise" or "choose to live," trudging against pressures and roles and expectations.

All my life I'd been searching for women to emulate. I left rural, backward, sexist Missouri where women were wives and mothers and little else, seeking women who lived full, passionate lives. I had not found what I was looking for. It was a shocking, life-changing disappointment. I was naive. I thought all I had to do was get on a plane, and go somewhere else, anywhere else, and powerful women would be waiting for me with open arms. The closest I'd come was Yuriko, and she was crazy.

"Earth to Queenie." Finn waved sideways to me from his bent-over position. "Hello!"

"What?"

He stared sideways at me, eyebrows raised.

"Sorry. What?"

He shook his head.

"I'm here now. What? What?"

"It's like you cease to exist on the planet. It freaks me out." He sighed. "What I said was we'd better get going or we'll be spending the night outside." He forced himself upright.

"Finn?" He started the slow trudge forward. "Finn, wait."

He turned his lanky body toward me. I wanted to talk to him about the temple. About how he found me. His eyes were as blue and wide as the sky, and I wanted him to understand. I wanted our love back. But these were things I had no words for. How could anybody understand? They'd call me crazy, and as they'd done before, they'd lock me in a padded room. I knew my reality wasn't crazy. I knew it wasn't normal, but I knew I wasn't mad. How did I say all of this to him?

I pulled myself upright. "Can we talk?" I said.

Nervous, he pulled hard on his Mighty. He started talking. It was like I'd opened Pandora's box. "What was that with the penitent? Jesus, Queenie! The owner of the house saw you out there, barefoot, and roused me. What were you doing?" We hadn't bathed in a week, and his white hair was ratty, matted and growing long.

"I guess I was trying to help." I left my pack on the rock and paced, taking deep open-mouthed gasps of air and smoking.

"How were you helping her? How was that helping her?" A hint of hysteria. I knew my visions scared most people, but there was something else going on here for Finn, some triggering. He seemed to attract craziness in women. His last girlfriend in Tokyo had tried to kill herself.

"I guess I was sleep-walking or something," I said. He didn't want me to be crazy, and I didn't want to be crazy, but there was the difference between what *was* and what one desired *to be*. "I think I wanted to show her the path to the temple. I figured she was stuck."

He rolled his eyes toward the ground.

"But mostly I think I was dreaming," I said, because it sounded less bonkers.

"Then at the temple, I'm out of my mind looking for you, and when you show up, you looked like something the cat dragged in. Your hair." He shook his head. "Your clothes were torn." He arched his back as if he suddenly had a backache. The weight of the pack pulled him backward and he stumbled and righted himself. "On second thought, I can't talk about this now." He stamped out his cigarette. "We need to just keep going."

I stared at his pack as we lumbered forward at a desperately slow pace. We'd bought matching backpacks for the year, his navy, mine green. Our packs carried the totality of our possessions. Mine held two pairs of trousers, one swimsuit, two shirts, a sweater, sneakers, underwear, socks, a journal, a camera and a book. These packs were the only home we had. I didn't want to lose him. I was losing him.

I said to his back in my mind: *We can't question "us," Finn. We can't fight, because there is no other ground to hold us. We are each other's earth. We can't rock the boat, because if we do, we'll fall, and we will both drown.*

By the time we stood on the edge of the dry river bed, we'd been trekking for six hours. We'd been told it would take six hours to the next village, but it was nowhere in sight. We were at the base of the gorge now. The wind traveled between the cliffs like an angry scream.

We threw ourselves down and let our packs fall off. From the packs, we pulled out nuts and candy bars and devoured them, chugged greedily at our water bottles. We didn't talk. In front of us was the riverbed, lined with fist-sized stones and mammoth boulders. With the headwind, it wouldn't be an easy hike. Looking at it made the path thus far seem like a picnic. We were running out of daylight.

We packed up, put our heads down, and trudged forward into the dry river bed. The wind picked us up and carried us backward. Two mighty steps forward, one back. There was no talking in wind like this. Below our feet, we had to maneuver boulders and rocks. Boots slipping, legs twisting, ankles wedging, the relentless wind shoving and snapping.

After thirty minutes, my face hurt like it was on fire. I reached up. The snot from my nose was blowing sideways along my cheeks, digging blood tracks into the flesh. My fingers came back covered in blood and mucus.

The pack felt like the world's troubles on my back. I thought of the penitent at the village. *For what sins was I punishing myself? What was my penance, tell me, so I could do it and be done with this torture?*

After over an hour, I sank to my knees. "What kind of vacation is this?" I screamed over the wind. Finn didn't hear. I stayed slumped on my knees, watched him slip and slide and stumble in front of me. "What are we fucking doing here?" I cried, the wind throwing the words back into my face. I started sobbing. The salt in the tears stung the bloody tracks.

Finn turned and saw me, dropped his pack. The wind was so strong it blew him toward me; I swore his feet left the ground. "I can't go on," I begged up at him as he leaned over me. "I can't do it. I can't." *It was your idea to come to the Himalayas. This is your fault. Everybody does it, you'd said, it'll be fun, where's your sense of adventure? All your god-damned fault.*

He put hands under my armpits and hauled me up. Walking beside me, he urged me on. Flat rocks, sharp rocks, slippery rocks, tripping, catching, falling, fumbling. We stopped to retrieve his pack. I was sobbing, sobbing. The relentless wind whipping, slapping hair, digging trenches deeper on the flesh of my face. Six hours grew to seven, then eight. And still no village.

The pack straps dug into my shoulders, the strap around my waist put tremendous pressure on my hips. I kept putting my hands behind me, below the pack, lifting the weight for seconds of relief. I bent forward, like a withered old woman, so that the weight rested on my mid-back. We didn't see any other foreigners on the path. It was just the two of us, tiny dots at the base of the world's deepest gorge, surrounded by vast mountain peaks that didn't care if we lived or died. In the distance, along a path on the ridge above us, I saw a local driving mules, a man with a team of yaks, and amidst rocks at the base of one of the cliffs, vultures danced over some unseen corpse, but otherwise it was only us, and we had no option but to keep moving forward.

Then it became worse. Then it became like some epic joke the gods were playing. We stopped and just stared. Dumbfounded. The path had become a raging river. The dry bed had a four-foot-deep whitewater torrent. It was difficult to even stand with the wind slamming against us, and now we would have to hop from rock to rock and avoid ice-cold water. I looked at Finn. I wanted to kill him, to bash his head bloody against the boulders. I wanted to rip the guidebook out of the front zipper of his pack and tear it to shreds with my teeth. I wanted to lie down and sleep, and let night fall and let myself freeze to death.

Finn's face fell, his eyes deadened. He had finally crossed the line that I'd crossed hours before. He slipped his pack off and dropped it where it fell. He had to come right up to my face to talk to me, to be heard over the wind. "I'm going up ahead to scout!" he screamed. He was covered in dust, his body the sand color of the river bed. I looked at my arm. I was covered in dust. We were being absorbed by the landscape.

He leaped onto a rock, balanced on one foot, hopping to keep his balance in the wind, leaped to the next rock—there was no way we'd be able to do this with our packs.

I fell onto a low, flat rock and let my pack tumble off me. The wind blew my hair so hard sideways, the sun burned my scalp. I could barely raise my head.

I saw motion near me. I blinked, sure what I was seeing was not there, that I was hallucinating. Someone sat in the middle of the river, squatting on a protruding rock. I was losing my mind. I squinted. He squatted Asian style with his butt not touching the boulder. I thought it was a mirage and tried to ignore it, but the presence was so strong that I looked up again.

It looked like Usui. I stared, hard. He was lanky, dreadlocked, and wore tattered clothes the same gray as the landscape. He waved. I raised my hand, just barely.

CHAPTER 12 ½

*"**I'm here, Purr-chan.**" It is as if he is whispering in my ear.*

"Not now, Usui. Leave me alone." I put my hand up, palm toward him. "Please! Dear god, go back to where you came from. I beg you. I have no time for you. I'm barely surviving here."

He settles himself down on the rock, legs crossed, hands on knees, the Buddhist meditation pose. When I met Usui in Tokyo, when he was alive, he was a Jesuit missionary, with a Shinto shrine in his closet and a stack of Buddhism and Christian books on the tatami. The mix of religions is the very essence of him. It took his death, it took my leaving Tokyo, to realize he wasn't just Usui, he was a Holy Man.

"You are on the path, Purr-chan. This is the path. You see with your eyes, but you do not see."

I untie my boots, take one off. The wind is screaming. Shut up. Shut up. Shut up. My socks are soaked with blood. I peel one of them off. A sore on my heel that I'd gotten with the penitent has reopened. There is an open sore on the back of my heel, too, where the boot has rubbed the flesh. My big toe is bleeding. I take a T-shirt out of my pack and pat at the blood.

"You think this other world you sometimes see, this spirit world, is

not real. You see only this world of rocks and blood. There are none so blind than those who will not see."

I wave my arm at my bloody foot. I wave toward the overwhelming landscape. "What am I not seeing, Usui?"

"This is the deepest gorge on the planet, Purr. Why you here? We're showing you but you're not seeing. Why you here?"

I have my own questions. "Why is yet another man telling me what to do or think or believe?" I can feel him reading my thoughts, about my father, about the Holy Cross priests, about the Christian god being male.

"You ask for me! You ask for man. Whether you know or not, we give you everything you ask for."

I sigh heavily.

"You see? No? We appear in manner of your culture. You understand? If you are Indian, we might be colorful god. For devout Christian, we maybe angelic."

I stick my bloody foot into the river and let the frigid waters cleanse it.

"Purr, you already on the path. You understand? You already progressing from time you left America, from time in Japan and now here. This is path."

"This fucking riverbed?" I yell.

"Why are you in this land? What you see?"

I sigh, shake my head. "The penitent?"

"Yes."

"The monk at the Temple of the Goddess of Fire?"

"Yes, but what you see is what you see." He stresses the second you.

"What?"

"You cannot know with brain. Brain is too big. Cannot see around it. Brain is in the way. You see, Purr. You always have been able to see. Must know in other places in self. Must accept that you have a knowing."

For a moment, the pain in my foot subsides, and I feel in my soul the knowing I've had as a small child, a deep connection to everything, a joy around simply being alive.

Usui laughs. "Yes, you are seeing now. The path is long. You will become tired. But, yes, this is the way."

I nurse my foot, numb now from the ice bath. "Yeah? Great. How will I survive it?"

When Usui doesn't answer, I look up. He is gone.

13

Finn stood above me, looking at me like he was waiting for an answer, like he'd spoken. I stared blankly. He leaned down and put a hand on my shoulder, put his face next to my face.

"Queenie?"

It was such a relief to feel his cheek. I just wanted my cheek against his. "I went up to the bend in the river. I didn't see the village. I didn't cross the river the whole way, though. Maybe we'll see it when we get there."

I nodded, looked over to the middle of the river. Usui was still gone.

"Where's your left boot?" I didn't answer. "Queenie?" Finn looked around.

"I don't know." I sounded like a lost child. "I don't know."

Scoured by the sideways wind, Finn stumbled around. Finally, he found it several yards away. I didn't know how it had gotten there. I must've thrown it.

As I pulled the sock on my foot, and crammed the boot back on, the pain sent me to tears. "What's the purpose of all of this?" I asked. Finn couldn't hear and put his face down and I screamed it again.

"The purpose?" He hauled me to my feet. "He squatted and finished tying my boots. "To get to the other side. Right then. Move."

I hauled my pack up onto my back, went to the river's edge. I didn't know what it was, the wind or Usui, but something or someone came up behind me and lifted me. I leaped like a balle-rina to the first rock, like a fairy, or a graceful bird.

And I missed.

And I fell hard to my knees in icy water. My pack landed face down in the river. My angels were demented, my fairies sick.

Gritting, I hauled on the water-logged pack, now heavier than ever, climbed back on to the rock, and leaped again. I missed again and hit the river hard, falling forward and stopping myself with my hands. My jacket was soaked. I looked back and Finn was watching me from the river's edge, head bent sideways, his hair and clothes whipping in the hard wind. I pulled myself up, and leaped again and again and again, falling off more boulders than I stayed on, fueled by some higher rage.

Throughout my life, when I wanted to motivate myself through hellish times, I'd think of my father. I would *not* let him win. He was my crazy violent nemesis, the wall that I used to kick myself off in the opposite direction. I promised myself as a little girl one thing: I would win. I would live a good life, and in that way he would lose the battle for my soul. With all my rage, all the willfulness, all the force of my almighty character, I leaped and fell and fell again. But by God, or by Buddha, I forded that fucking river.

Stumbling forward onto dry land, I fell to my hands and knees, sharp rocks biting into my palms and knees, unable to get up. Drenched, I shook in the bitter cold. Minutes later, Finn fell beside me. We didn't even try to speak in the roaring wind. I looked him in the face. His long chin was raw and bloody. I thought the wind had done it, like it'd carved the bloody snot tracks on my cheeks, but I wasn't sure. He looked scared. I called upon every ounce of strength left to me and forced myself to stand up.

I saw it almost immediately, the setting sun reflecting off the side of a low stone building in the far distance on a plateau.

"Finn," I yelled over the wind. He was on all fours. "Finn!" I grabbed him by the scruff of his jacket, pointed. With his fissured blue eyes, he followed my finger. He put both hands over his face, and started crying.

Space was deceptive at high altitudes. What looked close enough to touch didn't seem to get any closer as we walked. For the final three hours, we could see the village on the plateau, but it seemed to move farther away as we moved toward it. The sun was dangerously low on the horizon, and would set before we got there. My body was chilled so deeply I couldn't feel anything, as if arms and legs were not attached to the body. This worried me more than the pain.

When we finally made it to the plateau, it was dark. Our entire bodies shook from the cold. We were so exhausted, all we could manage were baby steps. Street lights are not a thing in Himalayan villages. We could barely see. We walked bent in half with exhaustion. The wet packs seemed to have tripled in weight. Local people passed us like ghosts in the dark, but we couldn't even look up to acknowledge them. One step, shuffle, trip, another step, shuffle. Finn pointed to a sign on the side of a low cottage. It was written in English, the letters awkward like a child's, and you could barely read in the dark. "Room for hikers," it said. We shuffled toward it.

A small woman in a woolen robe opened the door. She stepped back and gave us a look of fright. I stared up at Finn's blood-covered face. His look toward me said my face wasn't much better.

She showed us to a room using a kerosene lamp—two metal

beds with thin mattresses, walls made of local rock and adobe, an opening for a window covered by a thick wool woven rug, bitter wind whipping around the edges, dirt floor. We dumped our packs. My knees buckled as I flopped onto one of the beds. Finn threw himself down. She left the lamp on a side table.

Twenty minutes later, I bent and removed my boots and bloody socks. I undid my trousers, pulled them down inch by inch, slowly, so slowly, grunting. I brought the lamp over to see. There was blood all over my belly. I used a sock to clean it, and found the source. My hipbones were open sores. The pack strap had rubbed them raw. Two streams of blood trickled down my thighs, and now, because I was lying down, were trickling down my hips and ass.

I lay on the cot in my messy underwear. It was freezing, but I didn't care. We didn't talk. At some point Finn asked for the lamp. I handed it to him, his shadow dancing against the adobe wall. He took off his clothes. Thirty minutes went by, an hour.

Finn turned on his side and groaned. He held up the lamp, looked at me, in my bloody panties, my face striped raw. A laugh started in his belly, a low grumble. It burbled up. His thin body curled in the cot in a paroxysm of guffaws.

"You're no pretty picture either, Mister," I said. Turning on the bed to face him was a Herculean effort.

We were both snorting. Slap-happy, oxygen-deprived, beyond exhaustion; the giddiness like a relief. Finn always set the laughing world in motion. We hooted, rolled, cried in pain, laughed harder, held our aching bellies.

"Shh," I cried, hearing some movement in the dark house. We covered our mouths with our hands.

Hiccupping, errant giggles. The mirth had broken some storm between us. He'd taken off his shirt and even by the lamplight I could count his ribs. He'd always been thin, but I was surprised by how emaciated he was getting.

He reached out a long arm toward my bed. I reached out my hand. He held my fingers and squeezed them. Wind whistled in like dissonant music through the gaps in the walls.

14

For the next five days, Finn and I spent each day in bed, only getting up to venture ever so slowly to the bathroom, or to waddle over to the rug-covered window to peek out at the snow, and the desolate landscape. My body hurt in ways I'd never experienced. A lethargy in the muscles, deep aches. Stretching the skin on my face caused the tracks on my cheeks to bleed. Even turning over in bed would open the wounds on my hips and feet.

Still, Finn and I seemed to be in a bubble, a happy place. It was the kind of love we used to have, when we first met. Simple, and openhearted, and full of good will.

The woman who owned the house was called Etisha. She would knock on the door, open it, and bring in two trays of food. We'd sit with the trays on our laps, and scoop up dahl, vegetables and chunks of meat in sauce with chapatis. We were ravenous. Afterwards, we'd read, and sleep, and talk about simple things. For the first time in a long time, I was happy.

Etisha's forearm was aflame. Light seared from the window and set it aglow. As she placed dishes on the low table — dahl and rice, chapatis, a fat dollop of yak butter, homemade yogurt — she moved in and out of the fire.

It was the first time we'd been out of the room, to eat in the dining room with the rest of the trekkers. Apparently there was another room our landlady, Etisha, let out in the back of the house.

The dining table sat on short legs on the dirt floor. We scrambled to sit, and discovered a hole had been dug in the ground below the table. In the hole, embers. Our feet dangled over the heated pit. Charred wood smoke, the smell of goat shit wafting through the window, gluey greasy yeasty smells. Etisha's arm a work of art, a scratch-and-sniff Rembrandt. She stood at the fire at the hearth and stirred something there. I thought of Usui at the riverbed, and the love I felt now, and the child full of love I used to be.

Finn slathered yak butter onto a chapati. "Do you think she'd let me interview her?" I pointed to Etisha.

"For a travel article?" he asked, his mouth full of food and jumbled teeth.

"Yes?" I said it as a question. I didn't get what made a good or bad travel article. Most readers were probably just looking for fun, when I always went way too deep.

"Sure, why not?" he said, devouring the rice and dahl. We'd learned already in our few months of travel the necessity of eating as much as possible when food was placed in front of us. Already, several times we'd had no way to get food because of a jeepney or a bus ride that lasted more hours than expected. We'd learned to eat everything in sight when food was available.

I watched the woman cook. She wore a traditional, deep-orange robe sashed at the waist. Her hair was tied up, strands falling into her face. I could not see her eyes; she seemed always to be looking down. She moved from work table to fire in a poetry of motion, as if her cooking was choreographed. My mother used to have such simplicity and grace in the kitchen, steps from refrigerator to stove, almost like a dance.

I'd always felt a love-hate pull with traditional women. I'd watched my mother spend hours canning, baking, stewing. The only creative space given to the woman was the kitchen, the relentless rearing of children, the needs of the husband.

Asia was bringing all of this up again. Japan too. The women had their roles. What was it that Yuriko said to me, how countries become these epic canvases, and as travelers our souls are writ large? That we choose countries to move to for a reason. That each of us chooses the country that has the greatest lessons we need to learn. That we go abroad, and project ourselves there, our deepest issues exaggerated so we can see them. Really see them.

Even as young as five, I knew I didn't want what my mother had, what other women in Missouri had. Even as a very little girl, I vowed not to marry, not to have children. I wanted my own life, my own path, my own brain. Still, I had not found a place for myself. I didn't want the conventional and didn't know what else was open to me, what path to trek down, what riverbed to wade through. I was willing to work hard. I just didn't know in which direction to aim myself.

What would become of me if I didn't want to play a role? What role did I want to play? Did I have to play a role? *Usui, those are the questions you could answer for me. Those are the torrents that tear at me.* I heard Usui answer my thoughts, *"You give me too much credit, Purr. And why are you asking a man?"*

We took our first walk through the village. It was another cloudless cold day, the sun and the sky at this altitude brilliant in a way that made you lose your mind a bit. The village was comprised of a couple dozen shacks built into a stone cliff face, the earth a craggy gray, the buildings white-washed, sudden pops of color of threadbare prayer flags and woolen hats. It took us mere minutes to hike the entire length of the town. We stopped often so Finn could take pictures. He was a stellar photographer. His photographs were as good as anything you'd see in National Geographic, his visual acuity better even than his music. He didn't believe it, though. He knew his gift, but he didn't know, or he had forgotten, just as Usui had said in the riverbed. Somewhere we all know. Then we forget.

At the end of the village, we followed the path through some truncated trees and came to a flat rock that jutted out over the river. It was a platform, a stage, an altar, ancient and protected. The god behind the altar was the Annapurna peak. In the distance the mountain was low-shouldered, narrow-topped, ice-white. The Kali Gandaki River had a stronger current here. It raged toward us, flung itself below and beyond us, beneath the outcropping. And with its churning, it vibrated inside me like something alive and roiling. We both stood ramrod straight, chests out, taking in hard mouths full of air, the wind itself full of excitement and electricity.

Finn took out his flute and started to play. The guidebook was in my day pack. I read out loud: "Annapurna is called The Goddess of the Harvests... the universal and timeless kitchen goddess... the mother who feeds."

I sat crossed legged, and aimed my body toward the mountain. Finn played softly, his body undulating in waves. His hair was matted, and white strands stuck up from one side like a sudden idea. This is what I loved about Finn and me as a couple. If we loved something, we showed it. We loved that mountain and we were going to show it.

The mountain air left me winded, and heady with glee. The sun was brilliant. Finn put the flute down, came to me, took my wrist loosely, swung me up, twirled me. He kissed me wetly. We moved slowly against each other, like two seventeen-year-olds at prom. I put my head against his bony chest. We hadn't showered for many days. He smelled of dirt, sweat and river. *He loves me. He loves me. He loves me.*

He extracted himself and bent to get his flute and took it up again. That feeling I'd had as a child, where anything was possible, life was a great adventure, and the world was full of unending joy. I sat, circled my thumb and forefinger on my knees, closed my eyes.

I had always felt I'd been called to bigger things. But here was the thing about "being called." You could spend years trying to figure out what you were being called to do. You could know the urge deep in the belly as a child, it could go underground for years, you could be called again, and you could answer the call, but you didn't know who you were answering, or what you were answering. You had no idea how it translated into this one life.

I'd felt this call all my life, a subtle drum beat like the pulsing of a heart, but lately the drum was thumping faster, harder, and sometimes would reach a crescendo. *Fulfill your purpose. Now.*

Not long ago, at Tokyo Bay, after the earthquake, I'd bent in supplication and told the gods, "I'm ready." For what, I did not know. Some kind of giving over the ego to whatever bigger purpose was out there. It'd been many months, and no purpose had come to me. Now, here again with Annapurna as my witness, I sighed the heavy phrase. "I'm ready. I'm ready."

Something stirred, something forceful, inevitable. Something scary. Sad. Something as devastating as death. I understood I would have to step up and meet whatever this was. It would change absolutely everything I thought I knew.

I felt the limb I was crawling out on shake and tremble against the low-throated echo of the earth's pounding pulse. One small push, and I would tumble.

15

The sky was spitting snow, hocking miniature hail, and I stood huddled in my coat, waiting for people to pass in the slow, meandering life of the village.

Finally, a kid came by. He was barefoot. The way the locals could withstand the weather was shocking. "English?" I asked, pointing at him.

He shook his head. I motioned above my head to include the entire village. "English?"

He looked confused. I held my fingers inches apart. "Little bit English?" He nodded. His nod meant *No*. One of the other trekkers had told me that in Nepal and India head movements for yes and no were opposite that of the West.

A woman passed, hauling wood in a basket on her back. "Do you speak English?" She ducked and veered. A tiny old man put a bony hand on my arm, laughed up at me with a gap between his upper teeth. He spoke rapidly in Nepalese.

"English?" I asked him over his chatter. He laughed, kept talking in Nepalese and held onto my arm.

Up and down the road I went a dozen times. "English? English? English?" Real travel writers set up translators in the cities, and had them travel with them. Why did I have to be a duct-tape, jury-rigging, seat-of-the-pants kind of writer?

A lanky boy approached. "English?" he asked me.

"Yes. Do you speak English?"

He wobbled his head and worked his mouth, as if he were chewing on words, but then said simply, "English? Yes?" He started walking away. "Come." I didn't follow. "Come." He put up his hand up, with his palm toward me and waved me away. This had confused me at first in Asia, too. Waving *away* meant *come*.

I thought, *This is what I should do a travel article on, differing cultural gestures, body movements and facial expressions in Asia, and how Westerners take as a given the way our bodies move, the way we communicate physically, as if our physical expressions were the norm and not learned behavior. How our perceptions shape every inch of our world.*

I followed the boy at a distance. He was tall and thin and held himself crooked. Too short trousers exposed bony ankles and bare feet as we walked over patches of ice. He turned back to me. "London." Waved me away. "London." I stopped and stared at him. He motioned me backwards, forwards.

He stopped at a low wooden house, and I came up beside him. He pointed at the door, whispered, "London." He did a sweeping motion at his knees. "No more. Not good."

We went through a low door without knocking. People did not seem to knock in Nepal. My eyes had problems adjusting to the dark.

"May I assist you," a British accent, the outline of an old man on the floor, bent over a mat with a cup of tea. He looked into the tea as if he were reading the leaves.

"I'm Pearl Swinton." I put my hand down beside him and he looked up at it. I remembered the guidebook said the Nepalese didn't shake hands and was about to withdraw it when he took my fingers into his slowly. His hands were surprisingly soft, long and elegant. He was bald, pure Nepalese and middle-aged, with weary eyes. He stretched his mouth, and his teeth were chaos.

"I am Yash."

I explained my need for a translator. I wanted to interview Etisha, my landlady, about her life. When he turned to stare again into his cup, didn't respond, and the silence stretched, I asked, "Where did you learn English? London?"

He groaned his way to standing. His back was bent and he looked sideways and up at me. "Yes, I had a life in Britain." He looked like he wanted to sit down again, but kept standing. "Anyway, it is of no consequence now."

He agreed to do the interview, somewhat unwillingly. We set out down the village's one road. He wore a jacket, striped button-down shirt, and faded checkered trousers, and walked bent over at my side. He took baby steps and so did I, to keep pace. I huddled against the onslaught of sleet, but he wore a Western jacket, not at all suitable for Himalayan weather, and left it unzipped. I asked him about his fluency and his life in London.

"It is of no consequence. Not anymore."

We came upon Etisha outside the house, washing clothes in a beaten tin pan. Yash spoke to her in Nepalese. She looked frightened, nodded in refusal, and spoke barely above a whisper.

"She is saying no. She is not used to exposing herself, speaking about her life," Yash said. She nodded in dissent again and backed toward the doorway.

I told Yash I wanted to explain my intentions. I found that if a person knows your intention they are more likely to agree to an interview.

I wanted to write about a day in the life of a woman in the Himalayas for people all over the world to read, so that we could all understand each other better. I didn't say that I missed my mother, that I missed my women friends, that I just wanted a woman to talk to. Etisha looked up at me when Yash finished, into my eyes and moved her head from side to side in assent and smiled.

As we entered the hut, Yash and Etisha removed their shoes. I took off my boots. Finn and I had not taken off our shoes while staying here. Was it a custom? I didn't know. These were the pitfalls of traveling in countries where you didn't know the customs. You could insult someone so easily without even knowing it.

Yash and I sat on the dirt floor at the table. The warmth from the coals warmed the bottom of my wool socks.

"Will you sit?" I asked Etisha, pointing to the floor next to Yash. There was no other furniture. Yash shook his head, and whispered, "It is not done. She is the woman. She will stand. She will serve us."

Etisha went to the open fire in the corner, the smell of chai filling the room. I asked Yash, "Is my sitting here as a woman offensive?"

"You are a foreigner, so normal customs are not expected. But the way Western women act can be a great challenge for rural Nepalese women. Not just the rural ones, actually."

Not knowing the social context was a tightrope for a sensitive person. You'd make a faux pas and see a grimace and never know what you'd done. If you lived in a place long enough you could figure it out, but constant travel made understanding social graces nearly impossible.

Every expat had stories to tell about social mishaps. I had a few incidents that haunted me. In Tokyo, when I'd worked briefly for a publisher, my boss, Yashimoto-san, invited me to dinner to meet his family. His children and wife spoke little English, and my Japanese was rudimentary, so I created a grab bag to bring with me, for show and tell, a map, some pictures, an arrowhead.

In the foyer of my boss's house, his family gathered to greet me, his wife, a ten-year-old son, an eight-year-old daughter. Yashimoto-san introduced each of them.

"This is my stupid wife," he said. She smiled and bowed. He gestured to the boy. "This is my lazy son, and this," he pointed toward the girl, "this is my ugly daughter."

Something cultural was obviously happening. I'd find out later what all of this meant, but at the time, I didn't know what to do. I bowed. Grimaced. Bowed again. *Should I argue? Laugh it off? What did one say in Japan in response to their boss insulting his family, one by one?*

Their main room was surprisingly Westernized, with carpet, sofas and chairs. I knew such a Western design was a status symbol to someone like Yashimoto. I sat in an easy chair, and opened my grab bag to entertain the children. I extracted the crumpled map of the world. The girl and boy gathered around, wide-eyed. They followed my finger as I pointed to the U.S. and then to the state where I was born. I traced the rivers and told them stories of fishing and hunting, while their father translated. From the grab bag, I took out the mango-colored arrowhead, with its sharp tip and burnished sides, told them how the Osage Native Americans who used to live there.

I brought out the photo of my mother. I had only one. Dog-eared, faded, veined, it'd been taken after Father died and before her second husband, when she and I lived alone. She stood in front of a Christmas tree, shoulders thrown back, as if she were a little girl trying to make herself big for the camera. In Japanese because I knew so few words, I said, "This is my beautiful mother."

The children's eyes fogged over. They retreated to the sofa. Yashimoto-san cleared his throat. The wife left the room. You could cut the tension. I knew it had something to do with calling my mother beautiful. I should've taken my cues from the insults Yashimoto-san had lobbed during the introductions. *This is my distant, head-in-the-sand, throw-you-to-the wolves mother.* I felt their shame and willingly owned it as my own. I stared at the floor and sweated. My boss laughed awkwardly, changed the conversation, but the evening never recovered. All night, everyone avoided eye contact.

Much later, I would learn that by calling my mother beautiful, I proclaimed myself beautiful, and my family as better than theirs. From their perspective, I spat in their faces.

On some level, I knew this was why I traveled. These other cultures were the stone against which I sharpened my knife. How could I really know who I was if all my life I lived around everyone who was the same, people who never challenged me? How would I ever discover who I really was, beneath all the conditioning?

Just a few days earlier in Kathmandu, Finn and I had been walking down a sidewalk crowded with hundreds of tourists. A line of vendors at the edge of the street sat behind squares of cloth laid out on the road surface, selling Buddha figurines, incense and jewelry. It was impossible to walk there it was so crowded, so Finn leaped over one of the vendors to get from the sidewalk to the middle of the road. A collective gasp went up from the line of squatting men.

I struggled to get around the tourists and get to Finn in the street. A dozen vendors stared at him. The vendor he had leaped over leaned forward and fussed with his Buddhas, looking at Finn with a pained face.

Apparently, it was a sacrilege to point the bottom of your feet at sacred objects. Even exposing the bottom of your foot to someone sitting across from you was the equivalent of flipping them off.

The vendor collected up his wares. I didn't know what he'd have to do to cleanse them. Finn's face was twisted in mortification. We didn't know what to say or do, so we apologized, and ran away.

Etisha dribbled milky chai into tin cups at the table from a banged-up metal kettle. She placed a wood block below Yash's cup. I didn't know the custom, and looked at Yash quizzically.

"My tea now sits higher than yours. I am a man. I am of a higher position." I shook my head and snorted. "It is the way here," he said

I wanted that fiery tableau I'd had that morning at breakfast, the glow that lit the room like a painting, but it would not come. Now the light seemed diffused, the ground beneath my butt cold and hard, and I had a headache.

Etisha stood sideways next to us as we did the interview. Her husband was a Sherpa and was out with a group of climbers. He was gone for weeks and sometimes months at a time. As we spoke, Yash translated, and it was an odd juxtaposition, her moving lips, the male British voice, my questions, his translation, as if he were a ventriloquist and we were his dummies.

A typical day for Etisha—arising when it was dark, roaming the mountainside collecting sticks and dung for the fire. She showed me the woven basket she used. She milked the yak. Collected eggs. Churned butter. Ground spices. Sometimes butchered a goat. Supplies came up twice a week on the backs of little boys from Pokhara. Rice, dahl, chai, toilet paper.

She pointed to a dented tub. I bent to look. She was dying sheep wool. The water was the deep purple color of berries. This woman's life in a tiny village in the Himalayas was not so different from the life I'd lived as a child. We'd been dirt-poor in Missouri, living hand to mouth. My mother and I foraging, collecting, hauling, butchering.

Yash seemed to be growing heavy, his voice low and almost inaudible, his face inches from his tea cup. "I'm not sure you're going to get much from her daily life to fill a travel article." I gave him an annoyed look, and wondered who did *his* laundry.

I understood that Yash missed the sophistication of London. That this uneducated, subsistence life wore at him. I could see that, even if he hadn't told me. I had run away from rural Missouri for the same reason.

Still, even as a girl, I'd understood that a poor person's story was held in a low position by the literary, the educated, the cosmopolitan. Shouted down, or ignored or scoffed at or dismissed or thought of as something heavy to be pitied. My mother thought it, eager to be away from the earth, to get a house in town. And she'd succeeded. I was no better; I'd run away from it. How we were all so ready to dismiss our very roots.

Even as I tried to run away, the earth never let me go. The humility of the life—there was not a day I didn't think of the souls of the people, the animals and the land that I'd left behind.

Sometimes I felt like kneeling at the feet of these earth people, asking them to tell me their stories, and as they opened their hearts, holding their words like precious found objects in my palms. I'd always thought women like Etisha and my mother were humble. But now I wondered as I watched Etisha, whether it was humility or low self-esteem. Or both.

I'd long known that the earth itself wasn't held in high esteem and anyone close to the earth by association was held low. I'd seen it in America, and now I was seeing it everywhere. As a journalist, I witnessed liberal colleagues partake in arrogance against the earthy and dirty, and in the Tokyo newsroom it was no different. I understood how the denigration entered the blood of those close to the land, how it defined their personality, how it kept the lovers of the soil and sky unsure and painfully shy.

Etisha left the harsh beam of sun and disappeared into a dark corner. Back into the light, she brought out a handmade loom with a square of fuzzy orange wool. "For a sweater," she said through Yash's voice. "It is yak wool. My neighbor spins it, and I do the weaving."

The corners of the loom were awkward branches, and the yarn

was stuttered and uneven. Everything about it was earthy and homegrown. I ran my fingers over its stuttered imperfection.

It flew me backward in memory, my mother teaching me to sew at an old foot-pump sewing machine. She sewed all of our clothes, Father's, mine, Meghan's, the curtains, pillow coverings, table cloths. I didn't want to learn. Tiny threads, and lined-up seams were a straight-jacket life to me. She'd give me a task and I'd sew a seam crooked or warp the weave. I'd do it all wrong on purpose, until finally she stopped asking.

That square of yak wool reignited that push and pull in my gut. The beauty and comfort of these womenly creations, the trap of a lifestyle I was trying to outrun.

The door opened. Three Nepalese women entered. One had a baby on her back. Etisha followed them to the fire pit. One brought from a basket a ball of yak yarn and handed it to her. The other took up a pile of what looked like Western clothes in the corner.

"Unlike women of the West, Nepalese woman have many sisters," Yash said. Why did he always sound so bored?

"Her sisters?"

"Not blood sisters. Women live their lives in groups here. You will not find a Nepalese woman by herself for very long. It is different from the West. It would not be considered a positive thing if a woman were alone."

The women whispered and laughed, and jealousy burned in my gut. This had happened to me before in Asia. The plight of the women seemed so backward to me, so close to the Missouri I'd left, and I'd feel deep concern or pity, and then something would happen that would turn the pity on its head. Where were my women? Why were the women in my life so battered and fractured? Mother? Meghan? Torn apart. Divided. Jealousy burned scars in my belly as I watched the three women. Why was I all alone?

After the women left, we resumed the interview.

"What is it like to open your home to all of the hikers? What do you think of these Westerners you meet?" I asked. Yash translated.

Etisha stood to the side, holding her fingertips. Her face soft. She looked uncomfortable, and Yash spoke to her in low tones. When I asked what he was saying, he said again that women are not used to sharing their deepest thoughts.

Etisha's voice was barely audible as she started to speak. "I think with tourists who come, we are destined to meet. Each one that comes. They are destined to meet the spirit of the mountain, and I to meet them. In this way, we spread our spirit from one world to another world. This is why I agreed to speak with you for your article. There is a reason for it that is bigger than me, and bigger than you. All of us, all tourists and village people, we will meet in another life. We have met in many lives."

She knelt to put paddies of dung onto the fire. "You see this fire? The fireplace is *thapmig*, we say *fireplace with eyes*. You must never pollute fireplace by throwing trash into it or you will offend the spirits. But some of the tourists pollute the fire. Do you see?" She pointed back to the flames licking at the bottom of a soup pan.

"What do you mean about throwing trash into the fire? I'm not sure I understand."

She was quiet, thinking. "I will give an example. Shiva's sacred plant." Yash stopped translating, looked at me and said, "She's referring to marijuana."

Etisha continued: "For centuries, sadhus smoke it as they roam the mountain, seeking elevation of spirit. Only for expanding. Okay? Then the tourists want to buy, and the young people make money from what is sacred. Or young people smoke it, but not to find the expansion. Only to forget. You see, they only smoke to forget. This is trash thrown upon the spirit of the fire."

A waft of dark smoke blew out from the fire as if on cue, and burned my throat. I coughed. I thought of the woman back at the first village, who'd served us food when we were with the Germans, stoned out of our minds. It wasn't just Shiva's sacred plant. We were throwing trash everywhere onto nature. Everywhere we trashing the spirit of the fire, in ourselves, and outside ourselves.

A squeal came from the corner. Etisha went into the dark back area of the main room. The squeal turned into a gurgle. She had a baby. The child must have been around since the first day Finn and I arrived, but we'd never noticed. Etisha paced with the baby, singing softly.

I went to her as she placed the child back into a woven basket filled with straw. Yash followed. "Her name is Tunali," Etisha said. On the girl's head, an orange scarf that looked like a coffee bean bag. Her dress was red and embroidered. Her eyes were bright and glorious as only a baby's can be.

"She had two others, boys, but they did not make it," Yash said. "I was living here in the village when both of them died. Infant mortality is high here."

Dust swirled around the child in a beam of light from the corner window, hands grasping, as if the specks were a universe of stars. As I watched the girl, I fell into her soul, was pulled backward through many lives, saw her stories unfolding, and I could not stop them.

"Pearl."

The tales continued to play out, winding out like a rolled sheet in a strong wind. Snap. Snap. Snap.

"Ms. Swinton."

Then the story started moving forward. This child's life. The future that was meant for her. I wanted to throw myself between her and the world, do anything to protect her. *How would such a pure being survive? How would she make it?*

A grip on my arm. It was Yash. I was on my knees leaning over the baby. He pulled me to a standing position, not an easy feat with his curved back.

"I'm so sorry," I said, stumbling toward the table. I had to think of something to say. "What a beautiful child." I tripped over a shoe at the doorway. Etisha rushed to turn Yash's sneakers upright.

"Upside down shoes are bad luck," Yash explained. "Are you okay, Ms. Swinton." He said something to Etisha and she came back with bottled water. I took several swigs.

Elbows on the table, I held fingers to my temples. I had to recover, say something. The film reel in my head, I needed to interrupt it, change the ending. "What are your hopes for your daughter?" I tried to control my voice, but it came out with desperation.

Etisha walked to the table and looked down at me full in the face. A fire burned behind her eyes. She spoke to me directly as if I could understand the words. This was the first time she'd looked me full in the face. I grew mesmerized by her lips. Yash translated in his rough voice.

"My daughter will NOT be reincarnated a girl. I have made my sacrifices to the gods. I will ensure it. She will be reborn in the next lifetime as anything but a girl. She will not be forced to marry, not be forced. Even a yak would be better. A dog. She will be anything but a girl." Her voice male and British.

I looked at Yash angrily as if he was the one who had initiated the thought. He put up his hands and rolled his eyes. Again that heaviness on his racked shoulders. The child squealed. The mother went to the stove.

I was trying to recover when the front door opened, and two worn-out hikers stood with the same frightened look Finn and I had when we finished the trek. Etisha went to help them. Yash and I had to go. I held up my camera. I needed pictures.

I was growing to dislike sticking cameras in people's faces more every day, but what could I do? We got Etisha outside. I positioned her in the stream of light at the window with the loom, had her stand in the glow of the fire. Got a shot with the baby, but felt nervous about it and hoped they didn't use it. I felt so protective of the child. We moved outside. After several shots in front of the white-washed hut, I felt the love. In the last one, the wind carried her hair and the prayer flags in matching waves. I felt the soul of her, and I hoped the photo turned out, hoped the newspaper ran it, hoped her words would echo from this little village far across this scarred planet.

Etisha put her hands together and touched her fingers to her forehead and bowed. I did the same. I wanted to roam the mountain for sticks and dung with her. I wanted sisters who would be with me, who would not abandon me, who would knit and cook until we all felt warm.

Yash and I began our labored walk back down the path. As we passed Etisha's hut, through a side window, we spied the child in the beam of light. She was playing with her toes.

"Tunali means tender grass," Yash said. With his words, my fear for the child turned to rage. Yash seemed to notice. "You mustn't worry about what the woman said about her daughter. They are all full of old superstition here."

I shook my head. There was no way I could explain how I'd seen the past lives of the child and the future life of this child play out. I could hardly explain it to myself.

"Why does it have to be so bad for women here?"

"Where is it not so bad for women?" Yash asked, bent forward, speaking toward the rocky path. "London?"

"I certainly hope so."

"Should Etisha's child grow up and move to London?" he asked. I nodded. I was so angry and I couldn't figure out why. Yash grew visibly wearier. "What would a Nepalese girl alone do in such a place? I was a man alone there, and…"

I felt fisted up. "What role will that girl play if she stays here?"

"What role would you have her play in London or America?"

I didn't even know what role I wanted to play in the world. This thought did not help me calm down.

"It is all too complicated for this one conversation, or just one newspaper article," Yash said. He squeezed his nose with long fingers.

My hands were clenched at my sides. "Everywhere is so sexist. I can't find a place that isn't hateful to women. I left Missouri to find somewhere better. Where is it? Where?"

Yash didn't answer. I felt like punching something or someone. "What do you think of all the sexism?" I demanded of his bent profile.

"Who I am or what I do used to be of consequence. But that is over. What I think is of no consequence. None of any of this is of any consequence whatsoever."

Why are we always *looking for things to be better than they are right now?*

The snow bled into the bones, flopped inside ears, dripped from nose, waterlogged boots. We were on the move again, hiking to the next village. Three hours on a roller coaster of a trail, ascent and descent over shifting rocks. What went up, must come down. This was an equal-opportunity trail, where the trek upward and the movement downward were impartial in their difficulty and frustration. Our packs threw our weight forward, pounded knees and thighs and calves, then pulled our weight backward, pulling neck and shoulders and arms. The next village was supposed to take six hours to hike, but who knew how far it really was?

When we reach our destination, we very soon want to be elsewhere.

I held a thin paperback of Buddhist quotes in front of me and read as we hiked. I needed something to quell the rage. I looked at my feet, read a line, watched the trail, read another line. Every once in a while, I said the quote out loud for Finn. He seemed to be ignoring me.

The book was made wet by the snow. Finn complained loudly about a sharp pain in his left knee.

Why were we always striving to be somewhere else?

I'd had my hair cut. Next to Etisha's hut, a man was sitting outside and cutting hair, and I paid him to give me a boy's haircut. It took some convincing. Women in Nepal did not have short hair. Finally, he only agreed to do it when I tripled his fee. My hair was black and frizzy, and when unwashed stood out in wild directions like a scream. The barber sat outside on the ground, and I sat cross-legged in front of him. He had no mirror. I used a compact from my pack. With no hair, my face stood out. Men turned to stare and followed me. Always when my hair was short, men flew at me like hawks. As we hiked, snow drops melted against my scalp. I just wanted the hair gone, I wanted it off me, tired of critters crawling from the nest, tired, perhaps, too, of being a woman.

Don't use meditation to achieve a higher state of mind, see what is.

When we left the village that morning, it was Etisha I expected to miss, but it was the child I could not get out of my mind. I wanted to swoop in and save her. Tender Grass. I could not seem to remember her name in Nepalese, and in my mind she was always Tender Grass.

The night after the interview, I motioned to Etisha that I wanted to introduce Finn to the child. She smiled. I had him play the flute for the girl. She reached chubby fingers for the sounds, musical dust. Finn let her play with the instrument and she put it in her mouth, which made Etisha laugh.

I went back to Yash the day before we left. We had tea in his hut. He told me his story. I was good at listening. I might not know what made a relevant travel article, but people's stories fascinated me. I was good at holding the space for people to speak their lives. Even as a child, I'd understood that people just need to talk, that stories untold fester, that the meaner and the harder the story, the more no one wanted to listen, and the more the person needed to speak. I knew that untold stories lodged in the organs and grew like tumors until they made people sick.

He'd made us chai over an open fire in the corner. We sat on a mat on the floor of his hut and he told me his story.

He went to London for college on a student visa. After graduation he stayed on, like many Nepalese. He kept under the immigration radar for nearly 20 years, married a British woman, had two boys. His jobs were menial, but his tastes sublime, and he spent hours at the British Library and the city's art galleries, and educated himself on the finer things.

When immigration found him, when they deported him, he told his family to stay behind. They were all legal citizens. The boys were in good schools. No one would have money if his wife quit her job. Why should they suffer because of his deportation?

His family came to visit for a month each summer. It was all anyone could afford. You could tell that their absence left a hole in his heart too big to fill. He sat slumped forward. I knew asking anymore about them was not a good idea. We sat quietly for a long while. I also knew this as a little girl, how much silence, too, is part of the story, that there are whispers and spirits between the lines of every tale. I learned early how to hold as much space for the silence as for the words.

"It is not so much that I miss London," Yash finally said. "It is that my life is lived in the space between. Here is one border. There is another border, and my life is lived in the crack between the two. When I am here in this village, I miss London. When I was in Brixton, I missed the Himalayas. I am not saying the London life is better, I am saying that being exposed to it has ruined my ability to find life in this village acceptable."

My chai was cold and had specks of ash floating in it. I drank it anyway.

"I have tried to come to terms with my family not being with me. It is my karma, as they say. I will own that pain. What I cannot seem to balance is that my soul now must live between two worlds." His voice broke. "I do not know how to live divided in such a way. I fear that I am going crazy."

His hut was darker than Etisha's, with only one window facing toward the road. The beam of light from the sharp sun highlighted a chair behind us. We huddled on the floor in the dark. I understood that Yash preferred the dark.

"I cannot go forward and I cannot go back. I exist in a place inbetween. If there is a way to come to terms with this, to integrate it into my whole being, I cannot find it."

That night, our last night in the village, I could not sleep. I heard a noise outside, went to the window. Outside, in the night, Etisha sat on a rock wrapped in a woolen blanket, holding her daughter. I grabbed my coat from the nearby chair, and put it on against the bitter cold.

I went to where she sat. She pointed upward to the skies, to the light clusters in a velvet night, the glow of the far-off granite peak. She sang a faint song. She was singing to the girl. Or perhaps she was crying, I couldn't tell. She held the child as if she were an offering, as if she were giving her over to the will of the white-knuckled Annapurna.

How can we find any contentment, when we are always striving for elsewhere?

Up the path, down, bobbing, seesawing, crooked, erect, unstable, unsteady. Snowing harder, chilling to the core.

I worried that my life of constantly leaving was not good, like a bad habit I couldn't wean myself from. I'd already left so many places, voluntarily or I was thrown out, it didn't seem to matter how it happened. Whereas I left other places after years, now this trip through Southeast Asia was a new level of leaving, a departure after mere weeks.

Bring the mind back to the present.

One step, two, pull up, lower down. Frozen glove swiped over wet face. Finn's audible complaints. Slippery rocks, the weight of the pack, the relentless gray-and-white landscape, the shivering, the aching. This was me "being."

I used to run when I was younger. Long-distance. I could go far. Farther than almost anyone. People asked how I did it, other kids, coaches, grown-ups. I couldn't put words to it then, but now I understood. I didn't judge the pain as bad. I'd study it, go deep into awareness of the sensations happening in the body. "Is this pain, or is this just pressure?" The knee bend, ankle drop, lung burn. If you broke it all down, it was just sensation, pressure, force. Feet slapping on pavement to the inhale, exhale.

The mind is everything. What you think, you become.

"Fuck!" Finn yelled ahead of me. He was pitching forward, falling headlong down the path. I dropped the book, threw off my pack and slipped down loose gravel to him. He landed on his face, his pack pinning him. I hauled the pack off. He held his left knee, and rocked. "Something popped." He gritted. "Bloody fucking hell."

Bring the mind back to the present. See what is.

I hauled him up by the arm, and he stood on his right leg. We hopped off the path to a nearby flat rock and I lowered him down.

CHAPTER 16 ½

He calls me by the English translation: Tender Grass. He is trying to call me home. But I am too very far away. I am homeless.

I sit at the window, stare down from our third-floor flat as the cars and trucks and motorcycles and bicycles speed this way and that. I watch the people. They walk with purpose. They think important thoughts. They do not look up. This is London. This is the place that was once a magical kingdom in my childhood imagination.

Below me, there is a child playing in the front garden, in the narrow scrap of weeds between brick walls and rubbish bins. She is six or seven. Sometimes she looks up. Sometimes she waves. Often she doesn't.

My name is like a joke in this city because there is no grass. Only concrete. Only buildings piled upon each other. Only noise, and people who are too busy. We live in a place called Bethnal Green.

Before you sent me here, Mother, before you and Yash made my "dreams come true," I would hear such place names and imagine legends of castles and magical forests. It was all such a cruel joke, made with the best intentions. You think you saved me from your life of drudgery, from the life of a woman serving others, but still here it is drudgery. Here, too, I serve.

My cup of chai grows cold but I sip it anyway. I still drink chai. The British have not taken that away from me.

The children will come home and I will make them their supper and help them with their studies, but in my mind, I will be sitting at this window. He will arrive from work, often with a gift, I will accept and open it, some bauble or bottle of perfume, and in my mind I will be sitting at the window as I put on the necklace or as I lift the bottle to my nose. I will be sitting at the window as he eats, as we make love, as he tries in his small ways to bring me out of this dark place.

Mother, I know you sent me here for a good reason. I know that you and Yash thought it was best. You must be disappointed that I did not go further with my degree, do something with my life here. I know that is what you wanted for me. I fear the leap was too grand, like trying to jump a crevasse in the Himalayas. We believe we can make it if we only try. But the hole between this side and that side is too wide, and sometimes we fall into the chasm.

I stare at an intersection. Thousands of cars. Hundreds of people. They all look down at the concrete. The smell of exhaust wafts through the closed window and leaves a layer of something inside my nostrils. I wish I would learn to drive, but then I do nothing but drink from my cold chai and keep staring.

What are you looking out upon, Mother? The colorless land, the sheltered slopes? That big boulder stranded in the lone east valley? The negligent peak of Annapurna? It is summer there, and you will have hikers. You got me away so my life would not be about serving them. You thought they had it better than we did, Mother. But you were wrong.

I will not write these thoughts. I will not send them to you. I will never tell you them. I will let you believe you sent me to a place better than the one where you are. I will give you that gift of ignorance.

We do not see Yash's wife anymore or his boys. They are not boys anymore, of course, but men about town. They have their life in London. I cannot accept it here. I am sure this is why we grew apart. I cannot own the concrete and cars and therefore I am alone. I have no friends. Just my two girls.

I think he is afraid I will kill myself. He walks as if he is scared to break me if he is too loud, and he speaks in a whisper. I think he thinks I am on the edge of a cliff, high in the Himalayas, and I will just walk straight into a fissure. He doesn't understand that I don't even have the passion for that. I don't even have enough will left to end things.

The one hope I have is that when my girls grow a little bit, they will become my sisters. Like in Nepal, Mother, all of the women in the village who are your sisters. I will then have sisters, too. Right? Of course, in my happier moments, I hope more for my daughters, like you did for me, Mother. Of course, I hope for them joy and fulfillment. Of course I do. This is part of my grief. It is just difficult for me to see how they will be happy, Mother. I cannot invoke a vision of their happiness. I cannot see it in my mind's eye. I cannot see my own and I cannot see theirs and this on some days makes me hysterical inside.

I must stop thinking. The postal woman is dropping the mail through the slot below, her back bent from the weight of the bag. The elderly woman rolling her personal metal cart to the grocers is half an hour late today. It is raining today and instead of heads, mostly I see the tops of umbrellas.

Mother, I want to come home. I want to spin yarn and make sweaters and cook over fire. I want to teach my daughters to do this. Do you understand? We have a stove, and they call it progress, but I only want flames.

Please. I know it is ridiculous. We cannot move there. What will he do in a mountain village in Nepal? Will he suddenly transform into a man of the Himalayas? The children are British mongrels with their Nepalese and Indian blood. What would the girls do there in the mountains? When we come every year to see you, for that short week, I see in the girls' eyes, I see it in his eyes, that our Himalayan life—yes, Mother, I wrote "our" because it is my life too—I see through their eyes that it is foreign, and old-fashioned and something to wonder at, and later tell stories about, but it is something that must be left behind.

How strange what is called progress in the world. How filthy, and over-peopled and dirty this thing called progress. How the heart hardens with this "progress."

The children are home. I must go. I will not write this. I will never mail this.

17

I had no idea how we should go forward or go backward. It was mid-afternoon. Where was the next village? How long would it take to go back? Finn's knee was swollen to twice its size, the pain etched into his face. I was not a nurse. I'd watched other women throughout my life rush to the nurturing role when someone got hurt, while I stood back and watched. I watched Finn's knee swell. I watched as he beat himself up for being so weak. I stood back and watched, and occasionally lit his cigarette.

It was the sounds of music that saved us. It flowed like memories or dreams. It was a story that entered through a back door, a fairy tale that bubbled from the depths. At first it was there, but we didn't hear it, just a subtle backdrop heard only by the heart. It was like a scent, primal. It harkened the past, and teased the future. It was hope.

Finn heard it before I did. A banjo or a fiddle, an echo off the cold rock of the mountains.

We agreed I would go find the source of the music and try to get help. The sound grew in and out of focus as I walked, packless now, feeling so light I could almost fly. The tune was folksy, like Father's fiddle-playing in Missouri. It spoke the mood of the mountains, just as my father's carried the currents of the Missouri rivers.

I kept thinking the musician was just around the next corner, but it was an echo, the hard edges of the place creating illusions. This was a world of perceptions and misperceptions. But then the music grew louder, a folksy twang, wind and wood and screeching cheap strings. It foretold of someone lost, of hope buried deep inside a pit.

I found the man sitting on a stone outcropping over a deep valley, a tall, thin Nepalese man with a dark and narrow face, wearing a striped cap. He held a rough-hewn, squat fiddle in his lap and used a bow made from a tree limb to work the strings. At first I thought he was singing, but then realized the strings had a voice. He was looking out, listening to the land, calling to it, hearing it.

He stopped when he saw me, looked at me as if he were in a trance. He didn't speak English. I looked around but there didn't appear to be a village nearby. I gestured wildly, and his eyesight seemed to recover.

I pointed to myself. "Pearl. Pearl."

He pointed to his nose and said, "Sanjit."

I gestured for him to follow me back up the path. He wobbled his head and came with me. He had to slow for me, his gate long and strong. It was another hour before we got back to Finn.

Finn had taken his Swiss army knife and cut the legs of his trousers so his knee had room. It was fat and bruised. He was sitting at an angle, smoking hash. I packed up everything. I put my pack on my back, and Finn's on my front. Sanjit lifted Finn. We went at a snail's pace. Finn cried in agony. We stopped often to rest. To get both packs off me, I had to kneel until the bottoms rested on the earth, until the packs flopped forward and backward to the ground.

If I hadn't found Sanjit, if the snow hadn't ceased just after nightfall, if the clouds hadn't cleared, if the moon wasn't nearly full... we would have had to spend the night outdoors. Or we might have floundered off the path and fallen down a ravine. We might have died. We probably would've died.

At a house at the edge of a village, a woman lowered Finn to a thin straw mattress. I knelt to the dirt floor and released myself from the backpacks. She dipped a rag in water, came back and held it to his knee. Ghostly pale, Finn fell back and closed his eyes. I studied her as she went into a room and came back with a pile of wool blankets, how she folded them, lifted his knee, placed them beneath. She wrapped a rag around the knee to keep the wet towel in place. I stood with fisted shoulders and aching back and watched. Outside, beneath the full moon, in the distance, we heard Sanjit take up his instrument again, the music wistful and edgy.

I t was days before Finn could walk. We went out to exercise his knee. The clouds were heavy, and the far-off peak obscured. Finn hobbled on a stick over uneven ground. His knee was the size of a melon. I clenched his arm to help him walk. Our goal was to make it the length of the village and back at least once.

There was something moody about this village, drab. Forlorn. How the land could carry a temperament, have a character, hold a spirit. Eight huts were built on a curve overlooking a crevasse, a deep pit that was gray at the top and black-pitched in the middle. You could not see the bottom. The pit seemed to suck you toward it.

Finn heard the music first. The music whispered and echoed. It swirled like a waft of smoke and floated into the icy crevasse. Finn reached into my day pack and withdrew his flute.

He cocked his head and listened. There was something else behind the fiddle. A drum. I couldn't hear it at first, but he made me listen until I did. In Tokyo, when he discovered my musical illiteracy, he had me listen to Dizzy Gillespie, Ray Charles and Thelonious Monk. He'd ask me to pick out the instruments. It took me a while. My ears weren't attuned to it. When the instruments finally became discernible, when the strings flew from the stereo, then the wood instruments and the drums, and I could hear the cooperation of it, the serendipity; it was like the epiphany of snorkeling, all of those textured layers that I'd never noticed before. Whole worlds that existed that I knew nothing about.

Finn played a trilling burst on his flute, stopped, and listened. The music continued its distant whisper. He played again, his flute like a bird calling to its gaggle. The drum and fiddle went silent. We heard a wild relish from the fiddler. Finn laughed, raised his flute, called back. He and the fiddler played a call and response. The drummer joined in. The sounds echoed off the cliffs as if the mountain itself were another instrument.

Every day after this, we took a walk. Every day, mid-after-noon, Finn played his call and the other musicians sent their response. It was a week before Finn could walk well enough to go searching for them. They never came to find us, no matter how long we waited. A half mile farther down the path, we came around a bend and Sanjit and a drummer sat in front of a hut whose roof had caved in.

The three men laughed as if they'd known each other their whole lives. Finn held his flute up, and Sanjit waved him over. I sat on the hard ground as the three jammed. They sounded folksy, like something you'd hear in the backwoods of the Midwest. They sounded like home. A little girl in a torn dress came up the path with her mother. The girl ran to the musicians and began to dance, a primal turning, the sun flashing on and off behind her head. Her face was caked with dirt. The hem of her dress was ripped. I lifted my camera and took pictures of her and the musicians. I tried not to think of Tender Grass. I tried not to think of the little Missouri girl I'd left behind.

We came back the next day with a translator. It was surprisingly easy to find a translator in the tiny village, a young man from Kathmandu who was home visiting his parents. These musicians were a perfect idea for a travel story.

The drummer's name was Balmani. Where Sanjit was tall and thin with a long narrow face, Balmani was short with a head too small for his wiry body. Finn stood over by the crevasse, smoking a cigarette and waiting for me to finish the interview so they could get back to playing.

The fiddle was called a *sarangi*. With four strings, it was short-necked and wide, held vertically on the lap and played with a bow. Sanjit stood, walked to a red cedar, put his hand flat on the scaly bark. "This is the tree. One whole block of red cedar wood is used to make one *sarangi*. I am maker of *sarangi*."

He went into the falling-down hut and came back with a half-finished *sarangi* and put it in my hands. He placed his hand on the block of wood, and explained the carving of three hollow chambers. "The stomach, the chest, the brain." He smiled and nodded and I noticed for the first time his two front teeth were missing. The instrument reminded me of Etisha's square of weaving, of awkward and rough things made with the hands, objects with soul.

"A *sarangi* will hum and cry like a woman wailing and singing. It echoes, like someone in the mountains, the first cry, and then behind it another softer crying." Sanjit's eyes were so full of sadness. Red and half-closed and full of a heaviness.

I asked if he could make a *sarangi* for Finn, if I could buy it. He'd need to finish it in a week. Sanjit placed his long fingers on the half-finished *sarangi* in my lap, smiled and nodded. "Yes, this one will be for your love."

I asked them about their childhoods, their parents, the traditional music they played, how often they played, where they'd traveled, how they met. Sanjit looked at Balmani as he answered, but the drummer didn't speak, only nodded in a low-brow way, sometimes smiling and showing gaps where his teeth should have been. Their parents, and their parents' parents, had been musicians like this, traveling the mountains, for as long back as either could remember.

A group of young Nepalese boys came up the path and began yelling something toward us. The translator shook his head. "Please ignore them. There is much prejudice here. Especially in the mountains, but you find it in Kathmandu, too."

I looked at him confused. The boys began throwing rocks. The translator got up, yelled at them, and they ran off. He came back winded and whispered to me as if Sanjit could understand him. "Sanjit and the drummer, these men are Gandharbas, untouchables. They are musicians who travel Nepal and play. Treated like beggars, panhandlers, driven away like dogs." That was why they were staying at this abandoned hut. They weren't allowed in the village proper. That's why they hadn't come into the village, and Finn and I had to go looking for them.

"In old times," the translator said, "Gandharbas brought news from Khatmandu, like European minstrels. They sang the news to the villagers and got food or clothing. But this is romantic version, because life was hard. It still is hard. They cannot get education. They cannot get jobs. They depend only on people to give."

Sanjit spoke to the translator in Nepalese. Finally, the translator turned to me.

"Sanjit is asking me what I am telling you. I told him I am explaining why the boys threw the rocks. He would like to speak to you about this for your article."

Sanjit spoke, and my translator told me what he said. He talked about how the government was trying to give the Gandharbas some kind of cultural status to raise them up, but it hadn't really caught on.

"The traditional music is dying," Sanjit said. "The children do not want it. They change their last names so no one will know they are Gandharbas."

You could see the erosion of the self-esteem in the way Sanjit and Balmani smiled too much, and in the curve of their backs. The little girl in the torn dress came running back up the path, and clung to Sanjit's leg. The translator explained that this was Sanjit's daughter.

Balmani said the first words he'd spoken since the interview began. "It is hard to have nowhere to call home."

I knew this hang-dog look. I grew up with kinfolk who used outhouses and Sears catalogs to wipe their butts. I knew folks who would have nothing to do with you because of how poor you were, how that broke you down generation after generation, until you were nobody and your story was nothing.

I looked up to see Sanjit, the translator and Balmani staring at me. I'd apparently said this out loud, and the translator had said it in Nepalese. The three stared at me, and I said the first thing that came to me. "Where does the music come from?" The translator translated and the two musicians looked confused. "Is that a dumb question?"

"This is the best question. It is a question in words for something that has no words," Sanjit said. He looked around. "From there," he said, pointing to a woman in a sari coming up the path with a load of wood balanced on her head. "From there." He pointed to a pile of rocks on the side of the path. "And there." A line of tattered prayer flags hanging at the entrance to the far-off hut.

Sanjit went to the tree he'd shown me earlier, the type he used to carve his *sarangi*. "From here," he called over, clapping the bark with his palm.

"From here," the little girl said, holding the hems of her dress out like wings, and flying in circles.

Later, as Balmani and Sanjit played, and the girl began dancing, I snapped pictures. Being behind a lens always gave me some distance, and I could see the three now with greater perspective, how dirty, and bent, and scarred they were, how the music lifted them to the peaks, how I loved them, how I didn't want to be anywhere else in the world than with these misfits.

Later, as I was out roaming the village and taking pictures at dusk, I ran into the translator. He was tall and thin and wore a red Western sweater and a pair of dungarees. He spoke English with a British accent.

"I wanted to thank you for what you just did," he said.

"What did I do?"

"Sanjit said to me after you left, 'She has a gift for hearing the stories of the people. This is an important gift. We are honored to speak to someone such as her.'"

I wanted to tell the translator of my childhood, and how they were my people, but I just smiled.

He said, "I saw a lifting of the shoulders of the men. Something like pride. Sanjit is right. You have the gift of listening."

After I left the translator, I saw Finn coming back from jamming with Sanjit and Balmani. He seemed to glide over the path, even with his bum knee. Music always made him so happy. The sun was setting, and a beam came between two rock formations behind him, and landed upon his blonde hair. He glowed. I laughed, he laughed and he swooped me hard against him and kissed me like he hadn't kissed me in months. I went weak at the knees like some girly cliché. We glided together to the hut, to the makeshift room. The woman seemed to be out, but we made love as quietly as we could. I ran my palms down the flesh of him. I loved the animal of him, the wide stretch of mouth, stubble burning my chin. Neither of us had any fat left on us, the sex bone against bone, angular and hard.

Afterward, I watched as Finn's face softened into sleep. He looked so young, a ratty-haired boy. I could imagine him as a boy roaming the streets of London, darting here and there, looking in with wonder at the eccentric sights and smells.

I could see him listening for the music.

18

The accordion telephone cord reached several feet from the window of the hut to the street outside. We were back in Pokhara, back in civilization after one month of hiking down the mountain. My hair was growing and popped like exclamation points from the sides of my head. The walking had made me healthy and strong. My thighs were wiry with muscle and my shoulders wide from the pack. I'd been brought back to full primal strength.

On the Pokhara street, cycle rickshaws, trucks, bicycles, bells, whistles—clang and clatter, and rushing bustle. I wasn't used to the noise after the simplicity of the mountains. I handed the guy inside the hut the telephone number in Missouri. Somewhere on the hike I began to miss the girl I once had been and I needed to call home.

"Jason!" I yelled into the receiver, a finger in my other ear. His voice was deep and manly. The childhood boy I knew was now a man I didn't know.

"Pearl Elizabeth Swinton." He was the only one who used my full name.

"I can barely hear you," I screamed.

"Where are you?" he hollered back. I described the scene, just as a goat wandered past and bleated. He laughed, and I could feel his soul float toward me. I was always amazed by how someone so far away could be right there with you, and someone physically present could be miles away. The soul didn't know the boundaries of the human flesh.

Jason was lounging in his backyard with a Budweiser in that rural part of Missouri where I grew up. It was summer, and it was hot and the mosquitoes were out. I could smell the heat, the way a smell can pull you back in time and place.

"All alone?" I hollered.

"I got Lady right here." Lady was the dog that replaced Lady Luck.

He was watching the sun set. I told him I was watching it rise.

"Time travel," he yelled.

Jason, the only person who knew me beginning, middle and end. We were tangled together by story, written up in each other's flesh. We were friends, soul siblings, old lovers. We'd saved each other's lives. He was my Midwest root, organ, stem and root-hair. He was the last frazzled tether to my homeland.

I yelled to him about the final days of hiking, how Finn and I had our first shower in weeks in a concrete outhouse with a cut-out window that overlooked a mountain peak, and how the snow flew in as you undressed and how glorious it was to be naked and shivering. My socks stood up by themselves when I took them off. They gave me a bucket filled with luke-warm water and I stood naked and freezing, dousing myself.

How a story can force the soul of the other from their body. How Jason left his Missouri flesh, and flew across nations to be with me. How I could see his eyes and feel his touch, and see his paint-spattered boots on the dirty Pokhara road. In another life, Jason had been home to me.

I told him about the man who had God in his hands. I needed Jason to know about him. I needed the world to know about this singular man in the foothills of the Himalayas. I needed to tell his story. It was not an easy story to scream. He lived in a hut in the foothills made of newspapers. The hut was built of branches, and the walls of sticks, and they were covered with Nepalese newspapers, stories from around the country writ large across the shanty.

Outside, when the man squatted to make chapatis over an open fire, spirit or magic or something flew from his fingertips. Watching him make chapatis was like going to church, like seeing a god, like praying to a mountain peak. His hands moved like poetry as he shaped the bread in his palms. There was something so profoundly quiet about him, a peace in the depths. The crack and sizzle of the chapatis cooking in a banged-up pan. We were in the foothills, and surrounded by forests. The caw and bark from the woods as night fell. The guy's hands enveloped my vision. The sight of those hands made me lonely, so desperately lonely. I was calling Jason because of that hole in my heart.

"Lady likes to run," Jason yelled. Lady was a male. "He keeps getting out. Keeps digging under the fence." Now Jason was taking him running. I left myself there at the edge of the newspaper shack, on the busy Pokhara street, and I flew to the textured filth of mid-America. I saw the two running down the dirt backroads, farms and fields and forest gristle. I could taste the humidity. I could smell the stink of cow shit from a nearby farm. Jason's animal body, the pure physicality of him. Lady, whom I'd never met, became in my mind old Lady Luck, but a healthy version this time, a version of a dog that had not been kicked and abused and rescued. As I was thrust back to the streets of Pokhara, the loneliness became acute.

I looked up and thought I saw Yash across the street. I stretched the telephone cord to get a better look. He was with a woman and two children. He must've come down from the village to meet up with his wife and kids. They headed into a restaurant.

I didn't want to get off the phone with Jason but I was desperate to get to Yash, to talk to him about Tender Grass, to tell him of my vision, to stop a future that he and Etisha thought would be best for her, to assuage my guilt that somehow I had started the girl's destiny in motion.

Jason's voice cracked as I told him I had to go. "I'll call you back," I screamed.

"Don't be a stranger, Pearl," he yelled. As I hung up, I felt his hand reach out for me to pull me back, but already I was falling away.

I paid an exorbitant amount for the call and ran across the street. In the restaurant, I came upon Yash from behind and put my hand on his shoulder. The kids and wife looked at me surprised.

"I need to talk to you about Tender Grass."

He turned. It was not Yash. I apologized and left. On the way back to the hotel, all I could hear was Jason's scratchy, yelling voice filling my head.

"Don't be a stranger, Pearl."

That bittersweet mixture of love, of loneliness, of adventure, of fear.

THAILAND

Mother used to say, "Let Pearl talk. Don't try to stop her talking. She needs to tell her stories." She'd pick me up from school, my head filled with the events of the day. She used to say, "If Pearl can't tell you her stories, she goes to a bad place. You just need to let her talk."

I'd always loved stories, the who of them, the where, the how. I could see how others could tell your stories for you, and ruin you. We started as a blank page, and they wrote whatever they chose to upon you. By the time you were in your late twenties, so many voices and stories had been layered upon you, you could scarcely remember who you were.

Moving somewhere else didn't make the stories go away. I tried to outrun them. It didn't work. I'd lived for years now in other cultures. There was nothing to trigger "home"—not the earth, the language, the gestures. No cultural cues. It was a freedom. At first.

You could be anything, anyone, you wanted to be. At first. Your lungs opened up and you could breathe. Your soul became giddy with the lack of tethers. You could laugh and dance and fly.

Then the stories others told about you returned and spun in

circles inside your head. They screeched like harpies, danced their crazy dance, and burned like smoke that obscured the view.

———

The plane descended into a thick layer of dark fog toward the Bangkok airport. The pilot came on to tell us it wasn't fog, but smoke. In provinces in the middle of India forest fires were raging out of control, and a plume of smoke was traveling across the Southeast Asian landscape.

As Finn and I made our way from our hotel to Patpong Road, the city looked ghostly through the pall of smoke. Visibility was just a few feet. People were pale and distant in the smoke, many wearing surgical masks. They'd float in and out of the fog, apparitions in white masks. Car lights and neon signs flashed in otherworldly glow. When we stopped to buy cigarettes, another Westerner in line told us some Indian businessmen had been burning off forests to build palm oil plantations, and it'd all gotten out of control. The smoke was being blown across the continent like some dark primordial bird of prey. Apparently nobody wanted to spend the money it would take to stop the fires.

Patpong was the famous red-light district. We were a far cry from the grit and nature of the Himalayas here. Strip clubs and bars, foggy neon signs, dripped dollops of color into street puddles. Thai girls in hot pants. The tint of bubble gum and white plastic go-go boots, giggles in the swirling smoke at the entrance to clubs. A large Western woman was rocking out on the sidewalk, punching the air with her fists to AC/DC pumping through loud speakers. As we passed each club, we were assailed with different music, disco, heavy metal, hard rock.

Stalls sold suitcases, skirts, scarves, jewelry, handbags, wallets. The objects were factory-made, brown and black, with no soul. The stalls bled off the sidewalk into the road, and the street narrowed until it was just wide enough for one person to walk.

Somewhere along the way, the black dog showed up, nipping at my ass, yanking at me and pulling me down. It was the fires. It was leaving the glory of the Himalayas. It was talking to Jason and being reminded of a home I'd never be able to return to. It was the fact that everyone we passed was from somewhere else, and the only people who were local wore skimpy clothes and looked thirteen, or were local Thai men sidling up to Finn to sell him a piece of ass.

In the smoky haze, the girls were like bits of candy, like raspberry and lemon sweets. Older white men led young Thai girls through the thick decadent maze. Silver Pussy, Bada Bing, A Go-Go, Electric Blue. The neon signs were like dessert, the color of cotton candy.

The black dog settled. The black dog found its home deep in my belly. I seemed to be a barometer for the setting I found myself in. If I was in nature, I became like the mountain, the gorge, the river. If I was around this, I became this, wired, and sideways-glancing. What fun a person could have, though, in the dark. What trouble one could get up to in this place that so few people called home.

A girl in a babydoll negligee motioned with one finger for us to follow her. She led us into a club called Bon Bon. The flashing treats on the sign had cherries in the middle and looked like pulsing breasts. The walls inside were pink, the floors a confection lime. The girls on stage were topless, wore day-glo g-strings and hot-pink hearts on their nipples. They were not really dancing, but walking around and giggling. One girl tickled her friend. Some looked younger than thirteen. Tourists sat drinking, brown people hustled, serving. A young Thai boy sidled up, and Finn bought a bag of weed.

Someone yelled, "Hey, over here." A group of Westerners had pushed together tables in one corner. "Come join us," a big guy called to us. We went over. Everyone said hello. They were a mix of Aussies, Brits and Americans. A Thai waitress in a bikini served us drinks the color of blueberries.

Someone ordered pitchers of a hot-pink strawberry concoction. How many did I drink? Four? Five? I sat next to the Aussie guy who'd called us over. One of the Thai girls left the stage and was dancing around our table. When she got to the guy who called us over, a burly Australian with a tattoo of swords through a heart on his forearm, he pulled her onto his lap. "Musical chairs. I win," he said. She smelled like baby oil and cherry Lip Smackers.

I poured myself another drink. The Australian put his hands around the girl's waist, picked her up like a doll or a child, and turned her so she was facing me. Her knees touched my forearm, her nipple hearts at my eye level. She clutched a teddy bear beneath one arm. I looked into her face. She was just a child, and she seemed to be missing behind the eyes. She put a finger to the teddy bear's button nose and pushed on it, and made a sound like *boop! boop!*

I drank, lit a cigarette. The edges of the room were melting. The girl touched my arm to get my attention, took something out of an opening at the back of the Teddy Bear and handed it to me. They were two unused sticky-back hearts, like the ones she had on her nipples.

Finn had given me a tight, backless black mini-dress as a gift. I took off the backing and pasted the hearts on top of my dress, just over my nipples, stood and thrust out my chest. The table roared with applause. I moved to the dance floor, just me and the childish naked girls on stage, moving to the song "Cocaine." Colored strobes pulsed and raged as I found my place in the world of the dark.

We left about 2:00 a.m. I could barely walk. We stopped at a brightly lit display window. I didn't know what I was looking at. The smoke haze hurt my eyes, and made them tear up. I had to put my hand flat on the glass window, otherwise I would've fallen over. One girl sat in each window. They wore red bikinis and sat on stools. A light bulb dangled above each of their heads, throwing long, twisted shadows along the floors and walls. Written on signs propped in the windows were their names: Pudding. Cake. Plum.

The girls were for sale.

Just beyond sat a woman at a table; next to her sat a young girl. On the table was a sign: "Read the future, U.S. $5." I started to sit but Finn grabbed my arm. "Don't waste money, Queenie. Come on, it's late."

I sat anyway. "You're bloody drunk off your arse." He tried to pull me up, but I wasn't budging.

I fumbled with my money belt and put a five into the woman's outstretched hand. She was tiny, no more than four feet, with a lined face, thin black hair in a bun. She handed the five dollars to the girl, who put it in a small purse clutched in her lap.

With gnarled hands, the elderly woman took tea leaves from a brown paper bag and sprinkled them into a cup. She held the tea cup toward the girl, who took a bottle at her feet and poured in water. The woman put the cup close to her eyes, which bulged from the sockets. Even drunk, I could feel the energy of her, feel myself being pulled over a cliff. I looked around for Finn. I wished I'd listened to him, but he was now immersed in the girls in the display windows.

The woman made noises in the back of her throat, breathing in staccato gasps. She closed her eyes and spoke. The girl translated without looking up from her lap.

"Grandmother say, some things you must understand now as you go upon travels. As you pass through each country, you are treated well. You see, this is not true of people who live there. My English not good. I hope you understand me."

The elderly woman spoke in a long stream of sentences, and I worried the girl wouldn't be able keep up with her.

"You are just passing through. You witness all that you wish, and you leave. People here, they cannot leave. But you *can* leave.

"This is blessing. Very few in the world have such a good thing. What is word? Privilege? Yes, in your country many have privilege. But this is not true other place. You have the honor of leaving home and seeing the whole world. Do not hold such lightly. It is a gift given to you this lifetime. It is also a…" She struggled for the right word. " …responsibility. "

One of the hearts fell off my nipple, and I wove my head down to see where it might have gone. The woman squeezed my hands.

"Grandmother wants to know if you want to hear more."

I took one of my hands away, tried to search around for the fallen nipple heart but couldn't find it.

"Grandmother asks, do you want to continue?"

I sat up and nodded. She reached for my hand again and I reluctantly gave it to her. The black dog was nipping away.

"The journey is long. The purpose is to break you. Anyone on the path must be broken. Brain must be broken. You see? Light cannot come through. Then when broken, light comes through, and you can put back together in a better way. The journey is long, however, very very long. So very long." I noticed tears in the grandmother's eyes. "So lonely. It is long for this lifetime, and it is long across many lifetimes."

"The journey has already been so fucking long," I slurred. The girl translated. I felt sick. Grandmother spoke.

"And yet, sorry, you haven't really begun journey. Now you are just running away from journey. You have not begun to run toward journey. This is a journey toward heart." The grandmother touched her chest, then the girl touched her chest. "Now, you not want to be who you really are. It is frightening for you. It will be time."

"Why would I not want to be who I really am?" I said. I spied the heart on the ground, reached down and grabbed it.

"Grandmother say, this question is too big. It is best to be blind right now. It is best you do not know the path, or you shall give it up before the journey begins."

I pressed the nipple heart hard on top of my dress. The glue had worn off. I kept pressing and it kept falling off.

The girl said, "Grandmother wants to know if you have heard your message, and if are satisfied with her telling of your future."

I nodded, blinking, unable to focus. "Let's go, Queenie." Finn was next to me. He took me by the arm, and I let him lift me. As we walked away, I leaned heavily on him, now so deeply tired. I turned to take a last look at the woman. It was the girl who grabbed my focus. How close in age she was to all of those naked girls, how little and child-like she looked. How shy.

<hr>

Koh Samui was nothing like the island of Enchanted. We'd left Bangkok for the islands, but I seemed to have brought Patpong Road and the black dog with me, and couldn't shake it.

The boat boys were not like Raul at all. They were greedy and cynical, and had a look in their eyes, dark, as if they had too many times been deceived. As they ferried us around, I missed Raul, and wanted to run back, steal him away and protect him before Enchanted became like this place. The beach was lined with bars, filled with drunken Westerners in various levels of undress. Men wore tiny trunks, and women thongs, and you couldn't get away from the bulging flesh of their bottoms.

The forest fire smoke was no better here. Everyone wore the white surgical masks against the haze. Naked tanned bodies, the fierce white masks, the sooty haze—it was another world. Lining the beach were shack restaurants, '80s music blaring from boom boxes, and bamboo-fenced dance parties.

Finn had gone down the beach to find a musician to jam with. He had a knack for finding musicians no matter where we were. Finn could find a musician on a deserted island in the middle of the ocean. I stood on the rickety porch and watched him disappear into the smoke. We were in a cheap hut on the beach. You could see through cracks in the walls. One end of the porch had fallen and it slanted to the right. From the porch, the horizon seemed to tilt sideways.

I got into the hammock with my surgical mask on. Next door, an elderly woman sat in a white plastic chair on the porch of her hut. Her arms were crossed across her chest. I waved, but she didn't move and I wasn't sure she saw me.

I woke from a nap in the hammock a few hours later, and decided to go out in search of the next travel article. As I passed my neighbor's hut, I saw she was sitting in the same position, arms across her chest, upright in the chair. She did not wear a mask. I felt compelled to walk up to her. I pulled my mask down. "Hello," I called.

She seemed to snap out of a trance. "Hello." She looked me up and down, eyeing me suspiciously. "Nice outfit."

I'd purchased a light green bikini and matching long skirt, and I was proud of how it fit, how it flowed when I walked. I felt elegant in it. I rarely wore anything that made me feel elegant.

Uninvited, I climbed the stairs to her porch, and took the white plastic seat next to her. I didn't know what was compelling me. There was nothing in her energy or voice that suggested she wanted anything to do with me.

"Well, yes, help yourself then," she said, pecking her head toward where I was already sitting. "By all means, have a seat." She had a Boston accent. She eyed me up and down again. I drew my arms across my chest, just like her. The two of us, arms crossed.

She burst into laughter, a surprisingly hearty sound. "What's your story then?" she asked. "Are you another one of these tourists come to taste the Asian fruit?"

I blushed. I opened my mouth to speak. I *was* one of those tourists. Did it matter that I was writing travel articles as we spent a year in Southeast Asia? Did it matter that I'd already spent four years in Tokyo? I blushed again. She looked me up and down, nodded, and turned back to staring out to sea, or rather out to the band of smoke haze that obscured the sea. Why was I even here with this woman? I contemplated leaving but couldn't do anything but sit.

I studied her as her gaze fixed on the hazy horizon. Her cheek twitched like she knew I was staring at her and didn't like it. She had short, bristly gray hair, a lined face, jowls that drooped, and the heavy shoulders and arms of someone who did not do physical labor. She looked like one of the nuns who taught me as a child at Holy Cross.

"Stop staring."

"Sorry."

"Is there a reason you're here?"

"I'm asking myself that." The smoke haze seemed to be thickening. You couldn't see much of the beach now. I reached in my fanny pack, took out a cigarette and lit it.

"Nothing exciting here. Feel free to move on."

I didn't move.

"Just some old lady, ignored by almost everyone." She looked at me. Her eyes narrowed. "Why are you looking at me like that?"

I really could not stop staring at the lines in her face. They were etched so deep, like river beds. "I don't know."

"You think I look out of place, do you? With all of these naked bodies, cocktail drinking, slithering happy people?" The heaviness of her voice was like an oil spill slinking down a ponderous river. I wobbled my head.

"I didn't come here of my own free will. They made me take this vacation." She rubbed her nose. "You ever been burnt out?" She moved her arms long enough to put "burnt out" in air quotes.

I sighed, nodded. In Tokyo at the newspaper, I'd been plenty burned out. The dark circles under her eyes were the same circles I'd had for months and maybe even years in Japan.

"It's called compassion fatigue. They booked this ridiculous hut. Leave it to an NGO to have so little money that this is the only thing they can afford. As if this is relaxing." She pecked her head toward the smoke-covered sea. A group of hot young men and women in tiny swimsuits walked out of the smoke wearing the glowing white masks.

"What does your NGO do?"

"Work with the villages. Build schools, mostly. They're losing kids to the cities, way before there's any education. But that's nothing new. It's the story of all of Asia, this flight from the earth to the cities. The farther the kids get from the land, well…"

This woman would be the real article I should write. But could I write about something so heavy for a travel article? Not for the first time, I thought, *I'm writing the wrong stories.*

"The girls go into Bangkok and make the money and send it back to their families."

As she said it, I fished for another cigarette and came across the nipple heart, the glued side now covered in lint.

"There's always one event that's the last straw, you know." She blew her nose, a loud snort that reminded me of my father. "That one person that turns the compassion into such deep fatigue you can barely function."

When she didn't go on, I said, "Well tell me!" I didn't know why I spoke to her like we were old friends.

She blew out a loud, grunting sigh. Clicked her tongue. Her voice was weary and belabored. "We were getting some of the girls to come back home, back to school. Maybe having, what, about a ten percent success rate? We could keep one in ten from running back to the city. There was one girl, her name was Manee." She clutched her arms around her chest again as if to protect herself. "She was up to here with darkness." The woman rocked her head up and back to signify what she meant by "up to here," without moving her crossed arms.

"Boys return and become prodigal sons. Daughters return and become failures. At best. Abandoned, mostly. But this girl had…"

She signed again, "…something. The darkest ones always have something. It's the ones who live on the surface that don't seem to have such terrible trouble. So, she comes back to the village. She comes back to the tiny school we run. We worked with her. I knew we'd gotten somewhere when Manee started laughing again."

The old woman nodded. She kept nodding. I looked more closely and realized she was trying to shake off the tears.

"Then one day she was gone."

The woman whose name I didn't know leaned over her legs and draped her arms down to the banged-up boards of the makeshift porch. She was prostrating herself. She sat bent over, her body keening.

Then she sat back up, crossed her arms, and said too loudly in a clear, emotionless voice. "We looked for her in Bangkok. We talked to the pimps she used to work for, the clubs she used to dance at. Nobody would tell us anything. She was twelve years old."

She reached over and took the cigarette from my hand, took a deep drag, and coughed as she blew it out. She handed it back. Our hands touched. She squeezed my fingers for a moment, as if she were ready to fall off some cliff, and she was clinging to me to save her. She refolded her arms.

"That's not what broke this old camel's back. It was her mother. I found out her mother talked her into going back to Bangkok. Her mother was used to having all that money. Her mother was used to the status it gave her to buy gifts for her relatives. Her mother threw her back into the den of wolves."

I felt like apologizing, like it was my fault. Like my being at the club just a few days earlier made me complicit. Maybe it did.

Her body was rigid now. I wanted to go get her a coffee, or a tea, or a stiff drink, or a cupcake. I looked around but she didn't have anything around her. Just these two chairs, an empty table, and her arms across her chest.

We sat in silence. Whatever words I could say seemed trite and not good enough, so I didn't speak. She fell back into her trance, arms locked, eyes gazing far off, beyond the thickening smoke.

We sat this way for another ten or fifteen minutes. I was hesitant to get up and leave.

She spoke suddenly. "They found Manee's body in a seedy hotel in Bangkok. I went to the mother, ready to kill her." Her body shook. "I want to kill that mother."

I stood up. "Can I get you anything?" I asked, looking down at her, her body visibly vibrating. She looked up at me. Her eyes were brown and hard. Something happened. I seemed to fall down into her. I saw that she was cracked down the middle, and the only thing holding her together were those arms wrapped around her. I saw that the crack went way back, back beyond this girl named Manee, back to this woman's childhood, where someone else had cracked her open, had thrown her to the wolves, but I kept falling down and going back and back, until I was back generations, falling, falling, falling.

I seemed to leave my body and enter her. The soul of me, the still whole part of me, went inside her. I leaned toward her, and she shifted toward me, and I knew she was feeling it too. I seemed to be healing the rift in her soul.

This ability to energetically enter another person was not new. I had experienced it a few times. It was like the visions, but something different. But like the visions, I could not control it.

The woman loosened her arms. Her face broke open. The hard, brown fist in her eyes seemed to soften. A wail rose up and out of her throat. She stood, broke the connection, and stumbled headlong across the porch, and into her hut.

I sat down heavily, drained. Her stifled cries blew on the wind. I had no idea what had just happened. I didn't know what to do.

Did I knock? Did I go in? Did I have any rights here whatsoever? I didn't even know her name. I stood, paced, and smoked. Wavering at the porch steps, I could see in the window the mound of her on the bed. I needed some instruction manual for what was going on inside of me, some step-by-step guidance on what had just happened and what to do next.

I put on my mask and made my way down the beach, just needing to roam, to meander, to lose myself. I needed to find a travel article, but I wasn't able to focus. Inside me now was both the woman's crushing sorrow and the utter beauty of her. Behind her sorrow was a love so great it made my heart hurt. She would've died to save that girl's life. She would've died to save mine.

"Don't Worry, Be Happy." Bob Marley. At one of the bamboo-fenced dance parties, people danced in bikinis and Speedos in the waning light, like ghosts in the darkening haze. I paid the four dollars and went in. At the makeshift bar, I ordered a Long Island iced tea.

Dozens of bodies moved on the sand in slow rhythm. There was something beautiful about it. It wasn't just a cliché. The bodies moving seemed full of some kind of magic, or love. Some kind of miracle. To just be happy for once.

I took my drink to the middle of the sand dance floor. I let my body move. The lime skirt spun out like wings. I closed my eyes and let the music take me over, so open after that moment with the elderly woman on her porch. A big man in a Speedo came up and put his arms around me. I didn't stop him.

A light was on in the woman's hut when I got back. Finn was inside our hut smoking weed. He asked what I'd been up to. I said something about a travel article. He handed me the joint.

On the crooked front porch, later, I watched a night storm boiling along the horizon. The forest fire smoke had lifted. Monstrous black clouds marched toward shore. Finn was inside playing the flute, wood wind sounds mixing with the tempestuous waves. Wind gusts blew my hair and rattled the hut walls. I used to watch storms march across the landscape in Missouri. You could see them coming for miles. You'd still be in sunlight, while just on the horizon, a black dog pounded relentlessly toward you. It excited the gut, and raced the heart. Here on the wobbly porch, I watched the lightning strike in jagged fissures against the roiling ocean. I should have been afraid, but I wasn't. I invited the storm. I wanted it to savage me. The ocean swelled and spat as the clouds marched closer, ever closer, until I became drenched, and my flesh and soul merged with the ferocious gale.

The next morning, I went over to see the woman whose name I'd never learned, and she was gone.

CHAPTER 19 ½

Manee dances on the smoky stage with other young girls, moving her young body the way she was taught. Strobe lights pulse through dense fog. The fog becomes fire smoke, and the girls don masks and dance for the masked men who watch them.

Around their necks, each half-naked girl-child wears a price tag. The forest fires send plumes of smoke through the open door of the club, from burning trees that also have price tags, around their trunks. The girls and the trees are one.

The Women of the Light fly overhead in the rafters, rainbow arcs in swirling flashes. The Women of the Light rain pure energy down upon the children, and upon the men.

Manee giggles and turns to her friend onstage to tell her a funny story. The girl gives her a piece of bubble gum, and Manee laughs. Manee feels the light, the love, and it makes her giddy, and it makes her forget her village, or this choking stage. She pops the bubble gum in her mouth and blows a bubble, and it makes her sister-friend giggle, and soon all of the girls on stage are giggling. A masked man comes up to claim one of the girls and bring her down to a dark corner. The light energy dissipates and the girls turn back toward the men and move their bodies in the way they were taught.

The Women of the Light rain down their light energy upon the heads of the men. The earth's form and the mass of these men are thick, and when the light comes upon them, they cannot fathom it. They have not been taught how to comprehend it, its vibration out of sync with theirs. They do not know what to do with it, do not know how to live with it. They can only bend and shape it to what they know.

This childish heart-nippled dance. This mouth-foaming salacious witnessing. Above the light dance, below the dark. An echo.

Behind the seated, forward-leaning masked men, the mothers of these naked children appear at the club door. Someone has invited them to the dance. They too wear masks.

Some of the mothers head to the stage. Manee's mother appears and dances with her daughter. Some mothers go sit with the men and watch. They watch the men, and they watch the girls.

Some stand in dark corners, wanting to do something, anything, but not knowing what.

A few stand tall as witnesses. They see through the dense veil to the Women of the Light above in their spectrummed brilliance, down to the for-sale girls below in their dark metaphor, over to the mothers in their watching, tug-of-war confusion. These mothers witness what is, trying to figure out what to do.

There is a difference between what is, and what one desires to be.

A masked man approaches Manee's masked mother, and offers her gifts, a handbag, a pair of bejeweled sandals. The masked mother offers her masked daughter over in exchange for the baubles, and dances with her gifts in the burning club. There is a madness to her movements, as if she is trying to get from the gifts the light that she senses from above.

In a dark corner, obscured from the others by his broad back, the man tries to extract the light from the child. He has felt the light from the women in the rafters, and he wants it. He must have it. He takes from the child, but her form is too dense for the light that he senses, and anyway she doesn't own the light that the man is hungry for. It is not hers to give. He shakes Manee until the hearts on her nipples fall off, until she is a rag doll, until she is full of no light at all.

When he sees what he has done, he is shaking. He is upset, with the broken-winged girl twisted on the floor, with himself, with a world that told him if he just took it, he could have the light. He'd been told that this light belonged to him, and he was just trying to take what was rightfully his. He had been told too that the light in the trees in the forest were his, and he had a right to the forests, too.

The dead girl, and the burning forests are one.

The mother on the stage looks through the dense and denser smoke, to the dark corner. She senses a light has gone out in her world. She holds the shoes and the handbag to her breast. She looks but cannot see, and does not leave the stage for fear of what she will find.

Above, the Women of the Light begin a low song, and many below raise their heads to the rafters and see nothing, but sense something. The masked men, and the masked girls and their masked mothers can almost hear the music that is trying, trying so very very hard, to call them all home.

INDIA

The bus taking us from New Delhi to Agra seemed to be playing chicken with every other vehicle on the road. We veered, honked, rammed, thumped, and bumped, a swerving dash along a highway pockmarked with potholes. The traffic was insane. The view through the driver's windshield was obscured by a crude painting of Buddha's eyes, and the driver danced in his seat to see the road. Here too the forest fires covered everything with ash, the sky heavy and thick with smoke.

Finn and I sat on a two-person bench, crammed in with two others, people standing and filling the aisles, chickens and goats among them. Men and boys clung to the outside of the bus.

We'd only been in India thirty-six hours and already I did not like it. When we stepped out of the airport in New Delhi, the poverty shocked me. Children swamped us, tugging, begging. Everywhere, the homeless, sleeping outside the airport, on sidewalks, alongside the road. We'd had to step over bodies while auto rickshaw drivers hassled us, pulling at our packs to take them off and shove them in their vehicles so we'd have no choice but to go along with them. We'd been harangued, harassed, haggled, harried, hurried, hassled. It shocked me to my core, the poverty. It sickened my heart. It left me weak, pale, and so desperately dog-tired.

For Finn it was a different story. Of course he saw the poverty, and it bothered him too, but on another level, India was a dream, a mirage, a British fantasy of the exotic. He'd grown up imagining the magical properties of elephants and camels and sacred cows, women with dark eyes peering from chiming veils. Finally he was here. I was world-weary. He was excited. We were two weather fronts waiting to collide.

We veered so hard that the six people holding onto the outside of the bus at our window fell off. Another sudden turn, and I slid hard across the seat, smashed into the leg of the standing man next to me, and fell on my ass on the filthy floor. Finn reached down, grabbed my arm and pulled me back up.

I was trying to read a book about Hindu gods and it was making me nauseous, so I was just looking at the pictures. Elephant heads, too many arms, skin the color of ripe blueberries. Westerners had lost the mythology. Our gods were plain, too human, too all-suffering.

The bus driver had transformed his dashboard into an altar, and on it sat a fiery god. Between his thighs a muscled blue ram with golden horns. Flames shot from his head. He was white-washed and festooned with beads and flowers. I leafed through the book, jarring back and forth and up and down, and finally found him, Agni. He was god of combustion, a divinity on fire.

His flames transformed the gross to the subtle. He was the primal flame that broke through the primordial waters. His was the ultimate burning.

The bus reached Agra, home of the Taj Mahal, and disgorged its passengers like vomiting out a bad meal. We wove our way through a chaos of people and stalls to our cut-rate hotel. I wanted to stay in, find my legs, rest, but Finn was too excited to wait, and urged me to come.

Outside on the sidewalk we got separated. I didn't know if it was the noise, the color, the commotion, but somehow I lost him. Somehow I found myself at the end of a long alley by myself. But not by myself.

A woman was coming toward me, hand outstretched, begging. We'd seen beggars in other countries, of course, but the need in India was overwhelming. It was like a zombie horror movie.

A brown scarf covered her face so that only her eyes were showing. "Bakshish." Her voice was muffled by something more than the scarf. "Bakshish." Her long fingers implored. I didn't want to give her money. I'd already given out so much money. I tried to get around, but she blocked the way. She pulled her scarf from her face. Her cheeks were eaten away. Her nose was gone. Leprosy. She had leprosy.

I stood staring at the hole where her nose should have been. She reached toward my face to touch my cheek. I backed up. I kept backing up. I felt piles of garbage pressing against the backs of my legs.

When her fingers grazed my cheek, I threw myself back into the putrid rubbish as if she'd punched me. I twisted in the trash looking for my money belt, took every rupee I had and threw it up in the air like confetti. She scrambled for it. I got my footing in the trash, and ran around her.

I started crying. I was like a small child crying for her mother as I ran back down the alley. I did not like what India turned me into. From the moment we'd landed in New Delhi, I did not like the person I became around so much need.

In the light at the end of the alley, Finn was on the sidewalk, turning this way and that, looking for me. I rubbed my eyes, used my sleeve on my nose, tried to pull myself together. A vegetable peel was stuck to the back of my trouser leg, and I flung it off with sticky fingers.

When he saw me, he turned and gave me an upset look. I didn't say anything about the leper. Whenever he saw me so disheveled, he no longer asked me what had happened. It was for the best.

He had the map open. When I reached him, he said, "It's this way."

We turned left.

India was like skydiving. When you skydived solo, you began huddled in the belly of an airplane, terrified. When they opened the Cessna door, it was as if they ripped through a veil on reality. You were no longer connected to the earth, but were made of air. Below you the patchwork quilt of the far-off earth, around you the sky. When you jumped, the falling was a swirl and a rush. Few people remembered those first few moments. They called it "browning out." Solo divers are hooked by static line; the chutes pulled automatically. It was why so many people died on the first jump. You were so over-stimulated, so disconnected, that if something went wrong with the first chute, you wouldn't be aware enough to pull your reserve.

India was like jumping headfirst out of an airplane, an overwhelming plunge, a losing of the mind, a browning out of the senses. I was already disconnected because of the visions. India was worse. And if I lost my mind here, there would be no safety net. I would hit the ground hard. And when I hit the ground, which I would, nothing would ever be the same again.

How we ended up in one of the turrets of the Taj Mahal by ourselves, I couldn't say. All the chaos made me forgetful. Whole sections of time were lost in the morass. I woke up and we were in the Taj Mahal, alone in one of the turrets, in a small circular room with inlay work of precious stones, windows with screens of ornately carved marble, and high above us the bowl of a dome. Fractured light shot stars off the gemmed walls.

Legend had it that the white marble Taj was built by a 17th-century Mughal emperor as a mausoleum for the love of his life, his third wife, who bore him fourteen children and died in childbirth. Would he have built her such a wonder of the world if she had not wanted to have children, if she'd preferred to travel and know her own mind, if she'd been the emperor? Would he have loved her then? How many benefits did women receive from following what society expected of them, what suffering if we chose to know our own minds, to own our own selves.

Finn took out his flute. He loved such spaces for their acoustics. In Tokyo, he'd played almost every day at dusk beneath a footbridge, his sax echoing against the back of the concrete stairs. I'd spent hours, days, months in one room with the guy as he played his music. It was wonderful at first, but now I was tired of it. I was always the audience. It got old. He put the flute to his mouth, and my jaw clenched.

The sound was unexpected magic. With the marble and the precious stones, the echo was the call of a ship at sea, forlorn, hopeful and vast. Every note blossomed in the narrow dome that rose above us. The higher notes were like a wind chime in a fantasy world. My body uncoiled. The grip that squeezed my heart loosened. I could move my jaw.

The music rained like a meteor shower, shot sparks of something like hope, vibrations of something bigger than both of us. Something like god, or spirit, or soul. Not just our souls, but spirit of space, gods of place, passions of the architect who had built this great wonder of the world.

I looked at the freckles at the corner of Finn's closed eyes, at the way his lips kissed the wood of the flute, at the poetry of bone and sinew in knuckles. He had dreamed of this, this moment of breathing music inside the Taj Mahal. I was witness to someone else's dream made manifest in the world. How many dreams did we have that were never spoken out loud? That were never fulfilled, that were locked away in chambers, so deep and so lost, we couldn't even find the key. Finn was aglow with spoken magic. I went up and smooched the side of his face.

Two nights later, back in Delhi, we were on the banks of Ganges. Men, women and children washed themselves in the rivers, and prayed. Men and boys went in with white strips of cloth called *dhotis* around their wastes, and the women submerged themselves in their saris. Many prayed.

I'd always had an instinct about water, whether it was pure or polluted. I felt it in my body. I could feel the profound sacredness of the river. And I could sense how dirty it was, how toxic. I imagined it as snow and ice in the Himalayas, melting, roaring down into the Ganges. I remembered Etisha's words in the village in Nepal, how people were not holding the mountain sacred. I imagined the river entering populated areas, and it slowing down, weighted down by the waste of humans, sludgy and full of trash. Here it was a thick, murky color, and I mourned for the water.

Still, you could feel the sacred, too. Centuries of prayer pulsed up from the river. It was like entering a cathedral. Indians lived their lives outdoors. Women in bright saris bashed clothing against rocks at the river's edge. Families built small fires and cooked. The middle class and the poor swarmed around the homeless and the ill with outstretched palms. A sadhu with a long beard and longer hair and a painted face sat cross-legged, purifying himself with the smoke of some incense. We wandered toward a group of people building something, and only realized after several minutes that this was a floating funeral pyre; and they were setting a body on fire and floating it on the river.

As night fell, some sort of festival began. Women lit candles and set them adrift upon the river; meanwhile, in the distance the floating body still burned. A procession came toward us on the streets, a crying, calling, singing procession, where many held torches.

I needed a guide, someone to tell me of such rituals and their meanings. So much was being lost on us as we watched it all unfold. We followed the procession to a makeshift stage. Thousands of people were here now, holding torches, the pulsing of the crowd, the smell of burning incense, and the animal fat of cooking fires, human sweat.

Men on the stage were playing with fire, lighting balls at the ends of chains and swinging them overhead. I was being pulled out of the crowd. I could see Finn watching, smiling. I was being led up onstage. There were other foreigners like me up there. A young bare-chested Indian man was trying to show me how to swing the unlit ball and chain. I looked over at the Ganges, and saw thousands of floating candles flickering in the dark. I swung the unlit ball and chain. I looked at the other foreigners like me, doing the same. This wasn't just a trick for the tourists. We were being indoctrinated into something old and sacred. My guide lit the ball. It was on fire. He motioned for me to swing it. I did. The others did. Without grace. There was some power here, if I just knew how to harness it, if I just had more guidance. Some honor to this fire dance, some sacred purpose. I swung fire, and felt the vibration go up my arm, and enter my torso.

Looking out over the crowd, lit by torches, I had a flash of what India was—a juxtaposition of the dark and the light, two tectonic plates, one soulful and the other gritty and hard, one richer than any worldly treasure, the other a poverty of flesh, a festering. The two slammed against each other again and again. A searing of the heart. Something about India brewed in the depths and scared me. It terrified the piss out of me.

And we had only been here four days.

People had been vomiting for hours. We were traveling through the heart of India on a long-haul bus. These buses were not like the city buses—they had toilets and cushioned seats and air conditioning. People rushed to the toilet in the back, and every time the door opened, shit and puke roiled in waves. Some people vomited before they could reach the bathroom, before even they could remove their surgical masks. Littering the floor, a pile of the rancid glowing masks.

Dozens of people squatted in the aisles where chickens squawked from cages. One man held a frayed rope tied to a goat's neck. A chicken had gotten loose and was flapping madly from row to row, the owner too sick to care. People would shove it like a ball being bounced around a crowd. Its flapping was riling the goat, who made baying sounds like a child's screech. Finn's long body was curled next to me, his eyes closed, his face green. Out the night window, only our own twisted reflections thrown back. The night made darker by the pall of the unrelenting forest fire smoke.

At sunrise, finally, the driver pulled to a stop. We'd been traveling twelve hours, and had six more to go. We were in no-man's land, just a strip of road, and a worn-down shack that sold old packaged cookies, Coca-Cola in bottles, and nuts in brown paper bags. The driver put his arm around the man who owned the shack. I imagined they were cousins and this was why we stopped. The few of us that were not green with bile waited in line for the slim pickings on the stall's counter.

I noticed, hanging up on the side of the shack, dusty packages of what looked like aspirin. I pointed. The man reached for them, jiggled his head and said something in Hindi.

"Aspirin?" I asked. He wobbled his head, said something again in his native tongue.

Someone behind me said, "It is for motion sickness. It is not for headache."

I made a vast motion of my hands. *Give me all of them.* There were twenty packages, two pills in each. They were so covered in dust you couldn't read the label. I tore open two packages, took the pills with a gulp of Coke, and gave two to Finn.

Back on the road, more vomiting. The pills started to take effect, washing out the jerking motion, the hazy view, the riling stench. The chicken flapped in some far-off distance. I was just about to fall off to sleep, and I could hear the echoing of the retching as more and more people became sick. One person seemed to trigger another, with the puking carried in waves from the back of the bus to the front and back again. I roused myself, took out the packs of pills, opened all of them. There wasn't enough for everyone.

I maneuvered around the goat and chickens to the first row. The bus took curves so hard that I grabbed onto people to stay upright. I held my hand out, and handed out the blue pills to anyone who wanted one. No one even questioned what they were. Many did not even look up, they were so unwell, just picked pills from my palm without looking. The tips of their fingers in my palm like a caress, something about it ancient, those fingertips brushing my palm.

As I settled next to Finn, as the pills took effect, the line between past and present dissolved. The goat leaned his warm body against my legs. I was a little girl, maybe nine. Father held out a handful of change. It was Sunday. This happened only on Sundays.

We were allowed to take one quarter, Meghan and I. It was the kind of stinking hot Missouri day when the tar boiled on the paved roads. We walked to a truck stop two miles up dirt and gravel roads to the highway. It sold burgers, soft-serve and candy. The plastic window protecting the stash of candy was covered in sticky fingerprints. I had bangs that kept getting into my eyes. I picked five pieces for a nickel each, Chic-O-Stick, Pop Rocks, bubble gum and more. On the way home, the taste of the sugar sliding down the back of the throat, the slime of sweat in crook and neck, the fiery sun burning symbols into the top of the scalp. Meghan was still my sister then, so much older, so much wilder. When she ran away, it didn't stop our relationship. When someone leaves you like that, suddenly without warning, it didn't end the connection. You still had a sister, but she became a ghost. She was still there, haunting me, telling me jokes, always trying to shock me with stories about sex, giving me little gifts. Now, though, I had to build and maintain her with my imagination. I colored the vague outlines of her in with crayons. We still had this ongoing relationship for years, it was just no longer real.

On the sidewalks and in the streets, people washed laundry in tubs, cut each other's hair, prepared food over open fires, pounded carpets with brooms, purchased live chickens and dirt-covered vegetables. They went down an alley to piss and shit. The smells were a revolving carnival, slaps against the face, sickly sweet, bitter, nasty.

I sat at a cafe, at a plastic table on the sidewalk next to a pile of dog shit. Cars and trucks honked on the busy street. The smoke mixed with the smog, and the haze was thick here, heavy and dark and obscuring the distances.

A travel article was due. Finn was out somewhere with his flute. I'd banged out some clichéd drivel on Thailand for my last article, avoiding everything that had truly happened there. It was light and frivolous, something about how, despite the forest fires in India, tourists were not scared off, something about Bob Marley and not worrying and being happy. Nothing about children dancing naked, or psychics with messages that bore into the soul. Nothing about older women crushed by a devastating world.

I sat with the Indian guidebook, searching for ideas for another article. Nothing in the book piqued my interest. I removed my surgical mask to drink milky chai from a clay cup. People shattered the cups on the ground after use. At my feet, clay chips in piles.

A few doors up, a group of male drivers gathered around their rickshaws. I couldn't stop staring at them, tall and painfully thin, in rough-looking button-down shirts, frayed khakis and flip-flops so thin they were barely there, beneath their callused brown feet.

When Finn and I first arrived at the Delhi airport, when we took a motorized rickshaw to our hotel, the driver took a corner so fast, our open-air buggy side-swiped a sacred cow in the street. The carriage hit the flank of the beast, and caused a rectal explosion. Shit flung in several directions, some of it slapping Finn and me in the face, some of it hitting our chests and lap. It was the perfect metaphor for India, where sanctity meets the shitty.

As I approached the rickshaw drivers now, one of the men

took my arm and tried to steer me to his vehicle. "Hello, this way." I pulled away. Others gathered. "Hello, rickshaw. Cheap." "Good price. Happy trip." "Hello, rickshaw." "Hello." "Cheap." "Madam, no, this way. This way."

Four men surrounded me, standing so close I could smell the sweat. Personal space is an altogether different paradigm in Asia. It wasn't just that I was American, but growing up in the wild-open spaces of Missouri, I was bred on open spaces, wide fields and big skies. I'd recoil at the implied intimacy of the physical proximity. You could back up, but the people in Asia would just follow you.

I felt compelled toward one of the men. He didn't look different from the others, but something was in his eyes. He had a bicycle rickshaw that he had to power using his legs, whereas the others had fancier motorized rickshaws.

"Hello," I said.

"Hello." He put his hands in prayer position and bowed toward me.

"I would like to write an article on you, spend all day riding in your rickshaw, and interviewing you. Is that okay?"

His eyes were chocolate, and the whites of them cream. He put out his hands flat to say he didn't understand. His palms were lined, and reminded me of the forest.

I turned to the crowd, "English?"

Some of the men responded, "Yes, English," and pointed to their vehicles.

"Yes, please, English."

"This way, English. English."

I moved my head from side to side. "No. No." I stretched my hands wide. "Full English. All English." They looked confused. "Can anyone translate?" A man raised his hand, spoke rapidly in Hindi, and ran off.

"Pearl," I said to the man I wanted to interview, pointing to my chest.

He put his hands together and bowed again, and said, "Leo, Leo," pointing to his nose.

I checked out Leo's rickshaw, a metal car attached to a bicycle. The car had a double seat and it was spotless. At one time, a red stripe had been painted on the outside of the car, but it had been scratched into fragments. In front, his bicycle seat was covered with duct tape. The tires were bald, thin strips of rubber, as thin as the flip-flops on Leo's feet.

The man came running back, hurrying along a young woman behind him. She came up shyly. "Would you be in need of translation?" I was at least a head taller than she was. Her thin hair was tucked behind her ears, and she wouldn't look me in the face.

"I'm Pearl." I held out my hand. She didn't take it and didn't respond. "And your name?"

"Amra."

I reached down and took her dangling hand and shook it. "Hello, Amra. Can you tell this man that I want to interview him for a newspaper article? I'll hire him for the whole day, and travel around with him in his rickshaw, and I'll pay him extra for the interview. And I'll pay you to translate." I gave her two amounts.

"I'm afraid I do not have all day. My mother…"

"I will pay you for whatever time you do have."

She nodded, and spoke to Leo. He held his palms out as he answered her questions. He teared up and nodded.

Amra turned to me. "That is much needed money for him. He is very moved. He believes you were sent to him by the gods. Of course, he would be honored."

"Can you tell him to pick a nice place to take us to, perhaps a tourist destination, but one that he likes, that's not too far away, to take us both there and we'll sit and have an interview?"

"Yes, I will tell him."

As we got into the metal car behind the bike, I saw letters painted on the side of the metal car. They reminded me of Raul, so far away now. I pointed them out to Amra, and she spoke to Leo.

"It is the name of his rickshaw. It is Hayagriva, god with horse head. It is god of knowledge and wisdom."

Amra and I got in the back and Leo straddled the bike. I took out my book on Hindu gods and studied the blue horse-headed god, his many arms, the legends. I imagined growing up in India, and learning these wild legends, and what that would do to a girl's imagination. As a little girl, we had no books in the house, just the King James Bible and a farmer's almanac. I'd closed myself off in a bathroom to read the bible page for page, just for something to read. What if my head had been filled with these blue, many-armed gods? What would that do for the imagination? What would that do for the wildness of the soul?

The smoke haze left a cinder taste in the mouth. Leo had to strain hard to get the bike moving, the muscles in his emaciated brown calves small and hard, like golf balls. The streets were mad with motorcycles, bicyclists, rickshaws, and cars, no one staying in any one lane, the piercing honking making me flinch. On the sides of the roads, crumbling buildings, and small shops with wares spilling onto the streets. Most of the men wore faded Western clothing, and many of the women moved in flowing bright saris. The smells were of sewage and shit and goat meat sizzling over open fires. Above all of this hung a thick pall of smoke mixing with the smog, and it turned everything a mustard yellow. Amra and I put on our masks. To some, I knew this level of chaos might seem exciting, but to a sensitive soul it was utterly overwhelming.

We passed a group of musicians playing clanging music, and I tried to see if Finn was among them, but couldn't get a view.

I watched Leo stand up on the bike and pull the three hundred-odd pounds of people and carriage through the streets. This was the work he did. Rain or snow or burning forest fires, he had to make money. I moved the mask, and asked Amra what this ride would normally cost. She answered without shifting her mask, the words muffled. "Fifty cents for you as a tourist. Twenty-five cents for me as local."

There was something about the way that he held his body straight, his head up, as we maneuvered around veering trucks, how he took the exhaust fumes and forest fire smoke in the face, that was somehow regal. There was elemental freedom in it, face to the wind, the sweat, the pull of the muscles, the breath going so deep into the soul.

He stopped at a temple—columns topped by monkey statues, vines growing into their mouths, walls and stairs ancient and decaying. Everywhere the chattering and swinging of live monkeys.

He biked to a side area, where there were no tourists. We got out and made our way to a crumbling curved bench, behind us a wall covered in moss with muscular vines climbing the cracked stone, and next to us a massive twisted tree. Monkeys ran in a line on top of the wall, a cacophony of chattering, one of them crying out like a police siren. The whole scene was out of an Indian fable.

I interviewed Leo, a strange sensation, Leo's milky eyes, and Amra's tentative song-like rejoinder. I asked him to tell me generally about his life as a rickshaw driver, and he opened it up with money. Sometimes I did this, kept the interview general to see how the interviewee would respond, to see what was upper-most in their minds.

Leo told me the cost of purchasing the rickshaw, the price for a license, the monthly amount fee paid to the city, the rates for the riders, the amount he took home, the money he spent per month, as well as the cash he sent home, to his wife and two sons, far away in rural India. He spoke in minuscule amounts, spare change. The frugality of subsistence survival. Figuring of such tiny amounts seemed to deflate him.

He said that he wanted ultimately to get a motorized rickshaw, but this was all he could afford for now. Even for a bicycle-powered rickshaw, this was one of the very cheapest, as it had a heavy metal car attached. There were others now where the car was replaced with just a seat on wheels to decrease the weight the driver had to pull. But he could not afford even that.

"Do you like bicycling?" I asked.

He spoke in Hindi, using his hands, the fingers long and elegant. While I waited for him to finish and Amra to translate, I watched warily as a monkey hovered by the nearby tree, watching us. It seemed too smart, and too intent on us, and made me nervous.

Leo finished, and Amra turned to me. "He was given an old bike as a child. You see, no one had a bike. He let his friends ride it. That way, they all had a bike. It wasn't about the bike after that, it was about happiness, sharing the happiness, you see?

"There was a steep hill, and it would take all of one's might to cycle up that hill. Just at the top you could see the sea. He would come up over the hill..." She demonstrated this motion with her hands, echoing a motion Leo had made earlier. "...and imagine at the top, the bike would fly and he was flying, over the houses of his friends, over his house, and farther, out over the ocean."

I felt my soul become his soul as Amra spoke. I could feel Amra feeling it too. How one told story can tie us all together into magic. I saw the boy and the bike flying. I became the air-born boy.

I asked about his family. "He sees them once every eight weeks," Amra translated. "To take more time off and to pay the bus fare more often than that, means none of them have enough to survive."

"You live this life in a city you do not really want to be in because you want to go home to that life where you really want to be," Leo said through Amra. Just like with Yash and Etisha, it was odd to hear Leo's story told through the breathless high-pitched voice of a young woman.

"He is here only because he really wants to be in his village. There is no way to make money in his village. They cannot survive. So he comes to where he does not want to be, so that someday he can be where he wants to be. It is a world that has gone crazy. But, he says, you cannot think of these things or you will also lose your mind."

"When will you get to go home," I asked, "for good?"

"He would be glad when he never has to pedal it again," Amra said. "But he's afraid he will die on this bike. He sees no other way for there to be enough money for him, wife and family." I thought of this exodus from the earth across Southeast Asia, about my mother's frantic desire to get away from the farm and move to town. I needed to understand why everyone was in such a hurry to get away from the dirt. For Leo, it was financial. But why was it so? Why could they not live off the land? Why was everyone being forced away from their roots? It had something to do with money. It had something to do with a system that forced you outside yourself to survive. There was so much about the world I did not know.

We talked about the types of fares he picked up, who he liked most and who he liked least. I asked about his best fare ever, and his worst.

Once, someone stole from him, an Asian man, a rich man. He did not just stiff him on the fare, he reached out and grabbed money from Leo's hand. Leo spoke of this with such despair, that I was upset with myself for asking.

He said he preferred the white tourists because they gave guilt tips. He looked at me and blushed. He could tell a white person who had been too long in Asia by their clothes and tried to avoid them because they knew the real local prices and would never give a penny more. He bent forward and held his stomach and laughed. He said something while he was laughing. Amra laughed, and translated. "He cannot believe he is speaking such truth to you."

I wanted to get his philosophy on life but I did not know how to ask the question.

"Amra," I said, "I want to get more on Leo's life philosophy. Can you help me in asking the question?" I instinctively felt if I asked the question directly, it wouldn't get to the core. This was the problem with not speaking the language, with having to go through someone else to find the nuance.

Amra was quiet, thinking, smiled to herself, then spoke to Leo in Hindi. Leo looked at his open palms for a long time, at the branches and leaves of the lines etched into his flesh. The lone monkey was now circling our bench, looking for a handout. He scared me in his wildness, terrified me with his street smarts, like he might jump up and scratch any one of us at any moment, like the wild creature he was supposed to be.

"He spent much time in the forest when he was a child. These forests are now gone." He pointed to the heavy smoke haze in the air, and made a swirling motion with his hand. He stared at his palms. "If you see how a tree grows, a branch or a leaf, it has an intelligence. It knows: It is what is it. It isn't what it is not. It knows: I am a leaf. It grows accordingly." He looked up, and his eyes were far away.

"People think they are not what they are. They think they are something else. And so they try to grow like something else. It does not work. They get angry. They take things from you. They take and take. It is most simple, to be what is. But people think it is most difficult. They think it is the hardest thing, and they make it hard, but it is the simplest."

Amra's high-toned voice said the words as I looked at Leo—I felt myself falling into his eyes.

He stared at his palms again, saying nothing. A pall fell upon us. The monkey at our feet screeched the high-pitched wail of a child. I got up and went to a nearby food truck and bought us kebabs and Coca-Cola. Leo threw some of the food over the wall, and the monkey chased it. Other monkeys screamed and scampered after him. We had to eat quickly before the animals returned.

After we'd finished, Amra said, "I am so sorry, but I must get back to my mother."

On the ride back, I talked to Amra about translating. I was interested in the process. It seemed fascinating to me to interpret one person's question in one language and have to interpret the answer in another, going between thoughts, ideas and nuance.

Amra became animated. "It is a challenge between speaking the very words that are spoken to you, back and forth, and speaking thoughts between the lines. You must decide if these are your thoughts or the thoughts of the person speaking. It is a fragile business."

"After I do this translation all day, I go home, and the thoughts and words of the person become my thoughts and words. Do you understand? I do not know what it is that I think, and what it is that they think. I sometimes become lost inside them. It can take maybe ten days before I come back and know myself again." She was not a pretty woman, plain and soft-spoken, but she moved her hands while she talked as if we were both swimming in water.

"What did you say to Leo about his philosophy on life?"

"I asked, what would the gods say about the way people are today? What message did you think the gods would have for the people?"

Our shoulders were touching, and I felt like I was lifted out of myself, made into a stream of light, and lowered down through the top of her skull. It was the same thing that happened with the older woman on the Thai beach.

The light of me entered the soul of her. Amra was a surprise, a dynamic and dimensional intelligence, a genius. I had been lulled by her passivity and mousiness. It was easy to miss the depths of women; many of us were taught to numb ourselves out and dumb ourselves down, and it was easy to overlook the layer. Amra was astonishing. There was something of a physicist in her, someone who could see the coming together of things in the physical world. She did not live all of her gifts, but they were there, waiting.

She'd been taught to hide how smart she was. Some of us women even forgot it ourselves, like unused muscles, the genius atrophying and withering. We were taught to play small, and be demure, to not speak too much of what we knew and not look up because they would beat you for being so brilliant, they would kill you for your wild genius. I thought, *I must stop judging a book by its lack of self esteem.*

I was suddenly released from being inside her. She looked at me with astonishment. She knew I had seen her, that I really saw her. I did not know how many people had ever seen this woman. We stared at each other with surprise and did not speak.

When we disembarked, Amra bowed, tears in her eyes, and I was weepy too. We would probably never see each other again. It was difficult to see someone or be seen so deeply; it felt like a love affair or a moment of majesty, and then you had to let it go, then you had to go back to the hard-scrabble world and come to terms with being invisible, disappearing sometimes even to yourself.

Before she left, I paid her and had her arrange with Leo to bicycle me around, to take it slow, point at the places he loved, and to take breaks. I watched as Amra waved shyly, walked away, melted into the swarming crowd, became indistinguishable from all the others, and disappeared.

As Leo maneuvered around side streets, I thought about his family in the village, and the sending back of money. I thought about the Thai girls selling sex to send money back. How no one could survive without the selling of themselves to the highest bidder. All around us were Westerners being biked on similar cycle rickshaws, the white people big and hearty and heavy, bellies straining against shirts, fatty breasts straining against singlets, the brown men hauling them around rail-thin and wiry. The sight disturbed me. Leo was turning and pointing things out and looking for my reaction, but I felt ill. I tried to smile, but I was sure it came out as a grimace.

We stopped at a corner. Leo put out his thin hand for me to disembark and took me to a couple of men selling wares on the street. On a blanket on the road were wooden bodies, arms, legs, and dismembered heads. I'd become so overwhelmed, it took a while to realize they were selling puppets.

I tried different heads on different bodies. They reminded me of Usui and the dolls he made as a homeless man. There was a skinny woman with a hawk nose, and a beige dress with mismatched designs. I held it up to my face, and motioned from it to me. It *was* me. Leo laughed. I purchased it from the vendor. As we biked around, the head kept falling off and rolling around the back seat.

As we moved around the bustling city, I kept hearing Leo's thoughts. I'd always had some capacity to read people's minds, but sometimes, if I felt the person I was with deeply, their thoughts became my thoughts. Like Amra, who held their thoughts for days afterwards, I became a translation of them in my soul. Sometimes, if I was too much in love with someone, I wouldn't know whose thoughts were whose.

All my life, people spoke to me without moving their mouths. The thoughts in their minds were so strong they shouted out to me even when the person wasn't speaking, even when they were trying to keep those thoughts hidden.

And when they did actually speak, the words did not match the thoughts. I learned at a young age to pretend. Someone in shattering grief would say they were fine, and laugh, and I'd hear the wailing thoughts of pain and sadness, and I'd smile back and agree with them on how happy they were. I had gotten so good at pretending, I didn't know what was real and what was pretense anymore.

Leo's mind sought out the beautiful. I could feel him examine things for their beauty, always the landscape, never the people. Like me, he preferred the earth to humans. The energy of a certain neighborhood, the way the branches of trees surrounded it, protected it. How the sun at this time of day made a beam of light that turned the side road silver, especially after rain. Now of course, everything silver was yellowed by the forest fire smoke, but that too, in Leo's mind, had its own mystery. We came to a corner near the train station, and his energy and voice changed. This was where something bad had happened, I could feel it. His body clenched and went cold. His mind hardened.

I thought Leo's thoughts. This is the place where the Asian man stole his money. Leo bicycled as fast as he could past the spot, a corner of a sidewalk near a post office that would now always be haunted for him.

These were the kinds of stories I wanted to use in the travel article, this reading of minds, this nuance, but I couldn't. I experienced so many things that I could not speak of, that I could never write about or say out loud. At least not to the normal world.

We came to a hill. Leo stood on the pedals, leaned forward, used all his might to haul me and the metal car up and up. I could not imagine he did this every day, seven days a week, that he knew no other life.

I peered out of my metal box. It was an almost empty road, off the main thoroughfares. I saw as we got to the top, a strip of water in the distance, some lake or river. Leo looked back at me and laughed. It was a reminder of the street of his childhood, his mind told me. He came here often. I gave him the thumbs up. As we topped the hill, he spread his arms out and pedaled us hard over the edge.

And then we were flying. Leo had his legs stretched out, feet off the pedals, his laugh carried back to me on the wind. I stuck my head out of the car like a dog, and the wind took my hair. I was crying. I was sobbing. I could barely breathe.

Back at our starting point, as I paid Leo, I remembered one thing I'd forgotten to ask. I folded my hands next to my cheek and pantomimed, "Where do you sleep?"

The other drivers laughed and yelled the word for "sleep" in Hindi, or so I assumed, because Leo arced his arm in a flourish toward the seat I'd just vacated. He climbed in and curled into the fetal position.

Of course, did I think he slept in a hotel? He leaped out and again with a dramatic flourish, took hold of the edge of the seat and opened it. Tucked inside were a pair of trousers, a shirt, and a thin blanket.

"Your closet," I said, and he nodded. The other men opened their seats, too, to show me the totality of their worldly possessions.

Leo mimed to me with an eating motion. I nodded. Of course, that was a question I needed to ask, too, where did he eat?

He motioned for me to follow. We walked a block, and then turned down an alley, going deep into the dark, leaving behind any of the even marginal cleanliness of the shops on the street. The ground was littered with vegetable and fish debris, the smells rotten and pungent. Grime at the edges of the alley seemed to be ancient, bubonic. We came to another alley. On the corner was a shack, a piece of warped plywood for a counter. Behind the counter, a man stirred two pots on an open fire pit.

Leo ordered for me, a bowl of vegetables with bits of what looked like chicken, and a bowl of rice. He used his fingertips to scoop the rice. A roach skittered out of his bowl as he put the rice to his lips. I put my fingertips in my rice, and the motion upset a roach there too, the black insect topping the edge of my bowl and falling to the plywood. I looked at Leo, who nodded, and put the rice to my mouth and ate it.

I watched Leo as we ate. His soul was now my soul, but we would now go to very different lives.

———

I clung to Finn's body. He was malleable this evening. He had not been so pliable in a very long time. Something had happened to him that day, too, but we had not spoken. When I came into the hotel room, he was on the bed, writing an aerogram letter. I went to him without words, and put my body onto his.

I ran my hands along his back, neck, shoulders, down his long, pale torso, to his thin thighs. I was seeing less of him. I was sitting beside him for eighteen hours on a bus and I was not seeing him. I wasn't keeping track of him. How many days since I'd looked at him? When was the last time our souls were together?

"Queenie," he groaned. "What are you doing?"

I ran my palms in circles on his ass, tried to find a place at his waist to grab flesh, but he was too skinny now. We were both angles and bone, our bodies sharp and hard against each other. I took his ass into my palm. I needed the meat of him.

I was trying to live in flesh, to come back into flesh. Something about Leo had forced me out of my body. I did not want to float above. It was too painful. So much of me already had flown away, terrified pieces that could not bear the pain of mundane reality. You would think this would be a numbing, but there was a pain that came with it too. Now, with Leo, I was flying high above the landscape, and I needed to come down. I needed to come home. I wanted to come crashing back to earth, to be in this body, this flesh. With Leo on his bike, I had not come back down.

Finn got on his knees and grabbed me from behind. He entered me hard. He fucked me like we used to fuck when we first met, slap of skin against skin, an animal mounting, a grunting, a rutting, a guttural beating. Neither of us had showered, and you could smell the stench, sweat, armpits, the stink of pussy and junk. When we both came, the room grew full of the aroma of our fluids.

Afterward, lying beside each other, panting, our bodies slippery with sweat and cum, I ran my hand through sweat and semen up my stomach, felt the razor sharpness of my hipbones, squeezed my breasts. I was hoping, waiting, wanting, a full return to my flesh.

O**n the sidewalks,** the poor brought out their broken children and placed them on display. Withered limbs, missing legs, whitened blind eyes, mental handicaps, one child had hydrocephalus, his head as large as a watermelon, the rail-thin, starved body beneath. We heard reports that some parents were disabling their kids to beg for money.

I knew about poverty in India, but the magnitude of it was still a punch to the gut. There was no way to travel the country and not feel the need, the pain. There was no way to not see the slums, the shacks, the trash, the hungry children with distended bellies. No way not to smell the stench of open sewers. It brought me crashing back into my body, the sheer intensity of it crashed me hard back into my flesh.

In Nepal and Thailand, we'd met other travelers who'd been to India for yoga retreats or to stay in ashrams. They spoke glowingly of how spiritual the country was, eyes dancing, heads in the clouds, but they never mentioned the poverty, not verbally and not energetically. As I roamed the streets, I wondered how they could not have brought up the poor, how they could not have been affected by it. Did they take a taxi from the airport to their retreats without even looking out the window? Did they stay inside the retreat center without leaving? It boggled my mind.

For anyone, surely, seeing the poorest country in the world would touch them, transform them, call them to do or be something. For my sensitive self it wasn't just a call, but a howl that ripped at the core.

A woman, newborn, infant, and man curled in the dark corner of a metal dumpster. Through the side door, a sunbeam shot in like a message from the gods, a flame from the head of Agni.

The heat inside must have been excruciating. The black metal absorbed the sun. Sweat poured from dark flesh. The whites of eyes stood out in the dark, like fearful animals in the forests where I grew up. The baby was on its back on the filthy dumpster floor. It made no noise. The family was also quiet in their hovering place.

The dumpster sat in the alley behind our hotel. I was entering the hotel by the backdoor by myself when I heard a noise, and looked inside. For the rest of the day, the image haunted me, the family following me around the city like ghosts.

The next morning, while Finn was out, I took all of my clothes out of my pack. I took all the money I had. I folded a bill and put one in the front pocket of a blouse. I put another in the back pocket of a pair of jeans. I filled every pocket with folded bills.

It reminded me of Meghan—how small kindnesses done to you can last a lifetime in your soul. Meghan gave me a purse and a wallet the Christmas I was seven. The purse had a round front flap that was a big leather sunflower, painted bright yellow, red and green and sewn with thick leather stitches. The wallet was a round sunflower, too. I rarely received gifts that were so full of color. I found the first dollar bill right away, tucked away in the purse pocket. I kept coming upon folded bills even weeks later. It was a gift of magic. I carried the purse and wallet with me until it fell apart. I kept them in a box at Jason's when I was at college. I only threw them away after they grew mold and became covered in fur.

I took the pile of clothes down to the back alley. I leaned into the dumpster. The woman half sat, half sprawled next to the newborn, who seemed to be sleeping. The father and the other child were gone. I got on my hands and knees and crawled inside, handed the pile of folded clothing to the woman. She seemed too tired to move her arm. Or perhaps she didn't want the gift. Perhaps what I was doing was rude. I had no social context.

The sun beat down on the top of the dumpster. It was a sauna. I put the clothes on the mother's lap. She didn't touch them. I looked at the lethargic baby. Was he sleeping? I couldn't tell. Was he even alive? I took the woman's hand and placed it on top of the pile of clothing. She picked at the folds lazily. I squatted for a time and watched her, and then crawled back out. Outside the dumpster, I peered in occasionally, but the pile of clothes sat on her lap and she didn't move. Finally, I left.

For days afterwards, I thought, *I hope she found the money. I hope she didn't sell the clothing without finding the money.* Then I said to myself, *Don't be ridiculous, of course she found the money, or her husband did.*

I worried about that for days. *Did she find the money?*

Finn was giddy. I tried to keep up. So much stimulation. We were at an open-air bizarre, a tsunami of color, smells, and noise. Cars honking, people yelling, music blaring, goats bleating. Unrecognizable vegetables, fruits, live animals roaming the grounds, standing on tables, being hauled on shoulders. People squatting, sitting, spitting, coughing, careening. Growl of sewage, nectar of fruit, shit of goat and dog. And surrounding it all, that ever-present pall of forest fire smoke.

Daily, I felt on the verge of panic. I'd felt this before, but by the end of the hour or the day, it would calm down. Now, from day to day, the panic did not subside. Perpetual anxiety became the new normal.

At the end of the market stood a Hindu temple. Carved pillars, ornate domes, the statues of gods. I could not even begin to understand Hinduism, and I did not pretend to. After the austerity of Missouri, and the zen simplicity of Japan, the gods here created an explosion in the psyche.

My body seemed to vibrate at higher and higher intensities. I stood outside and waited for Finn and chain-smoked to bring myself down, but it did not work. I bought a beer from a vendor and drank it, and another, but nothing seemed to work.

A man in one of the doorways at the edge of the temple court-yard was smearing red bindi dots onto women's foreheads and chanting. I knew from the guidebook they were put on the third eye to represent divine nature. I stood in line with the rest of the women. I wanted a bindi. I needed a bindi. A bindi would help center me. The women in the line poked each other and pointed to me. They pulled up the edges of their saris and laughed behind them.

When I got to the front, I leaned forward. The man was bare-chested and wore a dhoti, rocked back and forth and chanted. His voice was high like a little girl's. You could count his ribs he was so painfully thin. He didn't look at me as he rocked and put his thumb into a tin bowl of red paint. Still without looking me in the face, he smeared the paint onto my forehead. I stood up and felt dizzy. Still the anxiety. I tried to breathe.

A man in a turban with intense eyes approached me as I leaned against a wall for support.

"See your future?" he asked. I was mesmerized by the dark

depths of his eyes and nodded. "I will read it for you. Yes? Inform you of what is to come."

He held out an opened hardback book. "Put rupee in book. I will read your fortune." He shook the book at me. I reached into my pocket and put the equivalent of a dollar into the open pages, like a bookmark.

He peered at me. He moved his head this way and that, danced around me, looking at me from the front and from both sides. He looked into the pages of his book, but he wasn't reading, just staring, wide-eyed. "You have great purpose." He said "purpose" like "poipose." He moved toward me. I backed up. He moved again. He held the book open again, to a different page. "Another rupee in book." I did as I was told.

"You seek poipose, but you run very far away from it. You run very very fast. Speeding very very fast away."

I fell into his eyes. He held the book up again, to a different page. "Rupee." I inserted the bill into the folds.

"Go backward."

I backed up. He followed. My back was against the crumbling wood doorway.

"Yes, you must go back. So far back. No going forward until you go back. Way back you will find that the path has fork," he held up his other arm, put his elbows together to demonstrate the fork. He had black grime beneath his fingernails. "You went one way on fork. You must go back to beginning and take left. It is like dying. You will feel death."

His words moved along my flesh in waves. He held the book up again. I took another bill from my pocket. Just as I was putting it into the pages, a hand reached from the side and snatched the bill away.

"Queenie?" It was Finn. He took me by the shoulders and turned me to him. "Are you kidding me?"

The man in the turban wedged himself in front of Finn and faced me. "I have more to speak with you about. Please."

"No," Finn said. The man shook the book beneath my nose. "No," Finn said again, taking my arm and pulling me away. I kept staring at the man in the turban as Finn pulled me down the street. "Queenie, for fuck sake."

The Indian man called after us. "Please, there is more."

Finn marched me down the street. "That's the oldest trick in the book. You're not that gullible." The book. I looked back over my shoulder. The man stood staring at me, his body vibrating. I wouldn't tear my eyes away. The book in his hand, now closed. Finn pulled me around a corner. My body was vibrating too.

CHAPTER 22 ½

Objects fly from cubbyholes. *They will not stay on the shelves. Rusted horse shoes, green glass insulators from electricity poles, thick railroad ties, rusted gears. Father finds the dirty shelf with its dozens of cubbyholes deep in a valley in the woods. Somebody has dumped it off the edge of a steep gravel road, and it has tumbled into a ravine. He is a lifter of heavy things, Father. He has much practice in lifting the heaviness of himself. He has brute strength and can lift things other men will never try by themselves.*

With his floppy way of walking, he stumbles down into the ravine. He rolls the shelf back up the hill, brutal grunt by brutal grunt. When he gets it back onto the road, he wedges it into the bed of his truck, drives it back miles through over rutted roads through the forest to the farmhouse basement. The shelving is massive, reaching to the ceiling and taking up one wall. Each cubbyhole becomes a compartment, a shadow box, for forest junk.

Father is obsessed with collecting trash left deep in the inscrutable woods. He'll hunt and fish and come across the detritus of mankind. He is gleeful about his finds, a poor boy who thinks finding a broken toolbox in the forest is like coming upon hidden treasure. His hoarding of the broken trash of man found in the depths of the mysteries of the forest is his way of trying to survive.

He will go out on one of his hunts, for wild beast and forest junk, revving his truck as it is parked in the grease-slicked basement next to the cubby shelf. He will back up, storm off, and come back with the carcasses of deer, duck, and pheasant, and the treasures of oxidized chains, broken compass, and duck call. He'll rev and leave again and come back again with trash, mostly, but sometimes with gems, Native skinning stones, and arrowheads and rocks veined with gold. He is a violent man, gleeful in his meanness, insulting, scary, and these parts of him are in the cubbies on the shelf, too —rusted wire cutters, a spent 12-gauge shell, bloodied fishing hooks, the wooden handle of a pistol.

I can smell the dank musk of the rotting potatoes kept in bins in the corner of the basement, hear the echo of the concrete walls.

The junk will not stay on the shelves. I've seen this before, somewhere, at some time, long ago and far away. The museum of forest garbage flies from the shelves and becomes a man, turns into my father.

Rusted saw arm, stone heart, chains for hair—it is as if Father goes into the forest to retrieve bits of himself that he's lost, as if he is obsessed with finding a lost self in this junk. He is recreating himself from the detritus and trash in the depths of the forest.

The objects fly off the shelf and make the man, then fly back again and new objects make a new man. He is trying on new identities, like changing clothes. He has no idea who he is. Is he an arm made of rotting wood, or a throat crafted from a hollow pipe? Where is he? What is he? He is never satisfied. He is nobody, nonexistent, invisible. He is the trash that man threw away in the mystery of the woods.

He is a little boy who was told he is nothing, who finds solace in the song of the trees, whose only recourse from the hate is a deeper and deeper retreat. With no one to guide him, he can only craft himself from what others discard.

E
very day for several days, I went back to the temple looking for the psychic, but in a city of millions, finding him was impossible. I came back and went to bed. I stayed in bed. I had no desire now to get out of bed.

Finn would rise early and grab his camera and flute and try to get me to go with him, but I wouldn't go. At first, as the sun set, I'd get out of bed and dress, pretending when Finn came home that I'd gone out too. But then I stopped pretending. I was in bed when Finn left and in bed when Finn returned. In the corner, the black dog snarled. If I just stayed still, if I did not leave the bed, I would not further poke the beast.

I didn't know if it was the heavy smoke that moved like a dark monster across the sun, shadowing the landscape. I didn't know if it was the sheer stimulation of India, the smells and the poverty and the intensity, and if I was just psychically overwhelmed. I didn't know if it was what the psychic said about going backward to find the fork in the road, but it felt like a death sentence, like being ordered back into the pit of the Midwest I'd worked so hard to escape. I didn't know if it was the vision. I kept thinking about the shelf and Father's junk, and how for years after he died, the objects were left untouched in the corner of the basement, collecting dust, how I'd run down to get potatoes from the bin, do it as fast as I could and run back up the stairs, fearing Father lurking in the shadows of that shelf. When I came out of the vision, I was in bed, back arched. I looked quickly to see if Finn had seen it, and I swore his eyes were open a slit, but when I looked again, they were closed.

When my days in bed stretched to a week, Finn began returning with offerings. He brought fruit from the market that neither of us recognized. He got a book on Indian fruits and vegetables. He started at the beginning of the alphabet. He placed the fruit on a brown paper bag on the bedspread, and searched for it in his book.

"This is *amla*," he said. A neon-green taut, round fruit. He took out his Swiss army knife, peeled it and cut a piece for me and one for him. Father used to take out his hunting knife when he had an apple and peel the red skin in one full spiral. Meghan and Mother and I would watch, as if it were a magical feat, mesmerized, until the spiral of apple peel fell to the table, and the four of us would break it apart and eat it. How someone could be dead for decades and they shot up in your memory like they were alive, how it could take you by surprise, how it could ring you out.

Finn propped my chin with his fingers. He handed me the book. He had me read it as we ate. Juice squirted from the watery flesh. It was bitter, like eating a whole lemon, sour, and astringent. Finn grimaced and laughed.

"Ayurvedic scriptures, Indian folklore and Sanskrit texts mention the fruit exhaustively. The famous Tamil poet Avvayar claimed that a celestial amla was given to Prince Adhiyaman to promote longevity. In turn, this would enable the prince to continue with his good deeds to the people. India's father of ancient medicine, Sushruta, wrote of amlas' rejuvenating health benefits during his life circa fifteen hundred to three thousand BC," I read.

Afterward, Finn took played his flute. I got out of bed, sat at the window and chain-smoked.

Night after night he brought home exotic fruit, sliced deep into the unfamiliar flesh. Burmese grapes that tasted like lychee fruit, sweet and brightly sour, *Calamondin*, with the look of tangerines, but a taste so bitter we could only take one bite, dragonfruit, sharp-edged peel but so bland it tasted of nothing, the yellow elephant apple, which the seller demanded we add sugar to before eating, and it tasted nothing like an apple at all.

When I didn't get better, when I still would only get out of bed in the evenings when he played the flute, and I sat at the window and smoked, Finn started returning with multicolored scarves covered in tiny mirrors, elaborate earrings that dangled to my shoulders, statues of Hindu gods he made me look up, a sari of diaphanous pink that he draped from the window, casting the room in pink light.

Two weeks into my visit from the black dog, Finn showed up with six large glass bottles of Kingfisher beer and four packs of Gold Flake cigarettes.

"Maybe you just need to get drunk, Queenie," he said. We sat on the bed and smoked and drank. Soon we were both slurring our speech. He kissed me hard on the mouth, but I didn't want to be touched.

The next night, he came home so drunk he could barely walk. He sat on the edge of the bed, weaving. He looked at me through dark slit eyes and wove a cigarette to his mouth and missed. He started singing in drunken slur.

Nobody likes me, everybody hates me,
I think I'll go eat worms
Big fat juicy ones,

Eensie weensy squeensy ones,
See how they wiggle and squirm

He jumbled the words after that and gave up, humming instead and focusing on trying to smoke his cigarette. When I had my down phases in Tokyo he used to sing this to me, some nursery rhyme from England.

He stomped out the cigarette and fell sideways onto his pillow with his back to me. I could see in his pale shoulders that he was about to give up on me, that he had nothing more to give. As he started snoring, I knew I had to pull myself out of this or lose him. Then where would I have to go? Then there *would* be nowhere to go but backward.

There had been other times where I had to pull myself off the floor, where I had to make a choice. Feel better, don't feel better, but stand up. Take a step. Take another step. People pitied you for your depression, but really you had the strength of a mythological god. There was more courage beneath the nail of the pinkie on your left hand than most people had ever known. Getting out of bed and living life took more strength than most people could ever imagine.

The next morning when Finn woke up, I was dressed. I wore the earrings. I'd already been out. I brought chai and kebabs to soak up his hangover. Throughout the day, while he slept, I brought him offerings from the streets.

It was Finn's idea. It was on the way to our next destination, so why not? We hired a driver. He drove us as close as possible, as close as we could go and still be safe.

We stood on a plateau. We had our masks on and still it was

hot and smoky, and we were all holding our hands over the masks, and still we were coughing.

The great forest fire marched forward across the landscape in front of us. This was the fire that had sent up black smoke that shadowed a whole continent. It was devouring the trees, at first each like a skeleton, then even the bones were digested and spat out as ash. It was more than a mile away and we could still feel the heat of it. We were at the front edge of it, watching it march forward. It smoldered, crept, ran, rolled, crowned and spotted. It spat, screamed, grumbled, moaned, clicked. It threw up fiery confetti, thousands of flecks of sparks like lightning bugs, or meteors shot up from the earth and out into the sky. It stank, and smelled sweet like burnt sugar. It was the smell of a fireplace. It could fool you with smells and sounds of comfort, pull you in and then scorch you.

Finn and I stood in silence, taken over, devoured, unable to speak. It was preverbal this burning, post-verbal. Proverbial.

The way fire shared itself. The trees in the monster's path, the ones not burned, seemed to lean back into the flames, as if magnetized. The not-burned trees seemed to vibrate with the fire of the burning trees long before they themselves burned, and that vibration would explode it into flames with a mere lick of fire. Even when you could make out individual flames in the monstrous whole, it was as if they were talking to each other, licking each other, urging each other on. There was no individuality here, just a whole system going up in smoke. Behind this great wall of flames, a void where a vibrant forest used to be. Black ash. Stumps. A lifeless hell.

When I was a little girl, I did not see myself as different from trees. Every tree was me, every sassafras, cottonwood, elm. Palm against bark was palm against flesh. Every crook in branch was the crook of my elbow. As we stood watching, I saw myself as a skeleton amidst the burning trees, burning with them. What of the animals that made this place their home, what of the people?

We'd passed burnt-out shacks. Where had the people and animals gone? Where would they go?

A fire like this filled the psyche of burning things. Fire here was becoming a story that was being told, passed around, with a plot we could not stop, an ending we could not change. It was like the falling people from the train accident in Tokyo—Finn and I were left with the metaphor of falling. Everywhere, we saw people tumbling. Such falling was so uppermost in our minds, it made us fall, too. It worried me how dramatic, traumatic events filled our collective mythology, so that now many people would go to bed with dreams of flames, and from that place wake to create more ash, and accidentally and collectively burn down the whole world.

This fire reminded me of the psychic's fork in the road. It felt like I wasn't the only one forced to choose. The fire felt like the call to death that I'd received staring at the white peak of Annapurna on that rock in Nepal with Finn. The flames danced in the distance, just as Finn and I had danced. As if my call was not separate from the earth, but aligned with it. Was this call I'd been hearing even mine? Or was it the earth's?

We had to get back into the jeepney and leave because we could not breathe.

2 4

Stories danced across thin blue parchment, tales of other lives, echoes of the past. We'd picked up letters from friends all over the world at the post office, the hand-written script music that became song in the reading voices of our minds. We needed the good news, the connection. We desperately needed the melody. This was the highlight of every country we entered—a visit to the post office to collect aerograms from Missouri, Tokyo, London. They were full of mundane tales of dogs, of bosses, of neighbors. They were like homing pigeons, creatures of flight that kept us connected. Messages from the clouds.

The post office was a crumbling British building, a throwback to the days of the Raj. Lines were not lines in Southeast Asia, they were mobs with no discernible middle or end. The echoes of so many voices across the high ceilings, smells of sweat, incense and curry. I got into a shoving match with a Sikh who cut in front of me. He was over six feet tall, with a turban and a long beard. He carried a symbolic knife in his waistband. I wasn't even thinking when I put both hands on his chest and pushed. He didn't move. He acted like I was not there. I pushed him again. Then he looked at me. I looked into his eyes and stopped pushing. *Do not push Sikhs who carry knives in their belts.* He stayed in front of me.

After two hours in line, after several more people pushed their way in front of us, and Finn had to restrain me from shoving them (even after the Sikh, I had a motto, *when push comes to shove, push back*), we came out with a fistful of letters each.

There were four for me, from Yuriko and Choko in Tokyo, from Bonnie and Jason in Missouri. Finn had gotten four as well. We started reading them as we were walking to a coffee shop, sat down still reading. We barely looked up when the waiter came over to take our orders for chai.

Finn threw his head back and laughed at one point, showing the inside of his large mouth. Why I found his British wayward teeth so sexy, I didn't know. It took me awhile to quit watching him and get back to my letters.

I read Jason's, but rushed through it, the fear of Missouri still too fresh. I didn't want to be sucked back into that reality. Didn't want to feel the love I felt for him, for that dirty rough place. I ripped open Yuriko's, tearing through the words in the flimsy aerogram.

She and her girlfriend Asha were coming to India. Asha's parents lived in Jodhpur. Could we meet them there? I could barely breathe. I hadn't realized how much I missed the company of good strong women until I read those words. I blinked back tears.

"Pearlie Girl," she wrote. "I have your itinerary hanging by my easel. I'm painting portraits of Asha, dozens of them. She's sick of sitting for me, so some of them are of her sleeping on the tatami.

"She's my muse whether she likes it or not. During one of these sittings, or lyings down, I looked up and noticed your itinerary. I suggested to Asha that we go to visit her parents in Jodhpur, and meet up with you and Finn.

"She took some convincing. She has a very different life here than the one she left behind. I don't how much you know about her. I know you met her for the first time the night of the earthquake, and I know how crazy our lives became after that." She wrote more about the rebuilding that was going on, and how she and Asha were still running the food bank.

"Anyway, back to Asha. She chose to go to university in Singapore to get away from her family. She moved to Tokyo after that. She's hesitant to go home, but I've convinced her. We're going to be there the last two weeks of September. I have no idea if you're sticking to your itinerary, but if you could meet us..."

I looked at the date on the letter. I tried to remember today's date. Yuriko wrote that they'd booked a hotel for a couple of days in Jodhpur so they could rest up before going to stay with Asha's parents. If I got the letter in time, she wrote, I should come to meet them at the hotel. She gave me the date. It was in two days from now.

I looked up at Finn and stared at him intensely. He didn't like Yuriko. The feeling was mutual. They were just on different bandwidths. He was intimidated by her, and she thought he wasn't good enough for me. No matter what, I decided, we were going to Jodhpur to meet them. It was about a half-day bus ride from where we were now. I just had to figure out how to pitch it to Finn.

He'd taken to wearing wire-rimmed glasses on the edge of his nose, cheap ones he'd found at some outdoor stall. I wasn't sure he really needed them. I thought he was just going for the image. With his long nose and wide-stretched mouth, that shock of white hair, the glasses on his long face made him look like an eccentric. I studied his face. I could never get enough of his face. A year after we started dating, when we were still living in Tokyo, I looked at his face once and realized his face had become my face. We shared a face. He looked up and caught my eye.

"How do you feel about Jodhpur?"

"It's on our list."

"How do you feel about Jodhpur in two days?" I held up the letter, explained about Yuriko and Asha.

He looked down. I didn't like the way he was shielding his eyes.

"We're going there anyway," I said quickly. "You're always the one going on about being flexible, right? We don't *have* to be anywhere at any specific time."

"Queenie," he said, and paused. Something was coming. I felt it in the hairs on the back of my neck. He pursed his lips and nodded, like he was figuring out how to say it. I held my breath.

"I've been wanting to ask this for a while now, but I didn't know how." He lit a cigarette, took a deep drag and blew the smoke upward. He clicked his tongue and sighed. "I want a few days alone. I *need* a few days alone. What if we go to Jodhpur and I take a few days to myself?"

He was leaving me. I was losing him. I wanted to scream. *Don't leave me, Finn. There is too much leaving. Too much loss. Please? I have nowhere else to go. You are my home.* The threat of returning to Missouri loomed monstrous.

I tried to smile. "That sounds good," I said.

He breathed a sigh of relief, stabbed out his cigarette, and went back to reading his letter.

When I said goodbye to Finn at the hotel in Jodhpur, the few-days break had evolved into two weeks. He kept adding days to his alone time while I sat staring at him, unable to speak. The new plan was for me to meet him two weeks hence in Jaisalmer, a twelve-hour train ride away, on the edges of Rajisthan. He wasn't clear with me how long he'd be touring around Jodhpur before he headed to Jaisalmer. He kept the details vague and I was terrified to ask.

I didn't question being a single woman traveling alone on a train in a foreign country. Maybe for most women this would be scary, but for me, my whole life had been lived alone. I'd done things by and for myself since I was five years old. Maybe I should've argued. Maybe I should've played the fragile girl card, but the truth was I'd done everything alone and by myself for as long as I could remember. As a child, my mother gave me free reign. I'd overheard her once telling an aunt, "Pearl can do everything by herself, so I just let her." I knew she meant this as a compliment, but what she didn't understand was that she set me up for a lifetime of being alone. Sometimes I blamed her. Sometimes I was sure she'd meant to do that to me. I was sure her punishment for me was this lifetime of solitude, as if my eager curiosity and my desire to see everything in this world was something to be punished for, or something she desired and could never have for herself.

With Finn, I said nothing. Nodded and agreed. I wanted to cry out, but instead I was mute. I couldn't find my voice.

Jodhpur was a blue city. The buildings were notorious for their blue paint, alleyways of cerulean, hotels of indigo, rows of shops painted the same sea-green. Women in white saris and men in white dhotis seemed to float through this oceanic landscape. White bulls with sharp horns roamed freely, like some abstract painting. The crowning glory of the chaotic city of squat crumbling buildings was a massive fort that towered over the skyline, high on vertical rock cliffs that were cut smooth; the fort appeared to be carved directly into the mountaintop.

I sat at a rooftop restaurant of the high-end hotel with Asha and Yuriko. The table top was covered with shattered mirrors and broken tiles that tittered in the waning sunlight. Around us, exotic plants flourished, each table surrounded by its own garden, with the view open behind us, looking out over the sky-colored city.

For months in Asia, Finn and I had been staying in cheap digs, which in Asia meant mold growing green on the walls, filthy bathroom tiles, skittering roaches, cold-water showers. This hotel was plush and rich with tapestries, and I thought I'd died in some remote jail cell and gone straight to an abundant heaven.

Yuriko and Asha too were lush and fat. They sat back in their chairs, legs extended, a comfort between them. I was on the edge of my seat bent forward.

"Pearl, you're getting too skinny again. You're disappearing. You're going to float away. Dear god, *eat* something," Yuriko said, piling my small plate with samosas and veggie cutlets.

They filled me in on life in Tokyo. Yuriko had always been tall and robust. She was half-Japanese and half-American. She'd left Seattle and moved to Japan to find the other half of her ancestry. Now she'd gained weight, and was even more imposing, her thick black hair longer now, to her waistline. She had a Japanese face and the wide hips of a Westerner. She took up space. She was like a warrior princess. Her paintings were selling. She was doing less English teaching. She was becoming a bit of a Tokyo fringe celebrity.

Asha was small, round, brown. You could fall into her and rest there. In Tokyo, she'd worn black, but today she wore light, loose-fitting Indian trousers that buttoned at the ankles, an anklet with bells; her jewelry jangled and chattered as she moved. Her perfume was light, like the sound of kids playing tag outside a summer window.

She was explaining that she had been promoted at her banking job. I was never sure what she did, but she was Indian and spoke Japanese, and I knew it wasn't easy for an Indian woman to make it in such a male-dominated industry. I never really knew how to talk to Asha. We were on different planes. I knew nothing about finance. Still, I felt good energy coming from her toward me.

Yuriko and Asha didn't touch. You could see their natural instinct was to reach over and touch each other while they talked. You could see them stop themselves. People touched a lot in Southeast Asia, but not if you were gay. I was sure they'd discussed it. No touching while visiting the parents. Once they started touching, they wouldn't be able to stop, and the consequences could be dire.

"We want you to come and stay with us at Asha's parents. Okay?" Yuriko said.

I nodded.

"We're not out to them," she said, playing with her napkin, not looking up.

I nodded.

Asha jumped in. "It is taboo here." Her voice changed, her Indian accent heightened. "They kill people for it. It is, and I quote, highly immoral and against the social order." She looked at Yuriko, but Yuriko wouldn't look back at her. "Well, let's not discuss it," Asha said. Yuriko looked upset. "You were the one, Yuriko-chan, who forced me to come on this trip. Remember that."

I couldn't even begin to imagine what it was like to have such restrictions on love. Finn and I touched all the time. Held hands. Kissed. The only thing stopping us from meeting each other's families was distance in his case, and estrangement in mine.

The sun set in streaks of yellow. I imagined Finn out there somewhere playing his flute with local musicians. He had a right to do his thing. I was all for independence. All my life, I believed a person had a right to be themselves. Lord knows that was the truth for me, too. The breeze coming in at dusk was not as full of smoke today, just the faint scent of what smelled like barbecue. I realized that the smoke had been dissipating for days now and I just hadn't noticed. The breeze was so gentle I found myself relaxing back into the chair. I ordered my favorite dish, chicken korma. We laughed and drank too much wine. The energy between Asha and Yuriko uncoiled. At one point, the three of us got up and danced, each of us alone, dancing in a circle in the fading light around the table.

Yuriko asked about my visions. I was drunk so I told her about the Usui sightings. How it was like he was right there in front of me. How when he didn't show up regularly, I missed him, how he was always trying to get me on the straight and narrow.

Asha perked up. I was surprised she found it interesting, with her business brain. "In Japan, they believe the dead ancestors visit often. For Japan, such visitations are normal," she said, wobbling her head. As she drank, her mannerisms became more Indian. "When I was a girl, I, myself, encountered ghosts," she said. "In India, we accept such things. We have tales of witches floating near the ceiling. Sometimes during reincarnation, the spirit doesn't enter another body, but just witnesses. We are not like Americans where everything must be practical and logical and fit into linear thought boxes, and be lined up and quantified. We call them *bhoot*."

"What?" Yuriko drunkenly turned toward her and reached out to put her hand on her arm but stopped herself. "You saw ghosts?"

"Yes, after she died, Grandmother appeared to me holding persimmons. She wore her special sari, and hold out the fruit and throw her head back and laugh with great mirth. I didn't remember her with persimmons in life. Later, I looked it up and persimmons mean the wisdom that comes after much transformation. Young persimmons are bitter. Mature ones sweet."

Yuriko leaned in to kiss her, but Asha ducked. "Why have I never seen ghosts? It's really not fair," Yuriko said.

Asha turned to me and said, "Yuriko has told me about your visions. You must not think this makes something wrong with you—that is the problem." She studied her wineglass. "Well, we all think that there is something wrong with us, do we not?" Her lips were stained red with Merlot. Yuriko and I watched her and waited for her to speak, but she just kept staring into her wineglass.

Yuriko asked me more about the visions, but I was too drunk. I didn't want to open that door. If I took my visions seriously, if I entered that world and accepted it as my fate or my karma or my purpose, where would I end up? Somewhere even worse than going back to Missouri. I shuddered at the thought.

I'd booked a room down the hall from them. It was my first night of luxury in many months. I took a forty-five-minute shower. The bed swallowed me up. All night I tossed and turned. I kept reaching for Finn, but he was not there.

Asha's house had a shrine. It was strung with fairy lights, bordered by tapestries, and on the altar were bowls of herbs and a necklace of flowers hanging from a statue of Ganesha. I had to force myself to sit politely and not dig my god book out of my backpack. The only "god" we'd had in my house growing up was a massive framed picture of Jesus, bloodied and hanging from the cross. Again, I wondered at the difference in the psyche between a culture whose god suffered and bled from your walls, and one where deities had dancing arms and the heads of elephants. I preferred the latter.

This was the first Indian home I'd entered since we'd arrived in the country. It was an Indian fable, ornate mirrors and tables, thick colorful pillows, tapestries hanging from the walls. A shelf of ancient glass bottles filled with colored liquid at the window threw odd blotches of rainbows along the heavy tiled floor.

Asha's mother was imposing in a white sari with golden trim, festooned with necklaces and earrings, anklets and bracelets. She was short, wore her dark hair up, sat straight, spoke carefully, and was always polite. She scared the hell out of me.

Asha's father twittered around, fussing with things in the

background. We drank chai and had pastries in the living room, and afterward Asha's mother moved us to the courtyard for dinner.

I had to stop myself from exclaiming. The courtyard was mystical in its ramshackle beauty. A carved round table in the center of plant chaos. Many of the trees drooped heavy with fruit. It was a succulent, aromatic, heady place. They'd hung stained glass over a low wall and colors blew like confetti across the scene. I wanted to grab Asha's thick, jangling wrist and exclaim at the life she was born into, but her eyes were downcast and her shoulders bent. Yuriko moved like a bull in a china shop. She was huge and awkward in the surroundings, and silent. I'd never seen Yuriko silent.

The dinner reached our noses before it reached the table. I had fallen in love already with Indian cuisine, but these aromas were altogether something new. Like an orchestra of smells, dancing around each other. Turmeric, chili powder, cinnamon, nutmeg, cloves, ginger, garlic. Indian spices reminded me of incense, and incense was sacred, something they wafted around during Catholic mass; the smells turned the moment into the divine. It felt like a dream, a dream full of beauty, and ghosts and monsters. A dream of shadows, and secrets.

A bent, elderly cook brought the dishes to a sideboard, and Asha's mother brought them to the table. The rice was speckled with cashews, raisins and almonds. A plate steeped with large, handmade naan. She named the dishes as she brought them over: baigan bhartha (eggplant puree), palak bhaji (fried spinach), tandoori chicken.

The spices played upon the tongue like music. I'd never tasted food so nuanced. I wished Finn was there so we could talk about it later. As the cook brought the dishes to the sideboard, I wanted to throw myself at her feet. There was magic in the food. I wanted to say this, but I looked up from eating and noticed Asha and Yuriko picking at their food, staring at their plates.

Asha began arguing with her mother in Hindi. Their voices rose. Everyone stopped eating. I looked at Yuriko and she gave me a look to say she didn't know what was going on either. Asha's mother angrily left the table. The father sat shyly and said nothing. He had a round puffy face and kind eyes.

Asha said, "She has set up for me to meet with a man. He is coming soon, for dessert. He is to be here in 30 minutes. She said she didn't tell me earlier because she did not want to cause me anxiety. She wants me to meet him, and consider him for marriage."

I watched Yuriko recoil. I left my body, floated above the scene, and looked down upon the heads of the four of us as we sat at a festooned table in an exotic courtyard, like figures of a bygone era, painted and drawn into a brightly colored picture book.

His name was Bishal. He was tall and awkward, and seemed like a perfectly nice person. As he sat down on the sofa in the living room, Yuriko excused herself. I followed, thinking she was going back to the bedroom that the three of us were sharing, but instead she went out the front door. She walked so fast down the street, I had to run to catch up.

"Do you have a cigarette?" she called back at me.

"You don't smoke." I coughed as I ran and caught up with her.

She gave me a look so withering, I took out two Gold Flakes, lit them both, and handed her one. She coughed with the first drag, and stubbornly took another hit.

She turned into a restaurant, sat at the first table, and ordered a Kingfisher. The waiter brought two glasses. She drank it down fast, and ordered another. Drank that one down. She was on her fifth or sixth glass by the time I'd finished one. We were drawing the attention of the others in the restaurant. When traveling, I didn't like to draw attention. It was better to be invisible. I was good at going unseen. I had an invisibility cloak I could muster at any time. People would act like I wasn't even there. I learned it as a child. The gifts that came with an angry father.

"It's not like I think she's going to get married," Yuriko said.

I had no idea what to say to this, so I said nothing.

"It's not being able to be who you are." She took a Gold Flake out of my pack on the table, lit it, inhaled and coughed.

Men were staring at Yuriko. I'd forgotten how much people noticed her. She looked like an Amazon Japanese woman. She used to fuck a lot of men, in all sorts of positions. I knew, because I lived on the other side of her paper-thin Tokyo walls. I knew more about Yuriko's sex life than anyone on the planet. Men found something about her that fit a fantasy—strong-willed sexual American with the face of a Japanese woman, and all that implied.

An older man entered the restaurant, stared at Yuriko, leaned as he passed our table, said something and smacked his lips. Yuriko made a fist and started to get up. I put my hand on her arm.

She sat back down, her hand still in a fist, and said, "You have no fucking idea how hard it is to just exist. I cannot stand not being allowed to be myself. To touch the person I love. To even speak about it. To live a lie like this. It's so much fucking bullshit." I kept my hand on her arm. She kept looking at the smacking lip guy who was staring at her, and I had no doubt she would get up and punch him in the face if I let go of her arm.

She ordered another beer. I didn't know how it would go down for us to go back to Asha's house with Yuriko so drunk she couldn't walk. "Should we drink coffee, Yuriko? I want a coffee. Have a coffee with me."

She looked up and burst into sobs. She put her forehead against my upper arm and sobbed. I didn't know how to touch, so I let her cry there, felt the tears on my arm. People looked at us, but instead of rank curiosity, there was something different now. I noticed compassion in the faces. I'd seen it before in India in a way I never saw it in the States. A level of compassion that only tough times and brutal poverty could engender.

An Indian woman came to the table. She spoke soft Hindi to Yuriko, and rubbed her back. She was bent and old and wore a tattered sari that was deep gold, but probably used to be bright yellow. Her front teeth were missing, and the lines on her face were a spidery web. It was a face that had seen much pain. Yuriko put her head against the woman. The old woman made clucking noises, and put gnarled hands against Yuriko's pale cheeks. It was an image that would stay with me.

By the time we got back to the house, it was past 10:00 p.m. Yuriko could hold her liquor. She could walk, and as long as she didn't speak too much, she appeared to be okay. The cook opened the door. She reminded me of the woman at the restaurant, a look in her eyes of deep knowing. She pointed down the hall to the bedroom. We found Asha sitting hunched over on one of the single beds. Yuriko fell into her arms. I shut the door. They cried together. I stood back and picked my thumbs bloody.

Asha looked up with a face streaked with tears, and said, "Pearl, what have we landed you in the middle of?"

"I landed Yuriko in the middle of my stuff plenty of times in Tokyo," I said, sucking my bloody thumb.

Yuriko got up and paced. "So, how was your new fiancé?" It came out hard, bitter and drunken.

"Do not blame him. You know, this is not his fault."

Yuriko spat, "Who should I blame?"

"Me." Asha took a pillow, buried her head in it and cried. Yuriko kept pacing. Asha reached out, but she wouldn't go to her.

"You have to come out to them, Asha. It's the only fucking way. So we're going to go back to Tokyo and they're going to call you and discuss your fiancé with you while I sit quietly in the background?"

Asha cried. Yuriko paced. I went to Asha, and put my hand on hers on the bed. I wasn't a toucher, or a hugger. It just wasn't done in the place where I grew up. I didn't know how to tell Asha, *I had to leave my family, too, to be myself. I had to leave everyone and everything I loved to be myself. It left a hole so big that it haunts me. You think you will meet someone and they will fill it, but they cannot. They cannot.*

Asha looked at my hand and into my eyes, and it was like she could read my mind. For a while, we remained this way. Asha crying. Me sitting. Yuriko pacing, grabbing her hair, swearing under her breath.

After a while, Yuriko softened. She came to Asha. I got up. They hugged. I worried about whether there was a lock on the door, and got up to check.

They could not sleep in the same bed without getting caught. Later, we each went to our single beds. I heard Asha throughout the night, trying to muffle her tears with her pillow.

The next morning, Yuriko was snoring like a sailor. Asha wasn't in her bed. I went out to use the toilet. Passing the kitchen, I saw Asha and her mother. I stood at the doorway and watched. They were leaning over the counter, drinking coffee, speaking in low tones, food that smelled like coconut and ginger brewing at the stove. There was a quiet peace about them. I thought of my mother. We used to have this, too. That feeling of simple belonging.

I knew then in some psychic place that this would be the last time Asha would ever have such a time with her mother. That quiet certainty of love. I had lost the same thing with my mother. I knew what that felt like. The severing. The desire not to break it right away, the need to hold on. I felt myself cracking open, and scurried quickly to the bathroom to cry, for such a loss, for my loss, and Asha's and for every mother and daughter torn apart. The crevasse it left, unfillable.

Taking the longer route back to the bedroom to avoid the

kitchen, I came across the father in the living room. His back was to me at the shrine, and he was plugging in the fairy lights and murmuring to the Hindu god. He went to the window with the bottles of colored water and rearranged them. I realized he was the one who had created all of the colors, light and beauty in the house. I'd assumed it was the mother or an interior designer, but it was the father. The idea surprised me. He turned, saw me staring and smiled humbly.

After a childhood of one brutal man, in my life kept appearing gentle men. Each time, their appearance surprised me—Jason, Usui, now Asha's father—the relief of their existence, the grief inside them.

"Would you like to see the shrine," he asked in strongly accented English.

"Yes," I said. "I would love to."

The golden metal statue of Ganesha sat in a metal bowl. The flowers around the statue's neck had been removed. Ganesha was one of my favorite gods, with his elephant head and gentle energy. The father took a small pitcher and poured water over the god's head.

"I am purifying Ganesha," he said. He closed his eyes and seemed to be praying, and then said, "I think every family wants what is best, even if many of us do not know how to provide that. I am asking for the best for my family."

When he'd finished washing Ganesha, he took a small towel and dried him. He removed the bowl of water and dressed Ganesha again with the strand of flowers.

"Here," he said. "Please, place hands out, with the palms facing."

I did so. He took a spoonful of water from the bowl and placed it in my palm. "Now I am offering you this blessing, too, that you will have the best for your family."

I felt like crying, kept my head down and nodded.

When I got back to the bedroom, Asha was sitting with Yuriko and they were holding hands.

"Asha is going to tell them as soon as we get back to Tokyo," Yuriko said.

"I just cannot do it in person. I am sorry. Not in person," Asha said.

I felt the death of her old life in her. I wanted to go up and hug her. Instead I sat on my bed. They told me that Asha was going to tell her parents that she was being called back to Tokyo on a work emergency and had to leave immediately. We'd be moving back to the hotel today. They couldn't stay in Jodhpur because someone Asha knew might see them. They were going to change their flights and go back to Tokyo as soon as possible. They apologized to me, but it wasn't about me. I would be okay. I was used to being alone, had taken care of myself since I was old enough to walk.

At the door a few hours later when we said goodbye, Asha's mother's face tweaked in fury, but she was ever so polite. They hugged, but when Asha tried to hold on, her mother pulled back. Yuriko was already outside the front door, standing on the sidewalk, watching. I was still in the living room, not having maneuvered myself well, caught in the torture of these final goodbyes.

The father came up and hugged Asha with force. I stared at Asha's face over his shoulder. He held on tight. She squeezed her eyes closed and stood very still as if any movement might open the floodgates. It came to me then, suddenly. *The father is gay.* It came to me as a deep truth, one the whole family knew but pretended not to. I understood that he knew his daughter was gay. That he knew who Yuriko really was. That he had lived a life of pretense, that he knew what it took to be and what it took not to be.

I watched the mother watching them. She knew too, somewhere deep down; she understood the truth about both of them. I didn't know if it was a conscious knowing or one she'd pushed so deep she didn't even remember it. Like my mother, she just wanted normal. All of her life, she just wanted something middle-class and normal.

As we said our final goodbyes from the stoop, the top of the mother's bent head as she looked down, the jangle of her bracelets, the slow closing of the door, I thought of my mother.

After I left, my mother thought I didn't love her, but it was the opposite. I loved her so much I was willing to give up myself for her.

That was why I had to run away.

CHAPTER 25 ½

I dance with her in the other world. She is the color of blue sky, I am the crimson hue of flames. Our souls in another dimension, giddy with light, have danced like this before. Many times, through many lifetimes. She is always azure, a shimmering. I am a flickering of red, a tinge of yellow and orange with a center of purple ice. Trailing from both of our arms and legs, the spectrum of the rainbows we throw off is like nothing on this earth, the way we compliment and color each other.

I am dancing with my mother. I am dancing with her in another realm. I have a memory as we dance. I am a tiny child in the kitchen of the farmhouse. She is baking, flour everywhere. Mixing, kneading, rolling. I go to a bottom drawer, tug and pull and fumble. I drag a pan to her, try to lift it up. My little girl gift to you, Mother, this pan.

"How did you know exactly the pan I needed?" She looks down at me in surprise. "Pearl, you are such a smart girl. You see so much, don't you?" She reaches down, takes the pan and keeps staring down, shaking her head.

It is the seeing that gets me into trouble. It is the thing that I do best that is my downfall. It is me being me that gets me thrown out.

Still we dance. In that other realm, souls have their own language. My mother and I may be estranged in this world, but in that other realm, *our movement never ceases. Tint and hue mix and intermingle, the spectral light we leave in our wake. All my life, when I see the color of sky, that oceanic refraction, if I see a scarf or dress or blueberry eyes, if I am in a city in India where every building is painted blue, I think of my mother, of our universal dance, and I miss her. I miss her. I miss her.*

Love never ceases. In that other world.

She used to say to people, "That Pearl, she can do anything she puts her mind to. You just have to stay out of her way."

But I don't want her to just stay out of my way. I don't want everyone to just stay out of my way. I am so tired of the storms, Mother. I need someone here to help calm the weather.

"Pearl," my mother replies. "Don't you know? You are the storm. You were born of fire and wind. There is nothing anyone can do. It is who you are."

2 6

I **opened my eyes.** It tried to focus. An Indian woman held my face and cooed, her arthritic hands awkward against my cheeks. A crimson jewel rested in her third eye, like a bindi, but this was a precious gem—her forehead glowed the color of amber.

"Mother?" I jerked and hit my head on the window.

The woman spoke in Hindi. Her sari was lavender and rimmed in gold. Earrings with sapphire stones dangled in her long hair. She had the lined face of the poor, the gnarled hands of someone who'd known too much work, the boniness of poverty.

It took a while to figure out where I was. Outside, the train rushed over a midnight landscape. The packed car was full of guttural snores. Somewhere a baby cried. I was on the top bunk of a sleeper car, speeding my way to Jaisalmer to meet Finn.

The woman reached out for me again, cooing, fingers long and nails dirty. I pressed against the dark window. My pack was on the floor. I assumed I'd kicked it off the berth during the vision.

The woman leaned to the bunk below, said something in Hindi to someone, and came back up with the offer of a single triangle of an orange slice. I accepted it.

I had no idea how to maneuver this mundane reality after that journey into the soul world. It was jarring, a leap. That the two worlds existed in separate realms befuddled me. That others only seemed to live in the mundane world scared me, as if the only way I could exist in this world was through constant, perpetual pretense.

The woman smiled and began to move away. I put my hand on her shoulder. She was surprisingly fragile. I said, "Thank you." She smiled and nodded, put her hand to my cheek.

I had to go to the bathroom. The urge was sudden and intense. I leaned my legs over the bunk. The floor of the train was jammed with bodies. The aisle was impassable. People were sleeping everywhere. Single bunks were filled with at least two people, and there were men jammed beneath the bottom bunks and the floor. And the middle aisle itself was a chaos of arms, legs, heads, feet and hips, men, women, children.

There was no way I could wait. I put my foot on the corner of the bottom bunk. The man, perhaps the husband of the woman who'd helped me, looked up at me. There was a compassion in his eyes that I didn't want to deal with. I surveyed the floor for some foot purchase. The train was lurching and I swayed as I clung to the bunk pole.

I swung one foot to the edge of the next bunk, like a monkey. Still nowhere on the floor to put my feet. I swung again to the next bunk. At each bed, the person woke up and stared up at me. I swung bunk to bunk to the end of the car. At the narrow door to the toilet, I realized I was barefoot. I opened the door. The squat toilet was crud-encrusted. The floor, the platform, the edges around the hole in the floor, all of it was covered with feces. I looked at my feet. I looked at the floor. I had to pee so badly I could barely stand still.

I grew up squatting in the woods. I didn't have a problem with squatting. The entire trip throughout Southeast Asia had been about squatting to poop and pee. We had come across some challenging toilets, places where you just knew the toilet could infect and kill you, but this surely was the worst.

Jiggling with the growing urge to pee, I turned, hooked my foot on the bottom of the bunk closest to me and made my way back hand over fist to my bunk. I grabbed my flip-flops and as I was swinging back toward the toilet, a voice in my head said, "The primal dance." I swore it was the voice of my mother. Like the dance we'd just done in my vision, this was the primal "pee" dance. From bunk to bunk, Mother and I danced our way back toward the bathroom. I laughed and people woke up and stared.

It was still four hours until we reached Jaisalmer. I couldn't sleep, and thought about Yuriko and Asha, thought about spending a life of pretense. After the two left Jodhpur, I spent the next eleven days roaming around the tourist sites. I moved to a cheaper hotel to save money. I expected to run into Finn, but he was nowhere. I imagined he'd just picked a place on the map, and grabbed a local bus. He was that kind of traveler. He could disappear like me.

I put on my invisibility cloak and roamed Jodhpur. I could have gone missing, and no one would even have known. I did disappear. And no one knew.

The article was boring, a run-of-the-mill piece on a tourist attraction. I kept wanting to write, "Blah, blah, blah," instead of words. The real story was Asha. But I wasn't telling those kinds of tales. I wrote the boring article, tried to play with the language to give it more depth, but nothing seemed to work. I couldn't shake the feeling that my whole life I'd been pretending, my whole life I'd been telling the wrong kinds of stories.

Travel was like my visions. It threw up sudden visions, singular tableaus, events without context, months with no through line. Travel and my visions were like novels without coherence, scenes that were riveting but led nowhere, characters who came and went, who didn't stick around to fulfill the plot. Life came in spurts, with scenes that were glorious or horrible, people who appeared and disappeared. And you were left afterward, shocked and moved, trying to make sense of it all.

Of any country we'd visited, India was most like my visions. Every day held sights and smells and situations I couldn't seem to wrench from my psyche afterward.

One morning, I was reading the guidebook and making notes on what I could write an article on, when a man entered through the french doors to of the old hotel where we were staying, into our room. I started up when I saw it wasn't Finn.

"Who are you?"

"I work for the hotel, madam. I give massages. I am here to give you a massage."

I felt no danger, just annoyance. "Get out."

"You need a massage. I can see it. You are full of stress." He grabbed my arm and tried to move it above my head.

"Get out!" I yelled.

He wagged his finger in my face. "Next time, you don't want massage, you lock door!" He went out. I got up and locked the door. Finn came back a few hours later, and we changed hotels.

That night, late at night, I found myself passed out in the middle of the cobbled road. It'd begun a couple of hours earlier at a cafe. Finn had been talking about the bhang lassis they served at cafes in Jaisalmer, long before we got here, yogurt drinks filled with marijuana.

On the glass were fingerprint smudges and smeared lipstick that was not mine. Finn sat across from me. He'd shaved his head during our time apart, and looked angular and hard, like a skeleton tree in the burning forest. His ears stuck out with his haircut, his face long and beautiful in its ugliness. Two other people sat in the cafe, an old man and what looked like his son. They leaned into each other and spoke in whispers.

Finn kept asking me if I felt something as we drank the bhang lassis. I didn't know what to say. I felt a lot of things. Fatigue mostly.

I'd had some time to check out the city. It was the India of children's books. The buildings were sandcastles built from the Thar Desert. The city rose from the desert like a mirage. Ninety-nine bastions encircled twisted lanes. The streets were cobbled and many of the massive doorways were arched and carved with pictures and symbols. The doors were thick and wooden and had handles bigger than a man's head. Our room had arched windows closed with old wooden shutters, embroidered blankets glittering with mirrors and dangling with fringe. It was a place I could sink and sink into, a place I might fall down into and never get up.

Finn asked again if I was feeling something. He'd had adventures while we were apart, and I was sure he'd only told me half of them. I noticed my nails had gotten as dirty as the Indian woman's on the train. I tried to scrape out the dirt with a miniature plastic knife. *What am I feeling? So many things, Finn. What are you feeling? The crevasse between us seems to be widening, deepening.*

It was my first time ingesting marijuana. I'd smoked it but had never eaten it. I had no experience. I scraped and scraped at the dirt beneath my nails. Soon, the edges blurred. my body movements slowed. I saw trails when Finn moved his hand. As my body reacted, my mind became clear. There was something about this that was making me upset, but I wasn't sure why. Hysterical even. My mind was sharp and clear, but my body was stoned. I felt like I had no control of my arms and legs. I grew more and more upset. Was it the loss of control in a place where I felt I already had absolutely no control?

We finished our pint glasses, paid and went outside. It was pitch-black. There had been no rain, but the cobblestone pathways were wet with some kind of fluid. Grime seemed to be deeply lodged into the building walls, into the corners, into every nook, every crack on every surface.

The only light streamed out from the few open shops. The street back to our hotel was narrow, like an alley, tall buildings on both sides. The hysteria inside me grew. I slowed and then stopped. I couldn't get my feet to move. *This was supposed to be fun? This was supposed to be enjoyable?* My arms wouldn't respond to my commands. I felt my chest go numb, and I grew terrified I would stop breathing.

Then I fell down. Into the slime on the cobblestones. I was on my back, utterly unable to move. Finn stood over me.

"I can't move my body," I cried. "I shouldn't have had so much. A teacup would've been more than enough." My mind was clear, but when I tried to say these things the muscles in my mouth had trouble moving and it came out garbled. I blamed Finn. He should've known better than to let me drink a full pint glass. It was his fault.

Men started to congregate around me as I lay on my back. One led over a sacred cow, and it too stared down at me. A dozen brown faces, Finn's and the heifer's. The buildings on both sides rose to peaks. In the night sky, stars glittered like halos around each of the men's heads. My mind remained clear. Stone-cold sober.

Finn said, "Let's wait. It'll wear off. You'll be able to move soon." I was mortified. I was sure it just wasn't done in India to be a woman lying in the middle of the road in the pitch-black night. I was scared for my safety, not just now, but later. That I had somehow marked myself as such a woman, a "fallen" woman in the real sense of the word.

Finn tried to help me up by pulling on my arm, but I flopped like a heavy wet mattress. The Indian men did not reach to help, and I was thankful, because I didn't trust them. I explained in gobbled words to Finn that he would have to carry me. He had never carried me before. He bent and picked me up. I flopped in his arms like a rag doll.

"Pearl, you're so slight," Finn said. "Like a feather." We walked away from the crowd, up the road, my head lolled back. Near the hotel, someone had strung lights. The twinkling lights like a universe of stars.

"If you don't start eating, you're going to blow away in a strong wind," Finn said.

On the far reaches of the old town of Jaisalmer, they were building a funeral pyre. Fin and I watched. It took all day. The three young men worked methodically. This was their business, a profession of fire and death.

A pile of narrow tree trunks had been dumped. Two young men carried a metal plate from a beat-up truck and placed it on the ground. The air and the wind were important. If you placed the logs on top of each other, and fit them too tightly, the fire wouldn't catch. Because I'd learned to build fires early in life, I was fascinated by them. As Finn and I stood watching, a breeze blew from the east. They angled the metal grate to take the wind.

The first layer of trees went one way, the second layer criss-crossed the first. They started out by creating a wide base. As the pyre grew to about six feet, they narrowed the platform until it was just large enough to hold a human body. They were careful to roll the logs this way and that to build an even surface on each level. If it was lopsided, it might burn too hard on one side, and whole thing might collapse, the body roll off.

I gave a running commentary while they worked. Finn looked at me sideways like *how do you know so much about funeral pyres.*

We were not the only ones watching. Mangy dogs came up and poked their noses, a cow roamed beside us, pushing air hard through its nostrils. Two goats were tethered to a young boy in tattered trousers who looked no more than seven years old. An old woman nearby squatted and rocked, folded hands to her fore-head. A group of young men watched from the other side. Every-thing in India was a spectacle.

Later we talked about it with the hotel manager. He told us the custom was to cremate the dead within twenty-four to forty-eight hours, so Finn and I went back often to the finished pyre. We were at a roof garden having lunch when a commotion stirred below. We ran to the building's edge. Four men carried a stretcher on their shoulders, holding a body swathed in white. Around and behind them dozens, if not hundreds, of people, women in wildly colorful saris, people calling, or crying, or yelling, or laughing. Amidst the people, dogs and goats and an occasional cow. This was the funeral procession we'd been waiting to see.

Finn ran back to the table, dropped a pile of rupees. We scur-ried down the stairs to the street. Soon, we were swallowed by the procession. I lost my hold on Finn—he slipped from me, driven along by the crowd. His head stuck up above everyone else and bobbed several feet in front of me.

The swarm was as thick and fast as a Missouri River current. I didn't like crowds. The sheer quantity of smells and textures and energy quickly overwhelmed me. I tried to turn back, but there was no way I could go against the current. I was moved relentlessly forward.

A woman next to me draped a pink scarf over my head. I looked down at her and smiled as we were jostled forward. A woman behind her threw a hasty sari over my shoulders. She motioned for me to wrap it around my front. I did this, almost falling in the process. A scarf came from behind me and wrapped itself around my neck. I didn't see who had done it but turned and smiled awkwardly. I was now festooned in saris and scarves of lemons, yellow-greens and lavender. Toothless laughter all around from the older women. Finn turned back, nodded at me, raised his camera and took a picture. The massive crowd continued walking. Several blocks in front of us at the end of the cobbled road was the area where they'd built the pyre.

I was finding it hard to breathe, mostly from the anxiety of the jostling bodies. Something halted the procession. The bodies were so thick, we just stood and waited. No one could move anything but their arms. The woman next to me said something to the other women around me, pointing at me and laughing. Several women laughed. Hands then came from all sides, putting scarves upon scarves on my head and around my neck. The procession started moving again, but the hands would not stop. I felt the women's hands all over my body, squeezing my breasts, touching my thighs, feeling my ass. Hands grabbed at my fanny pack around my waste, unzipping it, rifling through it. A fist came out with a handful of my rupees. I slapped at the hands, smacked and pushed, and yelled. Suddenly we were spat out of the narrow street into the open area where the men were placing the body on the pyre. I grabbed the hand with my rupees and yanked the money back, struggling with an elderly woman in a dirty white sari.

"Queenie!" Finn yelled and ran to me.

I tore away, throwing off the scarves and saris as I ran, leaving a trail of colored scarves behind me. I caught up with Finn.

"All right?" Finn took my hand. I pulled him along, away from the women. A group of men stood close to the pyre. I dragged Finn and pushed our way in.

The swathed form lay on top of the pyre. I breathed erratically and kept my hand in a fist around the rupees. A young man placed tree branches on top of the body, until the body itself looked like just another piece of wood. They'd added bright scarves at the top of the wood pile, circling the body, and they dangled and blew in the wind like prayer flags.

One of the stretcher bearers paced three times around the pyre, reciting something. Dogs, goats, and cows roamed. People laughed, danced, wailed. One of the pyre builders poured some kind of petrol onto the pyre, evenly from head to toe. The reciting man was given what looked like a large rolled sheet of paper. He lit it, and put the flamed paper at the base of the wood pile.

Flames licked upward, devouring first the lattice of lower trunks, up the crisscrossed pyre, the alchemy of fire and trees, the heat that was created in the transformation, the way the meat of the wood broke down, became something necessary and out of control.

The brightly colored scarves danced and waved in multicolored flames. Then the fire found the flesh of the body.

Flames engulfed the body until you could no longer see it. But the aroma was overwhelming. Nauseating, sweet, putrid, steaky—the smell so thick it was almost a taste. Pork fat, sizzling beef, burnt liver, the keratin singe of frying hair, a copper-metallic scent of boiling blood. Finn and I and the rest of the crowd backed up when the smell and the heat became too intense.

I thought about my father's death. Usui's. There were no smells in those civilized funerals. No animals to bear witness. Here the sweet scent was so strong it lodged in the back of the throat, as if we were all eating the flesh of this human, taking what was left of him into our physical beings.

Something here was heavy and old. Something in the West that we'd learned to hide, to put from the mind, to forget. Something we'd learned to sanitize. Something here was real.

That night, Finn and I fucked hard and long. He stank of death, wood smoke and the boiling of blood, and so did I. I had a fever or flu that grew to a delirium and I let myself lose my mind. Finn was more aroused than I'd ever seen him by my thrashing. We both came at once, screaming out our right to be flesh, our desperation at being alive.

2 8

Yuriko **always said** that foreign countries were our karma. We were drawn to certain countries for reasons. If you figured out the reason, you'd figure out the lesson. If you figured out the lesson, your soul could fly. She also said that a country is a huge blank canvas where we get to paint our soulful journeys. With the year Finn and I were spending in Southeast Asia, I felt faced with more lessons than I could possibly learn this lifetime.

At the table at the window in our hotel room, I lit a cigarette and looked out over the sand-colored city. Finn wanted to go out and explore, but I couldn't. It wasn't the burning of the dead man. It was stimulation. My body was vibrating in all sorts of ways, and I could not calm it down. I needed woods and earth, but got only fire. Finn was trying to coax me out.

"I thought we were finished with this after the psychic," he said, playing with my hair.

"This isn't the same thing. This isn't black dog."

"What did that psychic say to you anyway?"

I shook my head. In a small voice, I answered, "He said I had to go backward, like a death, to go forward."

Finn played with my hair for a while. "It's not just the psychic. What happened with Asha and Yuriko? You haven't been the same."

"What?"

"Since I met you at the station, you've been… disconnected." He sat across from me at the table, lit a cigarette. "When you fell down after the bhang lassi, I didn't think the falling was just the bang."

"You should've told me it was so strong," I answered.

He shook his head, picked up the guidebook and flipped through it. I had a quick image of how my helplessness on the cobbled street had appeared through his eyes. I was like an infant, needing to be carried, like a helpless child.

"Maybe the crazy psychic was right. Have you thought about going back to Missouri to see your family?" he asked without looking up.

My knee jerked and hit the underside of the table and spilled my chai. *You want to get rid of me.* I sniffed and pushed down hard on the tears.

"I think you're more upset than you realize," Finn hastened to add. "And I think it's not just what the Indian psychic said. I think something happened with Asha and Yuriko."

I sat and smoked and didn't speak. I didn't want to open that door. Didn't want to begin that discussion.

He put his hand on mine. "All right, Queenie. It's okay then. No worries. No one will make you do anything you don't want to. All right, love?"

I nodded through the tears.

Later, he packed his day pack, came to me and put his hand flat on my back. "You sure you won't come?"

I shook my head. He patted down the top of my frizzy hair, kissed the top of my head and left.

I thought all afternoon about what he'd said. The thought of going back to Missouri had summoned the black dog. Seeing

Asha make the decision to leave her family… I had no words for it. My body felt on some edge. If I thought too long or too hard about it, I'd fall over that edge into a bottomless pit and never be able to get up again.

Home. Where was home? What was home? We ran into expats all the time on our travels, and during our years living in Tokyo. Some went back to their home country often, kept the connection to the traditions of their homeland, and even while abroad, hung out with their countrymen and together spoke the language of their culture.

I was not one of these. I had been gone from the States for five years now, and I'd never had any desire to hang out with Americans. I wanted as far away from everything American as I could get. I did not celebrate American holidays, did not watch television of any kind, did not read American newspapers. Besides the letters from Jason and Bonnie, which were full of their daily lives and did not cover national events, I had no idea whatsoever what was going on in the States. And I liked it that way.

It wasn't just Missouri I'd left, but the whole nation. Not just the country, but the continent. I was proud of myself, moving farther and farther away from the conditioning of the culture. Still, I didn't know sometimes if I was gaining perspective or losing myself, or both.

We'd met so many expats who'd talked about living abroad as an opportunity to reinvent yourself, you could be whoever you wanted to be. I could never get my head around this. How could any human let go of decades of conditioning? How could anybody reinvent themselves from nothing? Wasn't this reinvented self then nothing more than pretense? Wouldn't it take years of a deep understanding of who you really were, behind, below, and above all of the conditioning to truly reinvent yourself?

With the expat life, with travel, you left your roots, and all that such tradition entailed. Without family roots, who were you, really? You left your state, too, and without the land that was the flesh of your soul, who were you? You left country, and culture, and you had no idea how much it dictated your behavior until it was no more. You were daily faced with people and systems with entirely different perspectives, each moment driving a wedge into what you thought was immutable in your soul. In short, you were stripped of all the layers of paint that had been splashed across the canvas of your soul. It was my journey of growth, this expat life. I knew it even when I was a little girl. I knew I would travel the world, and it would strip me of everything I knew. I knew even as little as age five, I wanted this challenge, this growth, this soul's path. I just did not know how hard it would be.

What travel did do was leave you a blank slate. What it did was create an epic questioning. What it did not do, was teach you truly how to reinvent yourself.

I'd also traveled the world to see where I fit. Throughout Tokyo and now Southeast Asia, there was no way I would fit. I floated above. So many cultures where I didn't fit. The Thai woman reading tea leaves had told me how privileged I was. I could leave. These people in Asia were stuck here, stuck in this poverty. I was privileged enough to witness it, to float above, and to leave when it all got too much. What she didn't understand was that I didn't want to keep leaving. I was trying to find a place to call home, and all I was finding was places where I did not belong. I didn't fit in Missouri where I grew up. I didn't fit anywhere on these travels. And the only person I did fit with, Finn, was on the verge of leaving. My body shook with the vibrations of truth, and even a cold shower couldn't help.

Finn told me to go back to Missouri, to go home, as if that were still home. I'd never told him the full story of the estrangement with my mother. How she'd met and married someone else, and they'd banished me, how I'd lived with Jason and his mom to finish high school and go to college, how my mother had a new life now. He thought I needed to go back to Missouri to reconnect, but it was a place of the deepest disconnection.

I let dangerous thoughts in. Might it be true that what I needed was the soil beneath my fingernails again, the vastness of the Missouri sky? To build a fire out of Missouri wood? Was it my people I was pining for, or the earth?

If I left, I'd lose Finn. It would mean the death of all that I had tried to build over the past few years. And for that reason, I decided, lighting another cigarette, I couldn't go back. I wouldn't.

My camel's name was Baba. A fly fluttered into my right nostril and lodged there, quivering. "One went up my nose!" I turned and yelled back to Finn.

An Indian guide on the camel next to me mimed holding the other nostril and blowing hard. I did this. The fly blew out and fluttered away. Soon, another entered my mouth.

It was Finn's idea, this trek through the Thar desert, just the two of us and our three guides beneath the boiling sun in the vast sea of golden sand. He'd had to convince me. For days, my body wouldn't stop its vibrations. My hands shook. It was the stimulation. Months of it, but no. Years. I'd curl beneath the covers and beg the flesh to calm down. He'd convinced me to come on this trek with whispered tales of being close to the earth, with visions of sand and sky.

Around us, miles of beige. Hectares of sand. A neutral ground meeting a deep azure sky. The unrelenting sun. Finn's camel, Akbar, walked long-necked and proud, on high-trotting bulbous knees. My Baba seemed put upon, his head bowed as he trudged forward. I kept slipping sideways. The trek a study in constant rebalancing.

Beneath a scorching sun in this sandy world, women appeared like illusions on the horizon, flashes of neon-colored saris, pots balanced upon their heads. A heat shimmer undulated on the horizon, creating mirages, playing with the mind. Hours or minutes passed, the camels loping forward. My mind became lost in time and space. It wasn't a bad feeling. Maybe it wasn't that I needed to find myself back again, embody myself, maybe I needed to completely lose myself. Maybe I needed just to check out.

As the sun became low on the horizon, the guides pulled us to a stop. One of the men hauled a bag of camel dung, and built a fire with it. I squatted and watched him light the patties. They burned slow and hot, heat pulsating from the center. I was mesmerized by the glow, fascinated by the difference in the way wood and dung burned, the difference in the output of heat.

The sun went down, above us an epic clustering of stars I hadn't seen since the Philippines. The cook took out stores of flour, water and salt, and mixed it into bread balls. He threw them into the fire, into the dung. They were large, and the dung had broken apart, and the bread balls and the dung looked the same. You couldn't tell them apart. I watched the bread balls engulfed in the embers, wondering which was the shit and which was the food.

He had tins of fiery red meat curry, chicken, coriander, and rice. We sat around the pulsing fire as night fell, drinking bottled water and eating the food with our hands. I took a full-mouthed bite of the bread that had been cooking in our camel's shit to the delight of the three guides, who watched me closely and laughed. I noticed since I'd been in India that men often liked to watch white women eat. On the train to meet Finn in Jaisalmer, three men stood by my bunk and watched me eat a piece of fruit. They wouldn't stop watching until I finished the very last bite, and after I swallowed, still they stood and stared.

These desert men in red turbans, long white shirts and flowing trousers were also fascinated with how I ate. I moved closer to Finn. As night fell, the men's faces were ancient in the flickering firelight, above us a sea of pulsating stars. The camels were hobbled nearby, and made grunting noises.

One of the men began a story in English. An Indian desert tale about a mother who was called Star, and her children Fire, Wind, and Moon. It was hard to follow, with the pull of the stars and the grunting of the camels, unseen somewhere in the dark.

The children went to a feast. Fire and Wind were wild and selfish, eating and drinking, with no thought of anyone but themselves. Moon, however, thought of her mother at home, and filled the tips of her long fingernails with morsels of every dish.

That night when the children came home, their Star mother first asked Fire if he'd brought anything back. He became enraged. No, why should he think of anyone else, the party was his time to celebrate! Enraged with her spoiled son, his mother banished him to become the desert sun, to burn up everything in his path, to cause heat and suffering to many. Wind too was blustery and sure of himself. Going to a feast was his right, and he didn't have to think of anyone but himself.

Star, now more upset, transformed Wind to be hot and relentless and reside in the desert, that he might scorch everything in his path—to be unloved because of his bluster.

When it was Moon's turn, Moon said, Get as many plates as you have, Mother. Moon brought from beneath her fingernails the delicacies, which she placed on each plate.

The mother, happy with her third child, told her she would be placed up in the desert sky as gentle light that would guide people at night, and everyone from below would look to her with gratitude and love.

Finn was right. It was here where I wanted to be, around this fire, glowing up at the wizened faces of these weathered dark men, beneath the moon. When it was time to sleep, one of the guides took the pads that covered the camels' backs and put them a few yards from the fire in the sand for our beds. We said goodnight to our hosts and lay on our backs, looking up at the moon and stars. The blankets smelled like the sweat of the camels, and a few flies still buzzed. We swatted them away. I reached for Finn's hand. Above us, the sky was an interrupted miracle of dark and light. Somewhere in the dark far behind us, one of the guides had started singing, more of a wailing or a hum than a song, and it bled out over us into the night.

Finn looked at me, and his eyes were full of the mysteries. This was deeper than this moment; he had refilled his soul on his two-week walkabout. We'd never really spoken about what he'd done during his time away from me, but it was clear since we'd met at the Jaisalmer station, that he'd found himself again.

My body became filled with the fire of the far-off stars, and I wanted to take Finn in the sand right there. I knew somehow I would have to learn how to refill myself with the mysteries, as Finn had done. I would have to find a way. I would have to fill and refill often. I would have to do this if there was any way I was going to survive.

Someone was calling my name. I awoke to the sound of it but at first didn't understand if it was the guide still singing or the grunting camels. I sat up and looked around. Finn was fast asleep. There it went again.

"Pearl," came the voice on the wind. "Pearl." The moon had set, and there was no glow to see by, but the stars were bright. I got up and looked around. There it was again. "Pearl." I followed the sound. The sand shifted beneath my bare feet. I passed over a dune.

A fire glowed in the distance. I went to it. Someone was sitting with their back to me. I almost didn't see him at first. His hair was black and his clothes the same color as the sand. He was singing. It wasn't one of our guides, I was sure of it. I walked barefoot through the sand toward him.

CHAPTER 29 ½

"Usui, what are you doing here?"

I sit in the sand facing him, the dung fire between us, patties stacked like saucers, flames shooting skyward. Usui's eyes are filled with eternity. When I stare into them, I see myself: I am Wind and Fire, Moon and Stars. I see my body explode into a million pieces, fly outward and lodge into the elements. Parts of me blow into the air, burn up in the fire, shine in the sky; fractals of me end up as stardust. This is what death is like. I understand that I am feeling what it is like to die.

"Do you remember when you were a girl, how parts of you kept flying away? You promised someday you come find those missing parts, bring them back, reform yourself?"

"Usui, why are you here?"

"Do you remember?"

I do not like this question. I fear where it is leading.

"You are not the only one whose heart is broken, shattered into pieces."

Behind Usui, I see my blue dancing mother, but she floats away and I am not sure if she is real or a mirage.

"What happens when person is shattered? They create from just a

247

little clay, all the clay that they have left. They create self that is not real. It is not just you. Many. So many. Me too, when I was alive."

I look around for Finn, but we are alone.

"We must go back. Find the pieces that are scattered to the winds."

I won't answer him. He sounds like the psychic. He is the fork in the road. I do not want to know.

"You promised. You made a promise to the gods. To yourself. To the earth, that someday you would gather yourself back again. When? When is it time to seek those parts, find them and bring them home?"

Usui's body appears to be made up of millions of particles of sand. I am wind and could blow him into a thousand pieces.

"You are no different," I say. "Look at you, all tiny particles."

"Exactly, I am no different. I went into the desert in Tokyo to look in the face of myself. That is what I am trying to tell you. You not alone. Many have the broken heart. Can you not see?"

"What do you want from me, Usui? Why do you keep following me? Why will you not leave me alone?"

"It is time, Purr-chan. You know what that means. It is time to go home."

"I do not know where home is, Usui. You asked me once, 'Where is home?' But you never told me. Where is it, Usui? Missouri? I cannot go back there. Please."

Usui stands and looks at me. He throws dust into the fire. The flames explode, so bright and hot they lick outward and sear the flesh.

"I will help you go into the fire. Resisting will make it worse."

"I will not!" I scream.

Finn was shaking me. I was out of my body, looking down on my physical self. My body flopped like a rag doll.

"For fuck sake. What the fuck?"

I was plunged back into my body, the jarring and heaviness of it. I looked around. We were in the middle of the desert. There was no Usui, and no campfire. I could not see our sleeping mats, or the camel guides, or hear the camels.

"I cannot believe I even found you. What if I hadn't found you?" Finn was whispering so loud, it was worse than shouting. He tried to pull me to my feet but I was too wobbly to stand.

"This is getting bloody fucking dangerous, Pearl." Finn only called me by my real name when he was deeply upset. He was still whispering. "I thought someone had carried you away and was raping you in the goddamned desert." He squatted, put his hands beneath me and lifted me into his arms.

"Put me down. I can walk."

"Can you? Can you, Pearl?" He stumbled through the sand. I had apparently wandered quite far. His jaw was clenched as he placed one foot in the sand, shifted my weight, then took another step. He said almost to himself, "What am I going to do with you?"

Above our heads, the glittering lights of the universe. There on the horizon, the moon was just rising, shadowing our passage through the sand. *If I could gather everything I feel, all of the love I have for this world, Finn, beneath my nail, I would. I would offer you a feast.*

"I don't know how to fix this," he said, shifting me in his arms.

———

Unlike the other visions, I did not recover from this one. I grew ill. Finn took me to a doctor. The doctor put me in the hospital until they could figure out what was wrong. I was skeletal, too tired to move my body. They were running tests.

The hospital room should have held four people but housed ten, beds nearly touching, just enough room for a nurse to wedge through sideways. I was told by a doctor that people came to this hospital only to die. I was so weak the first two days that I was happy to lie there. I stared up at the white ceiling, content not to function. I had started to write in my journal, but I couldn't maintain the focus.

The woman next to me was dying. She had some wasting disease. Her flesh was stretched tight over bones, elbows and knees sharp and angular. Large eyes peered from a bony skull. She would turn and stare, as if she were seeing the universe in my face. When her head was hidden in the folds, I often didn't even know she was there.

Our beds were so close that I could hear her despite her weak voice. Her name was Lucina. She asked me if we could talk. She needed to talk. She was dying and she had much to say. She spoke English with a crisp British accent. She spoke about her life with faraway eyes. "When you are dying," she said, "it is important… to tell your story, to… someone."

After every fourth or fifth word, she would have to stop to breathe. "Mother and Father wished… for me to have a proper… marriage. I'd been partially… educated in London, so we found a suitable… husband, one who'd also had… a British education."

They'd had a good marriage, she stressed it, and I thought she was trying to figure out if that was true or not. Their three children were in boarding schools in the UK, getting the sort of education she and her husband had gotten. I figured she was in her thirties, but the disease had ravaged her youth and she looked far older.

"What is it I see… you writing every… day?" she asked.

I told her about the travel articles. Between bouts of exhaustion, I was trying to write a piece on the monkeys that had chased us in the monkey temple in Jaipur. I was behind schedule on my submissions.

"You… are a writer, then." She said it as a statement, not a question.

I nodded hesitantly. *Was I?* All of the travel articles blurred into a ball of fluff.

"I was a singer, you… know." A light seemed to enter her when she said the word singer. Her voice grew stronger. She didn't have to stop to breathe as often. "I studied with vocal masters as a child in India, and in the UK. I learned…traditional songs of India. Then I studied Western songs…secular and religious. People often spoke of the beauty of my voice. But they said…my voice was too unique, and didn't fit opera or any…other standard venue." She paused and looked lost behind her eyes. "Can you imagine being told you…are too unique?"

I turned to stare at the white ceiling. I'd already counted the cracks. Two hundred forty two.

"As you die, the memories… that appear to you are surprising. They are… not what you expect. I see… the view that I was looking at as I was singing. These are my dying memories… now. If I was looking out the conservatory… window at Hampstead

Heath, or upon a temple in Bombay, it is these visions that come to me. A grey-haired gentleman in a black overcoat walking his small dog in the autumn leaves, a saffron-robed monk lighting long sticks of incense at the temple gate. You would think it would be the sight of my child's first steps, or my husband's shy smile… after we first made love, but no, it is mostly, almost exclusively, the views… from my eyes when I was singing."

Her husband showed up that afternoon at about the same time Finn did. Every time Finn entered the hospital room, shock registered on his face. I'd felt the same shock when I first woke up in here—it was truly a place full of death. The women in the other beds were in various states of decomposition, their eyes hollow and their bodies emaciated. But it wasn't the sight of them. It was the haunting look in their hollow eyes as they followed you across the room. It was the energy of death, so important and impotent, so shocking and fearful and not of this world. The women followed Finn as he walked across the room with their vacant eyes. You could see a desperate jealousy in them. Here was someone who was part of the world of the living.

He put a stack of tattered novels he'd gotten at a book exchange on my lap. I was too tired to move them. He had a bag full of candy, too.

"I saw the doctor in the corridor. He's been too busy to get to running the tests, Queenie." The sick and dying filled the hallways, too, beds lined up against both walls. I could imagine the doctor was too busy. Wedged beside my bed, Finn looked like a little lost boy. We had flights in a few days to travel to Sri Lanka. I reached out and squeezed his hand.

"It'll be all right. I'll be better. I just need a bit of a rest."

He told me about what he was doing—he was taking an Indian martial arts class. I'd begged him to do something to keep busy, to keep his mind off me. As he talked, I looked over and studied

Lucina's husband. He was small, a humble-looking man. He held his wife's hand as they spoke softly in Hindi. He looked like a perfectly nice man.

After the two men left, the nurses came in with lunch, rice and some kind of gruel. I sat up to eat and focused on the rice and ate the candy Finn had brought. The effort tired me out and I lay back down. I turned on my side. Lucina was staring with wide eyes. She seemed to be missing, and I called out her name, worried she had died.

A subtle shift of her head as she focused and looked at me. I breathed a sigh of relief. She started speaking, but her eyes were still unfocused. I wasn't sure if she was speaking to me or to herself. Her hand reached out from beneath the covers, and she gripped the bed rail. She was wheezing worse than before.

"My life has not been… bad. What I have to say will make it sound as if it were bad, but I promise you, it wasn't. It was as good a life as anyone around me had."

She inhaled an audible breath.

"I was a beautiful bottle. One day… a man came and purchased that beautiful… bottle. He took it home and put… it upon a beautiful shelf." I thought of Asha's father's bottles full of colored water, the way he moved them this way and that to reflect the light.

"How can I blame… my parents or my husband? It was the easy way, and I… bowed. I had a friend, you see. She was an… artist. Such color that came from… her. Color to remind… you of all the beauty in the… world. She did not take… a husband. She had no children. She… grew old, and even with… the beauty from her hands… she was so alone. I thought I did not want… such a… life. How can a person be so alone?

"I gave up… the music." Her eyes dominated her bony face. She stared a few inches above my head, as if she were speaking to a version of me that wasn't there. "I no longer… sang. I married and… decided… it was a conscious decision… my voice must go in the bottle... on the shelf. How else would... I survive the mundane world? Singing was not something... I could do while cleaning... dishes or sweeping... floors. The call would... be too strong. Like another... lover. If I could not do it in a grand... way, on a stage, or staring out... upon the sacred, I could not do it at all.

"The music would... be an affair. The lover would be so... wild and strong... My husband would... never be able... to compete with such an epic... love."

She took three deep labored breaths. She opened her mouth, and started to sing, a song in Hindi, but her voice devolved into a cough. In those few bars, I heard the jangling of her soul.

She was quiet then, and I closed my eyes. I was so tired.

I awoke hours or days later, time was bleeding into itself, to find the doctor and Finn standing at the foot of my bed. Finn had told me the last time I saw him that he was going to track the doctor down and force him to run the tests. A nurse had come to take a fresh sample of blood the day before. Was it the day before?

I was foggy, watching them talk, and felt like it was a dream. The doctor said that so far he'd figured out that I suffered from giardia and severe exhaustion.

I tried to listen. "...more, and I do not know what... Maybe depression. Depressed mind causes depression in the body. Medication will help giardia, but we will run... more tests. She must gain weight. She needs nutrition."

"How long?" Finn asked.

I wanted to tell Finn that it would be alright, that I would get better, but I was too foggy, too tired to figure out what was the best thing to say or do.

The doctor wobbled his head. "Another few days. Do not rush. She is not well."

I awoke some time later to a smell of burning, and to the sound of a song. It was Lucina. Her voice was raspy, but she wasn't coughing or breathing heavily after every few words. She sang sweet and low. I thought at first that I was dreaming. It was "Amazing Grace." It was the only song my mother had sung to me as a child, when I'd broken my arm, and she had lain beside me all night because we had to wait to see the doctor in the morning. It was a song that kept appearing and re-appearing in my life.

I felt such a grief boiling up as Lucina's voice floated around the room. Everyone was quiet, listening. Some women wept. Nurses congregated at the doorway, watching and listening.

After she'd finished, we remained silent, here and there coughing and wheezing. The song lingered in the air like smoke. Then I smelled the burning again. It seemed to be coming from right outside the window. I sat up and dizziness swooned me.

I sat for a few moments to get my bearings, and swung my legs over the side of the bed. It took another minute to stand. I wedged myself sideways between the beds and shuffled to the window.

I was surprised to see that right below the window was the funeral pyre, the same one where Finn and I had watched the cremation. A body was burning; from this vantage point a few stories up, the flame looked like the large flicker of a big candle. The smell was like a barbecue. Around the pyre, the ragtag assortment of women in saris, men, goats, chickens, and dogs. From this height, it looked like a carnival or festival, and I thought of Lucina's song, and wondered about the music's effect on this dead burning body, on its soul, or on the soul of the people below, even if they did not hear it.

The next morning they wheeled two corpses out of our room. Lucina and I watched, the gurney wheels making a nail-scratching sound. Eee. Eee. Eee. Eee. The women were quickly replaced by two other sick women from the corridor. Eee. Eee. Eee.

I slept, tried to work on my article, slept again, woke up to see

Finn looking down at me with such anguish on his face, put my hand on his to comfort him, then fell again into deep sleep.

I awoke deep in the night. The ward was closed down for the night, the beeping of monitors and the ringing of phones in some far-off place. The women around me coughed and moaned.

A group of people stood surrounding Lucina's bed, two men, a woman, and two children. They murmured something to Lucina. I lifted my head and looked around to see if anyone noticed, but everyone else was wrapped in their sickness and their dreams. In the people around Lucina's bed, I swore I saw the tall red head of my father with his back to me. I was sure I was dreaming. I stared at them awhile, then closed my eyes tight, and willed the dream to end.

T he next day, I couldn't bear to look at Lucina. I didn't know why. After breakfast of a bowl of fruit and a bottle of water, I tried to focus on writing the article. Tired out a few minutes later, I lay back down and without thinking, turned on my side and faced her. Her eyes were even further away. I was worried she'd died and no one knew.

"Lucina?"

She shook her head, looked at me, but still it took a minute for her eyes to focus. "Yes," she said softly.

I told her my dream. "I had a dream that I awoke to see people around your bed last night. It was a strange dream. I cannot seem to free myself from it today."

She looked me hard in the face. It was such a clear look, it was as if she was seeing me for the first time. "It was not a dream. My ancestors came. It will not be long now." She stared at me. "You see behind the veil."

A chill ran through me. "No."

Her eyes widened. "Oh I see it. You are frightened of who you really are. You are terrified with how much you see."

"It isn't who I really am." I heard the desperation in my voice.

She had tears in her eyes. "You know what they told me last night, the ones who came to prepare me? They said this illness is my… punishment for thinking I… could defy the gods, that I could ignore my soul." She coughed. "Do you understand? This cancer is… the karma for ignoring the beauty… of my soul, for ignoring my singing voice. As if I could trade in such… a gift… and not have… consequences." The hand she held to her mouth was translucent and purple-veined. "No…they did not say… punishment. That… is my… interpretation. It is more a discomfort that… eats at the body. Ignore… the soul and… you will… get sick."

She closed her eyes.

"If there is nothing else I can do in these… last few moments… of this life, it is to beg you… my new friend… to plead with you… please, oh please… do not ignore the soul. Do not… hate it. Do not put… it in a beautiful jar… on the shelf." She went into a coughing fit, closed her eyes, and did not speak again.

That night, I awoke again to find the group surrounding her bed. One was *my* father. How was the spirit of my father Lucina's ancestor? It made no sense. He was just next to my bed, his back to me. I could've reached out and touched him, but I didn't dare. I was unable to move, unable to close my eyes, unable to make it all go away.

He turned suddenly and looked down at me. When he was alive, lying down like this as he loomed over you was a dangerous thing, something I would avoid as if my very life depended upon it. I couldn't move. I was a terrified little girl again.

"Pearl?" he said. His voice was softer than the man I once knew.

"There was a lot I didn't get, Pearl. I'm real ashamed of a lot of it. My fear. It was my fear. My fear made you so afraid. And now you're scared. I was so scared of myself."

I could feel the remorse and grief bleeding off him. I'd wished him dead so many times, that I still deep down blamed myself for the hunting accident that killed him. I held a deep hate for the man, and somewhere behind that hate, a brokenhearted love.

"I'm working on healing here, where I am now. I have a lot to do."

Rage erupted in my gut. I spat, in my mind, as we were not actually speaking out loud to each other: "How can you be Lucina's ancestor? What are you doing here?"

"There is a lot we don't get when we're human. I cain't explain it now. You wouldn't get it if I did." Something was happening with Lucina. The other people were murmuring louder, and her body seemed to be arching. "I need to get back to her, but let me tell you one thing. There is a reason you are here, in this hospital, right now. You were put here beside Lucina. Do you understand? This ain't no coincidence. We're all connected much more than you can imagine."

The next thing I knew I was being awakened by the screech of gurney wheels. It was morning. The orderlies were lifting Lucina. She'd died in the night. I started crying. I felt I'd known her for many years. I felt like I was losing a good friend or a sister.

I spent all morning in a weepy state, thinking about what Lucina had said, and my father. The disease, the soul's calling, how my father was somehow an ancestor to Lucina, which still made no sense. What stayed with me the most, though, what I couldn't shake, was that it wasn't a coincidence that I was brought to this woman dying in an Indian hospital in Rajasthan. The only way, then, for me to be brought here, for me to be fated to meet this woman, was for me to get sick. Right? I didn't like it. It reminded me of the karma we kept hearing about in India, if your car wrecked or you were stricken with a fatal illness, it was meant to be, there was nothing you could do to stop it. The whole thing felt like my visions. There was nothing I could do to stop them. I wasn't in control. The gods, or the universe, or whoever could use me whichever way they wanted, and I just had to suck it up and deal with it.

I needed to get out of here now. I looked for my things, searched under the bed. When I checked in they'd handed me a hospital gown, a plastic bucket to puke and piss in, a roll of toilet paper, and a bottle of water. These were all stuffed under the bed, and amidst them, I found my street clothes. I struggled to sit up. It took some time because of the tiredness. I put on my clothes. Nobody paid attention to me. Already they'd wheeled in someone to take Lucina's place.

I turned my legs so I was sitting up, and stayed that way until the dizziness subsided. I got on my feet, and first went to the window, stood for a while looking out at the funeral pyre. It was still smoking, but long ago the body had burned up. I wouldn't stay in this hospital and watch Lucina's body be burned up. I didn't want to smell the flames burning through Lucina's flesh. I couldn't.

I shuffled out of the room, past the dozens of hollow eyes in beds lining the hallways, wondering how the nurses did it, how they managed so much death every day. I went to the front desk.

"I'm checking out," I said, breathing heavy.

My doctor saw me and ran up. "What are you doing? We are still waiting on tests. Please go back to bed."

"I'm checking myself out." I had to lean against the counter.

"You mustn't."

"I am." I looked him dead in the eyes. I would have no more of this, no more of the gods playing with my fate.

A nurse came running down the hall, spoke to him in Hindi, urged him to follow her. There was an emergency, and he was needed now. He ran with her, and looked back at me as he rushed away. "You must sign a waiver. You must free us from all responsibility." He yelled back instructions to the desk clerk in Hindi as he ran.

She filled out the form. I leaned heavily against the counter. Around me, the corridors seemed to be filling up more and more with sick bodies, moaning, crying, coughing. She slid the paper to me. I picked up a pen and with a shaky hand and signed it.

LONDON

When the plane landed at Heathrow, all I could think of was meat. Whatever was physically wrong me, whatever it was that had landed me in that Jaisalmer hospital, I'd pushed it down, shoved it gone, begged it away. I was slowly, very slowly, putting weight back on.

The bloody flesh of beasts. Fisted fat. After Asia and years in Tokyo, I just wanted to sink my teeth into the flank of some fatty creature. My body desperately missed the feral passions of my childhood. I'd built illusions in my mind of the fatted calves of my childhood, a fantasy of what my life was like in Missouri. When you travel, when you live abroad for years, your entire history, the length and breadth of the life you had before, grows to mythological proportions. You miss what you thought you had.

Finn humored me. There was no way he could stop me. I needed meat. We took the train from Heathrow to Piccadilly. We were in shorts, singlets and flip flops. The only place that would have us would be McDonald's.

Weighted forward by our heavy packs, we hobbled to Leicester Square. A dripping, frigid November day. Why hadn't either of us thought to purchase a single piece of winter clothing before flying into London in the winter? The sky was heavy gray, and the buildings gray, and the people gray. We were still on Asia time, slow and meandering, and people rushed us, knocking our packs. Every once in a while, someone would look up from the concrete and laugh at our our flimsy clothing, and the way our teeth chattered.

I tried to catch Finn's eye, to give him a look and make him laugh, but he had his head down, and the pack seemed heavier than normal on his shoulders. There was something wrong. This wasn't just about our quivering bare arms being hit by cold rain. I watched his profile. He seemed to sink somewhere deep inside himself. England was Finn's home. I realized I had absolutely no idea what that meant to him.

We sat on orange plastic chairs at McDonald's, leaning into our meat. Fat dripped onto the wrapper and congealed in murky glue. I ravaged the beef, sucking in fat bites, swallowing the entire thing in four mouthfuls, ravenous, back at the counter for another Quarter Pounder with Cheese. Outside, the winter rain beat like witchy fingernails against the glass. Tick, tick, tack.

It'd been years since I'd had red meat. In Missouri, my fingers ran red with the blood of animals, domesticated and wild. I'd butchered hundreds, skinned, gutted them. It was my job as a girl to bottle feed calves that were taken too soon from their mothers. The gristle of the fur on the tops of their heads, their eyes swarming brown orbs, the foaming drool that dripped into the dirt. Later, I'd help Father kill them, skin them, cut their flesh up into human-friendly parcels.

At dinner at home in Missouri, blood rimmed the edges of the plate, and with the wild beasts, our mouths filled with buckshot. We'd extract the tiny beads from beneath the tongue, and they'd roll around the edge of the plate in the blood. That had been a long time ago, though. That had been two or three lifetimes ago. That had been another life.

The last time I'd had beef was many years earlier at a McDonald's in Tokyo. The Japanese cut the beef with flour to make the burgers affordable. You could spread the patty with a knife. We only went to a Tokyo McDonald's once. I took the bun off and spread the meat with my hands like it was play-doh. It tasted like a greasy flap of nothing. In Asia, there had been no red meat. And by the end of our travels we were avoiding chicken and seafood, too.

The Quarter Pounders settled in my stomach, dark and heavy. I worried I was going to vomit. We couldn't leave the cold dark McDonald's until my stomach settled, until I'd been back and forth to the toilet. Even when we hauled our packs back on, my stomach roiled.

When you leave home, when you cut yourself off from the pack, when years pass and you forge your own path, or wander aimlessly seeking, you build a fanciful idea of what you left behind. You build a monument in your mind to what you are missing. Inside, a ravenous hunger builds, for what you thought you'd lost. My sickened stomach was a lesson in the fantasy of travel, a wake-up call around the mythology of home.

It'd happened for the years I'd lived in Japan. Food from home I could not get in Japan became idyllic. Idolized. Grilled-cheese sandwiches and fast-food french fries or the sun tea Mother put out on the stoop, legends of the mind. I'd travel back to the States, ravenous for them, dreaming of them, desperate for them like the arms of a lost lover.

I'd get to Missouri and gorge myself, tasting memory, imbibing the past, desperate to capture back all that had been lost. All such illusion did was make you physically sick, and you would not know it until it was far too late.

We had to make it to Clapham in South London. On the tube, people stared at our shorts and singlets. After India, everyone seemed so civilized, and so very boring.

We were going to stay with Charlotte and Michael, Finn's oldest friends. We got off at Brixton, and Finn pointed to the drug dealers on Electric Avenue as we hunkered past. By now, we were soaked to the skin, frigidly cold, and my pack seemed to have doubled in weight. It was a long, brutal walk.

When we climbed the steps to their door in Clapham it felt like I'd reached the end of a long journey, not just from the station, but across continents and cultures. The trip through Asia had lasted a year, but after four years in Japan, this felt like the end of a five-year heavy trek through the wilderness. We stood in the freezing rain, our toes almost blue from the cold, and I thought, *We've arrived. Finally, now I can rest.*

Michael was well over six feet tall, blonde, his skin lily white. Charlotte was tiny, brown, small and sharp like a caper. The height difference meant you could not look at them both at the same time. Talking to them was like watching a tennis match.

We went to their basement kitchen. Michael towered over vegetarian stew at the stove. He lit a spliff the size of a cigar and passed it. Finn held onto it too long. He had this habit. He'd take the joint as it made its rounds, and as soon as he had the thing, he'd start a story. He'd hold the joint up between his fingers while he talked. He'd drag the story out. He'd done this in Tokyo too many times to count. He knew if he had the spliff in his hand, everyone would watch him, waiting for him to take the hit, waiting for him to pass it. It drove a person crazy.

Michael and Charlotte were old hippies, older than Finn, almost my parents' age. Both worked with kids with autism. I'd never quite met anyone like them, passionate, conscious hippies. The basement kitchen filled with the thick smoke of weed and cigarettes as we talked until the wee hours.

The next day Finn and I awoke on the futon in their spare

room, still shivering in our meager summer clothes. We went to a local thrifty where we purchased pilly sweaters, too-big coats, and the smallest-sized trousers, which didn't remotely fit our emaciated frames. I got a green velveteen coat with a tail, a Sargent Pepper thing, a pair of black combat boots with massive heels that laced up, and a black tight dress. Finn bought a leather jacket with too many zippers.

It was New Year's eve. Charlotte and Michael wanted to show me London. At 10:00 p.m., we climbed aboard a double-decker bus, went up the stairs and took up the front seats. The lights of London passed through the wide windows. There was something about this city. I felt I knew her, like I'd lived here before through many lifetimes.

At Westminster Bridge, we disembarked and joined the hordes of people. Big Ben loomed. I knew this bridge, felt a relief in the reflected lights on the Thames, seemed to recognize the bridges that crisscrossed the river in the distance, felt I belonged with the mixture of so many different nationalities. It was cold and drizzling, strands of my hair damp against my cheeks, and for the first time in a long time, I felt like I might even be home.

Michael pointed behind me. A black stretch limo was pulling over to the sidewalk. Someone inside rolled down the tinted window. A hand emerged, holding a glass of champagne. Traffic was creeping by because of the thick wash of pedestrians. The man stayed in the shadows, and held the flute out as an offering.

"Take it, Pearl," Michael said. "Go on, love. It's meant for you."

I reached out and grabbed it.

We'd been in London only a few weeks when Finn found the band, or they found him. Idle Hands. The lead singer was Dublin Rick. He'd sometimes introduce himself as Rublin Dick. He was a man whore and he wrote songs about orgies and oral sex, and when I listened to his lyrics, I felt like I could breathe. Like I hadn't taken a breath in years. He'd scream into the mic, but his voice when soft was lyrical, magical, tender. He'd kick his legs in vaudevillian abandon.

We were down a long alley in the depths of Brixton, in a dark pub with fat musty drapes. Walls and columns flaked paint like disintegrating bark, and the color scheme of the club glowed red like hot embers. The stage was warped, the wood blackened from centuries of use. A blood-floral sofa sat in a dark corner, stuffing wrenched from both overstuffed arms.

On each round metal table, candlesticks dripped with wax, misshapen monstrous sculptures. Seat cushions on wrought-iron chairs were the same dirty velvet as the curtains. Everywhere the flickering of tiny flames.

Dublin Rick's lyrics were a long tongue licking out, catching flies. His face was dark, and his hair dark and long, and his eyes the black of winter death. His eyes and his voice fooled you. They could pull you in and make you think there was some earth beneath your feet, that there was some ground.

"The arms that once held you are now barring the way..." That gravel in his throat. The wash of him, the devouring, the soaking, the invoking.

The drummer and keyboardist, short muscular guys who were once circus performers, were named Ace and Fumble. They stopped playing mid-song and walked across the stage on their hands. They performed a double juggling act with four drumsticks.

I watched from the devouring sofa. Idle Hands finished their last set at 1:00 a.m. The girls swarmed. I watched from the shadows as the band descended off the stage, Finn's reaction as he leaned and smiled his big-mouthed crooked grin at the screaming girls. I wanted to throw myself between him and the swooning women.

My shadow self watched Dublin Rick, too. That dark lock that fell across his face, the way his joints seemed too loose, the pheromones of him that I couldn't possibly smell from this far away. The way he took a sideways drag from his cigarette. The girl he'd choose. There was always one. Usually she was dark and tattooed. Frail and crazy. The way he'd inhale her, sideways. The way she'd stand to the side, her body vibrating, waiting for Rick to pack up his gear.

CHAPTER 31 ½

You can leave. *You can go wherever you please, if you have the luxury. You can roam the world. But the souls you meet will follow you. They will fly after you on a rainbow bridge. They will talk to you in your sleep.*

Tender Grass sits at her window, her sadness turning the London streets to purple. I look up from the sidewalk, hair blowing in relentless wind, see her there and wave. She looks upon me with eyes the color of wet smoke.

Yash sits on the tube with his children and wife, heading to school, then off to work. The tunnels throw stripes of light across his brown cheeks. He is bored, the kind of bored that comes from being comfortable, from routine. The kind of bored you miss later, when your old life is taken away. I wave to him, but he disappears. Just his wife and two boys, and an empty seat where he once sat. Outside, Lucina sings to me in a lifting voice, as I fly with Leo on his bike into the sky.

At night, I am in a park, on my back, looking up at the stars. Raul appears. He is weepy, my little boy. I invite him to watch the Milky Way. On his back, the top of his head touching mine, he says he has no one to hear his stories now. The tourists are meaner, haggling too much, complaining always, enjoying too little. No one will hear his little boy adventures. I reach to the skies and take a handful of black, a fistful of stars, bring the blanket down and wrap him in the universe. "Talk to me," I say. And he does, his voice the sound of ocean wind.

The places too come forth, jumbled land and architecture from varied countries, golden baubles, dangling jewelry, snow-chiseled peaks, prayer flags like sacred laundry, ancient wooden doors, arched doorways carved with pictures of the gods, spinning prayer wheels worn by the laments of millions. The stench of it all too, wood fires, incense, shit. What a sanitized world we call "civilization."

More than visuals, it is the voices that haunt me, above, around, below, a tower of babble. Yash's British accent, his words emerging from the mouth of Etisha, Usui's thick Japanese-English, the broken American woman on the smoke-darkened Thai beach, breathy and full of gravel, and in Indonesia, the precise erudition of Amri as she speaks Leo's soul.

Something moves over and covers the light. It grows darker. Neon pink hearts pasted on girl nipples, giggling gangs of white men reaching like zombies, Leo curled like a cold fetus on the rickshaw seat, fat Westerners slobbering over massive meals as the brown people serve them. Above us all, a heavy cloud of smoke, unchecked flames feeding on the heart of a nation, purple fire flicking upward, exhaust floating eastward, a dark monster blocking out the sun.

inn and I found a top-floor bedsit in Russell Square. It was up four flights, with a shared bathroom on the third-floor landing. Our "kitchen" was two burners and a waist-high fridge on the landing outside our door, which we shared with a tiny woman from Iran with fiery red hair, a visiting professor of Persian studies at London University. We rarely saw her. Our room was about 350 square feet, with a queen-sized bed and an armoire. We owned so little, the few things in our pack, and the new used clothes from the thrifty.

While Finn fell into a dark place, I fell in love with London. Daily I walked to the British Museum to stare at artifacts from ancient cultures. I had no idea why mortars and pestles, hand tools, and tiny carved statues brought me such profound relief. I took the tube to the Tate, the National, the Victoria and Albert. For hours, I'd stare at the Turners, the Goyas, the Blakes. I knew that London was offering me something great, something I'd never had, access to masters. It was if finally someone held a fancy party and invited me to the table.

London was also dirty and mean, a rank old whore, and I adored that side of it, too. A hacking cough that came in fits when she laughed, drooping breasts, that vagina stench, deep etchings on cheek and forehead, lipstick caked into the cracked corners of her mouth. In fringed floral robes, she stood in doorways and talked to anyone who would listen.

I knew this woman. We'd had many lifetimes together. I was familiar with the droop and sass of her, with the mottled thighs that had embraced so many lives. This whore and I were old friends.

I was sure I'd lived in this city before, in some other lifetime. If I went down a certain street, I'd know the curves and edges, the river banks. Some parts of her were like a map I already had memorized. Old landmarks were as known to me as the veins on my hands. I knew the stench and breath of her.

Over the months, I merged with London, wore it like a cloak, took up its mannerisms, its accent, it terminology. I lost myself fully in the folds of her flesh. Our local pub governor, when hearing that I was American, could not believe it. I'd so adopted the mannerisms and accent that I fit in like a local. Walking the streets of London was the closest I'd felt in a long time to something like peace.

We lived a long train ride, and a longer walk, from Michael and Charlotte, but I found myself with Charlotte often in their sitting room, on pillows on the floor, talking, smoking cigarettes, and drinking black tea. She was a feminist. She gave me books. Our talks put into context so much of what I'd gone through my entire life, feeling so secondary, so invisible, as if my reality was not just less than a man's, but not even real. She opened my mind on those sitting-room floor talks, life epiphanies in the middle of Clapham. I looked up at her once, in a moment of clarity, at her brown hair, and small sharp face. She was not even five feet tall, and had a small body like a child's. I admired her. I'd been looking for women to admire, women I wanted to emulate, and here, finally I'd found one.

Mostly I listened. She was angry at everything, raging against the man, against the culture, against the government. Even though she was close to my mother's age, she was like no mother I'd ever met. When I told her my Missouri butchering stories, she thought I was making them up. "Nobody lives that way anymore."

My middle-American reality was not hers. Our Tokyo reality was not hers, nor was our Southeast Asian reality. When you traveled, when you lived in every country and no country, you often found yourself listening and not speaking. Few people could understand, and it was difficult to explain, so you went into silence. You knew so much, and could share so little.

London was now my new reality. I would have to learn to fit into it. To adapt. To say the right things. To mirror back to Londoners what they thought of as normal.

I was learning in my travels that there were all sorts of different actualities, different ways of seeing and knowing. People who lived in each culture took their way of knowing as the only truth. But there were many. Oh there were so very many.

And what of the truths behind the veil, Purr? It was Usui. *Yes, Usui, those too*, but then I pushed him hard away from me.

Meanwhile, Finn wasn't doing well. He loved Idle Hands, but spent too much time in bed afterward, or awake and stoned. He was so far down in the dark, that he couldn't find the words. It felt like I had to reach down into him, root around, find the real Finn and pull him out.

It was reverse culture shock, the pain of re-enculturation. For me, London was new; for Finn it was full of memories, lowered expectations, a path he'd refused to take.

We were sitting on the bed. He'd been up until 4:00 in the morning with the band, to a gig at the Elephant and Castle that I did not go to. It was now the afternoon. His hair stuck up from his face, and he had circles under his eyes. He smelled of stale beer and marijuana, and even depressed and smelly, I wanted to fuck him.

I begged him to talk to me, and he was, haltingly, his voice coming out like gravel, dark and sharp.

"One returns and is not the same person, but the place is the same, the expectations are the same, and it's as if you're invisible." I put the ashtray between us, lit a cigarette for him, and handed it to him.

"I'm this cardboard cut-out." He held up his long fingers. "They've got this cardboard cut-out idea, but it's the former self. They hold it up to the new self. Where it does not fit, they fill it in with their minds, color it in, until they can only see the person I once was. It is like I never left. They could not see the real me then, and they cannot see the real, newer, me now. But it's all the same. Who I am doesn't quite exist."

A chill ran through me. I thought of what it would be like to return to Missouri. I couldn't imagine London could be the same for someone as the American Midwest was for me.

He seemed to sink into the bed. "The British mind is twisted, taken up by hundreds of different philosophies, and if one cannot twist the mind to echo it, one is lost. The expectations of someone like me in this outdated caste system are so low, and I feel I must bow to meet them." Finn was working class. Even in Tokyo, he'd spoken to me about how much it hurt him that the mainstream British society had such low expectations for the working class, how much harder it was to break out of the class system in Britain, how much he dreamed of going to America, where anything was possible. Britain had broken his heart. He'd escaped to Japan for more than a decade, and now he was back as if nothing had changed. I moved the ashtray, got under the covers with him. We spent the afternoon holding hands.

———

You could be depressed or lost or jet-lagged or reversed in your culture shock, you could have visions and be barely able to cope, but still you had to make money. There was no room for the dreamer, the wanderer, the lost or broken soul. The need for money was like a drum beat, boom, boom, boom, like a whip, or a foreboding.

We'd saved thousands in Tokyo, but after the year in Asia, and with the expenses of setting up in London, our money was running out. Finn took a job teaching English as a second language. I wanted to get my foot in at the major dailies, but I couldn't find the doorway. There were other doorways that kept opening up, that were too compelling. But they were not doorways to practical survival. I tried. I pretended to try. I dallied. I was not good at the practicalities of living. My soul liked to leave my body and wander. Such a soul was not good for survival. My mother used to say, "Pearl, you ain't going to survive in this world with the way you see things." Almost daily, I worried she was right.

Finally, I had to take whatever was offered. What was offered was a job with an oil industry trade publication. The managing editor grew up in Missouri like me. She was harried, chain smoked, and spoke rapidly like a mad woman. She gave me a job I did not want for a publication I did not like because we both grew up in place I had so desperately wanted to leave. The black dog grabbed at my ankle and pulled.

33

L**ester answered the door.** He was weaving, holding the knob and leaning against the back wall to keep himself standing. "Hello. Ta then, come in." Finn introduced me. Les looked at the floor, and waved his cigarette in my general direction. "Come in." We took off our packs and put them in the corner. "Let me get this door closed. Out of the way, there." I made myself small so he could close the door.

Les was Finn's uncle. We'd shipped boxes from Tokyo, and sent a few from our travels to this address in Golder's Green. We'd taken the tube up with our packs to haul back our meager possessions. Finn had already been to visit, but this was my first time meeting him.

In the small sitting room, Lester drooped into a tall floral armchair, a sweating can of Foster's on a tray table next to him. On the telly, the Eastenders.

"Les, shall I make us all a cup of tea then?" Finn said, loudly. His uncle who couldn't seem to tear his eyes away from the television.

"Ta. None for me," Les answered, holding up his beer can.

Finn went into the kitchen and came back with a bloated

container of milk, green around the edges. "This is rancid," he said.

"Take your tea without milk then," Les slurred.

"Alright then. I'm off to the shops," Finn replied too loudly, an edge to his voice. We'd only been in the flat five minutes and already he was abandoning me.

Now, from his chair, Les lifted his Foster's can and jiggled it. "Pick us up some Foster's. Ta."

Finn's face turned heart attack red. "I'll be back," he said to me and slammed the front door.

I knew very little about Finn's childhood. Just the bare facts. We'd only discussed it a couple of times. He refused to tell me more, and never told random stories of his childhood, never even gave me pieces to a puzzle that I could later fashion into a whole. I was used to that. I'd grown up with a family that was also scared and brokenhearted over their pasts, a family whose form of communication was a silence that swam in tumultuous waters deep in the psyche.

Finn's mother was an addict and had died of an overdose when he was just a boy. His father left after that. Uncle Lester took him in. Finn left to travel Europe as a teenager as soon as he could. He left for Japan soon after that. He'd never come back. He'd never returned home. Until now. He had warned me on the tube ride only that day, that he and his uncle didn't get along.

This was the tiny flat Finn had lived in growing up. It was two bedrooms with a kitchenette and living room with dirty sliding windows that bled noise from the busy street. One of the bedrooms was no bigger than a closet and was now being used as such. In the living room, rickety furniture, drab carpet, everything a dirty beige. A matted cat squealed from beneath the warped sofa.

I had an idea, a way to broker peace. I'd never seen pictures of Finn as a boy. Perhaps if we looked at photos of gentler times, I could get Finn and Lester back on the same page. I sat on the sofa.

"Les, do you have pictures of Finn as a boy? I'd love to see them. I've never seen what he looked like as a little boy."

He looked over at me with lost eyes. He shrugged, and looked around confused. Then his eyes teared up. He brought up his arm and wiped his face with the back of his sleeve.

"He doesn't like me. Ne'er di," Les slurred.

"What?" I asked. Lester looked at me with hang-dog eyes.

"Our Finn. He nah like me. Ah di' me best." He spoke toward his beer can. "Ah knowed nothin' about shite kids."

His head rocked like a dashboard dog's as he wove his cigarette unsteadily to loose lips. He was tall and lanky like Finn, and had his wide mouth, but the drinking had aged his face into a riverbed of dry cracks.

"Ah was ne'er given nothin'. What did ah I have to give. Nothin'. His da scarpered, and his mum, that cun' junky." He mumbled something more, but I could not make out the words.

Finn's childhood enveloped me like a film reel. A mom obsessed with scoring heroin. I saw a picture of her once and she was dark and pretty in a heroin chic sort of way. His father left, just as Finn as a little boy had nowhere to turn. Even before they left him, he had nowhere to turn.

I felt dizzy, went into the kitchen and leaned on the counter. Dishes were piled in precarious formations, bits of crusted food on every surface, the yellow linoleum on the floor brown and curling at the edges. A kitty litter box was overrun with feces, a reeking of cat shit and rotten food.

"Ge' us a beer, love," Les' voice from the living room. "I think the's one left."

I grabbed the last tall can from the short fridge and took it into him. He held up his empty can, shook it and handed it to me. "Ta."

I had to do something. There had to be some action a person could take to make this better. I searched for cleaning supplies, found a bottle of glass cleaner, vinegar, and a dusty rag wedged between the fridge and counter. I was not a cleaner. I was not a woman who'd ever been keen on keeping a good house. Women in Missouri were relegated to finding joy in lemon soap and cuddly dryer sheets. *I don't want my tombstone to say that I was tidy.* Still Mother taught me well in the art of cleaning, and if I argued, my father's fist taught me even better.

When you ran away from home, you thought you were leaving a life behind. You thought you could build something new from scratch. But it didn't work that way. You just found the old life in a new way. You adopted someone else's life, as if it would be better than the one you'd run from. It didn't work that way. You just found the old life in the new, wearing different clothes, in different guises.

The dishes done, litter and food flushed, the kitchen smelled of glass cleaner. I was on my hands and knees, scrubbing the linoleum back to its original yellow, when I heard Finn. He'd been gone over an hour. When he came into the kitchen, he yelled, "What the fuck, Queenie. Get off your god-damned knees."

I looked up at him. He was drunk. I had just a small corner left of the floor. He slammed the shopping bag on the counter.

"Did you force her into this?" he screamed into Lester.

"Let the wee thin' he'p an ole man," Les cried. "Who you think I've got he'ping me? You have this goo' woman and you can nah let her hep me? Ah nah see you in years, and you come here givin' me this shite?"

"I don't see you in years, and you know we're coming and you don't do shite to bloody clean up?" Finn came back into the kitchen. "Queenie, get off your fucking knees now!"

I stood up.

"Thanks for nothing, Lester," Finn yelled. He went into the bedroom that was now a closet, and came out with our boxes. He threw them into the corridor, then when he'd finished, grabbed them one by one, took them to the front door and threw them into the hallway.

"Put the dish towel down, Queenie."

I held the rag tightly in my fist, scared of Finn, and scared of someone else who used to get this angry, someone who had died years ago but still lived in my soul.

"Put it the fuck down." Finn tore it from my hand and threw it at Les, where it landed on his beer.

"Ta," Les yelled. "Nice of you to visit."

Finn grabbed our backpacks in the corner by the doorway, pulled me into the hall and slammed the door behind us. He ripped open the first box and started stuffing his pack. I was three years old again. Shaking. Out of body. I wanted to hug him from behind, but his body was an unrelenting wall.

"Take care of your bloody box."

I did as I was told.

In one of the boxes was the *sarangi* stringed instrument that I'd gotten on our Nepal trek. I'd purchased it from Sanjit and had the interpreter ship it, in secret. I'd forgotten about it. Finn took it out of the box, held it up and stared at it, as if he didn't understand what he was looking at. His fist tightened around the neck. He looked like he was choking it. Then his body sagged and he seemed to sink, but he caught himself and threw back his shoulders, and stuffed the instrument into his pack with the other things.

On the way to the station, with the heavy pack, it was hard to keep up with his hard-driving anger. I picked my thumb bloody. I used to do this as a girl, blood-letting to get Father's evil out of me. I put the crimson thumb into my mouth and sucked on it.

On the train, he sat staring ahead. I started to talk to him but thought better of it. His family was so fractured. My family was torn apart. How did so many families get so broken up? What was the reason for generations of pain? Who started it? What caused it? What fueled it? Why were we all so homeless? The thoughts made me dizzy again. I thrust the wall back up and put the thoughts away.

When we got back, my body was shaking, the same tremors I'd had in India. Stimulation. Too much of it. I thought being enveloped in water might help.

Eight people in six bedsits in the house shared the same bathroom. It wasn't heated. Luckily it was free. It was so cold, my breath came out in clouds. I kept on my hat, gloves and coat, turned on the spigot and waited for the hot water filling the tub to warm the room. When the bath was full, I took off my clothes, hung them on the door.

I should've noticed the buzzing at the base of the skull. I was so cold, naked in the frigid bathroom, my head full of Lester. Finn. Fractured families. I arched back, naked, nipples hard in the freezing room. The vision felt like a hard fuck, sudden and deep. Liquid lapped at my toes. The water in the tub had broken over the rim, and at that moment, there was nothing whatsoever I could do about it.

CHAPTER 33 ½

I am five and my father is partaking in one of his favorite pastimes, catching me unaware in the hallway, bending down to my ear and whispering hate. *Ugly, fat, stupid. Nobody gives a shit about you, kid.*

Even at five I know one of these isn't true. I am not stupid. It is the other things that he says that get under my skin, that become a mantra for a lifetime.

My body transforms. I am no longer a little girl. Now I am Finn as a boy. I have a dizzy brain. My mother is high, rolling back on the sofa, eyes turned inwards, abandoning me by her lack of presence, yelling without a voice, "Finn, nobody gives a shit about you, kid."

As Finn, I see my father walk out the door and not come back, leaving everyone, just taking off, by his very actions not giving a shit. And then Finn is all grown up, and he's met me. My body is arching, my eyes rolling back. I am leaving him, too. With every vision, with every leaving of my body, I am his mother leaving him. His father leaving him. And then Lester leaving him, unable to give a shit because he has no shit to give.

Finn and I so alike it makes my body shake. Two train wrecks. Two shipwreck victims, clinging to each other like life preservers. The heartbreak in the little boy's chest. My little's girl's brokenness.

Ghosts appear in that frozen, breathy bathroom. Ancestors gather. Angry old men. Bitter women. The grief-stricken and the broken. This grief has been passed down over many generations. A man vicious as a rabid dog stands over my father, he as a little mischievous boy. The man, my grandfather, gives the child the message my father gives me. "Nobody gives a shit about you, boy."

The hardening of Father's unformed heart, the black impenetrable energy that envelopes it. The monster he becomes.

Finn's British ancestors whisper in ears, yell in faces, battering and bruising upon the heads of Lester, and Finn's mother and Finn's father, and all of this dumping of toxins going back generations, until there is no room in the bathroom and I cannot see where it all began. Until the water in the tub, like the Ganges River, goes from sacred at its source to toxic, where it meets the brokenness of humanity.

Something pops. In the middle of it, inexplicable peace. Usui is there. The others fade. Usui. His thick dreadlocks, those low-hanging trousers on narrow hips, his sensuality. I reach for him, like a buoy in a sea finally calm after a ravenous storm.

"Where did it all begin, Usui?" I ask him. "This story of worthlessness?"

"You not understand, Purr-chan. This is love. You think, this is hate. No, this is love."

"Nobody gives a shit about you? How can that be love?"

"It is the rage they feel from the lack of love. It is grief. But do you see? Behind it is love."

"I do not understand."

"I ask again, Purr. Where is home? Home has been taken away from so many people. Not just people who leave land to move to city to survive. Not just refugee who must run from home because of violence. There is deeper home inside ourselves that it seems we must give up to survive. We miss home. We lash out, have depression. All in the search for home."

"Why do you speak in riddles? Why can you not just speak clearly to me?

"So many people starve for it, Purr-chan. So many need to under-stand. It is not taught. It is not understood. The people they are so hungry, such starvation.

"This lack of love makes us crazy. We beg for it with bits of our spirit. We try to pay for it by giving ourselves away. To survive. Anything to not feel…"

Knock, bang, hit, slam. Someone was pounding at the bathroom door. I was plopped against the icy wall, my ass in a pool of water, shivering.

"Who's in there?" Pound. Pound. Pound. "Water is flooding the hallway. Hello!" Boom. Boom. Boom. "Is everything Okay in there?" Slam. Slam. Slam.

I crawled to the spigot and turned off the tap.

34

Finn was gigging with Idle Hands two times a week or more. They'd play small venues, old dilapidated pubs down dark alleys. Dublin Rick was writing more songs. Each set seemed to be wilder than the last, vaudevillian, chaotic, full of primal screams and nonsensical gibberish. In the corner of each pub, snarling in the dark, the black dog strained against his chain.

He'd kick his legs up and act the fool, Dublin Rick, while Ace and Fumble walked on their hands now more often than playing. Finn would close his eyes, tap his foot and blow into his saxophone, while the rest of them went wild. He was also learning the *sarangi*, and brought that onto the stage a few times too, the strings an echo of the Himalayas, some far-off world that seemed a lifetime away. Dublin Rick was losing it on stage, out of control. His music was getting so much better.

I sat on the speakers, smoked and drank pints of lager, or sat on the floor, or backstage or on some broken sofa. There was something in Dublin Rick's lyrics that got under my skin. The words jarred and clashed and woke you up. An ache grew in my belly, lower than that, too.

So many nights a week, I was Finn's audience. Dublin Rick's audience. It wore on a person, always being the object and not the subject.

S ome nights, I'd leave the pub and wander the streets of London. Only come back when the gig was over. Finn didn't seem to notice I was gone. Or I'd beg off, say I'm tired and not go to the gig. I'd go out and roam London at night, keeping to the shadows. As a girl, around Father's sudden rages, I'd learned how to cloak myself in invisibility. I'd leave my body and replace it with an absence of presence. It was something I used to keep me safe. How coping can become a super power. Invisibility on the London streets late at night was my super power.

I'd walk for hours in the dead of night, roaming for miles. Street lights echoed off water puddles in abandoned alleyways like starlight in some ancient reflection of the Milky Way. Only once was I noticed. Only once was I chased.

I'd ponder the path that had brought me there. All my life, I'd been searching for a place where I fit. My life had been a journey of shifting realities. First, my reality was dirt, shit, and blood, and the soil of a gritty Midwest. Then it was Tokyo's steel and metal; it was floating above. In Southeast Asia, it was a cultural hop, a paradigm skip, a metaphysical jump. Now, London—this marriage with the base and lowest self, a wedding to the whore.

This was life as a traveler, a minstrel, a roamer. Every reality became your reality. You had to let go quickly and live wherever you were. You had to adapt. You had to forget.

Somewhere I felt Usui hovering. I was supposed to be seeking out my purpose. *See, Purr-chan. Look.* I looked, and saw, and roamed. Aimlessly. Witlessly. Invisibly.

During the day, when I wasn't working, I haunted the galleries. The tortured paintings compelled me, dark lines, gruesome faces, murder—Goya mostly, Blake, Bacon, Munch, Caravaggio. Every visit was food. Dark sustenance. I did not understand why I was starving for such shadow delicacies. Here was a meal, a dozen suppers, scraps of food falling to the floor from a grand table and I was allowed to lick up the scraps.

I'd stand in front of paintings or photographs or statues for minutes and centuries, dangling from the wing of the plane like when I was skydiving, a force of wind so powerful I couldn't breathe.

The plunge below so steep. The form, the texture, the color, entering my soul like a dream or a vision. Walls crumbled inside my heart. I'd go away dizzy, stumbling back to the tube like a drunkard.

Meanwhile, elsewhere in the city, bombs were falling. Here and there and now and then, day and night, the ground of London shook. The earth rumbled and tossed. I'd be in a pub with Finn, and the glasses would rattle on the shelves behind the bar. We'd feel a roaring in the earth beneath the floorboards at our feet. "Bloody IRA," someone would say, and we'd go back to our beer. The IRA set explosives in trash bins and hid them beneath postal boxes.

One day, after a crater was left in the road in the financial district, while Finn went to play a gig, I put on my invisibility, took a night bus and got as close to the bomb site as the police and the caution tape would allow me.

Glass had rained down. Debris littered the ground like a fallen house of cards. The buildings gaped with open wounds.

Nearby in the Gulf, nations away, another war raged. Other bombs fell. The world was blowing up. Again. So many were perpetually losing their homes. So many were being thrown out. So many were being forced to roam.

Charlotte sat on the floor in a T-shirt and stretch pants. On a mat in front of her was a tiny girl with cerebral palsy, arms and legs spasming, eyes darting. I sat a few feet away. The child's mother was farther away, in the corner, in the shadows.

Scattered around on the floor were percussion instruments, claves, shaker eggs, cylinder shakers, kid's drums, bongos, woodpeckers, bells, a thunder tube.

Charlotte picked up the claves, and started clacking them. She focused on the girl, shaking the claves close to her. The child's name was Dotty. Her cerebral palsy was severe. She couldn't raise her head or her body, and her eyes rolled around, unchecked. She had thin blonde hair, blue eyes, and ivory skin. The two made a night-and-day pair. Charlotte jiggled the shaker egg. Dotty's leg kicked spasmodically. The mother sat hunched forward in the corner.

I'd already told Charlotte about Usui and his work at the handicapped center outside Tokyo, about watching the young man play the piano and Usui dancing with the handicapped boy. When she heard the story, Charlotte invited me to her own version of music therapy.

She told me it wasn't unusual that Usui had used the music method in Japan, that music therapy was used all over the place. Still I didn't understand why the gods kept putting me around the severely handicapped. Why the serendipity of the music therapy. There was some message there, some lesson. It seemed too strange a coincidence.

Dotty wasn't reacting as Charlotte had hoped. She wasn't responding in any new way to the claves. So, Charlotte picked up the drum. She beat it to a two-four rhythm and still nothing. She put it near Dotty's foot and the child in her spasms kicked it accidentally. Still, she showed no real connection. Charlotte tried again, putting the drum in the way of her foot. Another kick. This time, when Dotty's foot hit the drum and made a sound, the child stopped moving. It was only for an instant. She went back to looking around the room, her legs kicking in random motions.

Charlotte held the drum close to her feet again, took the girl's ankle, beat her foot against the drum, and let go. Dotty wove her eyes toward us. For a moment, I saw awareness. A wall came down, a door opened to another reality.

Charlotte held up the drum again. Dotty wove her leg until her foot made slight contact. The mother stirred in the corner. I burst into a cheer. Dotty's mouth opened in a sloppy guffaw. The mother in the shadows sighed. Charlotte held the drum up again, and this time Dotty's foot made repeated contact. Boom. Boom. Boom. She beat a sporadic tempo.

Mother, Charlotte, and I cheered.

Charlotte leaned to me and whispered, "Kids with CP get overwhelmed with sound, color, movement. If we can control their interaction, sometimes they shift. Perhaps they can understand they can affect the environment."

Charlotte motioned for the mother to come over. With Usui, I'd met one of the parents of a child with severe cerebral palsy, and she was overwhelmed. This woman looked like she'd dressed in the dark, a ratty sweater over stained sweatpants, mismatched socks. Her hair wasn't washed or combed, and strands of it stuck to her neck and forehead. Bags under her eyes, deep lines near her mouth. I felt so tired just looking at her. I couldn't even begin to imagine how difficult such a life was. I felt deep guilt for all the complaining I did about my own.

Charlotte put two small bongo drums in front of the mother and instructed her to play them. She kept a steady beat. Charlotte held the drum to Dotty's foot. Dotty beat an erratic rhythm with a leg she could barely control. Her mother kept up with the bongos. Charlotte began to sing, "Yes oh yes I'm playing the drum, playing the drum, playing the drum." She had an amazing, lilting voice. Her voice changed the vibration of the room. It was as if she had been professionally trained, the kind of voice that made you melt, that made you want to curl up. She reminded me of Lucina.

She noticed my reaction. Sang to me. "Yes oh yes I'm playing the drum, playing the drum, playing the drum."

Oh, Charlotte can see me! She can see right through me, the hurt, the handicapped part. She can see where I'm broken. I wanted to curl up on the floor right there, and rest. Just rest.

She waved at us to join her in the song. We added our off-tune voices. "Yes oh yes I'm playing the drum." Dotty's foot began to keep a more regular beat. I bellowed out the simple tune, feeling good and free and small like a child, so little.

The mother leaned over and smoothed the hair on Dotty's forehead, singing into the girl's face. The mother was crying. The child's eyes stopped roaming and looked directly into her mother's. In the girl's eyes something close to home.

As Charlotte walked me out, I thought about Finn, how he needed someone to sing to him, to smooth his hair, to look into his eyes, to find home there. How the whole world needed someone to sing to them.

"One moment. I've just remembered something. Stay here," Charlotte said. "I have something for you."

I looked out the windows near the front door. The Thames across the street flowed heavy and ponderous. I felt the pull of the river. Charlotte returned with a worn cloth bag full of tattered paperbacks.

"Read," she said. "We'll talk." I looked at her, wanting to say something, but not having the words. "I have Benny waiting," she was running away back down the corridor. "Go. We'll talk."

It took a while to find a place where I could sit by the Thames. In all the big cities, rivers weren't for sitting. Restaurants and businesses took up the space. It was annoying, and wrong. People should be able to go to the river bank. It was a primal need.

I found a concrete slab in a littered scrubby section of the bank. It was drizzly and cold, buildings, boats and bridges all swallowed in gray. I pulled my Sergeant Pepper coat tight around me, wound my striped scarf over my head. A rainbow stain of oil traveled the current. The smell was fishy and full of exhaust.

Betty Friedan's Women's Room was the first book in the bag. I looked through the others, all feminist books. Wet wind came in off the river. I pulled my knees up, hugged them and opened the Friedan book.

I used to hide in the bathroom and read the Bible as a kid. Squatting on the toilet lid, I read it page by page, book by book, Old Testament and New. I didn't read it like a religious person. It didn't move me that way. I was more interested in the transition of perception from the Old to the New Testament. Even at ten I was interested in how perceptions shift and why and how. Even then, I was interested in roaming Holy Men. The Friedan book seemed like an entirely different "testament," like an entirely new language. Not for the first time, I wondered, where were the roaming Holy Women?

When I looked up from the book, moments or hours later, the sun had nearly set. The river flowed like glue. The lights across the Thames had come on, the scene some gray, dark painting. My body ached, damp and cold to the bone. Around me, the homeless had gathered with their blankets.

CHAPTER 35 ½

Wild woods, moody forest, *a winter woodland, spruce and oak, ash and aspen, and the crumbling of fallen leaves upon hard-packed earth. Quiet woods, just the echoing plop and gulp of the Thames.*

I know that I am seeing one of the past lifetimes of the Thames, a distant past. This patch of earth, this bend in the river has had many lives, like a person or an animal is reborn in several incarnations. The river reincarnated. The land too has its own ancestral story.

Up ahead, I see in the foggy distance some kind of village along both river banks, but this area is still woodland. I walk among the trees, a moody winter wood. Stories whisper in branch and root on an even wind. Across the river, more trees, more forest. Below the surface of the water, a rich world of fish. Centuries ago, before London grows like a sprawling monster, this bend in the Thames is an earthy place. This land and water has its stories to tell, before humans came and imposed their narrative upon it.

The scene dissolves. I am being taken to another lifetime, another point in the Thames chronology. The earth blackens. Ramshackle buildings on stilts on the shoreline. Wooden buildings appear in heaps and chaos behind me, the town full of shit and mud, the river rancid. Across the river, a medieval monastery, arched entryways, walls made of black-

ened stones, men in dark robes. From this side, into the river flows streams of dank sewage. There are too many people, rough-hewn and heavy. They watch the sewage enter the river. They know that this is a hatred. They know they are toxifying their home. It worries them in their guts, but still, what can they do?

I watch as the Thames catches on fire. The river bursts into flames, a combustion of methane and neglect from the sewage. The heat of the licking flames back me up. Water on fire, I have never seen anything like it. The heat of it sears my cheeks.

This scene then dissolves, and another river life is born. Buildings go up on the bank, more and more, higher and higher, steel and concrete. It is like a sped-up film reel. Vehicles appear, dozens then hundreds, then thousands, then hundreds of thousands, then millions. Now as much sewage goes into the earth and air as lands in the river. The buildings edge closer and closer, forcing me backward until I am at the river's edge.

"Stop!" I yell, putting up my hands as if to push it back. "Stop!"

36

A voice called me back.

"Hey!" A shout.

I was rolling toward the river, close to dropping full body into the current.

"Hey!"

I sat up. Groggy. I was at the river's edge, litter and twigs stuck to my body. I looked around. I was surrounded by the homeless. This was the place the homeless came to put their heads down for the night. Another life of the river, unfolding in the present.

I tried to see who had yelled, who had broken the spell. Everyone was avoiding my eyes. *What I must look like to them*, I thought. *A hopeless woman, a girl without a home. I was one of them, and they knew. They knew this place of rolling helplessly toward the current.*

I looked down and noticed one of my boots dangled in the frigid water. My leg was heavy as I pulled it out, clothes filthy, hair tangled. I removed a chocolate wrapper that stuck to my coat, found a lolly-pop stick entwined in the frizz of my hair.

I stood. Through unclear eyes, I could see all of the river's past at once, the woods, the flaming water, the modern London. I couldn't seem to focus. The canvas bag was nearby, tattered books on the ground, pages flapping in the bitter wind. I collected my things, turned my back on the river and walked with wet and freezing feet to the tube.

I t was time.

The backpack had been sitting in the corner of the bedsit, unpacked, for months. After we'd picked up our things from Lester's, Finn had unpacked his in a fury, but I couldn't bear to open mine.

Inside were so few reminders of the past, but still I knew it would be hard to face them. Finn was out at a gig. I grabbed a Boddington's from the fridge on the landing, hauled the pack onto the bed. Haunted objects lay inside. It wasn't the pain I was afraid of.

On my third beer, finally I unzipped it. Clothes the color of black, thigh-high lace-up leather boots, slinky tops, short skirts, a few mini-dresses I'd bought or Finn had purchased for me in Tokyo. The clothes meant nothing to me.

Wrapped in a jacket was one of Usui's dolls. Made from left-over garbage, *gomi* dolls. She was the hefty one, with a thick waist, the body made of a heavy winding of wire, clothes hangers, wrapped in gauze, in a dress of multi-hued fabric. She wore a hood over a face swathed in black. Her breasts were heavy and her hips rotund.

Usui had made himself purposefully homeless, to find himself, to be away from society's expectations. Hadn't I done that too? Wasn't I still doing that? Wasn't I trying to find out who I was and what I thought and how to live separate from all the expectations? Wasn't every expat who left their birth families, their homes, and their countries making themselves homeless for a reason? Was this homelessness I found in my soul a good thing? A necessary thing? I didn't like all the questions. There were too many questions and not enough answers.

Usui, as a homeless man in Tokyo, had peopled his own universe with these handmade dolls, and later with his origami. He created his own world at the homeless camp in the park. He was a Holy Man searching for home, or creating it, or both.

I held the fat doll in one hand and dug in the pack for the other doll he'd given me, found her wedged into the opening of a boot. Wire-thin, bone, angle, sharp boobs, a short red miniskirt. She was small and childlike, unsubstantial next to the heft and gravitas of the bigger doll. I held the slender doll in one hand, the large one in the other. "This is you," Usui had said about the small one. "This is *really* you," he'd told me about the substantial one.

The memories were too much. I didn't want to miss Usui, I didn't want to love him. The pull of him inside me was hard, his soul tugging, leading me *to* somewhere, leading me *from* somewhere. He went in so deep, I could not find the root of him to extricate him.

I hid the dolls under the piles of clothes, and went and got another beer.

I held the letters we'd received throughout our time in Southeast Asia away from me so that I could not read the script. Disintegrating aerograms, histories of time and space. The writing on the wispy blue paper of the aerograms like the thin veins on an old woman's hand, a whispering of the roots. The earthy pull of those hieroglyphics. How many lives was I leaving behind, mine and theirs, and ours. I put them in the folds of one of Charlotte's books.

I unwrapped a package covered in Japanese fabric. It was one of Yuriko's paintings—a goodbye gift—sandwiched between two pieces of cardboard. I untaped it. A woman's face melted off the edge of the paper. Her eyes were green and far away and full of ponderings. I realized at that moment it was a portrait of me. Yuriko had given it to me the day I left Tokyo. She saw me study it. She must've been waiting for me to recognize myself then. I did not. The painting made me miss Yuriko, a pain in my solar plexus, a hole where she used to live.

How much Yuriko would love Charlotte. How we would talk about the tattered paperbacks while Yuriko smashed paint into the floors, chain smoked and worked on her canvases. This was the thing I hated about my vagabond life, the leaving behind. Life became a perpetual leaving. I did not know what these constant departures were doing to my soul.

Finally, the pouch. I used to wear it around my neck as a child, and then as a teenager. I couldn't remember at what point in Tokyo I decided to take it off. The brown leather was beaten up and stained, the neck strap pinched and ready to break. I put it to my nose, inhaled the meat of it, hints of clinging clods of soil, the musk of mammal. It was the jewelry of a feral child.

I poured the contents on the duvet cover. A small white feather, a pink Native American arrowhead, the monstrous-looking freshwater pearl Meghan had given me. I worried the pearl between thumb and forefinger, ugly, misshapen, the color of black and beige poop. Meghan gave it to me before she ran away. She used to call me Black Pearl. Where was that little girl who was once called Black Pearl? I wasn't sure. I didn't know.

And where was Meghan now? No one knew. So many lives left behind, roaming lost souls.

I picked up the arrowhead last. I shouldn't have. The vision was immediate, the arching of the back painful. For the next hour, I was pulled up and back, so far back, into so many lives, past life after past life, so many people roaming, so many lost, so many seeking home. My heart nearly burst with the emotion I felt from them and for them.

It wasn't the pain I was afraid of when I was afraid to open the pack.

It was the love.

37

To **balance my dislike** of the oil industry trade publication, I volunteered for the Gulf Report, a group of journalists doing independent reporting on the Gulf War, because the mainstream press was telling lies. Or hiding truths. Or keeping secrets. I was used to lies. I knew more about secrets than truth. This was my wheelhouse.

We sat around big tables in donated spaces. These were some of the greatest journalists in London. Gristly, war-beaten, soul-battered truth tellers. My people. Mine. Malcolm Moore, Elizabeth Harton, Richard Marrymore, international journalists with reputations for crawling under barbed wire to interview rebels in Afghanistan, reporting from the front lines in Iraq, witnessing mass murder in Rwanda.

Moore was a wizened guy who'd infiltrated a rebel stronghold in Afghanistan during the Russian invasion. He was the leader. This was supposed to be an egalitarian group, but such things didn't really exist. He sat at the head of the table as we brainstormed the new publication. Who would cover what and how, where and when.

I was giddy with nerves at the back end of the long table.

These were my people, the truth tellers, some of the greatest speakers of the truth on the planet. I swung my leg obsessively, tapping on the table leg. Tap, tap tap tap. Tap, tap, tap, tap. Morse code. Perhaps I just wanted to be noticed, just wanted to be seen. I knew things too.

Moore stopped talking mid-sentence and shouted, "Who's doing that?" I stopped. Blood red in the face. People around me stared, a wash of annoyed faces. It was like a father yelling at me, but this time it was someone I actually respected.

I volunteered to be the grunt worker. Over the next two months, when I wasn't doing my money job, I sat for eleven hours straight at a computer terminal, proofreading, preparing articles, doing layout. I was good at endless, mind-numbing hard work. I called myself a farmer/journalist. I was used to relentless hard work. I didn't get paid. No one got paid. I sat for hours and days doing minutiae that no one else wanted to do. I became the person that great tellers of hard truths could dump upon.

I would like to say that what we did made a difference, those grueling hours of journalists going behind the lines and sneaking the truth out beneath barbed wire. That seeking the truth always made a difference. I would like to think that.

After three months, however, the magazine folded. Apparently, telling the truth took too much time, and paid too little money.

From the Gulf Report, a journalism collective grew. We were only three souls, a lesbian, a Pole, and a Missourian, working out of a flat in Chalk Farm. One room, one desktop computer and one phone line. I quit my job at the oil publication.

Alex was a first-generation Brit-Pole whose parents emigrated when he was three. Eileen was an Australian, a lesbian, former soccer player with knee problems, short and heavy-set.

Sometimes she'd punch the top of my chest and say in a loud Aussie accent, "You're a right Sheila. I love ya!"

I'd hold my chest and say, "What do you do when you don't like somebody?" She'd wink and scan my body with lascivious eyes.

The three of us spent hours drinking black tea, smoking, brainstorming. We planned to write articles together and do other articles solo and sell them to the major dailies. We'd make enough money to live. That was the plan.

My first article was on Charlotte's work with Dotty. A glossy women's magazine picked it up, sent a photographer to the Chelsea center to take photos. It was a beautiful article, and I was proud of it.

Mostly, I was great at interviewing. Growing up, I'd been trained early on how to put my needs aside, how to focus on other people. I had no problem with being invisible, creating the space for the interviewee to exist in a greater form, to speak, and talk and elaborate. I would so absorb the other during these interviews it would take hours to extract them from my being, to inhabit again my own body.

Eileen mostly covered rugby. She was also good at research. We'd give her any question and she'd find answers to even the most obscure.

Alex's passion was pollution. He had asthma. His asthma was a barometer for the smog. He swore the published figures of pollution in London were false, sure they far exceeded European pollution limits. I went with him when he roamed the city looking for pollution detectors, small devices attached to city buildings. We found them installed far down alleys away from the streets they were supposed to be monitoring. He took photos.

He found that in some places, pollution was exceeding levels in Shanghai and Beijing. I'd been to Beijing. This was saying something. Alex had sharp features, an edged jawline and hawk-like nose. When he sat at the computer to type the pollution story, he bent forward, pecked at the keys, and looked like a bird of prey.

I wrote other pieces and tried to land them in major publications, but was rejected again and again and again. The subjects I picked seemed to trend later, three or so months after I submitted an article or idea. I was pitching them too soon. It was as if I could see what was coming next, but the rest of the world wasn't ready to hear it.

Finn grew annoyed at my inability to bring in money. I couldn't blame him. I couldn't figure out the balance between speaking my truth and making an income, the line between being myself and surviving. The two seemed to be mutually exclusive.

Dublin Rick was fucking a groupie. For hours. For hours and hours they fucked in the next room. Squawk, grunt, snarl, yap—the thin walls bled with their rutting.

"Six bloody hours," Finn groaned, his voice muffled in the pillow.

We were on the floor on a bare mattress, the buttons imprinting deep circle scars on our thighs. We'd left the Russell Square bedsit, and were just waiting for our new place in Brixton to open up. We were staying with the band for a week. They all lived together in a squat not far from the Brixton tube.

My body was a thin wire of electricity, absorbing the hours of licking, sucking, pounding. At the gig that night where he picked up the tattooed girl, Rick's voice and the lyrics seemed to crack open my flesh. He was getting beneath my skin. And now this.

I moved across the mattress and pressed naked flesh against Finn. He peeked out from his pillow and gave me a look with a bloodshot left eye. He sighed heavily and didn't move to touch me.

Dublin Rick was a machine. Finn and I didn't have sex like that anymore. We didn't have sex at all anymore. England was doing something to him. It was as if the country were a syringe that pricked his flesh and drew out his soul. He was bent over and weak, except when he was onstage, and even then sometimes, too. I knew Finn wanted to leave. America was a distant hope, beckoning, but I wasn't ready. I didn't want to go home. He didn't want to be home in London, and I didn't want to go home to the States. We were two weather fronts, waiting to clash.

Dublin Rick came with a hiss. The girl snarled. My groin throbbed. The house fell into a broken-down pall of silence.

The squat was a condemned three-story house whose outside had a surprisingly fresh coat of yellow paint. Windows were boarded up, a two-by-four cross nailed across the top of the front door. Someone had cut the door in half just below the cross and you entered through the bottom. You had to bend, squat, and waddle to get inside.

The living room ceiling had bay windows and high ceilings that fell in plaster chunks onto the scarred hardwood. Slats were missing from the banister, and it looked like the gaping mouth of a bag lady. There was only one piece of furniture, a filthy beige or once-white sofa, that either had a subtle floral design or was stained with red wine.

When we'd arrived the first day with our packs full of our only possessions, inside the living room, a girl with ratty pink hair was swinging by her knees from a rope swing affixed to a high door frame. Ace and Fumble ran with water rifles, shooting the girl, Finn, and me in the face with blasts of water. A fat man in boxers sat on the edge of the sofa, belly flopping over his shorts, dealing tarot cards between his knees onto the beaten-up wooden floor in front of him. I stood with my pack in the doorway, took in the scene and thought, *To all of these people, this is home.*

A week later, we moved into our flat, several blocks away from the band's squat. It was bipolar—full of locked doors and too many walls, a home divided, a place of no cohesion. A ground-floor flat, the living room and bedroom was one unit, and it was separated by a public hallway from the kitchen and dining room, which was another unit. The doors to the different areas of the flat would close and lock automatically, and we kept finding ourselves in the public corridor, locked out, in robes or sometimes worse. A bath and toilet sat on the second floor for the whole building to use, and we had our own outside toilet in the garden, a tiny square of concrete with weeds snaking through cracks in the walls. I couldn't blame anyone for this flat but myself. I'd chosen it. It was the only thing we could afford because I wasn't making enough money to contribute to the household. Finn retreated deeper into himself, so far down that no matter how deep I reached, I couldn't find him there. I couldn't pull him back up.

After work, he'd sit in the floral chair in the living room with the floral wallpaper, floral carpet and floral curtains. I called the design kitschy, but really it was dog ugly. He'd put on headphones and listen to jazz for hours, smoking weed. I'd come in from the kitchen across the hall, where I'd set up a folding table and an old desktop computer to work on my articles, and he'd have tears running down his cheeks. I'd ask him what was wrong and he'd say something about the music, some beautiful passage in some old-world melody. I wondered, though.

In Asia, we could be anything we wanted. People didn't know how to categorize you. Educated or uneducated, working class or middle class, it meant nothing in different countries with different class systems, as long as you were an outsider, as long as you didn't try to fit in. Rarely did the people around you judge you for the class you were back home. Missouri was exotic to them. Other travelers were fascinated with the stories I told about butchering and subsistence living, and they helped me see that just maybe my life was not just hard scrabble, but was also made of myth and legend.

Finn was a musician in Asia. He was a mini-god. So was I, in a way, but it was always different for women. Here, Finn's accent gave him away. He was working class. He needed to know his place. It bent him at the shoulders, the expectations or lack of them, dumped upon him.

When I could get him to talk, which wasn't often, he told me stories he'd never mentioned before. How he went to the school counselor as a teenager and was told to give up, to get a trade, that he'd never make it doing anything else anyway, so why try? Why bother?

I had no experience with how to care for a man. Father was a brute and his fear so shocking and crazy that I never learned about men's inner workings, what they needed, or how to be. I couldn't be a house frau. That was never going to happen. But I could be a good person. I just didn't know how to understand men. I'd be too soft with some reaction of Finn's when it wasn't required, and a sharp bitch when I needed to be soft. If he grew angry, which was rare, my fear of Father would be so intense I'd have to slap Finn down before he could hurt me, which he would never have done. It was a hard-wiring.

I didn't keep house. I flung myself into projects and forgot that everyone and everything else existed. I disappeared in a hundred of different ways, left the flat to roam, left my body. When I'd get back I'd be in a haze. I didn't vacuum, or scrub. I often didn't bathe.

I loved London too much to want to deal with the fact that he didn't. He wanted to move to America. He'd always wanted to move to America. It was a childhood dream. He wanted to be on a boat on the Mississippi like Huck Finn. He needed the adventure. I put him on the backburner. London was mine, and I had no desire to go back. For me, right then, London was home. And nobody was going to take that from me.

One day, I walked into the kitchen from the cooperative and a homeless man sat at the Formica table. He wore filthy clothes and reeked of vomit and alcohol. Finn came in from the bathroom.

"This is Rasco," he said. On the table were packs of cigarettes, a bottle of scotch, and a bag of weed.

The man was tall and hairy. He was on something much stronger than weed or booze or was coming off of it. His body shook with it. I didn't like him. He scared me. He was nothing like the gentle homelessness of Usui. I cornered Finn, and whispered that he needed to get Rasco out of my house. He slumped forward and said, "Where is your compassion, Queenie?"

I wasn't big on cooking. I went to the shop and bought chicken breasts, and cooked that and some mashed potatoes, something middle-American because it was easy and I couldn't think, because it was what Mother would've done, because it was what I thought a woman should do. Cook.

They sat at the table and ate, and I saw in their motions that Finn was this homeless man and this homeless man was Finn and I began to understand. I couldn't help all the homeless men in London, but maybe I could help Finn. Could I?

At one point, Rasco stumbled to our back garden and vomited.

It got bad. The crying. Too much grief as he sat listening to jazz. Too many days in a row. Too many nights without fucking, months, a year.

I had to do something. I had no idea what. I decided to take him again to Lester's. If home was our people, then maybe Les could help. It was stupid. I had no tools for any of this. I told Finn a notebook was missing from the box we'd shipped, that I needed to find it. He nodded, slumped. He was passing through life like he was walking through treacle. Lester was the only solution I could think of.

After Les let us in, he went back to the main room and flopped in the dirty recliner. On a small gravelly telly the BBC showing scenes of the Gulf War. Finn sat on the sofa. He didn't seem angry with Les this time, his passions pressed down into an unrelenting wash of feeling nothing. I looked at both of them, and realized they were no different. Two sad people.

I went to the corner shop and purchased a package of thin ham, a block of cheese, a cucumber and white bread. By the time I returned, the six-pack of Boddington's was gone, empty cans scattered on the floor near the two men. I went back out and got more.

They ate their sandwiches while I stood over them and watched. The room was thick with cigarette smoke, and there was that smell again of rotting food. The Gulf War droned in the background, beer tops popped, lips smacked, and car engines muffled on the busy street below. Finn didn't seem to be in his body. Lester was pounding the beer so hard, he could barely sit up. I went around Les and turned off the telly.

"Finn, control your woman," Les slurred.

"You guys are going for a walk," I said.

Finn scowled at me from lowered brows.

"I'll clean up, and see if I can't find that notebook."

When they didn't move, I went over and took Finn's arm, pulled him to his feet. "Go," I said, looking hard into his eyes.

It was a brisk winter day, the sun was shining, which in London was a miracle in itself. "There's a park across the street. Go to the park." Finn shook his head. Lester belched. Still, Les wiggled his way out of the recliner. They put on their coats and left the flat, marching in formation like two errant schoolboys.

I started cleaning. I would not clean at home, but here, it

seemed required. I felt my German mother urging me along, as I hit the sour-smelling kitchen hard and fast. Something possessed me, as if by scouring the linoleum I could clean up Finn's past, and make everything okay.

What I wanted to do was scrub the bank of sliding windows. The glass shadowed the room even when the sun was shining.

There was a new bottle of glass cleaner beneath the sink. Lester seemed to buy glass cleaner, although he didn't appear to use it. I found a rag. The tar came off with heavy scrubbing. *Out damn spot. Out, I say! One: two: why, then, 'tis time to do't. Hell is murky!* After an hour and a half, I was panting.

I turned to survey the room, and saw the problem with such cleaning. When you removed the dirt and scum, every other flaw became too evident. No amount of cleaning could change how ugly the room was. It needed to be gutted. It was like turning bright lights on in the face of a drunk and aged whore. No amount of new clothes was going to make her beautiful again.

I picked up beer cans, sandwich plates, emptied ashtrays. I found a push vacuum cleaner that did nothing to get the cat hair off the threadbare carpet. I pounded the pillows and released a cloud of dust. I scrubbed every surface. It would have to do.

The bedroom was small, just big enough for a bed with a narrow path around it. On the bed a pile of twisted blankets covered in cat hair. The sheets needed to be washed, but there wasn't time. No spare sets in the cupboard. I came upon Les' stack of porn. Bondage porn. Sadomasochism.

I knelt and flipped through the magazines. Women's breasts tied with rope. Women dangling from the rafters. Women gagged. Legs tied. Arms tied. Eyes covered. All sorts of awkward ass-projecting positions. I was so engrossed, kneeling forward on the floor, my face close to the glossy images, that I didn't hear Lester and Finn come in.

"Queenie?" The two men stood in the bedroom doorway, watching me. My face burned hot like fire. A magazine was open to a centerfold. A woman's legs and arms were tied spread eagle in a barn, a red gag ball in her mouth.

Neither men could stand straight. They'd obviously gone to the pub. Lester started laughing. I shut the magazine, stood up, felt dizzy, swayed like I was drunk, too.

"So, did you find your notebook?" Finn slurred. Lester's laughter degenerated into a frog in his throat that he tried to clear with barks of phlegm.

"No, I couldn't find it." I tried to shove a pile of clothes on top of the magazine, but the move revealed more magazines, opened to pages of more tied-up women, and all around me were women in bondage.

I stumbled toward the doorway. As I passed by Finn, he lost his balance and grabbed the door frame. Dizzy, I stumbled too, and grabbed onto his arm.

Lester propped his floppy body against the other wall. He wove his lighter erratically, trying to get the flame to the tip of his cigarette. He was too drunk, and could not get it lit, and he couldn't stop laughing.

Alex was cooking a batch of *bigos* for us in the small kitchen of his flat. Sauerkraut, meat, kielbasa, the aroma of cabbage swirled me back in time to Mother standing over the stove.

"It'll take months to research." He looked at me with his blue eyes that sometimes looked purple. He had a striking profile, a chiseled jaw line, and a large hawk nose. He had a piercing way of seeing the truth behind lies. I wondered what his parents' lives were like in Poland before they'd moved here.

He was talking about a story we could all work on together. He'd heard about abuse in government-run facilities for the severely disabled. Not centers like Charlotte's, but homes where handicapped kids were placed for longer stays. The abusers apparently were being transferred from home to home.

"We'll need to interview people all over England. It'll take a while to do the research. It won't be an easy story." He looked at me hard, like he was seeing something I wasn't. There was something driving Alex that was greater than just his own desire for honesty, but I couldn't put my finger on it. "We won't make much money off it," he said, holding a spoon of the *bigos* to my lips.

I blew on the spoon. "Yeah, I'm learning speaking the truth and making money seem to be mutually exclusive endeavors." I ate his offering. It was like swallowing Poland. Visceral. "Of course I'm on board," I said.

"Fools rush in…" Alex said, putting the lid back on the pot.

I did research on the structure and history of the government homes. Alex went out into the city and met with people who had contacts. He fed the contacts to Eileen, who worked to set up clandestine interviews with former and current employees and parents.

The organization was full of loving people like Charlotte, committed and passionate, trying to create a world where the learning disabled were treated as equals, supported, nurtured, where the families could get a break. It wasn't just talk. I knew these people. I knew Charlotte. The light of it made the darkness of the abuse all the more horrific. I felt guilty, as if I was just focusing on the abuse, and not on the good work they were doing. But it had to stop. I went around for weeks with a tar-darkened soul.

I tried to immerse myself when I wrote an article. I tried to become whoever I was writing about. But I didn't know how to enter the psyche of people who were severely handicapped. I was able-bodied. It wasn't acceptable to not be able-bodied in Missouri. It threatened survival. On a subsistence farm, you were not allowed to be sick or broken. There was no coddling. Sick or broken, you were expected to work. There was almost animal fury aimed at anything that was weak, man, woman, child, beast. You would be eaten by predators and left for dead. The fear around it was bred into the bone. Father would beat you if you were sick. You learned not to be sick. You learned to press the sickness so far down.

The research took weeks, then months. It circulated a darkness in my blood. I'd always worn black, but now my clothes seemed to cling to me like a dark cape. My face darkened, my eyes. My hair sank into a frizzled tar. The walk to the tube, the train ride back home to Brixton, the buildings I passed seemed to be cloaked in thicker and heavier soot.

I was going back to the flat one night. It'd been a long day of research into the evil secrets kept behind closed doors. The Northern Line passed the Elephant and Castle, metal wheels rattling on old track, lights flashing and strobing as the train barreled through the tunnel. It was eight o'clock.

Something happened. Panic rose in my throat. I couldn't breathe. My heart was racing. I was going to die. The chang, chang, chang of the wheels on metal tracks, the flickering of the lights, the smell of so many unwashed people. The fear and panic swelled me, then deflated me, then swelled me, then deflated me. I felt myself falling. I fell into the darkest pit. I kept falling. There was no bottom, a bottomless pit. Flop sweat poured from my face, flushed through the back of my hair. I couldn't breathe. I couldn't breathe. I couldn't breathe.

Gasping, choking, I thrust my head between my legs as passengers watched. I was going to vomit. When the doors opened at Stockwell, I threw myself off the train and fell onto a bench. I could see the blurred edges of the train as it left the station.

Sideways on the bench, waiting for the panic to subside, I felt frozen and utterly alone and on the verge of death. Every fifteen minutes another train came in and dislodged its passengers, and others boarded.

If I cannot get on this one, I can get on the next one, I kept telling myself. The last train was at 11:00. Nine o'clock passed on the overhead clock. More trains I could not get on. At 11:00, I had no choice. The last train. Sick, dizzy and in full-blown panic, I crawled onto the train. I sat and kept my head between my legs. Brixton was only one station away but if felt like an eternity.

The mother's name was Jaqueline. She came out of the front door, walked up to our car, and burst into sobs. We'd driven the M-5 to the north of England to meet her at her house, an attached home that looked like all the other attached homes around it, the only difference the vegetation and garden gnomes in the tiny square garden at the front.

Alex guided her back inside. She was hysterical, snot running from her nose and on the back of her hand where she kept wiping it. Alex was so good with people. He sat her in a straight-back chair, and we sat on the other side of a heavy coffee table on the sofa. "Just tell us what you know, in your own words," he said.

She was in her thirties, but the way her body bent at the middle, and the lines on her face, made her look older. Potpourri in a bowl on the coffee table sent waves of sickening perfume. A child and a small dog played in a cramped corner by the television. I didn't think they boy should be in the room. Jacqueline leaned forward, hands over her face. It was several minutes before she could speak.

She had a daughter who was fourteen, severely handicapped, could only move her eyes, emotional age of a three-year-old, could not speak. Jacqueline knew her daughter was being abused. She couldn't say the words; they came out of her as snot and tears. It was as if no one had ever listened to this woman before. She looked at us with such desperate need, and she kept breaking into wracking sobs.

At one point, she came around the heavy coffee table and knelt at my feet. She put her hands on my knees, and sobbed. There was nowhere for me to go. I couldn't back up and I couldn't move.

The sobbing woman, her hands like claws on my knees, the

little boy's fearful eyes in the corner, the yapping of the little dog —panic threatened in my gut. I made fists by my thigh, trying to hold it all down. Alex looked sideways at my fists and gave me a worried look. He stood up and guided Jacqueline back to her chair.

"Shall I go in and fix us some tea?" he asked. She nodded. I had a list of questions and considered asking her them while he was gone, but then thought better of it. He came back moments later with a teapot and three mugs. We drank the Earl Grey, and every once in a while the woman would emerge from her grief, and beg, "Please, please do whatever you must to help. Please."

We nodded and assured her. I knew I had a frozen look to my face but it was the best I could do.

When it was time to leave, we told Jacqueline we'd be in touch. She followed me to the door, her hysterical mucus gasping close to my ear. It was a sound I needed to run away from. We said our goodbyes and got into Alex's car.

"All right then, Pearl?"

I nodded. We waved to the woman as we drove away. Ten minutes down the motorway, I was gasping for breath, holding the passenger handle, my high-pitched, labored breathing like cries of some dying bird.

"What can I do?" Alex asked, looking at me frantically.

"Pull over," I cried.

"Okay."

I grabbed the door handle.

He yelled, "Okay!"

I opened the passenger door as he was still on the motorway. He swerved to the side of the road. I fell out of the car onto my knees in the gravel. My body pulsed with terror. I felt like I was having a heart attack. My heart was racing, my face covered in sweat. I pulled myself up and started pacing, holding my side, bending over as I walked.

They want me dead. They want me dead. They want me dead. It was the mantra that filled my head as a child. *They want me dead. They want me dead. They want me dead*, a broken record. I shuffled along the muddy ditch along the side of the motorway, pacing back and forth, back and forth, back and forth.

Alex stood at the driver's door. "What can I do?"

I shook my head. Paced. Shook my head.

He started to come toward me. I put my palm out flat, arm extended. *No.* He stopped. If he came near me and touched me I would lose it. I would have to go to an emergency room.

It was the same feeling I'd had on the bench in the tube. It was a feeling that was there all along, an old friend, or rather, a long-lost enemy who'd gone into hiding and now had come out to play.

"Just… a minute." I felt like I was going to wretch and went to the tall weeds at the edge of a scrubby no-man's land, bent over and gagged, but nothing came out.

It took a half-hour for me to calm down enough to get back in the car. And even then I wasn't sure I wouldn't panic again. Alex sat in the driver's seat looking ahead. He said again, "What can I do?"

I shook my head.

"Are you all right?"

I nodded. Of course I wasn't. I nodded again. "Let's go."

As he merged onto the motorway, he said, "Do you think you should get some help, therapy, talk to somebody about all that happened to you when you were a child?" I'd told Alex stories of my childhood in Missouri, the animal butchering, and a bit about Father's rage. I had not told him everything.

Nauseous, I looked out the car window at the drab field. "Sorry. I don't mean to be making this all about me. I'll get it together. This isn't about me. It's about those handicapped kids."

"Maybe all of this is about all of us, Pearl."

I leaned forward over my knees, and put my palm up to stop his talking.

Two nights later, another panic attack on the train home. An hour journey took me three hours. I had to keep getting on and off the train. My body was still shaking when I walked into the living room. Finn had his headphones on, sitting in the chair, listening to jazz. He had tears in his eyes.

I knelt in front of him. He took down the headphones. He was stoned. I could see it in his faraway eyes. He had his own demons to bear. I didn't have words for what was happening to me. I looked at him for a long while without speaking, holding his knees.

"I'm having these attacks or something on the trains," I said, almost in a whisper. "I can't breathe. I have to keep getting on and off the trains." I panted like a dog as I told him. Finn's eyes watered. "I can barely make it home. I'm scared. I think I need to go to therapy."

He put his hand to my face. His eyes were still teary.

I let myself melt into the feel of his palm. We sat this way for a while, the sounds of muffled Miles Davis emanating from the headphones dangling at his waist.

4 0

A card was on the floor mat when I got home. No panic attack on the train this time, but the erratic nature of the attacks made them even scarier.

I took the card, used the key to let myself first into the kitchen to grab a beer, and then used it to enter the living room. Finn and I would joke about how our lives were so compartmentalized, how one needed a passcode to enter the different parts of our existence.

The card was from Charlotte and Michael. I'd told Charlotte about my panic attacks. They were the only people I could think to tell. I held up the card. On the front was a bunny with a pink nose, a kitschy thing they surely purchased as a joke. "Happy Birthday," it read. I was going to be thirty years old that weekend.

I opened the card. "Go to South Kensington Station at 11:00 a.m. on Saturday. Inside the station to the right, you'll see a newsagent. Go up and say, 'Hi, my name is Pearl Swinton, and it's my birthday.' It was signed, "Love, Charlotte and Michael."

I showed Finn. "Do you know anything about this?"

"No."

"Did you remember it was my birthday?"

"You've only reminded me a dozen times over the past week, Queenie."

I had a thing for birthdays, not just mine, but other people's too. I liked to be celebrated and to celebrate. I'd had so little of it as a child.

"What should we do?" I asked.

"You should go to South Kensington on Saturday at eleven. It doesn't say I should go. So this is your celebration."

I nodded and stared at the bunny on the front of the card.

"Hello, my name is Pearl Swinton and today is my birthday," I said to the Pakistani man running the newsagents at South Kensington Station. I had a 101-degree fever. I was sick as a dog with a cold or a flu or both, and the snot in my sinuses made my voice sound like Daffy Duck.

The newsagent shook his head, waved his hand and ignored me. He went to help another customer buying an Evening Standard.

"Hello," I yelled louder over the din and echo of the busy station, "my name is Pearl Swinton and today is my birthday!" I looked around for Michael or Charlotte or Finn, but it was just the normal crowd of Londoners coming and going.

"Oh. Yes." He wobbled his head. "Yes, of course." The man's eyes brightened. "Oh I am so very sorry. I had forgotten. One moment, please." He dug beneath the counter.

"Happy birthday, Missus," the newsagent said as he handed me a Kit-Kat and another card. Kit-Kats were my favorite.

He turned and said something to someone in the back of the stall. A woman in a sari came forward. "Happy birthday to you," they sang in slow disharmony. I ate my Kit-Kat and watched them sing. They stood straight and didn't sway, sometimes forgetting the words. I tore open the card.

"Well done, Pearl," it read. On the front was a fluffy yellow baby chick. "Now go out the east exit in front of you, turn left, walk three blocks. On the right, you'll come upon Dee's Floral. Go inside, and say, 'Hi, my name is Pearl Swinton, and today is my birthday.'"

I did as I was told. The shop was full of heavy floral arrangements, but because of my cold everything smelled sterile. An older woman in pearls clapped, ran behind the counter and presented me with a half-dozen roses and another card. She had a young gay helper and they sang Happy Birthday in two-part harmony. Customers joined in.

The next card sent me to a chocolate shop, and the next to a novelty store where I was given a red hat.

Within an hour, I was carrying a journal, a book, a helium balloon and a stuffed bear, along with the flowers and chocolates. It was a brisk day, and my high fever made me delirious. I kept looking around at passersby, sure that everyone was in on it. I must have been giving them crazy looks, because they would give me a wide berth in my hat with my floating balloon and my crazy eye contact.

A card instructed me to go to a pub near the Chelsea Center where Charlotte worked. The Thames was swollen, and I felt its pull as I made my way. Finn sat in the low-lit corner. "Oh my God, are you in on this?" I said, laughing and kissing him hard on the mouth.

He held up a card of his own. "No, I got this the same day you got your card but I was told not to tell you about it." He showed it to me. On the front was a kitten. "Finn, for Pearl's birthday, we need you to go to the Chelsea Potter Pub at 2:00 p.m. Two beers will be paid for and waiting for you at the bar. Go to the bartender and say, 'Hello, my name is Finn, and today is Pearl's birthday.' The bartender will give you the beer. Do not tell Pearl. Love, Charlotte and Michael."

A pint of lager sat in front of an empty chair. Finn motioned for me to sit.

"The bartender gave me another card," Finn said, holding up the envelope. "We're not supposed to open it until we down these pints. Cheers," he said and winked.

I was so sick, I could barely taste the lager. Everything was misty in my feverish state, the dark pub with its low lights, shining wood, and table candles, like some distant memory of a long-ago London. I felt weepy. How long had it been since I'd had any fun?

"Okay, Queenie?"

I nodded, close to tears. Finn reached out a hand and held mine.

"Sometimes good things unleash the grief," Finn said, or I thought he said, but maybe he hadn't spoken. I was dizzy, and maybe it was a voice in my head instead or maybe it was Usui speaking from the land of the dead.

The next card instructed us to go outside and hail a black cab. Inside was another, smaller, sealed envelope. We were told to hand the cabbie the envelope. We did this. The cabbie showed us what was inside the card. It was an address and money for cab fare.

When the driver pulled up to a big top, I could not fathom it. I was a great lover of the circus. I had told Michael and Charlotte this during one of our stoned evenings.

The tent took up two massive parking lots adjacent to the Thames. We walked in to find on the bleachers in the front row people we knew: Ace and Fumble, Alex and Eileen, Charlotte and Michael. My body burned with fever, my nose a deep red from rubbing away the snot. Everything seemed as if it were a dream.

The lights went down. The circus performance began. They wheeled in a three-story-high fan and the air blew cold in my face, whipping my hair into a rat's nest. I would surely get pneumonia. Michael leaned over and handed me a program. This was Archaos, a French anarchist circus. They lit totem poles on fire in the center ring, the fan blowing them into flaming bursts. Men and women in leather biker clothes and trussed-up in BDSM gear flew on trapezes from the rafters.

They set a massive ring on fire. I could feel the flaming heat on my already burning cheeks. A man on a motorcycle flew off a ramp and through the fiery ring. I felt I'd died and gone to some form of hell, a place I wanted to live but wasn't allowed.

I spent the next week in bed verging on pneumonia, sick as a dog, in and out of consciousness. *Sometimes good things unleash the grief.* This time I was sure it was Usui's voice I heard.

41

Alex, Eileen, and I spent the next three months collecting case studies. Eileen found it difficult to sit for the hours needed to do the research, so she brought barbells to the flat. We'd hear the clink, clank against the hardwood as she worked out in the next room.

I assumed Alex told her about the panic attack because she came up to me, the front of her ample body thrust outward so her stomach touched mine. "I dig you," she said. "You're people." She punched me over my heart. "I'm here, girl." She punched me again.

The stories of these children not being able to speak, of their abuse, became a thick soot that entered my blood. I became someone else. Something else. Something dark and hard. I became two different people, two sides, one dark and one light. The dark started to win.

Eileen set up an interview for me with a well-known London psychotherapist who specialized in abuse. She'd found just a few articles where the therapist was interviewed, but there weren't many. In fact, overall there weren't many general articles on abuse in the UK. England was behind the U.S. in speaking openly about such things.

Linda Dunn's office was on the second floor of a historical building on Harley Street, in Marylebone in Central London. The wood was polished and the windows filled with warped leaded glass, which transformed the outsiders walking by into abstract images. As I made my way up the polished staircase, I wished I owned something other than thrift store clothes. I was in a black, long loose sweater, black tights, and lace-up boots. My hair snaked in tendrils around my face. No amount of makeup could cover the dark circles beneath my eyes.

I entered her office, and on desks and tables sat dozens of globes of different diameters, heights and hues. The light from the tall windows reflected off each, and it was all I could do not to go up and touch them, spin them. Although they were all globes of planet Earth, the office seemed to contain the entire Milky Way.

Dr. Dunn sat across from me in a plaid wing-back chair, beige skirt suit, legs crossed, hair coiffed. She outranked me by about six higher classes. I should have showered. Behind her was a wall of books stacked high, a ladder on a wheel track to reach them.

I had a professional way of interviewing. Usually I could stay in the intellect and cut off emotion. Tape recorder on the table, notebook opened, I let my brain take over. I peppered her with questions: about the culture of secrecy around the abuse, why it existed, the effects of the abuse on an able-bodied kid, then on someone severely handicapped.

I felt the panic rising in my throat like bile. I forced myself to click back into the intellect, to push the emotions back down into my belly. I felt like I was grabbing a small wailing child by the upper arms, shaking her, telling her to stop screaming, and shoving her into a broom closet.

"They have no protection," she said. When she spoke, you could feel her body vibrate with passion. "They have no voice. They will not grow up, and then be able to speak. They will never be able to speak about what has happened or is happening to them. This is why they're targeted."

She was looking at me. Hard. Like she was seeing right through me. I squirmed in my chair, crossed and recrossed my legs. Again the wrestling match with my crazy inner child. I was sure Dr. Dunn could see the depths of the darkness in me, the soot of my soul.

She asked about the journalist's cooperative. I felt silly and small describing it to her, surrounded by her posh office, her library (a woman with a library!), and the glowing orbs, like we were duct tape and she was satin.

"So you're outsiders," she said, leaning forward.

"Excuse me?"

"Your journalist's cooperative. First-generation immigrant, an Australian, an expat from the States. You're not *of* British culture."

I nodded. *Yes, I guess we were outsiders.*

"Some of the greatest acts of heroism have come from outsiders. Some of the greatest art. Some of the world's best thinkers. Do you know why?"

I shook my head, feeling dizzy. The dark cloak lifted off me, fell again, lifted again.

"Because being outside allows one to truly see." A ceramic globe sat on a table next to her chair, and she ran her palm over it. "This world needs outsiders to speak truth. You cannot play by the same rules because you do not know the rules. The norm doesn't reside inside you as a given."

My body was pulsing. She asked me about my personal history. I told her about growing up on the farm, living in Japan, working as a journalist, the travel in Southeast Asia.

"So you are a professional outsider. What a gift you've been given. What a purpose."

Being an outsider was my purpose? I sat stunned. I had no words. What did it even mean to have a purpose as an *outsider*? How could that be a gift, feeling you belong nowhere, having no point of reference? "It's more of a curse when one doesn't feel they fit anywhere."

She nodded, bent slightly in the chair. "Every gift is a curse," she said, her eyes heavy. She spun the globe, shook her head, sat up straight. "At any rate, the article you're writing gives these girls a voice. And that is the most important thing at this moment. And I applaud you for doing the hard work. You and your colleagues at the cooperative *are* their voice."

I loved her. I wanted to be her. The crazy little girl inside me wanted to run up and hug her. I finished the interview, collected my things, shook Dr. Dunn's hand, took one look back at her dream office, and left.

We pitched the story to a major London daily, and they accepted. We were given a deadline and a word count. We had to take months of research and boil it down to 800 words. The day came to compile the story. I had the file folder of notes, research and interviews, the size of a thick phone book.

Alex and Eileen disappeared. I didn't know where they had gone. I was alone in the office. I thought I'd just bang out a rough draft that we could hone and revise together. The words and thoughts roiled and boiled. My hands rammed and slapped the keyboard, like I was playing some kind of anarchist concerto. I worked at a frantic pace. I looked up and four hours had passed. The story was written. As if on cue, Alex and Eileen walked in with Chinese takeout.

"It's finished."

"What?"

"I wrote it."

They stood beside me and read the article.

"Do not change a word," Alex said.

Eileen punched my arm. Hard. "Good god!" she said. "Let's get those fucking bastards."

I knew somehow their disappearance was meant to be. It was my story to write. They just had to get out of the way.

We faxed the story to the newspaper and waited to hear from the editor. There was a relief and exhaustion in all of us. We celebrated by eating moo shu pork and chicken fried rice. I wanted to go out and prowl. I needed to prowl.

Alex handed me a fortune cookie. "All right there, Pearl?"

"They will not win," I said to him. "They will not win." I didn't know who the "they" was. Sometimes I thought even I was the "they." That was what tortured me the most.

"No they won't," Alex said.

"Fucking bastards," Eileen said, and punched me in the chest.

The shadow men drew up their dark hammers and slammed them against the graffitied wall. The force of their souls drove the hammer, boom, again, boom, again. Behind them the sun burnt symbols into their flesh at the back of their necks.

A 12-foot-tall mass of reinforced concrete. On top an enormous pipe that made climbing nearly impossible. Behind a gauntlet of barbed wire, soft sand (to show footprints), floodlights, vicious dogs, trip-wire machine guns and patrolling soldiers who might shoot any man, woman, or child on sight.

Soon, others joined the shadow men with their dark hammers, clawing at the wall with their nails, bloodying their fingertips, until plaster rained down, until small chunks gave way. Bulldozers joined the party, ramming the pockmarked edifice like a cock driving in and out, in and out. The people hammering the wall day and night became known as "wall woodpeckers."

Finally, the bulldozer loosened a slab. It fell away. The people screamed in frightening ancient delight. The man leaned heavily upon his mallet. The Berlin Wall was crumbling. East and West

Berliners flocked, drinking beer and champagne and sobbing. It was the greatest street party in the history of the world.

They had lived divided. Their lives were compartments. Truth sat in the bellies of Russian dolls stacked one inside the other, and each was locked with a key. Their lives had become the small compartments of a massive shelf, filled with forest trash, and now the pieces were flying out.

For the East Berliners, to get into their minds, you needed one key, into their hearts another, into their souls yet another. Now, suddenly the doors were flung wide. No one needed keys. No one knew the rules. No one knew this new definition of *home*.

Alex drove from London to Berlin to witness the crumbling wall. With him was a car full of his friends and family, Pole expats and Pole relatives. We heard nothing from him for a week. When he finally came back, he was unshaven, wild-haired, and stinking of armpit sweat and musty clothes. He came into the office where Eileen and I worked, holding out great chunks of concrete in the palms of his hands.

"So much work for so little gain. So much for so little." He kept repeating this as we fingered the chunks of wall. Some were painted with bits of red, and black lines, snippets of graffiti.

Something happened to Alex in Berlin. He was a different man. For weeks afterward, he rarely shaved. He hardly bathed. He rarely showed up at the cooperative. He had another delivery job that paid the bills. He was out delivering now most of the time.

When I did see him, he wasn't there. He'd fallen deep inside himself. *He is grieving,* a voice inside me said. Grieving so much loss, not just for the Berliners, but for his Polish ancestors. He wasn't just grieving for this generation, but for many generations. He was holding the sorrow of so many. I knew this, this collective grief. It was a heavy burden. *Sometimes good things unleash the grief.*

Meanwhile, our story on the abuse of handicapped kids in care created a snowball effect. Other journalists picked it up, bigger journalists, connected reporters. Dozens of articles followed.

There was an investigation. Policy was changed at the homes for the handicapped. Dr. Dunn was interviewed in article after article, and on the television. There were other general articles about abuse, too. TV presenters invited guests to discuss the issue. Our article seemed to have cleaned the tar off the window, and exposed how dirty the room really was.

Dr. Dunn called and left a message: "From your effort, a national healing has begun. You have no idea what you have set in motion. I am so proud of you."

I went to bed. I couldn't get off my mattress. The panic attacks were now inches from the surface. Besides sleeping, I would lie in a hot bath for hours, neighbors knocking, the room frigidly cold, water the only means of calming the vibrations of the flesh. I thought I would be relieved and happy, but I seemed to be getting worse.

***

There was something about Eastern Europe that was familiar, something about the oppression that spoke to me, a darkness of the familiar. Idle Hands was touring Eastern Europe, and I was their groupie.

The arched tunnels were dark, on both sides thick brick. The tunnels wound back into the earth, opening fluidly onto cavernous rooms that looked like they'd been blown out by explosives. Bricks and mortar flaked onto concrete floors. Walls were jagged and tooth-edged. We were in Krakow, Poland.

I followed Dublin Rick's voice down a long winding tunnel, into a domed room. Idle Hands stood on a round stage, and along the walls hung candles under glass. The face shadows were devilish. Finn was absorbed in his sax in the background. I stood right at the stage and stared at Dublin Rick. He played bass, sang, and stared back at me. He looked right into my darkness.

We traveled from gig to gig in a white van with no back

windows. They'd put down blankets and pillows and hung saris. It smelled like incense, weed and semen. Mostly semen. Ace and Fumble spent hours throwing drumsticks, juggling hacky sacks. I mostly lay on my back on the pillows staring at the metal roof of the van. Finn sat in the corner and smoked weed. Dublin Rick drove. Ace or Fumble or Rick would burst into spontaneous song, bang drumsticks on the van wall, shake gourd rattles, and the van would fill with dissonant clatter. I felt wrapped up in a circus bubble, and I never ever wanted to leave.

At night, Finn and I were almost always given a private room. It wouldn't have mattered. I threw myself at him, but he would not have me. Always some excuse. People in another room, too tired, not in the mood. I'd wear sexy underwear and rub myself against him, go down on him. He wanted none of it. None of me.

Eastern Europe was having an effect on me. Its darkness matched mine. I understood this heaviness in the belly. This secrecy. A furtiveness. My darkness did not have to hide. I wanted to let the crazy girl out to play.

We drove through the Black Forest. We were at a gig in a massive warehouse in East Berlin. There were four stages. When we arrived, I thought the people streaming through the front door were dressed for Halloween, but it was September. It took a while to understand this was the style, vintage '80s, mohawks, leather bustiers, big permed hair, frilly mini-skirts and thigh-high spiked boots. It was a throwback to the 1980s. It was Cyndi Lauper meets BDSM. The energy was giddy, sudden and out of control. Anything could happen. Anything was possible. Not necessarily in a good way. Darkness in this sudden vulnerable opening.

Four stages in four rooms. Idle Hands was playing on stage one. Again I stood and stared at Dublin Rick, letting the vibe of his guitar and his words jangle my bones. His energy rearranged me, broke me down, crumbled me into pieces. I stood at the stage and willed myself to be destroyed.

All my life I'd known artists. Jason, Yuriko, Finn. All my life I'd wondered at the way they crumbled bits of their spirit between their fingertips and finger-painted themselves upon the canvas of their worlds. It was as if no barriers existed between who they were inside and what they showed outside. Dublin Rick's voice rattled around below the skin, left shoulder, a word lodged in the womb, a phrase in the palm. I stared at his dark mouth and wondered if it was him, or if it was me, and how he did it. How any of the artists I knew did it.

Somehow I kept losing Finn. He'd wander off, and I'd go in search but I couldn't find him anywhere in the darkened warehouse. I drank at the bar in another room, watching a heavy-metal band slam instruments into the stage. I roamed. I prowled. Finn was nowhere to be found.

At the third stage, pinpricks of lights shot stars far up in the rafters. The room was choked with cigarette smoke, the metal band in the other room banging out discordance. On this stage, three people were performing some kind of sex show. Leather bondage gear, bare tits and asses, a woman using a whip and the sharp edge of her heel. Mouths close to leather crotches. I didn't know how far it would go.

I saw Finn by the stage. He was lost in it.

That night in bed, another struggle. We were alone in a room above a pub. The other band members down the hall. A row of single beds. We each had our own. I crawled beneath his covers, did everything I could to entice him. Nothing. Nothing. I went limp beside him. Hopeless.

"What is it?" I cried in his ear. "What's wrong?"

His eyes filled with tears. He wouldn't speak.

I went to my own bed, stared at the ceiling, boiling and churning inside.

The next morning, hungover and hacking from too many cigarettes, I went down the hallway to use the loo. There was a knock at the bathroom door.

"Queenie, I've got to use the toilet." It was Finn. "I'm going to take a shower."

I went back to the room, fell into a light sleep. The door opened. He sat behind me on the bed. He turned me over. I opened my eyes. It was not Finn. It was Dublin Rick.

He looked at me with cracked eyes, like he was searching for something in me, some answer, or some clue. I couldn't speak. The smell of him was rank. I loved it. He leaned in. I arched my body hard. He kissed me. I kissed him back hard, wanted more, wanted to be transported into his darkest places. He cut me off, sat back, looked at me with such profound confusion, said not a word, stood up and left.

Finn entered the room ten minutes later.

43

I **couldn't find Finn.** *I'd lost Finn. I was in a warehouse again in some dark Eastern European country, painted faces beneath big hair all turning to stare. Laughing. Trussing each other up. I kept roaming, but no Finn. I searched and searched, but never found him.*

I awoke in the flat we shared in Brixton. In the flat we *once* shared. He was not in bed next to me. He would never be in bed next to me again.

The breakup. The sobbing. The loss. Loss piled on top of loss. So many people I'd loved now gone. Abandoned, me abandoning them or them abandoning me. Did it matter? So many hauntings. *I loved him. I loved him not. I loved him.*

A month after the breakup, I had to leave the Brixton flat. I couldn't afford the rent or the memories. I couldn't afford the smells, his forgotten boots in the corner of the closet, his favorite block of cheese in the refrigerator. I couldn't afford the radio stations tuned to jazz. I couldn't afford the empty floral chair, the missing headphones. It was all just too expensive for my soul.

I moved in with a friend of Charlotte and Michael's. He held Bible study every Tuesday in the living room. Every few nights in the single bed in my room at the back of the flat, I fucked Dublin Rick. He took me hard from behind, ramming and slamming. He fucked my mouth, yanked my hair, growled like a dog. I sucked his dick and he came on my tits. I wanted to be destroyed by his cock, to be pounded into forgetfulness. One night, the candle on the table started the tablecloth on fire, and we fucked while it burned.

I didn't know what my new roommate thought, with his Bible and his discussions about God. I'd awaken late, and go into the kitchen in a long T-shirt, searching for some coffee. He was always kind to me. He was always nice. I suspected I was a soul he was desperate to save.

The cooperative fell apart. I got a job as an assembly line journalist at a magazine group. We churned out pap, sitting at a desk in an open-plan office with dozens of others for ten hours a day, typing in meaningless stories, editing, proofreading, feeding it into the system. Women's magazines whose whole purpose was advertising. I chain-smoked at my desk. People came up behind me with stop watches to time my typing speed. No one could believe I could type that fast. I was crazy and dark and on an edge.I snarled at anyone who got too close.

Then it got worse. Before, it was visions with a beginning, middle, and end. Now I was visioning all the time. Some barrier had collapsed. I could hear people's thoughts; even the trees were talking.

At night, spirits came and sat on the edge of the bed. People would appear in the corner of the room. This had happened before, but it was rare and sacred. Now it was perpetual and scary and far from sacred.

On the tube, thousands of thoughts, mumbling and tumbling. I knew I was reading minds and not just hearing voices. I knew I wasn't going crazy. I knew that whatever "gift" I'd had before had just upped the ante of its power. I knew it in my bones. This wasn't madness, this was my "gift." God help anyone who had such a gift.

The panic attacks too still happened. Sitting on tube benches all over London, waiting to die.

When I lost so much weight I was paper thin, Michael demanded I see a counselor. He gave me her name and number. He pushed me until I finally called and made an appointment.

44

As I drew near her office, a feeling came over me. *You are coming home. This is the feeling of home.* I didn't even know this place or this woman I was going to see. How could the feeling be so strong? My heart ached with it. I didn't understand it.

She had long, gray-brown hair, wore a loose dress. She was a hippie. Her office smelled of incense. A purple crystal sat on a round side table. Her lamps were fringed. Her name was Shirley.

We sat across from each other. I told her how I'd felt a strange sense of home as I'd walked there.

She ran fingers through mousy hair. "I had a group here last night, and we were doing spiritual work. I'm imagining that's what you felt."

I burst into tears. She watched me and said nothing for minute after minute. Finally she asked, "Why are you crying? Talk to me." But I had no words. It was all stuck in my throat. I couldn't breathe.

I have no home. It's been so long since I had anything close to a home. I have no idea what home even means anymore. I've lost my family, and my earth, and my country, and, now, my love. I cried into my hands, great wracking sobs.

"Talk to me," she said.

I couldn't. I cried until she told me the session was over.

In the next session, I told her about the panic attacks, and how water, a bath, was the only thing that calmed them. She kept saying that she wasn't sure she could help me. That my trauma was greater than anything she'd ever dealt with. She wanted to send me to someone else.

"No. Please, no," I cried. This place was the only feeling of home I had left. Dublin Rick was coming by less and less often. Soon, he would be fucking someone else and he too would be gone. Not that it mattered, many nights I was still out on the prowl. Dublin Rick was no different than I was. It was just that he could do it publicly, and I had to do it secretly. Because I was a woman.

It took more than a month of weekly sessions before I told her about the visions. She sat forward on her love seat, her energy electrified. I told her how they started when I was thirteen years old. How they scared my parents. How I couldn't control them. I told her about the Osage woman who came to me so many times in Missouri, wanting something from me but I wasn't sure what. I explained Usui to her, how I'd met him in Tokyo as a real live man, and how now his ghost guided me, even when I wanted him to go away. I explained how some visions seemed to be about past and future lives, and some were spirits visiting me, and others were great works of fiction, revealing a truth unseen by the mundane world.

She smiled and leaned forward like what I was saying was a

good thing. When I finished, she started laughing or crying, I couldn't tell which.

"It's not funny," I said, my head in my hands.

"No, it's that I gather why you are here now, with me. Before I couldn't fathom it."

"Why?"

"Because you have a gift, a spiritual gift."

"It's a curse," I spat. "I'm so sick of people saying that."

Shirley gained control of her face and looked at me more seriously. "Tell me why you think so."

From my mouth flew a torrent, a purging, a vomiting of words, how the visions came upon me like a rapist and took me unaware, how spent they left me afterward, how I could barely function in the normal world, how it was all getting so much worse. How I would never fit anywhere. Never have a home anywhere. I hadn't fit in Missouri, and I'd moved abroad to Japan, thinking in my naiveté, that surely it was just the American Midwest where I didn't fit, then of course not fitting in the Far East. I'd gone on the walkabout across Southeast Asia trying to find myself, but myself wasn't there. I felt at home in London, but now Finn was gone, and who could love me, the real me, when I had this side of myself? I was sobbing so hard, the words fumbled out like half-masticated food.

Shirley was kneeling beside me, her hand flat on my back. "But don't you see, these visions, that world, *is* your home."

I wailed.

I moved flats again, a one-bedroom railway cottage with bars on the windows beneath a rail line south of Brixton, near Electric Avenue, closer to the squat where Dublin Rick lived. I was addicted to him. He was pulling away. I needed to be closer, to get my fix.

My landlady was a visual artist. I didn't know why my life was always full of artists. Her studio was a long, narrow storage unit next to my flat. I'd sit on a stool and watch her paint scenes of fat Brits on holidays at the coast, while trains barreled overhead, the clanking sound a solid comfort.

I sat on the floor with colored markers and colored a woman with an exploding womb. I showed it to the landlady and she cringed.

Things got much, much worse. The psychic opening became a litany of dark spirits who visited my bedroom at night, the weight of them actually pressing on me as I clung desperately to the bedspread. I called upon Usui, but he wasn't there. *When I need you, you will not come to me,* I cried into the darkened room. Nothing from Usui; only these monsters from another world. I'd shiver beneath the covers and pray for the sun to rise.

To avoid the visitations, I went out at night and roamed. Electric Avenue filled me with dread, so I went there. Often. I circled around to Dublin Rick's and knocked on the shutters. He was there with someone else. I went again another night and knocked until I found him alone.

I wanted Dublin Rick to destroy me with sex. I wanted to burn up, to turn to ash, to feel nothing but his physicality, his monstrosity. We were two monsters, trading in the basest animal functions. I saw him twice a week, when he would let me.

We progressed to bondage. It was Rick's thing. I didn't say no. In his bedroom in the squat, there was a hole in the ceiling that he'd covered with a sari so no one on the second floor could see.

He kept the lights on, three small desk lamps sitting on the floor next to the bare mattress. I watched the shadows of us as we fucked.

Red ball gag and ass flesh squeezed by ropes. My shadow self was a winged black creatures with hair streaming in dirty wind, arms stretched hard and tethered behind my back. My shadow flew like a trussed-up chicken. Like the Women of the Light I'd seen in Nepal, here I was a Woman of the Dark. It didn't scare me. I liked these shadows, as much as I'd liked the light.

My dancing shadow embedded into the ceiling and the walls, like the shadow blasts left by the Hiroshima and Nagasaki bombs, after the people disintegrated, the outlines of their bodies were left as imprints on walls and concrete. Rick's room became a medieval mural, floor to ceiling full of contorted writhing shadowed me. Some bigger darkness was entering me. I wanted a master artist to paint my flying shadow, Goya or Blake or Caravaggio.

Then Usui's voice: *"Home is in the darkness too, Purr-chan. Truth not just in light, but in dark too."*

Rick left me trussed, and circled me. Arched like this, unable to move, I ached for him to touch me, to hold my breasts, cup my ass, yank back my hair.

Usui was circling, too. *"Many think home is only light. Many think darkness is other. It is outside. It is a misunderstanding. More dark comes of such misunderstanding."*

The two men, the one alive, and the one dead, circled me, not touching.

"You must understand."

Touch me, Usui, I thought. His ghost swirled in the darkness, like a vulture with no teeth.

Rick began plunging in me from behind. Gagged, I grunted, received him. Time had no meaning. I wanted this pain, these sensations to block out everything.

Someone beat on the shutters, "Dublin Rick! Man. You there!" It was a man. Rick was fucking men, too. The man must've heard us. "When's it my turn?" We were both addicted to Dublin Rick. He was like a drug. Rick and I fucked until the man beating at the shutters retreated.

When I put my clothes on, I had large button imprints on my knees from the mattress. My jaw hurt. My shoulders were sore.

Dublin Rick went over to a broken shelf to fix a hit of heroin. He held the filled syringe up to me. "A hit before you leave?"

I looked at the syringe. *Why not?* My hand reached out toward it like a child reaching for a shiny bauble. Oblivion. *Why not?*

I looked up into his eyes. He looked into mine. He pulled the syringe back. "No. No, I don't think so, love. This isn't a line you should cross."

I lit a cigarette. I let myself out as he stuck the needle into his arm.

Shirley gasped when she opened the door. I was worse. Darker. Harder. Haunted. Dublin Rick hadn't given me the heroin, but still my blood flowed with darkness.

"I thought we'd made real progress last time," Shirley said, hopelessness in her voice.

"Perhaps you underestimate the curse of this so-called gift." The words came out hard as granite.

She seemed to shiver. She knelt by my chair.

"Let's lay it on the line, shall we, Pearl?" Her words were no nonsense, but her voice was soft. "You are rare. This gift is unusual. I do not know how to handle it. You and only you are going to have to learn how to manage it. No place on earth is going to help you deal with this. No person on the planet is going to help with this. No man is going to complete this."

"Is this supposed to be making me feel better?" I said to her freckled face. Actually it did make me feel better and I couldn't quite understand why.

She looked about to say a whole lot more, but she just stared, nodded, got off her knees and sat back down. She folded her legs. "Now, let's start talking about what *does* work for you, shall we? Where do you feel best, and why. Let's explore that. Shall we?"

I shivered with sex withdrawals from Dublin Rick. It was several weeks later. I'd come weekly to therapy. The veil between me and other realities continued to grow thinner. Dublin Rick had moved on and was no longer available. He'd taken his heroin and moved on to some other man, or some other woman. Did it matter? In some recess of my mind, I thought he'd left me out of love. How he'd refused me the heroin, and how he was leaving me alone, and how for me that was the best I'd ever get out of this thing called "love," someone who chose *not* to destroy me.

Charlotte knew what a mess I was in. Her house in Clapham was close to where I lived, and she came to my flat, with its bars on the windows, and brought offerings. Fruit from the market. A homemade nut loaf. Cookies. Novels, biographies, and histories on the feminine condition. She'd sit on the floor, a hard peanut of a woman, and make fists in her passion to help. I knew if she could, she would have had me lying on my back, like little Dotty, playing musical instruments for me and singing.

Over the weeks, Shirley, the therapist, grew more and more unsure of her ability to help me. I begged her more than once not to send me away. She said: "Your gift is out of my league. This is beyond my capabilities." Still I begged. Still she let me come to her.

We were in a session, and she was sitting staring at me, studying me, and saying nothing. I couldn't smoke in her office, and played with a cigarette. "Okay, Pearl, this is it. This is the end of the line. We figure something out, or I'm going to have to commit you."

I looked at her aghast and left my body, floated near the ceiling in the corner of the room. It would never happen again. I hadn't told her about being committed to a psych ward as a teenager. I would never see Shirley again if that's what it took. The thought made me burst into tears. I'd rather become homeless and mad than go back to such a place.

Shirley took a pillow from beside her and held it across her lap as if to protect herself. "There are parts of you that are missing," she said. "The vacuum left by the missing parts of you is allowing this darkness to grow."

She said nothing for a while.

"I'm struggling with this," she said, working her mouth as if she were tasting the words before she spoke them. "I'm not sure I should say it. There's a message that keeps coming to me."

"That bad, huh?" I coughed.

She took in a breath loudly and blew it out. "Okay, this is it, *She needs to go back. She needs to go back to the States.*"

"Back?"

"To the States."

"Missouri?"

"There are parts of you that are missing, and you will never find them in London."

The Indian psychic. *You need to go backward.*

When I was little, I would watch the parts of myself fly away, balls of light spin from the top of my head, fly up and out. Father would burst into yet another rage fit, and another side of me would escape, run away. With each loss, I became more of a shell. I knew even then at some point, I'd have to figure out how to retrieve the parts. I'd have to go find the lost pieces of me, put them all out in front, connect the dots, recreate my constellation. Reform myself from the dust and light of the universe.

"I do know one thing. You will never be able to manage your gift, if you cannot get your body healthy. You have to do some healing, okay? Before you understand the visions, before you look up toward these other realities, you have to go down. You have to excavate yourself, and heal. You've had a tremendous amount of trauma.

I smashed the cigarette in my fist.

"What I'm really struggling with is that as a counselor, I can clearly see you are not in a good place to make an international move. We'll need to figure out a way to help you get your strength back prior to any such decision. And even then, when you get back to the States, you'll need to focus on healing. Health first, visions second."

She stood up and went to the drapes along one wall. I thought they covered windows, but she opened them to reveal a pair of large, mirrored, sliding closet.

"Come," she said. I got up and went to her. "Look at yourself." I kept my head down. "Look!"

I looked up. I was thin and small. The sweater hung on me like a potato sack. My jeans were too big and slipped down off my hipbones. I looked like a small child. I was the 13-year-olds with hearts over their nipples dancing on the stage in Thailand. I was the little girl me who'd had her first vision in the garden. I thought of Usui's dolls. The thin one that was me, and the big-breasted, heavy one that was "really" me. I was a girl terrified of her power. I was a girl who was refusing to grow up.

"Do you think this is attractive?" Shirley asked.

"I feel like shit. What do you expect?" What was she telling me? That I was ugly? I knew that. I was told that as a child by my father. I was in total agreement with her. I was ugly. I burst into tears. She led me back to my chair.

"Listen, I don't know what words to say. I'm trying to snap you out of this downward spiral. What trick will turn the light back on?" She sat back down and leaned forward with her elbows on her knees. She had on socks with patent leather shoes and her ankles were hairy.

"Okay, I also know that some of this darkness isn't yours. You've picked up something. I think it's very old trauma. And now, you're picking up new demons, too."

I stared at her, frightened. I'd always thought I'd carried

Father's black dog around with me, that somehow he'd put his darkness into me. It was the first time I'd ever heard the thought verified.

"I keep getting the word exorcism. We need to exorcise this. It is not yours."

"My father's," I said and shivered. He wasn't just a mean man, my father. He was full of murder. I'd thought more than once growing up, *This man wants me dead. If he could get away with it, he'd kill me.*

Dublin Rick had that darkness too. The currency Dublin Rick and I traded in was our mutual deviance. The darkness we batted back and forth in bed had come from others before us.

"Somehow we need to figure out how to extract that."

I nodded.

"For now, I have homework for you. I want you to draw a picture of your father. Purchase a long roll of butcher paper. Make him life-sized. Tack him to your wall. Can you do that?"

I looked at her horrified. Hang my father in my flat?

"Can you do that for me?"

I burst into tears.

"We'll work out a plan for you," Shirley assured me, handing me the box of tissues. "I'll be here for you in the transition to prepare you to go home."

What she already knew, and what neither of us was saying, was that I had no home to go back to.

The Thames was on fire. The river itself was aflame. It'd been hundreds of years, and now the waterway was shooting flames again. All across London, people gathered to gawk. A sewage barge rammed a bridge girder and spilled its toxic guts. It was on the news. I was watching at 3:00 a.m. to drown out the spirits crowding into my bedroom. People were on the bridges and shores as the water shot with flames.

I threw on my darkest clothes. My hair was a wild afro. I was sure I looked homeless, crazy. Electric Avenue was unpredictable this late, and I threw on my invisibility cloak as I walked. I was so open that I was picking up other's thoughts. This happened all day, but it was worse at night. Around me the minds of the people spoke their hopes and fears, their relentless worries, their obsessions and addictions. Their minds were befuddled on wine and drugs — the sloping darkness of their thoughts.

As a child, when I went into the forest at night, I became it, as if my body was made up of the sounds of crickets and frogs, wind through branches, the web of stars overhead. Here, too, in London, my body became a twittering universe of passersby, the sounds of cars and buses, of so many different languages. My body was the buzzing Tower of Babel.

On the night bus, there was only one other person upstairs, a goth with purple lips and a dozen piercings who was snoring. I thought about the last several sessions with Shirley.

The picture of Father hanging on my wall in my flat did nothing but send me over an edge. I kept it up for two weeks, but the black cloud around me grew. Shirley told me to take it down. She said again that my problems were out of her league.

She gave up the notion of extracting the evil that was there. It seemed too overwhelming a task. Instead, she decided we should focus only on the things that I loved. My life was full of what was wrong and what could go wrong, and we needed to "put our awareness to" what was right and good.

I told her about my love for the art galleries, and all of the artists I had known throughout the years. I explained my deep adoration for books, my passion for story, how as a journalist I'd committed my life to hearing other people's tales. I talked about Missouri, and my love of the earth. I didn't realize it until saying it out loud, how desperately I missed the soil, how no matter how much I felt at home in London, the earth came only in small patches; the sky was parceled out too, chopped into slivers that appeared between tall buildings. I missed muddy boots, the texture of bark against my palm, the animal stench of the forest, the wide rumbling clouds in a fat sky. She asked me about my belief in a god. She said if I was looking for home, I'd find it in spiritual work. I told her I did not believe in the white man's God. A childhood of Catholicism had scared God right out of me. She said that was why we were focusing on what I loved. We needed to find what I *did* believe in.

"With so much shit going on in the world, how can you believe in anything?" I asked her.

"With all that is going wrong, how can you not?" she replied.

"You don't have to believe in any 'God.' I'm not saying that. You just need to know *what* you believe in."

Session after session, I did begin to feel a bit better. I gained a few pounds. The old me flickered in some far-off place, like a ghost.

One day, the story of my life came out of me in epic fashion. I gave her the sweeping tale, about the forest behind our house and being a runner in Missouri. I told her about leaving the Midwest for the Far East with only a few hundred dollars and an address to a Jesuit mission, about my adventures in Japan, the death of Hirohito while I was editor, the earthquake and Usui's death in my arms, the trip across Southeast Asia, the people I'd met, the stories they had to tell.

I'd never given her the whole story like that. Before, it'd been about debilitating trauma, upsetting stories about visions I could never seem to fully understand. And lately, of course, snippets of the things I loved. But I'd never told her the entire tale. When I finished, I was standing and gesturing and nearly dancing in her office. She looked up at me, taken aback.

"What's wrong? Sorry. Am I talking too much?"

"No. No." She shook her head. "You've had quite an impressive life. You know this, correct? Or do you not?"

I wobbled my head side to side. What was she saying?

"Your journey has been writ large. Can you see this? Someday I will look forward to reading your books about your life."

I burst out laughing. "Sure. Yeah. Right. Books!" I said, but then I burst into tears.

"Why are you crying?" she asked.

I didn't know. I shook my head. I had no idea.

But in that moment, something clicked. She was right. I had to go back. I had to return to the U.S. The journey of my life needed to go full circle. There was no other way.

On the day Finn and I said our goodbyes, he looked at my face and said he'd never seen me so sad. He said in all the years he'd known me, he had seen me upset, but never full of such deep grief. I told him I had to go. I had to continue my journey on my own. I had to find myself, and I could not take care of anyone else while I was doing it. It wasn't just a choice; I would truly be incapable of giving to another person on this next leg of my journey. He sat on the floor and wept. He kept repeating, "So many memories. So many…memories." Watching him, more pieces broke off my already broken heart. I had to be strong. All my life, I'd had to be strong, and it was a habit this bearing down, this holding my nerve, this fierce commitment to knowing myself. I'd made a contract with myself lifetimes ago, a promise to journey to wholeness. I had to go. I had to grow—even if it meant turning to own the visions, even if it meant facing the black dog.

I got off the bus at Chelsea and made my way down to the river bank, near the building where Charlotte worked. It was the bit of the bank where I'd been before, when I'd been given the past-life visions of the London landscape, when I almost rolled into the current. Parcels of land, like people, could have a power of you. This bend in the Thames had such a physical effect on me.

The homeless slept on the ground; a few paced like shadows. On the river, flames moved in languid motion, undulating over the water, a primal fire dance. Fire boats were in formation. The barge was on its side against the bridge. Flames ran from the barge to the bank. When I was little, I could not discern myself from other living things. Every tree was me, every creek. The Thames entered me and I entered it, both of us so full of sewage. The river felt heavy and I was heavy and we were one in this heft. Grief filled me. Grief filled the Thames. The flames licked, burning. The river burned, and I burned with it.

Usui was there, a black outline against the flames.

"I've come to say goodbye," he said. "I must leave now. It is time."

I reached out, he reached too, his fingers on fire, and our fingertips touched like god and man on the ceiling of the Sistine Chapel.

"Yes," I said.

"You gave me too much credit, Pearl-chan. I was weak man, when alive. You gave me your strength. You must now keep your strength and not give it away."

I flashed on Usui depression the day I found him on his futon at the Jesuit mission in Tokyo, the sickly weakness of him, and the truth of what he said. It reminded me of what I was reading in the books Charlotte was giving me, about women and giving up power.

"I love you," I said.

He nodded. He knew. "You will see me no more. You must listen only to your wisdom now."

"Yes, not from any other place, not from any other person, not from any man."

"Not from any man," Usui repeated. He was fading, disintegrating.

"Goodbye." So much loss. So much love, and so many goodbyes.

His voice was fading. He was entering the fire, his ghost body bursting into flames, turning into ash. His last words were faint: "Not that you ever listened to me anyway."

I laughed. I held my stomach and belly laughed, flames my epic backdrop.

The panic attack was swift and sudden. I was unable to breathe. My heart pounded, face slimed with sweat. It felt like death. The black dog snarled, fang-toothed and murderous. A wall seemed to crumble inside me.

Beneath my feet the ground opened. I started falling. I couldn't stop myself. I fell into oblivion, plunged into the netherworld.

There was no ground. There was no earth. Like the first time I skydived, dangling from that Cessna strut, my fingers pried loose, a tumbling, a wailing, a flailing.

When I hit the ground, which I would, nothing would ever be the same again. What would rise from the ashes would be dark, and what would rise would be light. Nothing would ever be the same again, when I hit the ground.

Which I would.

BOOK GROUP QUESTIONS

1. In the beginning of this novel, Pearl has a memory of
   what happened in Tokyo when looking at a meteor
   shower in the bay of Enchanted.

*People falling from the sky, on fire, was a memory. The other, watching
a meteor shower on my back in the bay on the Pacific Ocean, that was
reality. Reality and illusion—sometimes one wasn't more real than the
other. Sometimes the veil between today and memory, between the water
lapping through sodden wrinkled fingers and a broken rail bridge in
another country and another time, between a meteor shower and children on fire flailing through sky, was cut from the thinnest, most
diaphanous cloth. Sometimes the veil was missing altogether.*

What part does memory play in FIRE as a whole? How do past
memories affect you and your story?

1. When Pearl is floating in the ocean in the bay of
   Enchanted and turns into little boy (Enrique), what do
   you think is happening? Is she dreaming? Is it a memory
   of a past life? Do you believe in past lives?

2. Pearl meets the baby of her "landlady" in a Himalayan village. The child's name, translated to English means Tender Grass. What is the significance of that name? Why do you think Pearl has a vision of Tender Grass growing up and living in London?

3. In Thailand, when Pearl is sitting with the woman who works for the nonprofit on her porch, Pearl feels herself fall into her, what do you think is happening?

I seemed to leave my body and enter her. The soul of me, the still whole part of me, went inside her. I leaned toward her, and she shifted toward me, and I knew she was feeling it too. I seemed to be healing the rift in her soul.

1. What part do the forest fires in India and the cloud of smoke moving across continents play in the theme of the book?

2. Thai girls leave their villages to go make money in Bangkok, the rickshaw driver in India, Leo, leaves his village to go make money in a big city. How does this affect the lives of the displaced people and their families?

3. Why do you think the author added the story of Yuriko and Asha coming to visit Asha's parents in India? What role did the story of their love, and Asha's ultimate future estrangement from her family, play in the book? What does it say about the concepts of family security and being your true self?

4. Pearl's deceased friend from Tokyo, Usui, keeps appearing in her visions, across several countries, and in different circumstances. Why? What do you think is their connection? (Usui is introduced in AIR, the second

novel in the series. Please read AIR to learn more about Usui's story.)

5. In the hospital in India, what does the dying Lucina have to say about her life, and giving up singing? Do you agree with her? Why or why not?

6. At the beginning of the book, the author talks about bodies falling and hitting the ground.

When they hit the ground, which they would, nothing would ever be the same again. Nothing would ever be the same again, when they hit the ground. Which they would. Something would rise from the ashes, when they hit the ground. What would emerge would be dark, and what would emerge would be light.

This idea, and some of the same wording, is echoed at the very end. What do you think this means?

More great reads from Art of Storytelling, a book coaching, editing, and publishing service, run by author Caroline Allen. ArtofStorytellingonline.com.

Earth and Air, novels
Caroline Allen

In the first two books in the Elemental Journey Series, protagonist Pearl Elizabeth Swinton is rooted in the grit of farming and butchering on a small farm in the American Midwest. Told with fierce lyricism, Earth is a story about the importance of finding one's own truth and sense of self in dire circumstances and against the odds. It is also a story about the link between understanding ourselves and our relationship with the earth. In Air, Pearl moves by herself to Tokyo, a place where she knows no one, has no job and doesn't even understand the language. Here she can float above the culture and gain perspective. She meets a Holy Man who makes himself homeless to disengage from the "real world", just as Pearl in leaving her rural American home has made herself homeless. Air asks: "Where truly is home?" Available at your favorite online bookseller.

Nothing Ever Goes On Here, a memoir
Ellen Newhouse

The story of a charming but cruel father, an intelligent yet mentally ill mother and a child who, against all odds, breaks through the chains of generational abuse to become a healer to others. It's raw examination of a deeply dysfunctional family reveals how the lines are often blurred between love, loyalty and betrayal. Available on Amazon.

Dancing into the Light
A Spiritual Journey of Healing
Arlyn Hope Halpern

This heartwarming memoir captures one woman's transformative journey of self-discovery by making peace with a family at once extremely dysfunctional, yet oddly endearing. A meeting with a college professor, and their subsequent marriage, set Arlyn down the path of Buddhist practice. In India, they received teachings from Tibetan Buddhist masters, and Arlyn undertook the rigorous study of Indian classical dance. Buddhism and her love of dance sustained her as she experienced heart-rending challenges. Arlyn never wavers from looking inward, facing her demons, and using adversity as a path to develop greater wisdom and compassion. Available on Amazon.

Emotional Witness
My Seven-Year Journey as an Aid Worker into the Heart of Honduras
Ellen Finn

Ellen Finn was in her 60s when she left Seattle for a home-stay visit in Honduras. What began as a two-week vacation became a journey that would change her life. For seven years, she found home in Copas Ruinas. Through financial contributions from friends, she started supplying teaching materials to rural schools.

This is no academic treatise or intellectual look at a Central American region beset by poverty. A searing, soul-searching testimony of one woman's love for a country and its people, this memoir details Ellen's struggle to understand cultural differences, and her deep despair over the inequities of the world's haves and have-nots. Available on Amazon.

WATER

BY CAROLINE ALLEN

Book Four of the Elemental Journey Series

Rain fell upon concrete in confusion. The rain knew there was something wrong. For more than a century, it had been searching for the forest it once knew, for the slap of drop on leaf, the absorption into soil and roots. For more than 100 years, it'd been searching for itself, in the drenching of the earth. Rain could no longer find its purpose.

"Gettin' a little wet there, ain't ya?" The prostitute carried a child's torn rainbow umbrella in one hand and a water-logged cigarette in the other. "You look like a rag doll, like you was ridden hard and put away wet." She had a bloody smear on a front tooth, the criss-cross ties of her *bustier* were so tight her breasts spilled over.

I lifted a strand of heavy black hair from my cheek. My sweatshirt and sweatpants were sopping. Somehow I had no shoes. I picked up one foot, and my sock flopped liked limp puppet.

"What are you doing way over here?" I asked. The prostitutes usually hung out a block away on Aurora; this was residential neighborhood, if you could call the dilapidated row of apartment houses residential.

"People need me here as much as they need me up on the borealis," she said, trying to drag on her soaked cigarette. "I gotta pay my bills just like you."

I sighed. She snorted a laugh that turned into a cough. She stared at me for a while, neither of us talking. Then she went on her way down the sidewalk, the heavy rain pelting the child's umbrella like a fist, rain pouring into the back of her laced-up combat boots.

I looked around. I was outside the duplex, a divided house. Back in the States three months, and I still couldn't figure out what I was doing here, in rainy, dark, and grey Seattle. I didn't know either how I'd gotten out in the front yard in the rain. Time was elusive, and slipped through my fingers like water.

I sloshed down the sidewalk, and as I entered the house, a man rushed out of my neighbor's door. As we passed, he reached a hand toward my hair, as if he was going to rub my head. I pulled back.

He smirked, put his hand down. "Nice knowing ya, then." He stank of sex and marijuana. My neighbor had a stream of not so savory (and sometimes savory) men parading in and out. I hadn't met her yet. I could hear the fucking through the thin wall, a wall that had been constructed not with serious intent, but simply to turn one house into two.

It'd been a bad day. The worst, though it was difficult to qualify bad days when there had been so many of them. In the three months that I'd been back, the veil between worlds had disintegrated. I have visions daily. It was impossible to hold down a job. I took on menial tasks, sweeping sidewalks, cutting keys, swabbing boat decks, and still it was impossible. I'd lost another job that morning, typing into small boxes on a computer screen the sales of wood products at a lumber company, while a big woman in a floral mumu rained criticism. Still, I knew it wasn't their responsibility when a vision left me crying on their industrial carpet.

That afternoon, I'd walked in the rain to the food bank.

Drenched, I waited in line. They were giving out frozen chickens. I walked home with the thing, heavy and as hard as an iceberg. Pelted by fat drops of rain, I sobbed. My parents had been right: I would never survive in this world feeling the way I feel. I would not survive being me.

I kept thinking as I walked Aurora that I could murder someone with that chicken; it was so frozen, so heavy, so rock hard. I could swing the plastic bag at a passersby head, and crush their skull. Then I could go home and eat the evidence. Sodden, carrying a frozen chicken, I cackled at the thought as I passed two prostitutes who looked about 13. They looked me up and down and cackled, too.

(CarolineAllen.com)

———

ABOUT THE AUTHOR

Caroline Allen worked in newsrooms around the world before being called to give up journalism and follow her passion for the arts, both literary and visual. At the Yomiuri newspaper in Tokyo during the death of Emperor Hirohito, at the Independent and Financial Times in London during the death of Princess Diana, and as a travel writer for a year through Southeast Asia, Caroline learned the power of story to transform lives. Caroline started a book coaching business, and today coaches writers of memoir, fiction, nonfiction and scripts around the globe. She lives in Oregon where she works out of a yurt art studio/writing space in the woods. CarolineAllen.com.